SLIDING
AWAY

BY
BAKER CROW

ISBN 9798440987845

ONE

"I bet you can't catch this one!" Tag yells before he heaves the football down the field.

Billy Ray Quick takes off like a rocket. As he streaks down the field his muscular legs are pumping his Nikes so fast it appears as if he's a video game stuck in fast forward mode. These powerful pistons are driving his body forward at an amazing speed. The fastest high school athlete in the state according to his track records and the stop watches of college recruiters. It's difficult to see his weight-room-built, strapping arms because they're equally pumping just as fast to generate maximum speed and maintain balance. The muscles in his neck bulge as they smoothly rotate his head so his eyes can track the flight of the ball and adjust his direction to snag it before it strikes the ground. The rhythmic, machine-like grunts emanating from his throat, as his lungs rapidly inhale and exhale to provide fuel, signal this is a powerful biological machine dashing down the field. Just as gravity appears it'll win the race for the football, Billy Ray, who prefers to just be called Billy, leaps off his feet. His arms seem to extend magically like the child's toy Stretch Armstrong. His six-foot two-inch frame is parallel to the ground when his hands snag the ball in an instant before he crashes to the earth. He skids on the manicured grass, rolls to his back, and holds the ball aloft to show Tag he caught it.

"No damn way!" Tag mutters amazed by his best friend's catch. As Tag jogs down the field, Billy sits up and holds the ball high above his head in his right hand. As he gasps for air, his head is bowed facing the grass between his powerful, spread-eagled legs.

When Tag reaches his friend, Billy looks up with a squint and a wide grin, "You're buying right?"

"Yeah, yeah, that was the bet," Tag reaches down, grabs Billy's extended left hand, and pulls him up. They're both glistening in sweat due to the mid-morning July heat. Billy's recovered quickly from his Herculean effort. His ripped chest is no longer heaving for air when he stands. This doesn't surprise Tag. Anyone looking at Billy will clearly see he's in excellent shape, even when held to an elite athlete's standards.

"Hey, you alright?" Tag points at fresh blood on Billy's right elbow. "You must've skinned your elbow when he slid across the grass."

Billy rotates his arm to look, "I'm fine. Looks like another strawberry, though." Billy grins, and changes the subject, "You thought you had me, didn't you?"

"Yeah, I didn't think you could get to that one."

"When are you going to learn, I was built for speed!"

"Don't let it go to your head, you'll always be Billy Ray Dumb Ass to me. Let's get your strawberry patched," Tag grins at his weak attempt at humor, "and then you can pick out your favorite Powerade from the vending machine, once again, on me."

Billy guffaws while placing his left arm around Tag's shoulders, which is easy for Billy since Tag's only five-feet ten-inches tall.

As they walk off the field toward the Rock Slide Avalanche's gym, Billy flicks Tag's ear with his left forefinger.

"Ouch, you jerk!"

Billy takes off running toward the gym laughing wildly. Tag does too, but he knows there's no way he can catch him. He'll find Billy eagerly waiting beside the vending machine for Tag to settle the bet.

Every weekday morning for the past four weeks they've met on their high school football field to prepare for the upcoming season. This is a new summer routine for them. Preparing for the season is important, but the real reason for this practice is to help Billy prepare for college football.

Billy burst onto the radar of college recruiters last year during his junior season. Frankly, it was by luck he was noticed. He was already making a name for himself as a track star. Many college track coaches became aware of him because he was winning sprint events at high school track meets as a freshman. After the state track meet his sophomore year, where he dominated the sprints, college recruiters reached out to Billy's high school to start their due diligence process. They requested tapes of his track meets to review.

Rock Slide School is not a large school. All the kids in Pocket Watch Valley attend the school. It's pre-K-12. There are slightly less than six hundred kids in the entire school. Due to its small size, they're in a seven-on-seven football league. To the best of anyone's memory, no one from the school has ever been offered an athletic scholarship from any college, in any sport. Heck, most of the graduates don't even attend college!

When Coach Jasper was contacted by college track coaches requesting film on Billy, all he had was footage from football games. Due to a very sparse athletic budget, they didn't film track meets. The only thing Coach Jasper knew to provide were outtakes from football games showing plays where Billy was running and being chased by the other team. There were many plays to choose from.

When college track coaches reviewed these outtakes, they quickly noticed his athletic skills were not limited to track. They shared the outtakes with coaches on the football staff. That's when all hell broke loose.

Every Friday night during Billy's junior year there were college football recruiters in the stands watching him. Also, the college football recruiting services began to take notice and share information nationally touting Billy's skills. Going into his senior season he's a consensus "four- star" college football recruit as an "athlete," meaning there may be more than one position he can play. Five stars is the highest ranking a high school football player can achieve, and very few achieve that ranking. With his high national ranking, all the college football powerhouses are recruiting him.

As for Tag, he's ignored by the colleges. He's seen in the pass play outtakes, but merely as a supporting actor. His job was to receive the snap from the center and then throw the ball downfield before he was tackled. Billy would out-run everybody, catch the ball, and then streak across the goal line for a

5

touchdown. This combination worked extremely well last year. The team averaged eighty-four points a game, an unheard-of number for any level of football, all because of Billy. The Rock Slide Avalanche were undefeated and won the state seven-on-seven high school football championship. Their first championship in any sport. They're favored to win it again this year, all because of Billy. By the way, when Coach Jasper calls a running play, Billy's in the backfield. Billy takes direct snaps from the center, and if he finds a hole in the line of scrimmage, no one can catch him.

Billy and Tag plop on a bench shaded by the red oaks in the Rock Slide village square. The breezes swirling through the mountain valley cause the deep green leaves to dance and sway. These breezes, along with the cold, ice blue Powerade spilling down their throats, are refreshing, and invigorating. Billy bends his right elbow back and forth trying to loosen the new bandage over his strawberry. He doesn't like that it restricts his movement. Tag's confident it won't be there tomorrow when they practice.

"Hey, what's that?" Billy asks pointing at a freshly installed plaque in the town square.

"That must be the new historical marker I heard they were putting up to celebrate the two hundredth anniversary of the town," Tag says rising from the bench to get a better look at the plaque.

"What's it say?"

"I'll read it." Tag positions himself in front of the marker. "Pocket Watch Valley acquired its name in the late 1700's from pioneers who discovered this serene valley while searching for a more prosperous life beyond the Appalachians. From the ridge tops surrounding the valley, the lake resembled a pocket watch, thus giving the valley its name. Pocket Watch Lake is one of the largest lakes in the Appalachians covering over two thousand acres with twelve miles of shoreline. It lies twenty-eight hundred feet above sea level making it the largest elevated lake in the eastern United States. It's fed by the Thread River before it spills into the Great Tumble, the name given to the granite gorge. The lake was created when tons of granite cleaved from the side of the gorge creating a natural dam."

"Cleaved, like cleavage?" Billy interrupts with a smile.

"No, like 'split from' you idiot! Get your mind out of the gutter. Do you want me to finish?"

"Sure, this is enlightening! I'm hanging on every word."

"You come read it yourself then!"

"No, I'm kidding, go ahead and finish it. My arm hurts too much."

"Yeah. Right. Where was I. 'Early pioneers found the soil around the lake rich with silt making it perfect for growing crops. To meet the needs of the early settlers, Angus McEachin established a trading post near this site in 1806 and named it 'Rock Slide' so travelers would know its location on the trail through the mountains.

Unbeknown to the settlers, the valley was sacred to the Cherokees. The constant roar from the falls in the Great Tumble caused the Cherokees to believe 'thunder beings' lived in the valley. Afraid the presence of the settlors would upset the 'thunder beings,' on the frigid night of January 9, 1808, the Cherokees massacred the settlors in the valley and burned all the buildings to appease the 'thunder beings'."

"I never knew that. This is getting interesting."

"My dad told me about it. Let me finish, there isn't much more. 'After the Cherokees were moved west, settlors returned to the valley. They retained the name 'Rock Slide' for the new settlement. Without the threat from the Cherokees, the settlement began to slowly grow over the next one hundred years. In 1938, the U. S. government constructed the current dam where the lake spills into the gorge to create hydro-electric power for the valley and surrounding areas. The construction of paved roads, the prevalence of automobile ownership, and post-World War II prosperity led to real estate developers marketing the shoreline for vacation homes. Home construction created numerous jobs causing the population of the sleepy village of Rock Slide to triple over the next fifty years. Today, the population in the valley almost doubles each summer when vacationers arrive to enjoy the cooler temperatures and the recreational activities on the pristine lake and in the scenic hillsides. Pocket Watch Valley

7

is a preferred destination for vacationers from throughout the eastern United States.' That's it."

"Nothing about 'Glides' and 'Slides'?"

"Why would they put that on a historical marker? I can just see the reaction of the vacationers reading the marker and learning we call them 'Glides' because we think they're elitist gliding across the lake in their big boats. Come on! Yeah, they call us 'Slides' because we're locals and serve them, but we call ourselves that, too."

"It's the truth, though."

"It may be, but it doesn't need to be broadcasted. That might seriously hurt our tourism." Tag returns to the bench next to Billy.

An old beat up, red Ford pickup stops at the curb in front of their bench. The driver hollers from the open window, "Hey Billy how ya doin', uh…and you too Tag," Tag's used to this treatment over the past two years. He wonders if his diploma will read "And You Too Tag Ryder."

"Hey Mr. Ted," they both unenthusiastically respond with a quick wave of their hands.

"Billy, you decided where ya goin' to school yet?"

"No sir Mr. Ted. Not yet."

"I hope you choose a SEC school. Ya know, that's where they play the best football. It'll prepare ya for the pros."

"I definitely will consider one Mr. Ted."

"Great! Look forward to seeing y'all play this year. Back-to-back state championships ain't never happened around here before. Y'all are putting our small town on the map, boys! It's excitin'!"

"Thanks Mr. Ted," Tag responds. "We'll do our best."

Mr. Ted waves and drives off.

Tag sips his Powerade. He lowers the bottle from his lips. Staring at the bottle he offers a random thought, "I think you need to talk to coach about substituting Gatorade for Powerade. The Florida Gators might drop you from their list of recruits if they catch you drinking Powerade."

"Ha. Ha. I bet you're a scream during nap time at the old folks' home!"

Tag smiles at Billy, but there isn't a smile on Billy's face.

Tag backpedals, "I'm sorry. Just trying to lighten it up a little."

"No need to apologize, but this recruiting process is getting old. I'm ready to get it over with."

"So, have you decided?"

"Ain't my decision."

"What do mean?"

"Just what I said, it ain't my decision!"

"Why do you say that?"

"My dad says he's gonna decide for me."

"He can't do that! It's your life!"

"Makes no difference. He's gonna decide."

"Why does he get to decide?"

"He just does."

"Come on Billy, give me more? This ain't right!"

"I can't tell you anymore."

"Why not? Aren't I your best friend?"

"Yeah, you are."

"Then come on and tell me. I might be able to help."

"You can't help."

"Why not?"

"You just can't!" Billy snaps with an angry look.

"Billy, come on! We've shared secrets all our lives. I haven't squealed yet have I?"

"Not that I know of."

"Remember last summer when you dyed Miss Pearl's cats pink? Man was she pissed! She accused everyone in town of a hate crime. For weeks everyone could tell when one of Miss Pearl's cats was on the prowl. Everybody, but Miss Pearl, loved it!"

"Yeah," Billy giggles, "I was lucky to pull that off."

"I didn't squeal on you, did I?"

"No, you didn't."

"I won't now either. Come on. I can tell this is bothering you. You need someone to talk to. We've always been able to trust each other, right? After all, you agreed, I'm your best friend." Tag grins.

"Yeah," Tag sees Billy's demeanor softening. He can tell Billy wants to tell him but is debating it internally. Billy takes another swig from his Powerade. He stealthily scans the area making sure no one is near, and then whispers to Tag, "You can't breathe a word about this. It'll get me and my family in trouble."

"I promise I won't ever tell," Tag whispers while leaning in close. He's suddenly anxious about what his best friend's about to reveal.

Billy hesitates. He looks Tag in the eyes. Tag's stunned when he notices Billy's eyes begin to well with tears. "My dad's gonna make me sign with the highest bidder for my services,"

"What!" Tag screams.

"Shhh! Shut up Tag," Billy cautions as he quickly wipes his eyes and looks around hoping no one's curious as to Tag's loud reaction. "You can't breathe a word of this!"

"That's illegal," Tag firmly responds, "uh well, not illegal, like going to jail illegal, but it's against the NCAA rules. You could lose your scholarship if anyone finds out!"

"I know. I know, but there ain't nothing I can do about it."

"Just tell your dad it's your future and you'll decide what's best."

"Come on Tag. You know I can't do that. You know my dad."

Billy has a point. Mr. Jimmy, Billy's dad, is maybe one step above a scoundrel, but it's a very, very short step. As far as Tag can tell, Mr. Jimmy's never held a steady job, yet they always seem to have enough money to get by. Billy's hinted that his dad works jobs that might be frowned upon by most decent folks. Tag's not sure what that means, but it can't be good. Mr. Jimmy's intimidating. He tends to leer when he's looking at you. He gives Tag the creeps. He's shorter than Billy, about Tag's height, but very wiry. Many men have learned the hard way that you don't cross Mr. Jimmy. There are legends about his fights as a younger man where he beat his adversaries to a bloody pulp. Tag's parents never let him spend the night at Billy's house. Mr. Jimmy can be very mean. He rules his family with an iron fist. It's his way or no way in their family.

There's one fact about Mr. Jimmy that everyone in Pocket Watch Valley will agree upon, he worships Billy. Since Billy attained celebrity status, Mr. Jimmy's been even harder to be around. He's constantly bragging about Billy and belittling everyone else's sons. His arrogance has worn thin with everyone in the valley. It's become an embarrassment to Billy. When Mr. Jimmy enters a room, others are looking for the exit. At Billy's football games, Mr. Jimmy sits by himself. He rants and raves at the referees, coaches, opponents, Billy's teammates, and even Billy.

"Can't your mom help?"

"She tried. Dad shut her up quickly. Since then, she just puts up with it. She keeps telling me that he only wants what's best for me. I don't believe that, and I can tell neither does she. She's just trying to maintain peace."

While Mr. Jimmy's bad news, Miss Florence, Billy's mama, is a saint. Everyone loves her. She's so kind and thoughtful. She'll help anyone in need. If there's a death or a sickness in a family, Miss Florence is the first to bring food. She'll stay in touch until the grief or malady has passed. She's at the Baptist church every time the doors open, dragging her boys with her. Mr. Jimmy won't darken the doors. Tag doesn't understand how Miss Florence ever married Mr. Jimmy. They truly are an example of the well-worn term "opposites attract." Billy will do anything for his mama, as would anyone else in the valley, but he avoids his dad. Tag's parents always refer to Billy as their "other son" since he's always at their house.

"Does your dad understand you could be declared ineligible if you get caught?"

"Sure, he does! He says getting caught only happens to the stupid people who break under the pressure of an investigation. He says if the schools are willing to risk being put on probation by offering money, then he ain't worried about it. He says getting money under the table happens all the time in college athletics. He says it's our turn. He's also laying a guilt trip on me."

"How so?"

"He said this money will make a huge difference for Mo. He says when I reach the pros, I'll have more money than I can say grace over, but Mo ain't ever gonna have anything. The more I thought about it, the more that made sense, but I'm not sure I'll

11

ever be good enough to make the pros. Also, I'm not sure dad will set the money aside for Mo."

"Hell yeah you'll make the pros! Remember, I'm gonna be your agent."

Billy smiles, "Damn straight, buddies for life!" as they high five each other.

Tag understands why Mr. Jimmy's reasoning about Mo makes sense to Billy. Mo, Montgomery is his legal name, is Billy's little brother. Mo was born with a severe intellectual disability. He's ten years old. They've tried to mainstream Mo in school, but at times he's become violent striking other kids in his class. He's very anxious when Miss Florence isn't around. He seems to be fine in church, probably because Miss Florence is never far away.

Mr. Jimmy's embarrassed of Mo. You rarely see the two of them together. He crudely calls Mo his only mistake. Miss Florence calls him her angel. Billy loves his brother and has confessed at times he worries a lot about what will happen to Mo if something happens to his mama. She's a large woman who periodically suffers with health problems. Mo appears to have inherited her physical characteristics. Billy's never mentioned it, but Tag believes one of the reasons Billy has worked so hard this past year to impress recruiters is so he'll be able to obtain the education he needs, or receive a lucrative pro contract, so he'll be able to take care of Mo.

"I'm sorry Billy. I guess you truly have a conundrum."

"A what?"

"A conundrum. Look it up soon to be college boy."

"Later. Speaking of cleavage, I saw a group of hot Glides on the lake yesterday hanging out near where Branch Water Creek drains into the lake. You up to checking 'em out?"

"That's the best thing you've said all morning. Let's go! But first, promise me that you'll leave at least one pretty one for me?"

They both laugh as they rise from the bench and jog the block to the school parking lot where Tag's car's parked.

TWO

"Look, look, look, Tag! Over there! They're back where they were yesterday!" Billy shouts gleefully when they cross the bridge over Branch Water Creek.

Tag peers from his open window as he slows the "Magnet," the name he's given his topless, used Jeep Wrangler. It's short for "Chick Magnet," a sarcastic attempt at humor since no female would find it attractive. Aside from a couple of awkward dates with Maggie "The Magnificent" Musgrove, the only other "chick" who's ridden in the Magnet is his mom, and that only occurs when she doesn't have a choice. Billy's unbuckled his seatbelt and is standing in the floorboard pointing over the windshield in the direction of the lake. Tag spots a Sea Ray deck boat anchored in the cove of Branch Water Creek. He's quickly distracted by the boat's shapely occupants clad in revealing bikinis. A wave of pleasing, anxious excitement surges through him.

"Park in that driveway!" Billy points as he drops to the seat.

"That's somebody's house! I can't park there!"

"Pull over damn it! You can move it if there's someone there."

Tag pulls into the driveway of the first house past the bridge which backs up to the lake.

"Did you see 'em, Tag! Did you see 'em! Gorgeous! Looks like we're gonna have some fun today!"

"Calm down Billy. They may not want to have anything to do with a couple of Slides. Plus, they're too far away for us to tell how pretty they are."

"Who says we're gonna tell them we're Slides," Billy hollers as he leaps from the Jeep. "With bodies like that, they have to be pretty!" Billy's favorite past time this summer has been fishing for Glides. He knows what bait to use to make them bite. Billy pulls off his t-shirt to reveal his bulging pecs and washboard stomach. His torso resembles those of the statutes chiseled by ancient Greeks of their gods. He may only be seventeen, but he can easily pass for someone in his twenties.

As Billy jogs toward the back of the house. Tag decides to back out of the driveway and pull on to the edge of the grass next to the bridge. Parking there shouldn't cause any problems. He hops from the Jeep and jogs across the grass toward the back of the house. By the time he gets there, Billy's on the dock already in a conversation with the girls.

Tag jogs up next to Billy. Billy glances at Tag, "See here he is now. Tell 'em Tag?'

Tag panics. "Tell 'em what?" Tag whispers under his breath to Billy.

"I promise ladies, this is his parents' house. Tell 'em?" Billy's giving Tag a look that screams you better go along with this buddy or else.

Tag clears his throat, "Uh, yeah, this is my parents' house. We came up last night to do some yard work." Billy rolls his eyes at Tag. "Uh, but we're finished now and want to have some fun." Billy smiles.

The boat's about thirty yards from them. There are four girls, all in teeny bikinis, lounging in the boat. One girl has light blonde hair, one is a dirty blond, and the other two are brunettes, but Tag isn't focused on their hair. Tag recognizes a Cold Play song wafting over the water toward them. One of the brunettes and the dirty blond stand. Tag's heartbeat quickens as he hears Billy utter "whoa" under his breath.

The brunette challenges Tag's statement, "Prove it!"

Even though the question is for Tag, Billy answers, "Prove what?"

"That it's his parents' house?"

"How?"

The dirty blonde screams, "Get us some beers from the frig!"

True to his name, Mr. Quick responds, "We drank them all last night. We haven't made it to town today to restock. We're hoping y'all might have some to share." Tag's impressed with Billy's response.

"Well then bring us some soft drinks."

"Out of those, too," Tag quickly answers. He's proud of his response.

The girls talk among themselves, but not loud enough for Billy and Tag to hear their words. Their giggles are audible, though. When they finish talking the shapely, brunette goddess shouts, "Then go inside and get us some ice from the refrigerator for our cooler."

For a brief, few seconds Tag and Billy are silent, then Mr. Quick responds, "If we leave the dock, we know you girls are just gonna speed away. That'll break our hearts. Come on girls, come pick us up. We just wanna have some fun!"

The girls giggle and again talk among themselves. Once again, Tag and Billy can only hear the giggles. When the girls finish talking, the shapely, brunette goddess speaks, "We know that's not his parents' house."

"Yes, it is!" Billy pleads confidently.

"No, it's not. It's my aunt and uncle's house. I know they're not here this week. That's why we're parked off their dock. It's a safe place for us to drink beer and not get caught. Busted!" Now all the girls laughing hysterically.

Tag and Billy are instantly deflated. How embarrassing! Slides are "outed" again.

Suddenly the shapely, brunette goddess speaks above the laughter, "Even though you're horrible liars, we give you an 'A' for effort. We also think you're pretty cute." Tag isn't sure that line was only meant for Billy, or it encompasses both of them. He assumes he's included. "We have plenty of cold beer. If y'all want to join us, then swim over!"

Billy's in the water immediately. When he surfaces, he's swimming toward them holding his t-shirt in his right hand and still wearing his Nikes as he kicks.

"What the hell!" Tag dives into the lake wearing his t-shirt and his Nikes. Tag instantly notices how cold the water is, but it's warmer as he nears the surface.

Billy reaches the boat first and climbs the ladder. He removes his shoes and empties the lake water collected inside them over the side of the boat.

As Tag climbs the ladder his heart skips a beat. He recognizes the silent brunette. Tag works part time at the Pocket Watch Lake Marina cleaning boats, filling them with fuel, and moving them among the slips. He saw her this past weekend at the marina. He couldn't take his eyes off her. In fact, he spilled some fuel in the water while filling up a boat's gas tank because he was paying more attention to her than to what he was doing. What are the chances of him climbing on to her boat? Wow, this is going to be a great day!

As Tag's peeling off his wet shirt, he hears Billy introduce himself and Tag. The shirt is difficult to remove because it's wet. While struggling to get his head through the collar, he feels someone else tug it. Once his shirt pops off, he sees this same girl holding his shirt and shyly smiling at him before she looks away. The other three girls are focused on Billy. Not surprising, Billy has a body most men would love to have, and women want, plus a charismatic personality. Tag hears the three other girls introduce themselves as Caroline, Millie, and Virginia, but he's not sure who's who because he's focused on the one whose name is Suzy. Suzy looks away from the others at Tag. Their eyes meet. Tag knows he must be smiling at her because she breaks into a smile. His body isn't as chiseled as Billy's, but he has muscle definition he thinks is attractive to women. Tag removes his shoes and empties the collected water into the lake. Tag wants to pinch himself to make sure he's not dreaming. Here he and Billy are, clothed in just their gym shorts, surrounded by four beautiful young women in bikinis.

Over the next fifteen minutes there's a lot of hormonal induced conversation and body positioning. Billy and Tag grab beers and koozies. The warm sun feels good after their brief, brisk swim. The aroma in the boat is a mixture of generously lathered sunscreen, outboard motor fuel, sun-heated plastic, muddy, puddled lake water, and spilt beer. Depending upon your position in the boat, and the swirling breezes, one smell will briefly dominate the others.

Billy's holding court with the other three girls while Tag's focused on Suzy. Tag learns from Suzy that the other three girls are college sorority sisters who will be entering their sophomore year in a few weeks. Of course, Billy's already gleaned that from the girls. Billy quickly shared that he's a highly sought-after football recruit. He's pretending to be interested in their embellishment of their school as they try to recruit him to attend. He's listening for clues to help him narrow in on the one he feels he has the best shot at romancing.

Tag's learned from Suzy that the shapely, brunette goddess, who was challenging them while they were on the dock, is Suzy's older sister, but to Tag her beauty pales in comparison to Suzy's. Like Tag and Billy, Suzy will be entering her senior year in high school. She lives in Pineville, which is a wealthy suburb of a larger city in the foothills. It's about eighty miles away. Tag's aware other residents of Pineville have vacation homes on the lake.

Suzy scoots closer to Tag. Unconsciously, his glance at her face becomes a gaze as he commits her gorgeous features to memory. Her tan skin, aside from a few freckles on her cute nose, is flawless. He resists entrapment by her captivating eyes. Her quickly forming, timid smile is alluring. His heartbeat quickens. Suddenly, he senses his gaze is awkwardly too long. He averts his eyes. They instinctively drop to examine her body. Her pleasing shape could have been crafted from his unspoken dreams. Her tan lines are uneven where her bikini straps shifted in all the right places. Forcing himself not to stare where he shouldn't, he looks down. He spots her chipped, red toenail polish on her tan, slender toes as they gently knead the shallow mix of lake water and spilt beer bilge.

"Tag," he glances up at her smooth face and locks onto her sultry dark eyes, "do you work at the marina?"

Tag's stunned by her question. His heart leaps for joy as he realizes she must've been watching him as he was watching her. "Yeah, I do some part time work for the marina to earn extra money." Trying to play it as a cool as possible he adds, "If you were there on Saturday, you may have seen me."

"I was!" Suzy answers gleefully. "I thought I recognized you."

Tag's ashamed he didn't admit he also saw her on Saturday. He's somewhat tongue tied as to how to respond to this beautiful girl who admitted she was watching him. Fortunately, her sister saves him.

"Let's go tubing!" Suzy's sister announces. "Who wants to drive?"

"Let Tag drive," Suzy enthusiastically answers. "He works at the marina."

"Tag, do you wanna drive? The rest of us have had a few beers." Tag's only had a couple of sips of his beer.

"Sure." Tag answers as he rises from his position on the rail and steps over Suzy's long, gorgeous legs on his way to the helm. He left his beer sitting next to Suzy. He looks at Billy who winks at him.

"Who wants to tube first"? big sister asks.

The dirty blonde says she does. Tag marvels at the scantily clad female body in motion as the girls take the large donut shaped tube from the bow section of the boat, pass it among themselves toward the stern, attach the rope hooked to the tube to the cleats on the stern near the transom, and push the tube into the water. The dirty blond squeezes on a life jacket, while Tag and Billy gawk, and then she jumps into the water. She swims over to the tube and pulls herself on top of it.

"Please don't go too fast!" she hollers to Tag.

Suzy straddles the seat across from Tag and places his beer in her cupholder. Tag fires up the outboard and eases the boat from the cove letting the rope slowly stretch out. He's trying not to jerk the dirty blond off the tube. Once the rope's taut and the tube's moving with the boat, Tag gradually increases speed. The sound of the outboard is deafening, making it hard to have a conversation. He suddenly imagines himself as a wealthy tycoon gliding through the water in a powerful boat with the wind drying his damp hair, the spray from the wake lightly misting his skin, and a beautiful, bikini clad goddess by his side. Even though he wants to stare at Suzy, he needs to keep his eyes on the water ahead to avoid any lurking obstacles. Suzy rises from the seat next to him, cups her hands around her lips, and places them next to Tag's ear.

"She's waving that she wants to go faster."

18

Tag nods and increases the speed to about fifteen miles-per-hour. Suzy grabs Tag's bicep to steady herself while standing. Tag glances at her. The wind's slapping her shoulder length hair across her face. When she rakes her hair away, he notices she's smiling at him. He's not sure he's ever enjoyed a better moment.

After about ten minutes, Suzy squeezes his arm. He looks at her. Her other hand is making a slashing motion across her neck. He understands that she's telling him the dirty blonde has had enough and wants to stop. He throttles slowly to an idling position.

The dirty blonde slides off the tube and swims to the boat. As she climbs up the stairs, she's regaling everyone about her ride. Big sister looks at Billy, "How about you Mr. All American?"

"I'm ready, sister!" Billy grabs a life jacket, adjusts it to fit, snaps it closed, and jumps in. He swims to the tube and climbs on.

"Hey Tag?" he screams once he's settled. "I bet you can't throw me off!"

"Same bet?" Tag counters.

"Yep!"

"You're on!"

Tag throttles the engine slowly at first to begin Billy's ride. As he increases speed, Suzy grabs his bicep again to steady herself. He looks at her and smiles. She smiles back. Tag steadily increases the speed.

There are only a few other boats on the lake. Every time they come near, Tag steers the Sea Ray so that it crosses the wake of the other boats making Billy and his tube briefly airborne while skipping across the converging wakes. Tag glances over his shoulder. Billy's smiling and laughing while hanging on for dear life. Tag pushes the boat faster. Billy continues to hold on tightly. The girls encourage Tag to drive faster. The wind slaps their hair across their faces. Tag scans the lake for Billy's next challenge.

Tag spots a big boat crossing in front of him slowing towards its dock. The slowing motion causes the bigger boat to dig deeply into the water causing a huge wake. Tag decides he'll steer into the other boat's wake, turn sharply and whip Billy and his tube across the huge wake. If this doesn't get him off, nothing will.

Tag skips the boat across the wake, bouncing his female passengers as he takes a sharp left turn. The tube and Billy whip and bounce violently and quickly across the wake. Suddenly, Tag feels the boat lurch forward. He glances over his shoulder. He's horrified when he notices the rope's snapped. Billy and the tube are skidding across the top of the water sliding out of control directly toward a dock about twenty yards away. There's nothing any of them can do to stop him. Suzy's grip digs into his flesh. The girls scream as Billy and the tube slam into the dock. They can't hear the sound of the crash due to the deafening roar of the outboard, but they all instinctively flinch when they see part of the pier splinter, the tube explode, and Billy disappear under the dock.

Tag screams in terror. He whips the boat one hundred-eighty degrees and heads for his friend. Suzy's bruised Tag's arm where she squeezed too hard. Tears are flowing from her eyes and she's deeply wailing. This same level of deep distress is evident in the other girls. One girl's thrown up in the boat. As the boat nears the site of the accident, Tag, with tears streaming down his cheeks, screams at Suzy to take the wheel. When she grabs it, Tag dives in to rescue his friend.

When he reaches Billy, he's repulsed by what he sees. Billy's bleeding profusely from shards of wood penetrating his body. One side of his face is unrecognizable where it caved in. All Tag can do is hold his friend and wail as other boats speed in to help.

THREE

Tag's in shock. He slumps on the bench in the hallway of the Rock Slide Police Station. He's waiting for his parents. A few feet away they're finishing their discussion with the sergeant and detective. He's not sure what they're discussing. The police told him, and his parents, he won't be charged with a crime, but it still doesn't change the outcome. His best friend is dead, and he killed him.

It was an accident. A horrible accident! An accident Tag feels he could've avoided. Those horrific few seconds are seared in his memory. If he hadn't been so intent on winning his stupid bet. After living in his friend's shadow for the past two years, was winning the bet that important that he put his best friend's life in danger? A bet for merely a dollar and change! Is that worth risking someone's life? Hell no!

Tag clenches his fists tightly in anger and frustration.

The girls. Suzy. Was he so intent on impressing her that he allowed his infatuation to distract him from being smart and cautious? The girls backed his story. It was an accident. How was he to know the tow line was frayed? He didn't examine it. It wasn't his rope. It wasn't his boat. The girls are the ones who set-up the tubing, not him. It's their fault! It's his fault! It's no one's fault. It was an accident. His best friend's dead.

Tag supports his elbows with his thighs to hold his bowed head in his hands. With his palms he rubs his eyes which burn from having shed buckets of tears.

He's afraid to close his eyes. Every time he does, he sees the shattered face of his friend. It frightens him. It repulses him.

Billy was invincible. How could this happen? In the blink of an eye, Billy's bright, skyrocketing future was over. Done with! Finished! All because of Tag.

Everyone tells him it was an accident.

Suddenly, Tag's jolted from his melancholy by a blood curdling howl. Mr. Jimmy, in a rage, is bursting through the glass double doors of the police station. One of the door panels shatters as it bangs against the wall.

"You kilt my boy!" is all Tag can make from Mr. Jimmy's incoherent ranting. Mr. Jimmy's eyes are bloodshot and burning with hatred. He's headed straight for Tag. Tag's frozen in disbelief and fear.

Just before Mr. Jimmy reaches Tag, the sergeant and detective grab Mr. Jimmy. His shrieking like that of a wounded animal fighting for its life. He's swinging and kicking wildly trying to break free to devour Tag. Tag's dad jerks him off the bench and pulls him away from the melee. Suddenly, more police officers appear and help subdue Mr. Jimmy. He continues to rant and lash out as they drag him down the hall away from Tag.

"An eye for an eye! An eye for an eye!"

"Get Tag outta here!" the sergeant screams.

Immediately, Tag's dad rushes Tag outside with his mother closely following. She's in tears. They pile in his dad's pickup and drive away. Tag's mother hugs him as they drive off. Tears continue to stream down her face as she tightly holds him. Over his mother's shoulder, he sees Suzy leaning against a parked car. Their eyes briefly lock as the pick-up approaches. Tag feels an instant connection and senses her deep sorrow. As the pickup passes, Suzy breaks the stare. She slides into the driver's seat of the parked car.

When they arrive at Tag's home, which is only a few blocks from the police station, Tag finds his Youth Minister, Wayne Winder, sitting on the front porch swing. News travels fast in a small town. He guesses the Senior Minister is with Miss Florence and Mo.

Tag and Wayne spend thirty minutes by themselves on the Ryder's back patio. Tag and Wayne are close. Tag's active in his church's youth group.

Their conversation is comforting to Tag, but it still doesn't change the outcome. Wayne can't satisfactorily answer Tag's question as to why God allowed this to happen. It's hard for Tag to accept that God's plan is perfect when Tag continues to see Billy's crushed face when he closes his eyes. Tag didn't think he had any tears left, but they begin to flow again as Wayne and Tag jointly pray.

After their prayer, with Tag's permission, Wayne invites Tag's parents to join them. Also joining them is Tag's black lab, Buddy. Buddy, sensing Tag's sadness, sits erect on his haunches next to Tag. Normally he would be bouncing around anxious for someone to start a continuous game of fetch. Tag strokes Buddy's black fur as they all talk. It soothes Tag.

When they finish a tearful family prayer, Tag walks Wayne to the street. Wayne walked the few blocks from the church to Tag's house. After a crushing man hug, Wayne walks away toward the church with his head bowed. Tag notices Wayne drag the back of his hand across his eyes.

It's late afternoon and the sun's setting behind the mountains. The leaves stirring in the trees from the mountain breezes cause the sun's golden rays to playfully dance in the street. It appears to Tag as if some of the shadows are waving. Tag's never paid attention to this routine act of nature. He's immediately overcome with a sense of peace as he feels his friend's using nature to tell him goodbye and he's now safely in God's arms. Tag still can't imagine life without Billy's physical presence. This is all so sudden and harsh.

When he turns from the street toward his home, the headlights of a parked car flash. He stops and stares at this odd behavior. The driver's side door opens, and out steps Suzy. He walks toward her. She points to the passenger side door and then she disappears into the car.

Tag opens the passenger side door. "Will you sit with me for a minute?" Suzy implores. Suzy's eyes are bloodshot. Her face portrays deep sadness.

"Only for a minute," he answers as he slides into the passenger seat leaving the passenger door open. Tag notices she's wearing a loose t-shirt over her bikini. Tag's still awed by her beauty.

Suzy weeps uncontrollably, "It's my fault! It's my fault! I'm the one who asked you to drive. I'm so, so sorry Tag!"

Tears begin to well in Tag's eyes as he's overcome by how much she's hurting for him. Only a few hours ago they were strangers, even though they had ogled each other at the marina without the other knowing. It seems this tragedy has caused their fates to intertwine. It's as if they're the only ones who can soothe each other's pain.

"It's not your fault. It was an accident," Tag parrot's what others have said while wiping his eyes.

"Can we go somewhere and talk?" Suzy pleads.

Oh, how he wants to tell her "Yes," but he knows he can't. His parents are going to be watching him closely, especially after hearing Mr. Jimmy's threats. "I can't. My parents are worried about me, and they want me close by."

"Please Tag! I need to talk to you!"

Tag clearly sees the disappointment in Suzy's face. "Let me go talk to my parents. I'll be right back."

Suzy nods. She raises the bottom of the t-shirt to wipe the tears from her cheeks and eyes. Tag averts his eyes.

"Thank you, for caring about Billy. I agree, I think it will also help me if we talk."

Tag steps from the car and closes the passenger door. He's conflicted by his overwhelming sadness over the death of his friend and his excitement about his quickly budding relationship with Suzy.

"I convinced them to give me two hours," Tag tells Suzy as he closes the door of her car. He waves to his parents standing on their front porch. As Suzy drives away, the bathing glow from the front porch light accentuates the concern etched on their faces. They're deeply worried about their son's health and safety. They're concerned about what Mr. Jimmy might do to him. They know his reputation. They're not happy about Tag going off with this girl who they don't know. They think it's a bad decision on Tag's part, but since this horrible situation comes with no instructions, they're hopeful that this two-hour window will help their son, and this poor girl who witnessed the accident, be able to cope better in the aftermath.

Suzy tells Tag that the place where she finds the most peace is in the hammock by the shore of the lake behind her parent's lake house. As they drive to the house, Suzy wants to know all about Billy. Tag regales her with stories which brings both laughter and tears. He finds that talking about his friend is comforting. He notices Suzy's relaxing.

Suzy parks in the driveway. As they carefully walk side-by-side in the fading light through the backyard toward the lake, Tag learns that Suzy's parents aren't here. He hears music wafting from the home. Through a large plate glass window, he sees Suzy's sister, and her friends, sitting inside at a table covered with various bags of food and bottles.

When they reach the lake, Tag finds a hammock attached to two wooden posts. It's located in a small bare area underneath sugar maples and hidden from the house by robust mountain laurel bushes. The beautiful white blossoms resemble a light dusting of snow in the fading light. The view of the lake is spectacular as it reflects the sunset's mosaic of colors. The lights from homes surrounding the lake appear to wink at them in the surging darkness. He understands why Suzy finds peace in this secluded location.

Suzy drops perpendicularly into a seated position on the hammock, bisecting it between the headrest and foot. The hammock sags where she sits and gently sways back-and-forth.

"Sit here," she softly suggests while patting the cords of the hammock next to her.

Tag gently eases into the hammock and the weight of their bodies forces the hammock to sag further causing their bodies to slide together. Tag braces his feet against the ground and scoots away to create a little space between them, but when he does, Suzy slides into the gap. Tag doesn't complain. His excitement of being alone with her is building. He hopes she can't feel how rapidly his heart's beating.

Suzy lays back in the hammock. Her head barely remains on the cords as her long, gorgeous, tanned legs dangle off the edge. "Lie down," she sweetly implores.

Tag eagerly complies. The hammock quickly swings back-and-forth when his feet leave the ground. He tenses for a moment thinking they're going to pitch out. She giggles. Their heads are only inches apart.

"So, do you think he's watching?" Suzy asks.

"Who?" panic wells in Tag, He prepares to rise to see who Suzy's referring to.

"Billy."

"Billy?"

"Yes, Billy. Do you think he's watching us?"

Tag notices Suzy's staring into the heavens. Looking skyward, Tag sees the pinpoint lights from numerous stars piercing the darkness as the light of day is almost extinguished. A day Tag's sure he'll never forget.

"I don't know. I believe there's a Heaven, and I'm sure Billy's there because he accepted Christ as his Lord and Savior, but I'm not sure he can see us. Frankly, I hope there're more exciting things to do in Heaven than to watch us."

"You're funny," Suzy giggles.

"Thanks, but I wasn't trying to be. I really do hope he's at peace and not missing being here. I sure miss him," a tear slides down his cheek into his ear.

"I'm sorry! I didn't mean to make light of Billy."

"No offense. I think if he could, he would tell me to get over it, just like he always said when I made a mistake. He simply wanted me to focus on getting better, not dwelling on mistakes."

"He sounds like he was a great friend."

"The best!"

"Do you think we could ever be as close as you and Billy were? Maybe even closer?"

Tag's shocked by her bold question. "Why do you ask?" is his startled response.

"What I saw today was horrible. But amidst that horror I saw something else. I saw a person with great character, who took control when others froze, who dearly hurt because of his love for his friend, and who was willing to accept responsibility for what happened when it wasn't his fault. I was physically attracted to you when I saw you at the marina, and even though you didn't admit it today, I saw you watching me. I think it's cute that you were too embarrassed to admit it to me. When you climbed into the boat, I almost had a heart attack!" Tag turns his head toward her. Their eyes meet. "I became emotionally attached to you when I saw the maturity and character you

26

displayed today during this awful tragedy. I knew then I wanted us to have a special relationship. One that I could treasure for eternity."

Their lips are so close that Tag can feel her breath. It's warm. It's sweet. It's inviting. He's confused by her candid nature. He's never met a girl this outspoken, and this beautiful. He wonders if he's correctly interpreting the meaning of her comments due to the shock of the events of the day. Never has life moved so fast for him as it has today.

Suddenly, life moves faster. She firmly presses her lips against his. Joyfully, yet bewildered, he presses back, and they roll together. They embrace and he feels her delicate tongue enticingly flicking his. Immediately instinct and passion conquer all inhibitions. If Billy's watching, it's time for him to turn away.

FOUR

"Daddy. Daddy! Tell Jase to stop it!"

Mazie's plea for help jolts Tag from his daydream. Jase is clutching a large rubber snake and he's hissing loudly while chasing Mazie through the house. The snake usually resides in the large rhododendron bush growing by the front steps to keep the birds from nesting in it. Jase has decided to put it to another use.

To halt the little terrorist, Tag grabs Jase when he runs near him. Mazie's hiding behind Tag's leg. When Tag raises Jase to eye level, Jase pokes the head of the snake toward Tag's face with a loud hiss. Instinctively, Tag jerks his head back even though he knows the snake isn't real. Although with Jase, you can never be quite sure. As opposed to most kids, Jase doesn't seem to fear creepy, crawly creatures. Tag closely watches what Jase brings into their home, and especially what Jase has crammed in pockets.

Maize runs off.

"Alright big guy. That's enough! I think your sister's had enough of scary snakes today." Jase still pokes the snake's head at Tag's face and hisses while Tag holds Jase under his arms aloft. Jase's legs are peddling as if he's trying to run on air.

"Let me have the snake," Tag instructs as he lowers Jase to the floor.

"Aw dad!" Jase complains pulling the snake back away from his dad.

"Come on big guy. Hand it over." Tag sees Jase is crestfallen when Jase raises the instrument of terror toward his dad. Tag takes it, and with a big smile ruffles Jase's hair, "Thanks big guy."

Tag quickly changes the subject to redirect Jase's attention, "It's stopped raining. You might be able to find some earthworms for your dirt pile wiggling around on the wet concrete." Jase breaks into a big toothy grin.

Now it's Tag's turn with the snake. Tag leans over and pokes the snake at Jase while hissing loudly. Jase quickly raises his hands. With a loud, fake scream Jase dashes for the door. Tag laughs as he rises and drops the snake on the counter. He marvels at how much he loves his kids.

Tag flinches at the sound of Jase slamming the outside door leading to the front porch. Tag watches Jase scurry across the porch, hop down the steps, and run on the sidewalk toward the driveway while he intentionally splashes in every puddle.

Before Tag was interrupted, he was distracted by his memory of the events of fifteen years ago today. It's hard to believe that it was fifteen years ago today that Billy died. Almost half of Tag's life ago. As he watches Jase dig with his fingers for worms around the edge of the concrete where it meets the grass, he wishes Billy were here to see his namesake, William Jason Ryder, aka "Jase." Tag couldn't call him "Billy," "Will," or "William." Emotionally that would be too hard.

Jase is four years old. He's the spitting image of his dad. Jase is into everything a four-year-old boy should be into at his age: dinosaurs, animated TV shows, Power Rangers, bulldozers, excavators, mud, dirt, bugs, scary animals, LEGOs, rough-housing, anything loud, terrorizing his big sister, leaving a wake of disaster wherever he goes, …oh, and of course, rubber snakes and earthworms. Now he seems to be fascinated with aliens. Where that came from who knows. When he meets someone new, a serious countenance appears on his cherubic face as he poses an important question, "Do you know E.T.?" The surprise looks from these unsuspecting souls is priceless, as are the awkward responses. Jase's pre-school teacher describes him as "precocious, very active, and curious, but in a good way," whatever that means.

Maize is Tag's six-year-old princess. When she was born, Tag had never experienced that depth of love before, until of course Jase was born, and Tag found there was room for two in this select group. Maize, though, will always be special because she was the first. Tag's very protective of her.

Maize runs their household, even though none of them will admit it. Tag thinks perhaps he and his wife may have taken the princess thing a little too far at times. Tag doesn't believe Maize is spoiled because she doesn't throw the temper tantrums normally associated with a child who doesn't get her way. She just seems to be confident and commanding in her opinions. She normally chooses where they eat when they dine out; what they watch on TV; what she plans to wear that day (which can change hourly); what games she will play with her friends and Jase; when she will have a snack and what it will be; what time she will go to bed; etc. Again, Maize runs their lives. Maybe it's because she can wrap her daddy around her finger. She knows he loves her. He will do anything for her.

She can be sugary sweet, attentive, and loving to her parents. She loves to perform for them. She'll break into a random, made-up song and/or dance at any time, which will make everyone laugh, unless of course she's using it to taunt her little brother. She loves dressing up, children's make-up, Barbies, animated TV shows, teenage girls, arts, crafts, butterflies, soccer, cheerleading, flashy fake colorful jewelry, flowers, nice animals, tea parties with her dolls, ice cream, jelly beans, picture books, dollhouses, swinging, picking on her little brother, and cuddling in her daddy's lap. She's shy around adults and bold around children. She's very pretty. Breath-taking to her dad. People constantly tell her how pretty she is, which is maybe why she's always performing in the mirror when she dresses-up. She has completed kindergarten and is already reading, so she must be smart. On a weekly basis she switches from wanting to be an actress, a doctor, a teacher, or a mommy when she grows up. All Jase wants to be is a dam worker.

"Hey hun I'm back," Tag hears his wife, Liesl, announce as she opens the door Jase exited a few minutes ago. She's returning from their next-door neighbor's house. It's a young couple who recently had a baby and the mother is constantly asking Liesl to come check every rash. Liesl is a physician's assistant for the local franchise of a corporate health clinic. Rock Slide is too small for a full-time doctor, but Lord knows you can't throw a rock during the summer without hitting one on the lake. "I saw Jase in the driveway. Are you sure he can tell the difference between a baby snake and an earthworm?"

"Yeah, I think so. He still quotes the limerick we made up, 'If it has a mouth and eyes, then it's not wise.' Of course, curiosity can cloud the judgment of a four-year old."

"Yeah. Let's check his pockets anyway before he comes in. I already saw him stuff a wiggling creature in one of them."

"I agree, that would be a scary surprise, especially for Maize."

"...and me."

"I hate snakes, too. Like this one!" he grabs the rubber snake off the counter and tosses it toward his wife. She jerks back her arms and lets it smack on the floor. Tag's smiling when she looks up at him after realizing it's fake. She's not smiling.

"Jase?"

"Yep. I'm not sure where our son got his gene of not being afraid of snakes. Fortunately, being this high up in the mountains, we don't have to worry about copperheads and water moccasins."

"Let's don't even talk about that. It makes my blood run cold," Liesl shivers. "Where's Maize?"

"I think she's in her room. Jase was chasing her with that rubber snake," Tag points at the snake on the floor. "When I intercepted him, she took off in the direction of her room. That was only about ten minutes ago. I'm sure she's had time to go through three outfits by now," Tag rolls his eyes with a grin.

"Probably so. Hey, now's a good time for you to run out to the cemetery. I should be here the rest of the day unless there's an emergency. If so, I'll call you, or we can go with you if you want us to. Up to you. I know how important this time is for you each year. I can understand why you prefer to be alone. Are you okay?"

"Yeah, I'm fine," which is a half-truth. The feelings of guilt have subsided, but the sadness has not. "There's no reason for y'all to come. I think the kids running around the cemetery would make me nervous and upset. Also, if we were to run into Mr. Jimmy and Mo...well, let's just say the kids don't need to be there. It could get ugly."

31

"Makes sense. I'll see you when you get back," Liesl gives Tag a kiss on the cheek. He doesn't return it. He feels guilty that he doesn't. He has no desire, though.

Tag grabs his keys and exits the house. He pauses, "Hey, if I have to show a house, I'll call you." He closes the door before he hears a response.

"Hey big guy, what's in your pocket?" Tag asks Jase when he reaches him.

Jase digs in deep and pulls out three earthworms knotted in a tangled mess. He grins confidently as he holds them up for his dad to see.

"Good hunting bud! Looks like you've done well. Make sure you only grab earthworms. What do we say?"

Jase furrows his brow, then with a wide grin he confidently recites, "mouth and eyes not wise."

"That's right! Stay away from the snakes. Now move over to the grass while I back my car out, okay?"

"Yep!"

"What was that?"

"Yes sir," Jase says softly peering at the ground in embarrassment.

"That's right. Now move over to the grass. I'll see you in a little while. Think of something fun for all of us to do when I get back, okay?"

"Yes sir!"

There's that smile again!

FIVE

Tag rolls up to the curb below the Pocket Watch Valley Cemetery. When it was dedicated over 150 years ago, the cemetery was on a secluded, gentle-sloping hillside outside the city limits of Rock Slide. That was for health reasons. Today, homes surround the cemetery causing unsuspecting visitors to believe it might instead be a sloping park, at least until they take a closer look. It sits high enough on the mountainside so in the winter the lake can easily be seen, but of course that view is wasted on the cemetery's occupants.

The old wrought iron fence surrounding the cemetery has been patched, repaired, welded, and propped-up numerous times over the decades. Tag believes the thick, tangled, clumps of weeds and grass which grow underneath and weave among the fence posts is the primary reason the fence hasn't already collapsed. The lawnmowers can't quite maneuver close enough to chew them. Every now and then there's evidence that a weed-eater made a feeble attempt to shear the tops of the weeds. For years, friends of the cemetery request funds from the city to replace the fence, but it's never been a priority item when money's even tight for the living. Tag isn't sure if the fence was built to keep the living out or the dead in, but it could do neither very well now.

The congregations of the local churches take turns maintaining the cemetery. Many of their kinfolk are buried here. Tag believes there may only be room for two more generations of Slides.

The pungent "green" scent of wet, mowed grass is pervasive when Tag exits his car. Obviously, volunteers from one of the congregations have just completed their turn.

Tag carefully avoids the muddy puddles from today's shower as he steps to the gate. He raises the latch on the wrought iron gate. Battling resistance from the thick grass, he shoves it open. It loudly announces his presence to the cemetery's occupants as it squeaks and grinds from decades of rust and age. He chuckles to himself at the sound. It seems to be straight from the archives of an old "B" horror movie. All that's needed to enhance the scene is thick, milky mist, a moonless night, and ear-piercing, high pitched, creepy, annoying music.

Tag knows the way to Billy's grave. It's half way up in the northwestern quadrant. Tag's grandparents rest in the southeastern quadrant. There's still room in their plot for a few more graves. He's in no hurry to fill them.

After he climbs the hill stepping over graves while dodging markers, headstones, dead flower arrangements, over turned cheap vases leaking chunks of green Styrofoam, and ant hills, he finds Billy's grave. It appears no one has recently visited it. Tag's convinced Mr. Jimmy no longer visits the grave. He guesses it's too emotional for Mr. Jimmy, and frankly Tag's glad he doesn't visit the grave, at least on the anniversary of Billy's death. It prevents a confrontation. It's emotional for Tag, too, but more than anything it's now therapeutic and cathartic for him to have this time alone with his best friend.

Tag creeps up to Billy's grave as if he's trying not to disturb Billy. Every time he visits, he first reads the inscription chiseled on Billy's granite headstone:

> "The time you won your town the race
> We chaired you through the market-place;
> Man and boy stood cheering by,
> And home we brought you shoulder-high."

With the family's permission, Tag's high school football team raised the money to have the first stanza of the A. E. Housman poem *To an Athlete Dying Young* engraved on Billy's headstone. It was important to them that they honor their lost hero. They felt the lines from this poem captured who Billy was for posterity.

It turned out to be a miserable year for the team. They didn't win a game. After Billy's death, they just seemed to go through the motions of playing. Their hearts weren't in it.

34

Tag's carried a backpack with him to Billy's grave. He removes from it a plastic bottle of cleaning solution and a rag. He sprays the solution on the rag and wipes off the face of Billy's headstone. He also wipes off the face of Miss Florence's headstone. Billy would want Tag to do that for him.

Billy loved his mama. She died a few months after Billy. The old folks said it was the "melancholy" that killed her. Tag had to look up the definition of this strange, unknown disease.

Tag also cleans the top of their headstones where birds left their droppings after serenading the dead. There are no tears mixed with the cleaning solution anymore. The tears stopped a few years ago. His early years of emotional pleas for forgiveness have evolved into a soliloquy of revelation and confession. Even though Tag doesn't expect responses from Billy, he does at times sense that Billy reaches down from Heaven and touches Tag's soul with an epiphany.

Tag once again apologizes to Bertram Howard Frink who died in 1955. The back of Mr. Frink's headstone faces the front of Billy's headstone. Tag sits, or leans, on Mr. Frink's headstone while he talks to Billy. He starts with a lean.

"Well Billy, like a bad habit, I'm back again!" For some reason Tag's visit each year makes him nervous. This awkward attempt at humor seems to help him relax…kind of. "Best friends for life, right! No need to worry, I'll never forget you. Although, I hope you aren't sitting around in Heaven waiting for me to drop by a few times a year."

Changing to a more comfortable subject, "You should see Jase! He's growing like a weed! I think he has your speed. Just the other day he beat Maize in a race across the yard winning his pick of the last two popsicles in our refrigerator. Of course, Maize conned him into switching popsicles with her. Just like you, he can't say no to women. Unlike you, he seems to be very smart," Tag needles with an uncomfortable grin. He glances skyward to ensure a bolt of lightning isn't headed in his direction.

"Work's going well. You won't believe what these Glides are paying for houses on the lake! There's not a house on the lake selling for less than a million dollars unless it needs razing. I could sell more homes if there were available inventory.

35

Do you remember Dumpy Doug Shaw? He put together a group of investors to purchase the old Jester farm. You know, the 120 acres about a quarter of a mile from the lake bordering Mossy Creek. Dumpy Doug and his group of investors created a plan for an attractive development of clapboard garden homes. It'll be a gated community with a clubhouse, pool, walking trails, a park with a stage, and a playground. He hired me as the exclusive agent to sell the homes, which should be a goldmine for a few years. I'm considering purchasing one of the new homes myself, but I'm not sure the development will survive Jase. Also, Liesl has her mind set on purchasing a home on the lake. I told her to dream on at these prices, although right now we seem to be doing pretty well financially.

Oh, you'll find this hard to believe, I was talked into running for city council this past year, and surprisingly, I won! I'm not sure I like seeing how the sausage's made, though. For instance, Rock Slide has an exciting opportunity which will create additional jobs for our community and additional tax revenue for the city, but it may be controversial.

Unbelievably, casino gambling's now legal in the state. The voters approved it late last year. Never thought you'd see that did you, but of course where you are this is probably frowned upon. The city council was approached by a gaming company who wants to build a casino, hotel, marina, and golf course across the lake from the town. They have options on a couple of large tracts of land that Branch Water Creek bisects before it drains into the lake. They've agreed to allow us to annex the development into the city in exchange for some initial tax breaks. They need our water, sewer, trash pick-up, etc. They estimate it will create approximately 250 new jobs, with most of them being full-time jobs, which as you know this valley desperately needs. Also, the tax revenue will be significant once the initial tax breaks sunset.

As I said, I'm afraid this is going to be controversial. The churches may try to oppose it. I'm sure it'll be a very lively debate. I'm hopeful the various congregations will recognize that the benefits will far outweigh the moral concerns. Afterall, since casino gambling is now legal, they're going to build them somewhere, so why not have the citizens of Rock Slide benefit.

I'm expecting to publicly become an unpopular member of the First Baptist Church of Rock Slide, but I'm confident many members will tell me privately they approve it. Afterall, if it weren't for the Baptists, many of the bars in Rock Slide would be out of business," Tag chuckles.

Tag changes the subject again, not wanting to get to the matter which he really planned to talk about with Billy, "I mentioned Maize earlier. She's so smart and pretty. You would love being with her! I would love to see her twist you around her finger like she does me. It's hard to say no to her, but I know I need to. I know I must be a father first, not a playmate. I need to make sure I teach her to respect others, and just as importantly, to respect herself. I need to encourage her to focus on being the best she can be, to be courageous but not foolish, and to be safe but not scared. Liesl and I make sure she attends as many church activities as possible. We recognize that the greatest gift we can give her is the gift of Jesus Christ, because we know He will be with her when we aren't. Man, let me tell you, it's hard being a dad!" Tag sighs.

"I don't know how often your dad comes by to see you and your mom. Hopefully, he does on a regular basis," Tag doesn't know why he feels he has to make excuses for Mr. Jimmy. "He still hates me for what happened. I've tried to meet with him, but he refuses. I worry about Mo. He still lives with your dad, but he's rarely seen. I can tell you that Mo's huge. If he had been on our football team, no one would've stopped us! I think we could've run behind him forever. The other team would get out of his way or risk getting hurt. The last time I saw him he had on overalls and a t-shirt. He had long hair and a big bushy beard. Unfortunately, because of his size, appearance, and disability he frightens many people, especially children. Some of the older members of our church have reached out to your dad over the years to try to help with Mo, but he refuses. Your dad quit taking him to school when your mom died, and he refuses to take Mo to church. I feel for Mo, but I'm the worst person to get involved."

Tag now stands quietly while internally debating whether he should broach the uncomfortable subject he wants to talk to Billy about. Tag believes talking to Billy about it will help him deal with it. He has no answers for his dilemma. The stress, though, is beginning to take its toll on him.

In the distance a clap of thunder rolls over the mountain ridges. The weather forecast calls for intermittent thunderstorms today. It sounds like the next one is almost here. These storms can quickly appear out of nowhere in these mountains. Tag knows time is running short if he intends to broach this subject.

Tag glances at the gunmetal sky. He's comforted when he notices that dark clouds have yet to appear above the valley. The wind's cooler causing him to briefly shiver. Before beginning, he looks around to make sure no one's in earshot. Seeing no one he begins, "Billy, I have something important which I need to talk to you about. I don't really know how to deal with it, so I thought talking to you would help me think through it. I'm falling out of love with Liesl, and that scares me to death. It's not anything she's done, in fact I consider myself fortunate to have such a loving, responsible wife like Liesl. She's beautiful, a great mom to our kids, and well respected in our community. In fact, many people call her 'Doc' because they truly see her as their doctor.

I guess you don't know Doc Flowers died five years ago. He's buried over there," Tag points to the northeastern quadrant of the cemetery. "As you know he was the only doctor in town. Dad had been trying to get me to come back to Rock Slide to take over his real estate business, but there wasn't a job for Liesl as a PA. She knew how badly my dad needed help and she loved visiting the area, so she talked to her boss after Doc Flowers died about the possibility of opening an urgent care facility in Rock Slide. After a fairly quick due diligence process, they agreed that the valley was a great spot for one. That's why I moved back to Rock Slide. I don't think I've ever told you that story.

In any event, my change in feelings for her is not her fault. It's my fault. I'm to blame. It's my problem, but if my feelings don't change it becomes our problem." Tag drops his eyes to the ground and begins to paw at the grass with his New Balance shoes. "I can't imagine the pain I'll cause if I seek a divorce, and I don't even want to consider what it'll be like if I can't be with Maize and Jase on a daily basis," Tag offers fighting back tears.

"This is all so stupid on my part!" Tag loudly exclaims as he raises his eyes to Billy's headstone. "I can't believe I still have feelings for Suzy!" There. He said it...out loud. He's admitted his deep, dark secret.

"I believed our relationship was almost spiritual because of the trauma we shared over your death. She was bold, and I loved it! I was a willing participate in whatever she wanted to do. It was exciting. I was enchanted, lustful, mystified and deeply in love. It was also extremely painful, and personally devasting when it ended. My struggles with your death and her abrupt, unexplained split from me almost drove me crazy. I've never talked to you about her because our meeting resulted in your death," tears begin to well in Tag's eyes.

"It was tough. Liesl came along at the right time. She was truly a blessing. I thought my love for Liesl was pure but lurking deep in my soul I've discovered this unresolved fantasy about Suzy." A tear leaks from the corner of Tag's left eye and begins to meander down his cheek. He quickly wipes it away with his upper right arm.

"Moving back to Rock Slide has awakened this fantasy. I drive by places where we shared intimate moments and the incredible memories of our passion rush to the forefront of my brain. Even when Liesl and I share intimate moments, I've begun to pretend she's Suzy. There seems to be a lustful beast clawing and gnawing its way out of my soul. It desperately desires to be with Suzy again. The more I try to suppress these memories, the harder it fights. I'm afraid it's going to consume me and destroy my life." Tag's confession is emotionally draining. He sits on Mr. Frink's headstone.

"Okay, your turn. I can already hear you, 'Grow up Tag! Forget her. It's over. Don't be an idiot. You're gonna blow it.' I keep telling myself all of this, but it doesn't seem to be working. I just don't understand how I can truly be in love with a memory, a fantasy, someone who deeply hurt me when I already have an incredible wife, and kids who I treasure. Heck, I don't even know where Suzy is now! She may be happily married with a bunch of kids, or she may even be dead."

I've thought about discussing this with my pastor, but it would be too embarrassing to admit. He'll think I'm a nut job,

39

and he may be right. I've tried to seek help from reading Psalms, because I equate my feelings for Suzy with the way David felt about Bathsheba. I feel David's pain, but his writings just don't speak to me in a way that solves my problem, except to recognize my sin and seek God's grace. Perhaps the solution is that simple, but it hasn't worked yet.

Maybe I need to move away, but how do I explain it to Liesl, 'Hey honey, we're moving because I'm in love with someone else who I haven't seen in almost fifteen years.' Yeah, right." Tag stands and begins pacing between the graves. "Boy, I sure do miss you! Especially during times like this. I could really use your advice. If you can hear me," Tag looks up at the darkening sky, "please, somehow, let me know." Tag stops pacing, stands still, and closes his eyes hoping for a response. Initially all he hears is the constant hum of his blood rapidly being pumped by his racing heart through the blood vessels in his ears. Slowly the rush of the wind, the chirping of birds, and the incessant barking of a distant dog creep into his ears piercing the quiet. No small, still voice, though. No epiphany. No sign.

Suddenly, the wind shifts direction. The breeze is distinctly colder and uncomfortable. The sharp smell of ozone tells him rain is very near. Tag approaches Billy's headstone, he places his hands atop it, bows his head, and offers a quick silent prayer. A drop of rain splashes on his hair. Then quickly a few more drops pelt him. "Thanks for listening, buddy. I miss you." As the pace of the rain quickens, Tag turns and carefully jogs down the hill trying not to trip over obstacles or slip on the wet grass.

SIX

Jimmy Quick's never amounted to much of anything. He was a failure in school. He graduated by the skin of his teeth. He's never held a job very long due to his explosive temper and poor work ethic. He failed as a husband. The rage caused by the death of his oldest son blinded him to his wife's suffering. She died, ignored, of a broken heart. He failed as a father because he couldn't protect his favorite son from being killed. He failed as a man. His defective sperm created a disabled second son. Jimmy's angry that he's saddled with caring for him, but at least this son's government disability checks provide cash flow which they desperately need. Jimmy's part time jobs just don't generate enough income to support them.

His rage and bitter disappointment over the death of his son still consumes him. His son was being highly recruited for his football skills by colleges from across the nation. His son's athletic prowess finally gave Jimmy the upper hand in life. Something he always craved. People had to respect Mr. By Damn Jimmy Quick and do what he demanded, by God! He was the king of Rock Slide, and everyone praised him. Then suddenly, it was snatched away in the blink of an eye. A stupid boating accident…they said. Frankly, it was negligent homicide on the part of one of his son's buddies who was trying to impress some rich girls. The boy walked away free because this town has no respect for Jimmy Quick and his family. He'll have his revenge.

The money Jimmy was planning to squeeze from a college for the privilege of his signature on a scholarship was going to be life changing. It was aspirational. It was going to buy him continued respect. No one would laugh at him or a Quick anymore. Then poof! None of these fancy colleges cared about

Jimmy Quick when his son died. His dreams of respect and riches were shattered.

When his wife died the stable income for the family vanished with her. All the do-gooders descended upon him. That just pissed him off. He sold his home, bought a cheaper home deep in the woods in a holler in the mountains, and put up a gate to keep the do-gooders out. The excess money from the sale of his previous home disappeared quickly. It was soaked up by alcohol purchased to soothe his demons. His new home was already old when he bought it, and because of lack of maintenance it has fallen into horrible disrepair. Mr. Jimmy Quick doesn't care, though. He's focused on avenging his son's death. Afterall, they say revenge is a dish best served cold.

This afternoon, though, Jimmy Quick doesn't have a care in the world. He's splayed on a ratty couch, which reeks of spilt beer, old sweat, and mildew, in an alcohol induced stupor in his filthy living room. Crushed empty beer cans litter the floor, some of which lie in a scattered heap at the foot of a heavily dented wall where they landed after being thrown in anger and frustration. This has become his tradition on the anniversary of his son's passing. He'll be out for hours.

Mo's learned to avoid his daddy when he's drinking his beers. When his daddy awakens, he'll be saying bad words Mo's mama wouldn't allow Mo to hear or repeat. Mama now lives with Billy, God, and Jesus in Heaven. Mama said Mo should never do anything which makes God angry. God doesn't like the bad words his daddy says. He sticks his fingers in his ears when he hears them.

Normally, Mo wanders in the woods when his daddy acts this way. He loves the solitude of the woods. He knows these woods like the back of his hand. There are no scary people in the woods. People hurt his feelings. Daddy says to stay away from people. Although, Mo craves to be with children. He can watch them play for hours.

The animals, trees, and flowers are his only friends, though some of them are bad. He tries to avoid the bad ones. He knows which animals are good and which are bad because of his picture books. He loves his picture books. Unfortunately, they're becoming worn, torn, and smudged due to over use.

Today, due to the rain, he's spent most of the day in his room watching his videos. His old TV and tape player still work. His mother gave these to him when he was a child. They were old then. His mother was able to convince her pastor to give these to her for Mo when the church was replacing its video equipment.

Included with this gift was a box of Veggie Tales VHS tapes. These are Mo's favorites! He watches them over and over and over. His favorite characters are Larry the Cucumber and Bob the Tomato. He laughs, claps, sways, and hums along with the music. The stories he continually watches become imbedded in his psyche. These stories, and the characters, are his world and his tool for learning. They've become his truth, his basis of "right and wrong." Watching them also reminds him of happy times with his mama and Billy. In fact, when he sees a scene from a video that he remembers watching with them he'll holler out in glee "'member dis mama!"

Mo's currently hairless. His daddy found a louse crawling on the couch. He decided it was from Mo's unkempt hair. His daddy ordered him into the yard. He shaved Mo's head and face to eliminate these pests. Mo's peach fuzz is prickly when he rubs it. He likes the way it feels. It makes him giggle. His lack of hair has accentuated his long face, big ears, and droopy eyes.

Mo's mama spent hours helping him overcome his disabilities. He can somewhat care for himself and function on his own. His daddy, though, has done none of that. Mo's relationship with his daddy is subservient at best. His daddy orders him around and treats him horribly. His daddy has learned, the hard way, that Mo needs a routine. His daddy has experienced firsthand the destructive power of Mo when he becomes frustrated. Mo's 6'5" and weighs 280 pounds. A lot of this weight is muscle. His daddy has numerous strenuous chores and low-paying jobs for him to complete which have made Mo physically very powerful. When Mo begins to act out his frustrations his destruction is devastating. Their home bears permanent scars from his outbursts. Mo wakes up, eats breakfast, eats lunch, eats dinner, and goes to bed at the same time every day.

Mo's glad it's raining today because he's sore. His daddy had him working with a logging crew the past few days. Daddy said not today because it's raining. They were thinning timber on a steep hillside. They needed Mo to help drag the fallen trees up the hill to the machines which pull them from the woods. Mo's daddy sat on a stump laughing and talking to the men while Mo dragged the logs. Mo was glad he couldn't hear what his daddy was saying because he was afraid it was bad words. Mama wouldn't like him hearing bad words.

A clap of thunder startles Mo. He stands and ambles to his window. He smiles when he sees the rain spilling through his vegetable garden. His Larrys and Bobs will grow big and strong, along with his other friends in the garden.

SEVEN

"Hey Homer...Virgil," Tag greets the old men sitting closely in the cramped reception area of the office suite he shares with his dad. They've become fixtures the last few months. Based on the look of relief in Ronette's eyes, they must've been waiting a while for Tag to return from showing a property and a prospect lunch meeting. Ronette, Tag and his dad's assistant, says they make her uncomfortable. They never call for an appointment. They just show up and wait. They sit silently in the cramped reception area and watch her work. She's tried everything she can think of to coax them to make an appointment, but they just respond, in unison, "No thank you mam, we'll just wait." Being the subject of a peep show is not what she bargained for when she took this job a few years ago. Every time she glances up from her work, they're staring at her.

"We need to talk," Homer states hurriedly.

"Yeah, and right now!" Virgil adds with a sense of urgency.

"Why sure gentlemen, let's step out back on to the boardwalk."

Homer and Virgil are the Jester brothers. These are the brothers who sold their family farm to Dumpy Doug. They're twin, seventy-four-year-old bachelor brothers who still look identical today. They're wiry old men with gnarled hands and perpetually tanned skin. The creases in their skin are so extensive and deep, it looks like a bushel of corn could grow in the furrows on their faces and necks. Tag thinks it's a wonder they haven't died of melanoma by now, but these are tough "old birds." They're probably bald on the top of their heads, but since they never appear in public without wearing their grimy baseball caps, that's still a mystery. The only way you can tell them apart is Homer's missing the top part of his left ear. Tag wants to ask why, but that would be rude. He finds himself absentmindedly staring at it sometimes when they talk.

The Jester boys have lived on their parents' farm their entire lives, scraping together a meager living by farming and performing various odd jobs in the valley. They're good men. Salt of the earth men. But no one would confuse them for intelligent men. They know farming, hunting, fixing stuff, and the Bible. It's rumored they also know something about making moonshine.

With the sale of their farm, their lives have been disrupted. Of course, most people would be pleased with a six million dollars disruption. That's what Dumpy Doug and his investors paid Homer and Virgil for their land. Homer and Virgil haven't adapted to the life of millionaires. Tag's not sure they ever will. Tag sometimes wonders if he did the right thing by convincing the Jesters to sell. He believes he was honest and ethical in his conversations with them. He doesn't spend much time fretting over it because this sale generated the largest commission he and his father ever earned. Tag put his share of the commission aside for college educations for Maize and Jase. His dad took some of his share of the commission and did the same by purchasing 529 college saving plans for Maize and Jase.

Under the theory that "no good deed goes unpunished," Tag has become their unofficial advisor on everything. Thus, the reason they've become fixtures in his office and are the source of Ronette's discomfort. Since Ronette was paid a nice bonus from the sale of the Jester farm, she's put up with their piercing stares. If this goes on much longer, she's told Tag she's not sure her bonus was worth it.

Homer and Virgil fall in line and trail Tag down a narrow hall, which bisects the office suite. They pass the doors to Tag and his dad's offices, which are across the hall from each other, and exit the building onto a large boardwalk.

Before Tag returned to Rock Slide, a developer took this section of Rock Slide, tore down the dilapidated buildings which backed up to the lake, and built an attractive, three-story development. It resembles a strip mall on the ground floor with two levels of condominiums on top of it. The developer made the development appear as if it were numerous different smaller buildings which share common walls. It won architecture awards for its design. In the center of the development is a breezeway which allows for a beautiful view of the lake and the mountains. The building rests on an underground parking deck which is accessed at either end of the development. The elevators for the condominiums and underground parking are located in the breezeway.

Along the front of the building, at street level, are the entrances to the various businesses. Aside from Tag and his dad's real estate office, there's a law office, an accountant's office, a gift and treats shop, a clothing store for all ages, a sandwich/coffee shop, a mini-grocery store, a casual restaurant, an upscale restaurant, and two currently vacant units available for rent. Along the lake front is a long boardwalk stretching the entire length of the development. All the retail rental units have space dedicated to them along the portion of the boardwalk immediately outside their units. The area of the boardwalk outside the space dedicated for the retail rental units is dedicated for the public to enjoy. Benches have been placed every few yards. Also, at the eastern end of the boardwalk is a dock where the Glides can dock their boats when they want to shop or enjoy a meal. People also fish off the dock.

Tag and his father have decorated their outside dedicated boardwalk space. They use it for meetings and conversations with clients and prospects. They've furnished it with rockers, chairs, and a round table with a colorful umbrella in the middle of it. At the border of their outside space and the public boardwalk, they built a long, two-foot-tall flower box in which they've planted a vibrant array of native flowers and plants.

Homer and Virgil plop in the rockers which are currently shaded. Tag grabs a chair and drags it across the wooden planks so he's facing them.

"So, gentlemen, what's on your mind?" Tag realizes he forgot something important, "Oh, I apologize. I should have offered you refreshments. What can I get you gentlemen?"

"Nothing," they respond in unison, each with a serious visage.

"Your secretary already asked us," Virgil adds.

"Pretty view," Homer deadpans.

Tag, without glancing over his shoulder at the lake, and glad that Ronette performed her job as instructed, answers, "Yeah, we love it. It's a great place to view the lake and mountains. It's also a popular place on the Fourth of July. I hope you'll join us next year. I'm sorry you were unable to be with us this year," which is a bit of a white lie. He was concerned how these hayseed brothers would fit in with the Glides who normally attend the party, so he was glad they declined.

Tag and his dad invite their clients and prospects to a Fourth of July party every year which they host on the boardwalk outside their office. They provide a generous feast and then everyone stays to watch the fireworks which the village shoots over the lake. Their clients are allowed to bring guests. It's a great way for Tag and his dad to stay in touch with their client base and meet new prospects for their real estate business.

"Go ahead. We agreed you would tell him," Virgil prods while looking at and elbowing Homer.

Homer, looking very sheepish responds, "We want our land back."

"Excuse me?" Tag responds not wanting to believe what he just heard.

"Yeah, just as Homer said, we want our land back!" Virgil responds loudly.

Tag's surprised, but not shocked by their request. He's noticed they seem uncomfortable with this major change in their lives. It's like they're lost with nothing to do. They've been allowed to live in their house until construction starts. Tag's tried to show them some other properties to purchase, but they don't seem interested. He knows Dumpy Doug is ready to begin construction since the final plans for the development have been approved. "I'm sorry gentlemen, but that's impossible. The sale closed and the developer is ready to start soon."

"Yeah, we know," Virgil responds.

"They told us we need to get out," Homer adds.

"I have some properties I would like to show you, but to close quickly is going to be difficult, even if we find something today." Tag believes they'll be better off if they move to a retirement village in one of the larger cities outside the valley, but he's been reluctant to address this issue with them.

48

"We don't want to move," Homer counters.

"It's our home," Virgil defiantly expresses.

"I'm sorry, but it's not. You sold it. You don't own it anymore."

"Break the sale!" Virgil demands popping out of his rocker.

"Calm down Virgil. Have a seat." Tag nervously glances around hoping that their now animated conversation is not causing a scene. "I can't undo the sale. It was a legal sale. If you have any concerns, then you need to talk to an attorney. But first, to save yourselves some money, you may want to talk to Ned Scales. You know, he was the attorney who closed the sale. I think he'll tell you what I just told you. It was a legal sale. You no longer own the land, and can't get it back, unless, of course, you buy it back. Based on the plans I've seen for your land, that's not going to happen."

"Yeah, we know Ned," Homer confirms. "He explained it all to us at the time, but we've changed our minds. We want it back."

"I can understand why you're experiencing seller's remorse. It's perfectly normal for people like the two of you who sell family land and don't have a plan for what comes next. Fellas, you received a king's ransom for your farm. Frankly, you need to count your lucky stars. Think about it for a minute. Both of you worked hard to make that land productive, just like your daddy did and his daddy before him. There are no more Jesters after you pass. At your ages you need to be thinking about your health. If you hadn't sold the land and one, or both, of you had a serious health problem, which required long term care and recovery, you couldn't have paid for it. You would have been stuck in a county nursing home and there's the possibility that some court appointed conservator would have been ordered to sell your land and pay your expenses. The conservator probably would have sold it quickly at a much lower price," Tag's subtly promoting his ability to obtain a great price for their land.

"You guys were smart. Since you sold the land, you won't have to worry about that. You sold it on your terms at a fantastic price!" Tag again promotes his skills. "You now have the luxury of enjoying your remaining years without the stress of a farm. You can do anything you want to and live about anywhere you want to. If you have a health scare, you can now choose where you want to be treated. You can be in the best care facility in the state, or country. Again, I understand why you're having second thoughts, but it was the right decision for so many reasons." Tag stops to wait for a reaction. He hopes they bought it. It sounded convincing to him.

The twins sit in silence staring at him. Tag now understands how Ronette feels. Tag desperately wants to break the awkward silence, but his sales training and experience scream at him to wait for their response.

"Makes sense," Virgil finally responds.

"Does," adds Homer. "We'll think about it."

"Think about what?" Tag asks confused.

"If we want to break the sale," Virgil answers standing.

"But you can't!" Tag responds exasperated.

"Like I said, we'll think about it," Homer now stands.

Without shaking Tag's hand, the twins turn and reenter the building. Tag's dumbfounded they can't grasp the situation. He removes his cell phone from his pocket and begins searching in his contact list for Dumpy Doug's number.

EIGHT

"Jase is running around naked again!" Maize screams from upstairs.

"Tag, will you go check on him," Liesl hollers from the kitchen. "I'm in the middle of making brownies for the daycare workers at church. Also, it's about their bedtimes, will you take care of that?"

"Sure," Tag answers rising from his chair in the den where he's working on his laptop to complete a contract for the purchase of a house for a client. He can finish it later. He's happy to have this temporary distraction from his work. Putting his kids to bed is a special time for him.

"Thanks!"

Tag steps into the hall and is immediately greeted by a naked four-year old who's bouncing on his bottom down the stairs.

"Excuse me naked boy, where are your pajamas?"

"Too itchy," another step's conquered.

"How about your underwear?"

There's thoughtful hesitation, then a short answer, "Wet."

"Wet?"

"Yeah."

"Yeah what?"

"Yes sir," is the mumbled reply with slumped bare shoulders and eyes averted to the carpet.

"How did it get wet?"

"I dunno?" with a shrug of his bare shoulders and uplifted palms.

"Jase, how…did…your underwear…get wet?" Tag asks slowly trying not to laugh seeing in Jase's visage that his young brain is crushed it's forced to fess up.

"Uh…Uh…I didn't make it to the potty in time," Jase ruefully replies with sad puppy dog eyes.

Tag climbs the few stairs to Jase and lifts his somewhat remorseful, naked son by his armpits. As Tag lifts, he begins tickling Jase. Jase laughs uncontrollably as he writhes trying to escape his dads torturous wiggling fingers. "How about not waiting until the last moment next time naked boy," Tag laughingly instructs as he climbs the remaining stairs carrying Jase.

The second floor of Tag and Liesl's home is the kid's domain. To the left of the landing at the top of the stairs is Maize's room. To the right is Jase's room. The rooms are connected by a Jack-n-Jill bath.

Tag steps into Maize's room carrying his writhing son, "Maize go brush your teeth and come in Jase's room. It's bedtime. It's Jase's turn to read a book in his room." Maize's back is to Tag. She's sitting at her child-size vanity table peering in her mirror. When she turns, Tag forces himself not to burst into laughter. She has generously spread bright red child's lipstick around her mouth making her appear clown-like and her application of blue child's eyeliner broadly encircles her eyes making her appear to have two black eyes.

"I see Jase's bottom! I see Jase's bottom!" She tauntingly sings.

"Pffftt," comes spurting from Jase's pursed lips.

"Chase! Nasty!" Tag reprimands with a gentle spank to Jase's bare bottom as they all start laughing.

"Maize, go wash the make-up off your face. Your mama will be mad if you get it on your sheets and pillow case. Oh, and if I haven't told you already, brush your teeth, too."

Maize rises from her vanity and skips toward the bathroom repetitively singing, "I see Jase's bottom!"

Tag exits Maize's room, carrying Jase while Jase is still "Pffftting." Tag tickles him so he'll stop. Tag finds Jase's wet underwear next to the empty toilet. He picks it up with a towel and gently wraps the towel around the hazardous clothing. He helps Jase pick out clean underwear and a t-shirt. Jase puts the clean underwear on his head and begins jumping around like a monkey. Tag snatches it off Jase's head and struggles to get it on his silly-acting, writhing son. Next comes the struggle with the t-shirt, and again with a gentle tap on the bottom from Tag, Jase is off like a flash to brush his teeth.

Maize comes skipping into Jase's room with a make-up free face. Bounding behind her is Jase with some toothpaste still on his chin. Tag wipes it off with a Kleenex he pulls from his pocket. Tag's found carrying a Kleenex is a necessity with small children.

"All right little monkeys hop up in Jase's bed," immediately Maize and Jase imitate monkey noises as they climb onto the bed. "Which book tonight?"

"Tell us a story instead, daddy?" implores Maize.

"Yeah! Yeah!" adds Jase as he jumps on the bed.

"What kind of story?"

"David and Goliath," Jase hollers enthusiastically. Maize rolls her eyes.

"Maize, how about it?"

"I want another one. I know that one," Maize whines.

"David and Goliath! David and Goliath! I want David and Goliath!" Jase chants.

"Maize, it's Jase's turn."

"Oh…okay, but only if you act it out," Maize smiles cunningly.

"Alright, you got it! Jase stop jumping and climb under your covers. Maize, you sit here," Tag points to the end of Jase's bed. The kids scramble to their appointed positions and anxiously stare up at their daddy ready for action.

"A long, long time ago in a land faraway in what is now the country of Israel, two great armies peered at each other," Tag raises his flattened right hand to his face and places it against his eye brows, so it shields his eyes. He then squints and acts as if he's looking at something far off, "across a valley from their positions on opposite hills." Tag lowers his hand.

"On one hill were the Israelites, the good guys," Tag smiles big "Okay lets cheer!" The three of them cheer wildly. Jase climbs from under his covers and jumps on his bed again causing Maize to bounce. "Okay, okay, that's enough. Calm down now. Shh!" Tag instructs with his right forefinger resting against his pursed lips.

"On the other hill were the Philistines, the bad guys." Without encouragement Maize boos. Jase quickly mimics. Tag again places his right forefinger to his pursed lips, "Shh!"

"Now the Philistines had a soldier named Goliath who was a giant. He was nine feet tall!" Tag stands on his tiptoes and raises his arms above his head and scowls at his children. They giggle. "Goliath was mean and scary. All the Israelites were afraid of him. Every day he would shout at the Israelites to send one of their soldiers to fight him," Tag swings and stabs with an imaginary sword. "Goliath said that if he lost the fight the Philistines would become their slaves, but if he won, the Israelites would become the Philistines' slaves. Goliath did this for forty days," Tag flashes his fingers four times, "but, none of the Israelite soldiers would accept his challenge. They were terrified of Goliath," Tag wraps his arms around himself and shakes as if he's terrified. His children giggle again.

"Now three," Tag holds up three fingers, "of the Israelite soldiers had a little brother named David. David was too young to go to war, so he stayed with his father and tended to their sheep. One day his father gave David some food and told him to take it to his brothers. He did as he was told and left," Tag walks in place acting as if he's holding an imaginary sack over his shoulder.

"When David reached his brothers, the Israelites were lining up for battle," Tag marches in place and constantly salutes, "but when Goliath stepped out and issued his challenge again, the Israelites ran back to their hill," Tag runs in place while constantly looking over his shoulder with a look of fear on his face as if someone is chasing him. Tag stops, "Now David saw all of this."

"David asked the soldiers about Goliath. Saul, the leader of the Israelite army, heard about David's questions and sent for David. When David met with Saul, he told Saul he would fight Goliath," Tag puffs his chest out as if he's strong and brave.

"Saul told David he couldn't fight Goliath because he was only a young man and Goliath was a mighty warrior. David said he had already killed a lion and bear," Tag raises his hands, forms claws and growls, "David said God had protected him from the lion and the bear, and he would protect him from

Goliath. When Saul heard this, he agreed to let David fight Goliath."

"Saul gave David armor and a sword," Tag acts like he's putting on armor, "but after trying them on and walking around, David took them off," Tag acts like he's taking off the armor, "because he was not used to wearing armor. David went to a stream, reached in, and took out five smooth stones," Tag opens his left hand, looks at his palm, and with the forefinger of his right hand he pokes his palm five times as if he's counting imaginary stones, "David took the stones and put them in his pouch," Tag acts like he has a pouch in his other hand and dumps the imaginary stones in it.

Tag puffs his chest out again and marches in place, "David walked out into the field in front of Goliath. Goliath laughed and started making fun of David. Then Goliath walked toward David," Tag stomps like a giant, "so he could kill him. David ran toward Goliath," Tag runs in place. Maize and Jase are entranced. Maize takes her hand, places it over her eyes, and spreads her fingers just enough so she can see her dad through the crack. "David took one of his stones from his pouch, placed it in the slingshot he was carrying and flung it," Tag raises his right arm above his head, rotates it in a circular motion, and then pops his wrist as if he's let go of something. "The rock struck Goliath in the middle of his forehead," Tag taps his forehead with his finger, pops his head back, makes an awful face, with his tongue sticking out, and gently falls to the ground quivering. His kids nervously laugh. "The rock killed Goliath. All the Israelites started cheering," Tag stands, raises his arms, and then pumps them while cheering. Jase joins him in cheering, but Maize doesn't. "The Philistines turned and ran. The Israelites chased them away. The end. All right, bedtime!"

"Aw!" Jase utters.

"Under your covers big guy," Tag tucks Jase in and kisses him on the forehead. "Don't forget your prayers."

"Carry me daddy?" Maize implores. Tag leans down and scoops her up in his arms. When he reaches the door, Tag stops, turns back to Jase, "Good night. Love you"

"Good night daddy! Love you, too!" Tag flips off the light. "Leave my door open!" Tag hears Jase holler from the darkness.

Tag carries Maize into her room and lays her on her bed. He tucks her in. "Daddy, was Goliath a monster?"

"No, he was just a very big, mean person. There are no such things as monsters."

"Carrie Anne says there are. She says there's one in our town," Maize's defiant.

Tag incredulously asks, "Where does Carrie Anne say there's a monster in our town."

"She saw him at the Dollar General. He made an awful sound. He was a scary giant! She said she ran to her mama. Her mama said don't be afraid, it's just Mo, but she could tell her mama was lying cause her mama acted afraid."

Tag's surprised, but not shocked, by Maize's statement. He can see where Mo would make people uncomfortable, and could scare children, but he is sad to hear that they think of Mo as a monster. "Honey, Mo's not a monster. I know he looks different and acts different from other people, but he's not a monster. I don't want you to think of Mo as a monster. You tell Carrie Anne that Mo's not a monster, that he was born with a disability."

"What's a dis-bil-ty?"

"It just means he has some," Tag's trying to search for a word that Maize might understand, "...sickness, which makes him different than everybody else."

"Can I get his sickness?"

"No, you can't sweet pea. You get it when you're born. Don't be afraid of Mo. I knew Mo when he was your age. He was a nice little boy. I think he's probably still nice. Have you seen him?"

"No. I am afraid of him. Carrie Anne says he's a monster."

"He's not, honey. I promise you he's nice. If you ever see him, just be nice to him. He may look and sound scary, but he's not. Okay, for me, will you be nice to him?"

"I'll try daddy, but Carrie Anne says he's a monster."

56

"Who are you going to believe, me or Carrie Anne?" Maize hesitates.

"Well, you better say me!" Tag smiles and tickles her.

"Okay daddy, stop!" Maize laughs.

Tag quits tickling her, pulls her covers up to her chin and kisses her on the forehead. "Good night sweet pea. I love you. Don't forget to say your prayers." Maize smiles at him.

As Tag flips off the light and leaves her room, he's disappointed that the kids in town think of Mo as a monster. He knows Billy would be upset by it. Tag wants to help the kids get to know Mo, so they won't be afraid of him, but he knows Mr. Jimmy won't allow Tag to get involved. Tag's overcome with a deep sense of sadness as he descends the stairs.

NINE

"Tag, sorry to bother you," Ronette interrupts, "but Magnolia's on the line and she says she really needs to talk to you."

"That's fine, put her through."

Magnolia Winter-Blossom is on the city council with Tag. Many might consider her a liberal female because she hyphenated her name when she married Ted. That's far from the truth, though. Frankly, she says she just did it because she didn't want to be called "Magnolia Blossom," although Tag thinks "Magnolia Winter-Blossom" is not any better. She says that if it weren't for Ted's good looks, she never would've married him because of his last name. With that said, she was very creative in how she took advantage of her unique name when she ran for public office. The only items which appeared on her campaign posters and stickers were the word "vote" and a picture of a magnolia blossom. During her campaign, these posters inundated the town's lawns, streets, and business windows. Due to the proliferation of magnolia blossoms throughout Rock Slide, it was obvious she was going to win.

Magnolia is Rock Slide's most successful cosmetologist. Her hair and nail emporium serve a sizable percentage of the female, and even some male, citizens of Rock Slide. Her male customer base might even be larger if it weren't for their wives. Magnolia has a big personality which is only matched by the size of her bosoms, which she loves to display in very tight, bright, low-cut dresses and blouses. Unfortunately, her tight skirts, diet, and age have strangled her mid-section into submission until it has blossomed into a muffin top which bunches and sags over her waist line. Some might describe her appearance as "trailer trashy." Magnolia's favorite activity is talking, and people love to talk to her. The gossip which flows through the rotation of

58

females in the chairs in her shop isn't printed in the bi-weekly Rock Slide Gazette. It's much more juicy, raw, and salacious. If you want to know who's rumored to be fooling around with who or who's on the verge of bankruptcy, just spend a day at Magnolia's. It's better than any podcast. You won't need curlers to curl your hair, and you sure don't want your husband hearing the gossip in her shop.

"Hey Mags! What's up?"

"Hey hun! You missin' me?"

"Always. You know we were meant to be."

"Sorry. Big Ted beat ya to it. He's my hunk of burnin' love."

"Kismet."

"Kiss who?"

"Kismet, you know, fate. It's kept us apart."

"You know, I ain't never attended college. You need to keep it simple for this mountain princess."

"More like mountain gossip queen. Anything worth knowing in this town starts in your shop. I bet if you published what you've heard from your customers over the years it would be a best seller. You and Big Ted could retire off the royalties.

"It's good, ain't it. If I were to blackmail folks, I'd own this town!"

"Yes, you would. Yes, you would."

"Hey hun, aren't you a member of the First Baptist Church?"

"You know it, why?"

"Well, I heard from Clarita, who heard from Lorena, who heard from Jackie Ashworth. Do you know her? She sings in your choir. She's the rail thin woman with the bob cut, which I hate. Not her, the cut. I told her she looks like a refugee from a concentration camp with that cut. She won't change it, though. Says it's easier to keep. She'd look better..."

"Yeah, Mags. I know her."

"Well, she told Lorena, who told Clarita, who told me that Pastor Honeycutt is tryin' to hold a prayer meetin' outside city hall when we're holdin' our meetin' to vote on the new casino. He supposedly wants to encircle city hall with a human chain of people holdin' hands and prayin' for us to avoid temptation from the Devil and not approve the casino."

"Really?"

"Yeah, that's what Clarita told me today while she was sittin' under the dryer."

"Huh. I haven't heard that."

"Tag, hun, we don't need Bible thumpers chantin' and hollerin' outside our meetin.' They're gonna intimidate those citizens who want to attend the meetin' and support the casino. Plus, it's gonna be bad for our biznesses. You need to talk to your preacher and tell him to stop. Tell'm if he don't, I'm gonna start telling folks what Jenny Birdsong said he tried to do to her!"

"Well, I can try. He's already been lobbying me and preaching from the pulpit about the degradation which will follow if a casino is built in our quaint village."

"There ya go with them big words again, dead-gra-who?"

"Breakdown. Collapse of the community because of the evil of gambling."

"Gotcha! We saw the plan rolled out by the casino owners. Do you think that's gonna happen?"

"No, not really."

"I got the feelin' at that meetin' that you were for it. Do you still feel that way?"

Tag pauses before he answers, "Yeah...I think it's the right thing for the community. It'll create jobs, tax revenue, and tourism dollars. If they don't build it here, they'll just build it somewhere else. That community will then reap what our community needs. Heck, these days, you can gamble about anywhere. I really don't believe we'll have any significant problems in the community by having a casino here. Those gambling today are still gonna gamble tomorrow whether Rock Slide has a casino or not. Those who haven't already gambled probably won't, even if we have a casino. I surely don't believe organized crime is involved in this casino, but you never know. As a council, we'll have to watch it. I believe the good outweighs the perceived bad."

"Just makin' sure you weren't wafflin' on me."

"I'm not. If what you're telling me is true, I'm not so sure how large a crowd he's going to get. I've had a number of folks from our congregation tell me they support it. Now, I'm not sure how many will go on the record, but I think many of them would if pushed. They surely won't show up for the prayer meeting."

"I don't wanna take that chance. You talk to your preacher man and convince him to stay away. A'ight?"

"I'll try, but he may not listen to me. It might be better if someone who's not in the congregation try it first."

"No, you try it first. If he don't listen, I'll talk to him. I'll make him listen."

"So, what did Jenny Birdsong tell you?"

"You gotta become a customer of Magnolia's to find out."

"I'll think about it."

"Come see me hun."

As Tag cradles the receiver, he's worried this vote is going to become more stressful than he imagined.

TEN

The ancient pick-up rumbles to a stop in a remote parking spot at the Dollar General. It burps and wheezes to a halt when the key to the ignition rotates to kill the engine. A wasp swiftly enters the cab through the open passenger side window. Its buzz disturbs the cab's occupants. Watching it hover in mid-air, the truck's passenger is more fascinated by the skill of the insect than afraid of the pain of its sting. He knows it has wings, even though he can't see them due to them beating at an incredible rate of speed. He marvels at God's creation.

Swiftly, a rolled-up, ratty auto parts magazine smashes the wasp against the console bursting it into a gooey mess. The driver who wielded the instrument of death rakes the splattered insect onto the floor of the truck leaving remnants of its sticky guts stuck to the console.

"Damned insect!" Mr. Jimmy growls. "He won't sting anyone anymore." Mo frowns and sticks his index fingers into his ears. "Get yer fingers outta yer ears boy and listen up!" Mo obeys. His frown remains. "I'm goin' in the store for some supplies. You wait here. I'll be back in a few minutes. No one should be messin' with ya parked over here."

"Anmul quackers."

"What you'd say?"

"Anmul quackers."

"Don't know if I got 'nuff money. We'll see."

Upon exiting the truck, Mr. Jimmy pulls the wad of cash from his pocket. He'll have to see how much he has left after he buys their necessities… and his case of beer.

Mo watches his daddy disappear between the automatic doors. Mo's fascinated by this magic. All the doors in his home can't be opened without turning their knobs. These doors have no knobs, and no one pushes them, yet they open.

Suddenly, Mo's ears capture the laughter of children at play. He jerks his head from side to side but can't see them. He realizes the sound is coming from behind him. The back window of the truck was broken years ago and is now covered by a crude, cut-out piece of plywood screwed into the metal to hold it in place. Mo steps from the truck hoping to glimpse the children at play. He smiles and claps when he does. The Baptist church playground is across the street, and the five and six-year-olds are enjoying themselves.

"Look Carrie Anne!" Maize exclaims as she holds up her clover chain bracelet.

Carrie Anne quickly glances up from her weaving. "Uh huh." She raises her hand to shade her eyes from the bright sunshine. "I'm not finished with mine. I'm making it bigger so I can give it to my mommy." She plucks a flower at dirt level preserving the stem so her tiny fingers can tie it to the chain of clovers she's weaving.

"I'm going to make one for my grandma," Doris brags.

"Me too," Daisy chimes in.

"Shoo bee!" Liza Jane commands as she waves away a bee which landed in the clover where she intends to pick a long stem flower. The bee quickly darts through a link in the fence and lands in the clover next to the sidewalk.

The girls are splayed in the clover just inside the chain link fence which separates the church playground from the village sidewalk. The lawnmowers don't cut close enough to the fence to whack away all the clover. The clover grows longer in this blade free zone until the hungry weed eater arrives. The girls are delighted they got here first.

Maize's suddenly embarrassed by her carefully woven bracelet. She thought her friends would be impressed by her creation. She slides it over her tiny hand onto her wrist. She thinks it looks great as she rotates her arm to view her hand-crafted bracelet. Not to be outdone by the other six-year-olds, she brags, "Well, I'm gonna make a great big one for my mommy!"

Suddenly, a large shadow shades Maize and Carrie Anne. They look up and spot Mo looming inches away on the other side of the fence. Carrie Anne shrieks, "Mo monster!" The girls, except for Maize, scream, scramble to their feet, and run away leaving their unfinished creations scattered in the clover. Maize, terrorized but determined to be nice as her daddy instructed, slowly rises to her feet. Her eyes never leave the giant's face. His facial features are unusual, but due to his large grin she doesn't find them frightening. His eyes seem to radiate joy as they beam at her. She senses he won't hurt her.

Trembling, Maize shakily asks, "You Mo?"

He nods his head.

"My daddy's Tag Ryder. He says for me to be nice to you. He says you were friends when you were little."

Mo's facial expression briefly changes to quizzical and then his smile becomes wider than before radiating greater joy as his deep voice resonates, "'member Tag! Billy's friend."

Maize now has a quizzical look on her face not knowing what that means. Mo places his enormous hands on the chain link fence causing it to bend toward her. His meaty fingers penetrate the links. Maize's eyes widen.

Mo senses her fear, "No hurt! You friend," Mo soothingly speaks. "You friend. You name?"

Maize calms, "Maize."

"May-Z, new friend," Mo beams again with his wide smile.

Maize returns a nervous smile. Even though she's calming, she's still wary of this giant.

"Mo likes." His meaty right index finger points at the clover bracelet on her wrist.

Maize glances at her bracelet. Daddy said to be nice. "You want it?"

Mo beams a smile and claps his hands in joy. Maize removes the clover chain bracelet from her wrist and holds it up. Mo sticks his right index finger through the links and curls it in the shape of a hook. Maize carefully places it on his curled finger. Suddenly, Maize's startled by a loud commanding voice erupting from behind her.

"Hey! You get outta here! Quit scaring these children!" She turns to see her day care teacher, Miss Edna, swiftly walking toward her gesturing her arms. Her class is following behind her at a safe distance. Maize turns back to Mo and notices a combination of fear and sadness etched in his face as he steps away from the fence. A new voice joins the shouting.

"Hey boy! What ya doin' outta the truck. Get yer ass over here, now!"

Maize sees an older, wiry, unkempt man carrying bags walking toward them from the Dollar General. Mo turns and scurries toward him.

Miss Edna hollers at the man when she reaches Maize. "Keep him away from these kids! He's scaring them to death! You need to watch him more closely. If not, I'm gonna call the police! Also, don't use those types of words around these children!"

"No worries mam. I'm sorry!"

Miss Edna stoops next to Maize, "Are you alright dear?"

"Yes mam."

Miss Edna stands and instructs the whole class, which is now gathered around Maize, "Children, let's don't play so close to the fence."

As Miss Edna walks away, Maize's class showers her with praise. She's met the monster up close and survived. She's earned a level of enhanced respect. She swells with pride, although she's slightly angry because she now knows Carrie Anne was wrong and her daddy was right. She strains to peer past her friends so she can see across the street. The old man kicks at Mo when they're close. Mo scurries to an old truck and squeezes inside. Maize's sad for her new friend.

ELEVEN

Tag marvels at the beauty of the lake as he strolls on the boardwalk. He watches the expensive boats skipping across the water thrilling their passengers. On cloudless summer days like this he wishes he were a Glide instead of a Slide.

Myrtles has the best cheeseburgers in the valley. It's always packed at lunch during the summer with Glides and tiny Glides. The wait for a table can be unbearably long, especially for a busy real estate agent. Even worse than the wait is the cacophony of noise from the unruly kids. Having sold the actual Myrtle her home, he gets special treatment. He called her this morning and said he would be by at 11:30 to pick up his Fantasy Island combo. It's one of his guilty pleasures, a thick, juicy patty topped with melted American cheese and smothered in a mixture of Thousand Island dressing and Heinz 57 sauce dressed up with a smattering of sweet pickles. It comes with a side of thick fries caked with sea salt and dusted with ground cinnamon. A small tub of Polynesian sauce is added as a dip for the fries. Since today is rain-free and a cold front caused the outside temperature to be pleasant, he devoured it on the outside patio of his office suite. He's convinced himself that if he strolls the boardwalk ten times after this massive intake of calories, he'll offset its negative effects. He's on his sixth trip.

He stops to stare at a mama duck paddling by with her four ducklings noisily following close behind. Suddenly, a soft pair of hands extend from behind him and press against his eyes covering them.

"Guess who?"

He instinctively raises his hands to force away these strange hands covering his eyes.

"Oh no! Not until you guess who!"

The voice is female and eerily familiar, but he can't place it. The lotion on her skin has a pleasing odor. He senses his ears growing warm with embarrassment.

"You got me. I don't have a clue."

"Oh, come on! It hasn't been that long!"

"I'm sorry. I don't know." He reaches up, grabs the soft hands, and forces them away ending this awkward child's game.

He turns hoping to be able to identify the mysterious woman. When his eyes meet hers, he's rendered speechless. The shock of seeing Suzy's beautiful, radiant smile again sucks the air from his lungs and shocks his emotions.

"Surprise!" Suzy squeals excitedly. "Gotcha!" She tightly embraces him.

Tag's mouth is agape. He's truly stunned.

Suzy releases him and steps back. Her smile evaporates when she notices his confused expression, "Don't you have anything to say to an old friend."

Tag gathers himself, "I'm sorry Suzy, but you totally caught me off guard. What are you doing here?"

"Aren't you glad to see me after all these years?"

"Of course. Of course, but seeing you here…now… is such a shock. Why are you here?"

"I need a good real estate agent."

"Seriously?"

"Seriously! I want to purchase a lake house."

"Seriously?"

"Seriously!" Suzy chuckles. "Is that all you have to say?"

"I'm sorry. I'm still a little stunned." Tag's eyes drink in Suzy's natural beauty. He remembered her as a teenager. Now that she's matured, she's filled out nicely in all the right places, and she's even more beguiling than he remembered.

"I completely understand. I felt the same way when I searched online for a real estate agent and saw your name. I had no clue you were still in Rock Slide. Not that that's a bad thing. There was no doubt who I was picking when I saw you were a real estate agent."

"I appreciate it. Frankly, I've only been back a few years. My dad's business had grown to the point where he needed help and he wants to eventually turn it over to me. It's been a great decision on my part."

"I'm happy for you."

"Suzy, just being totally honest with you, I'm not sure I can help you."

"Why's that?"

"You hurt me pretty badly when you just disappeared from my life. Billy's death and your rejection really messed me up. It took me awhile to recover. For you to just pop back into my life acting like everything's great is not alright with me. I'm very confused right now. My emotions are a mess. I'm sorry. I'm not sure what I'm saying."

"I'm sorry. You deserve an explanation. Many might disagree, but my life hasn't been easy either since I broke off our relationship. I want to make amends. That's one of the reasons I'm returning to the lake."

"Well, I appreciate it, but I need to think about it."

"I'm sure you remember how impatient I am. Do you have time this afternoon for us to talk?"

"I don't know Suzy."

"Please! I owe you an explanation."

Tag pauses unsure of what he should do. He quickly decides that maybe meeting with her will bring closure and slay some demons swirling in his head. "Okay. I do have time late this afternoon. How about 4:30?"

"Great! Thank you. I rented one of the condos above your office," Suzy points. "Just come on up when you're ready. I'm in 308."

Tag hesitates. He's not sure it's a good idea to meet in the condo, but he knows if he's seen meeting with her in public or after hours in his office it will generate gossip. No one will know about a meeting in her rented condo. "Okay, see you then."

"Thank you! There's a lot we need to discuss. Please bring your listings, regardless of the price." Suzy again hugs him.

"I will," Tag responds without returning her embrace. He quickly scans the boardwalk hoping no one he knows, or even worse Liesl knows, notices Suzy's affection.

Suzy releases her embrace, steps back, and with a captivating, radiant smile and cock of her head wiggles her fingers on her right hand in a wave which is alluring to him. As Tag watches her walk toward the breezeway of the building, his private memories of their teenage intimate moments rush to the forefront of his brain. They excite him. He's never felt so alive as he did then. He craves more. He knows it would be wrong. These salacious memories frustrate him. They've threatened his marriage. Now there's a greater threat. She's back.

The ring of his cell interrupts his thoughts and his enjoyment of watching Suzy's gait. "Crap! How does she already know?" he mutters. Liesl's name appears on his cell's screen. His anxiety spikes as he answers his cell.

"Hey! What's up?" he offers hoping he sound's calm.

"Hey daddy. I saw Mo and wasn't scared. Carrie Anne was. She ran away. I was nice like you said. I gave him my bracelet. He said he was my friend. I want to be his friend. Miss Edna and a mean man made him leave. I was sad." It's hard for Tag to understand Maize since she's talking so fast and on the speaker.

"So, you saw Mo today. Where did you see him?"

"At church. Next to the fence."

"And you weren't scared of him?"

"No sir! I was nice like you said, and he was nice back," Tag can hear Maize's new found confidence in the tone of her voice.

"See, I told you. There's no reason to be scared of Mo."

"Carrie Anne and my other friends were. Everyone said I was brave!"

"Yes, you were. I'm proud of you!"

"When can we go see him? He's my new friend."

"I don't know sweet pea. We'll have to see."

"I like Mo. He looks scary, but he's not!"

"You're right. Hey Liesl, is everything alright?"

"Oh yeah. I just picked her up for a mother daughter lunch, but your daughter was so excited about her adventure today she had to call you as soon as she got in the car."

"I'm glad she did. Maize, again I'm so proud of you!"

"Thank you, daddy!"

Tag clears his throat, "Liesl, I may be a little late tonight. I have to gather some listings for a new client who wants them this evening. I should be home by dinner, if not, I'll call you." He didn't tell her a lie, but then again, he didn't tell her the entire truth.

"Thanks for telling me. I'll see you when you get home. Love you! Maize?"

"Love you daddy!"

"Love y'all, too!"

Tag's disappointed in himself as he hangs up. He knows he must resolve these feeling for Suzy quickly, or the stress is going to affect him even more than it has. He can't continue meeting secretly with Suzy. If he's caught by Liesl, it will be much worse than if he just tells her about Suzy. He just can't tell her everything about his new client.

Tag's too stressed to walk the remaining four laps on the boardwalk. Maybe the additional stress will burn the unwanted calories. Man, he wishes he had Billy to talk to! Suddenly, he wonders if Billy didn't arrange for this to happen after his confession to him at his grave a few days ago. It would be just like Billy to try to bring things to a head just to watch him squirm.

TWELVE

"Say ah?"

Lilla's pressed hard against her mother while clinging to her. Even though she's not feeling well, she's terrorized. She believes before she leaves the room, she'll be shotted.

"Come on honey. Please open your mouth for Doctor Liesl. She needs to look at your throat to help you feel better," Lilla's mother Karen softly pleads.

"I promise Lilla, this won't hurt. I just need to look to see what's making your throat hurt so I can make it go away," Liesl adds.

Lilla presses her lips tightly together and buries her face in her mother's chest.

Karen's embarrassed and exasperated by her daughter's refusal, "Lilla, this is ridiculous! Turn around and open your mouth!" she harshly commands.

"Hold on Karen. I have an idea." Liesl opens a cabinet and removes from it an Elsa doll from the *Frozen* movie. She presses a button on its back and a brief tune emits from the doll. Lilla whips her head around. Her eyes grow wide with excitement.

"Look Lilla! It's Elsa!" Karen exclaims.

"Would you like to hold her?" Liesl asks. Lilla nods her head. "Then all you have to do is open your mouth. Will that be okay?" Lilla pauses, then she nods her head. "Good! Then here you go." Liesl reaches out to Lilla with the doll. Lilla takes it and hugs it against her body. "Now open up Lilla and say ah."

Lilla opens her mouth. Her eyes quickly well with tears as the giant popsicle stick with a yucky taste is pressed against her tongue and the strange-shaped, silver flashlight is shined into her mouth.

"Now say ah?"

71

"Ahhhhhhhhhhhh!" Lilla relaxes when the popsicle stick's removed from her mouth.

"I don't see any sign of an infection in her throat, nor did I see any in her ears. I think she just has a bad cold. If you don't already have it, get some Motrin from the drugstore, and follow the instructions on the box. Also, she can have all the popsicles and ice cream she wants to soothe the pain. You'd like that wouldn't you Lilla?'

Lilla's nods enthusiastically. She loves ice cream and popsicles! Her smile reappears, primarily because she now believes she's going to escape without being shotted.

"If she's not better in a few days, I'll need to see her again."

"Thanks, Liesl. I'm glad that's it. I'll watch her. When can she go back to day care?"

"Why don't you hold her out tomorrow, and if she's not any worse, she can go back to school the next day."

"Thanks. I will."

"While I make some notes in Lilla's file, do you have any additional questions?"

"No, I think I'm good. Lilla, do you have questions for Doctor Liesel?" Lilla shakes her head signaling "no" while pressing the button on the back of the Elsa doll. "I'm glad you said she could have ice cream. I took Lilla over to that shop near Tag's office for ice cream at lunch. I almost didn't bring her because she felt better after eating it, but in an abundance of caution I did. I'm sorry I wasted your time."

"You didn't waste my time. That's what I'm here for. It's always better to be safe than sorry."

"Thanks, by the way does Tag have a sister who's just came to visit?"

"No. Why do you ask?" Liesl finishes her notes.

"I was just wondering," Karen now wishes she hadn't said anything.

"What makes you think he has a sister?

Karen has no choice but to answer now that she's cracked that door open. "Lilla and I sat out on the boardwalk while she ate her ice cream. I saw Tag on the boardwalk talking to some woman who gave him a hug. He looked like he was very surprised. I thought it might be a sister who surprised him with a visit. She appeared to be excited to see him."

"No, he doesn't have any siblings. Not sure who that might be. I'll have to ask him. Perhaps he was able to obtain an attractive offer on a home for her," Liesl responds trying to hide any concern, even though she's now curious as to who this mystery woman might be. She knows she can't ask Karen anymore questions without causing Karen to become suspicious.

"Yeah, you're probably right. She sure was pretty..." Karen could kill herself for saying that.

"Alright Lilla. Elsa needs to go back into the cabinet. Some other little girls might need her help to be brave." Lilla reluctantly hands the doll back to Liesl. "Do you know my little boy Jase? He's in your class." Liesl's trying not to let Karen see that her comment is bothering her, but she's very curious about this pretty woman who's showing public affection for her husband.

"Oh yes, Lilla talks about Jase all the time. I think they must play together a lot. They have a great class!" Karen's also trying to move on from her slip of the tongue and she's hoping she hasn't caused a problem. She mentally scolds herself. She needs to think first before trying to force conversation.

Karen lifts Lilla from her lap and stands her on the floor. She then stands and takes Lilla's hand. Lilla's terror has disappeared now that she realizes she won't be shotted. She wiggles as she peers up at Doctor Liesl with curious eyes.

When Liesl see's Lilla's imploring look, she realizes she forgot something very important to Lilla. "Oh, Lilla, I'm sorry. I almost forgot." Liesl reaches into another cabinet and removes a jar full of colorful suckers. Liesl bends down so Lilla can reach into the jar. "Pick out the color you like Lilla?"

Lilla's smile has disappeared. She has a very serious look now that she must choose among the assorted colors of suckers. She's very thoughtful as she studies each sucker before grabbing one.

"Come on Lilla. Pick one. Doctor Liesl has other patients to see."

Lilla grabs a red one. She lifts it from the jar, and then immediately drops it. She's changed her mind. She grabs a purple sucker and removes it from the jar. She rips off the thin, clear covering and sticks it into her mouth. Liesl places the jar back in the cabinet.

"Alright, let's go Lilla. Thanks again Liesl."

"You're welcome. Just take this file to the receptionist to check out." Liesl hands her the file.

"I will."

When Karen and Lilla leave the room, Liesl's thoughts again turn to this mysterious woman Karen saw. It wouldn't normally concern her, but she's noticed Tag's seemed distant and less affectionate recently. Probably nothing to worry about, but she needs to resolve this issue quickly so it doesn't eat at her.

THIRTEEN

Tag paces outside the door of 308. His emotions tug at him. His secret fantasies lie on the other side of the door. His reality doesn't. If he walks away, he's worried he'll always be haunted by not knowing. If he walks in, he's worried his life, and the lives of his family, will change forever. Curiosity has led him to the door. He must know why Suzy ditched him years ago. He must know which fork in the road he's destined to take. He snickers at Mags comment of "kiss who?" during their telephone conversation. It briefly relaxes him. Be courageous. His Kismet has arrived.

He knocks. His heart's racing. His iPad's cupped in the fingers of his left hand. It bounces as his fingers nervously roll. He waits. He paws at the tile with his shoes. No answer. Tag checks his watch. It's 4:33 pm. He knocks again, harder this time. He waits. Still no answer. He doesn't want to create a scene by calling her name. Frustration and confusion build. Did he have the wrong time? Did he remember the right condo number? Did she change her mind? He decides to knock one more time. Three strikes and you're out. He'll leave if she doesn't answer this time. He'll even be more confused about their relationship than he was before.

Suddenly the door opens. He gasps! Suzy stands in front of him in a revealing bikini, like the day they first met. What's dissimilar is she's wearing a diaphanous cover-up and her body is now fuller and more seductively shaped.

"I'm so sorry Tag. I was out on the balcony soaking up some sun in this beautiful mountain weather and fell asleep. Your knocking woke me. Please come in."

Tag steps into the room. Suzy closes the door behind him. He can't speak, and even though he knows he shouldn't, he can't avert his eyes.

"Let me go change into something more appropriate for our meeting. I'll be right back. Please help yourself to the bar, or I have Coors Light in the refrigerator. If I remember correctly, that used to be your favorite beer."

Tag's a frazzled bundle of nerves as she walks away and closes the bedroom door behind her. Thankfully, no *Basic Instinct* moment. The thought of her changing on the other side of the door is more than he can handle. He needs to calm his nerves. He makes a beeline to the bar. He's shocked when he finds a bottle of Pappy Van Winkle bourbon. He can't pass it up. He's always wanted to try it, but a single shot usually costs more than most expensive bottles of bourbon. He pours himself a one finger, neat glass, and drinks it. Its rich pleasing taste soothes him. He now understands why bourbon drinkers all over the world will pay so much money for a single shot. Maybe this shot will provide him a shot of courage.

He opens his firm's website on his iPad and taps the file containing all the current listings on the lake. He hopes there's a business opportunity, but he's not sure he can emotionally handle rekindling the relationship. He's still undecided whether he can be her agent. He's very anxious about being here. Perhaps another shot will help him.

Tag pours himself another one finger, neat glass. As he takes a sip, the door to Suzy's bedroom opens. He almost chokes. There's an immediate burning sensation. He's sucked the expensive bourbon into his sinus cavity. Suzy walks toward him wearing a skin tight, powder blue spandex top. It has a mock turtleneck and wide openings for bare shoulders and arms. The hem of the mock turtleneck is tucked in under the waist line of her tiny white shorts. The cloth of the shorts end at her crotch, accentuating her long, shapely, gorgeous, smooth legs. Those legs have tantalized Tag since their first meeting. Also, it's terribly obvious she isn't wearing a bra. He shouldn't be here, but he can't force himself to leave.

"Now that's better. Did you find something to drink?"

"Uh…yes I did. I had some of your Pappy. I hope you don't mind. How'd you get some of that? It's very rare."

She stops so close to him that the lack of space between them is uncomfortable to Tag. The alluring fragrance of her newly applied perfume fills his nostrils masking the bourbon's burning sensation.

"It was a gift from an admirer," Suzy winks. "I'd never heard of the stuff, but people seem to go ape over it," she snickers. "I usually don't bring it with me when I travel. I only bring it when I need to impress someone," she smiles, "like you."

Tag's tongue tied. Suzy brushes past him, grabs a wine glass from the cabinet, opens the refrigerator, and removes a half empty bottle of Chablis. While she's pouring herself a glass, Tag gathers his wits.

"I have my iPad which contains all the listings on the lake. Where do you want to review them?"

"So, you've decided to be my agent?" Suzy sips her wine while leaning against the kitchen counter. Her flawless, gorgeous legs are crossed at her ankles.

"Maybe, but let's see if you find anything of interest first."

"Oh, I've already found something I'm very interested in," she smiles.

"Excuse me?" Tag's heart beat spikes.

"I've already been looking online, and found one I'm very interested in. What were you thinking?" she narrows her eyes while her smile widens.

Tag's afraid he's blushing. Scrambling he offers, "I'm sorry, I didn't understand what you initially said."

Suzy laughs. Tag senses she's very skilled at these types of encounters with men.

"Come join me over here," Suzy walks to the couch and sits. Patting the seat next to her she adds, "Sit beside me, and first let's talk about what happened fifteen years ago. It's time for you to know."

Tag decides to pour one more finger before sitting. He sits next to Suzy and places his glass on the coffee table. Now that he's inches away from her, he marvels that she's more beautiful than he remembered. He's glad the couch isn't forcing their bodies together like the hammock did on that wickedly, amazing night.

"Where do I begin," she sighs. "I guess I'll start with the first time I saw you at the marina. I thought you were gorgeous! I knew you were interested in me because when you thought I wasn't looking, you looked at me. I thought it was so cute when you overflowed the gas you were pumping, and it spewed out into the lake. You were distracted, and I knew why. When we sped off in our boat, I was wondering how I could meet you. Then, a few days later, up you popped out of the water into my boat. I nearly died! I could tell you were also pleasantly surprised. Unfortunately, that meeting turned into something so horrible I don't want to mention it," Suzy looks away from Tag.

"You don't have to."

"Thank you. I knew that us sharing that awful event created this unbreakable bond between us. I knew I had to be with you that night. How something so awful could create something so amazing was surreal. My memories of that night still excite me," Suzy blushes.

Tag's neck warms from a spurt of emotion, or perhaps ole Pappy's beginning to kick.

"Those passionate days and nights with you are still the most memorable of my life. They say you never really forget your first true love. I've found that to be true," she shyly smiles.

Tag now knows it's not the Pappy which is causing the flushing in the veins in his neck.

"I cried all the way back home when I left the lake. I wanted to be with you, but I knew I couldn't. We were too young. My days soon revolved around your texts and phone calls. If you'll remember, our plan was to run away together when we graduated in May. I was determined to make that happen."

"Then what happened?!?" ole Pappy's dynamited Tag's inhibitions.

Suzy pauses…then stumbles ahead, "My parents. I got mad at them. In anger I revealed our secret plan. They grounded me. Took away my phone. They were incensed by the frequency of your texts and calls they noticed on my phone. They bought me a new phone, with a new number, and they checked it every day to ensure I wasn't contacting you. I cried and cried, but what was I to do?"

Tag's gut tells him that she's not being completely truthful. It seems she would have found someway at the time to let him know as opposed to leaving him twisting in the wind.

"I threw myself into my school work. I was already near the top of my class. I graduated in the top five of my high school class. I was accepted to the University of Virginia where I majored in business. I dated numerous guys through college, but I never felt the same way about them that I did about you. I figured you were so mad at me, that you had moved on and probably never wanted to talk to me again."

"Hell yeah! You were right about that!" ole Pappy's now barking loudly.

"I'm sorry. I never forgot you, and still missed you. After college, I was lucky to get a job on Wall Street. I was working almost 24/7, and when I wasn't, I was partying. Drugs were very prevalent on the Street, and money was plentiful. The cocktail of drugs I took daily kept me from collapsing. I quickly learned that men, even very powerful men, desired me. I didn't disappoint them," Suzy's voice softens as she drops her eyes to the floor.

"These men would tell me about business opportunities in which they were investing and how incredibly profitable they were going to be. Sometimes I invested in them, and sometimes they gave me some shares due to the favors I was showing them," she's still staring at the floor.

Suzy averts her eyes from the floor so that she's now staring into Tag's eyes, "Some of the investments did well and some of them didn't, but one did really, really well. The money I made was unimaginable. I still can't believe it today. It's generational money. I'll never have to work again. I could, and still can, buy almost anything I want to. I was a wreck though. I had to escape that world and get off the drugs. I left the Street, went to rehab, and though it was very difficult, I kicked the drug habit. I was very rich, but very lonely."

"How much did you make?" Pappy's curiosity immediately embarrasses Tag for asking such a personal question and not being empathetic. "I'm sorry. I shouldn't have asked you that. That's none of my business." He's surprised that Suzy doesn't seem offended or upset by his question.

"Let's just say I'm worth low nine figures," Suzy's countenance is serious.

Tag quickly calculates that's a helluva lot of money! Pappy speaks again before Tag can stop him, "I'd think you wouldn't be lonely with that much money." Again, he's embarrassed, "I'm sorry, this bourbon's gone to my head. I apologize."

She laughs, "No need. It blows my mind, too. Yeah, I'm sure I could buy many gorgeous men who would want to be with me and help me spend my money. But I want a real relationship. Not one I'm paying for. That's why I came back to the lake." Suzy places her hand on Tag's thigh.

Tag's heart beat once again spikes, "Uh...Suzy...uh...I'm married."

"Then why are here?" Suzy's isn't laughing.

Tag glances away, "I shouldn't be."

"But you are. If you were happily married, you wouldn't be with me...in this condo...by ourselves."

"I have two kids," is his only response.

"I can't have kids."

"I'm sorry."

"Once I was pregnant. I was afraid to tell my parents. A friend of a friend of a friend put me in touch with someone who could get me an abortion. It worked, but this person butchered my ovaries resulting in me never being able to have children again. Not something any woman should ever have to deal with, especially during her senior year of high school."

Tag whips his head around. He's staring directly into those gorgeous eyes which have always melted his inhibitions and brought unfathomable joy. Those eyes are now quickly welling with tears. Her beautiful face is contorted in a distressed and serious look. "Me?"

"Yes, you," tears now cascade down her flawless cheeks. She wipes them away with the palms of her hands. A few tears escape, kissing her lips, something Tag loved and craves again.

Tag's dumbfounded. He doesn't know what to say. How do you respond to someone who was once carrying your child, and you never knew it?

"Why didn't you tell me? I could have been there for you."

"I was scared to death!" Suzy wails. "I didn't know what to do. I sure couldn't tell my parents! I used most of my savings to pay for it. It was all I could do to hide the physical pain from them for a few days! They thought I was just sulking from being punished."

"We were going to have a child?" Tag repeats dumbfounded.

"Yes! Do I need to spell it out for you? I was too young! We were too young! Maybe it was a rash decision, but I just couldn't tell you. It would have ruined my life...your life."

"This is a lot to take in. I'm really at a loss for words."

"You don't have to say anything, just think about us...together again. I've dreamed about it, and when I found you on the internet, I knew it was possible. Don't you ever dream about us together again?"

Tag stands, places his hands on his head, and walks to the bar. He turns. Suzy's perched on the edge of the couch, anxiously anticipating his response. She looks even more beautiful and desirable in her wounded state. This can't be happening he scolds himself. If he doesn't leave now, it may be too late to save his family.

"Suzy, I'm sorry. I need to leave. This is just too much." He grabs his iPad and makes for the door.

Suzy stands, "Please Tag! Think about us together again. The passion reignited. All the money we would ever need!"

Tag doesn't look back before the door closes behind him. He quickly jogs to the stairwell. He can't wait for the elevator. His life just became very complicated and confusing.

FOURTEEN

"Good," Tag mumbles. The door to his office suite is locked. His dad and Ronette have left for the day. Right now he can't face anyone he knows. Especially someone who knows him well. They'll easily see how flustered he is.

He locks the suite's door behind him and hurries to his office. He opens its door, flips on the light, and heads to his desk. He yanks open the bottom left drawer. He removes his toothpaste, toothbrush, and mouthwash, essentials for someone in real estate sales. He heads for the bathroom, flips on the light, turns the water on in the sink, and begins vigorously brushing his teeth. Once he washes out his mouth with water, he repeats the cycle again. After the second rinsing, he pours the mouthwash in his mouth, gargles, and swishes. He spits it out and repeats it. After his second rinsing, he cups his hands over his mouth and nose and exhales. "Good!" he congratulates himself. The smell of the Pappy has been washed away. It wouldn't be good for him to return home with alcohol on his breath when he's supposed to be meeting with a new client.

He glances at the mirror above the sink. He doesn't look any different after such life changing news, but he is different. The thought that he could have a teenager today is sobering, strange, weird, and sad. Would it have been a boy or a girl? Would she look like Suzy? Would he look like him? He can only imagine how his life would be if Suzy had made a different decision fifteen years ago. If she had, it blows his mind to think that he probably wouldn't have Maize and Jase, the two humans he loves the most. It's bothering him that he's not mourning the loss of the child he never knew.

Right now, he doesn't like the person staring back at him. His mundane life became boring. He was wanting more excitement, especially in his love life. He was embarrassed to discuss it with Liesl, so his memories of his passionate times

82

with Suzy caused his brain to create new make-believe fantasies. They were pleasurable experiences only for him to explore and enjoy. An escape from the mundane. He thought he could manage it, but his fantasies were pushing to become realities. It was affecting his marriage. He knew he needed to accept his reality, but he just wasn't ready to end his affair with his fantasy. It was safe. He always got what he wanted. He thought he was in control, but now, staring in the mirror, he's not so sure. He realizes he'd fallen in love with his fantasy. How sad and demented is that! Now, the main subject of his fantasy has appeared in the flesh, and what gorgeous flesh it is! It's threatening to become his reality. "Idiot! Fool!" Tag hollers at the mirror. He flips off the bathroom light and slams the door behind him.

Tag removes a bottle of water from the refrigerator in the small break room and storms back to his office. He believes drinking the water will dilute the effects of the buzz from ole Pappy. He's certain Pappy's igniting his emotions over this life changing news.

As he sits at his desk swigging the water, he can't help but notice the many framed photographs scattered around his office capturing happy moments in his life.

There's the one taken last summer by Liesl at the beach with him on all fours in the sand, Maize on all fours on his back, and Jase on all fours on her back. What isn't captured is the laughter which ensued when a biting fly caused their family pyramid to quickly collapse.

There's the professional photograph taken two years ago for their church directory. He's amazed at how much Maize and Jase have grown in just over two years. What's even more amazing is how calm they all look in the photograph. He remembers it was a battle to coax them to be still. They look so formal in clothes they never wear except for Easter and weddings. No doubt the kids have already out grown them.

The photograph which bothers him the most is the one of Liesl and him at their wedding reception. It convicts him. He thought at the time he was deeply in love with Liesl, and he'd flushed Suzy, until memories of Suzy crept back the past few months igniting those pleasurable cravings.

Liesl rescued him from depression. She was his savior from that horrible darkness. The one-two punch of losing Billy and Suzy ditching him was too much for a seventeen-year-old to handle. He just didn't care about his future anymore. His parents kept a tight leash on him because of fear of reprisal by Mr. Jimmy. For his last semester of high school, they shipped him off to live with his aunt and uncle to keep him safe. He knew no one at his new school, and he didn't try to make friends. He kept to himself, pining for Suzy.

After graduation, despite the pleas of his parents to attend college, he hit the road. He was hoping to "find" himself as he toured the country taking odd jobs to finance his excursion. The only thing he "found" was a nomadic, impoverished life was not for him. To his parents' delight, he enrolled in a college. It was near Pineville. He chose that college for one reason, it's near Suzy's hometown. He was hoping to find her and address this unresolved matter which continued to haunt him. He never found Suzy, but he did find Liesl.

To earn extra money, Tag took a job at a casual restaurant as a waiter. Working on staff with him was a beautiful coed named Liesl. She was focused on achieving her life goal of becoming a physician's assistant. He was still distracted by his search for Suzy. They enjoyed working together and scheduled their shifts so they could. After work, they hung out at the restaurant enjoying free meals of unsold cooked food and discounted drinks. They would laugh about the events of the night, talk about their lives and their plans for the future. He became infatuated with Liesl. His pining for Suzy disappeared. He emerged from his depression and was enjoying life again, all because of Liesl. They fell in love.

When Liesl left to attend PA school, it was difficult for Tag. Since he was two years behind her in school, he remained behind to finish his degree in Business. As opposed to how he felt about Suzy, he didn't feel abandoned when Liesl left. They continued to talk daily, sometimes multiple times a day. During school breaks they were together.

He proposed to Liesl while she was in PA school. She accepted. They married the weekend after Liesl graduated. She was able to secure a job with a large medical care chain offering primary and urgent care in the college town where they met. Tag took a job as a mortgage banker. His dad was unsuccessful in coaxing him to move back to Rock Slide. There weren't opportunities for Liesl as a PA. Then, when Doc Flowers died, they were able to return.

Financially it's been a great decision for them. Also, Liesl and the kids enjoy the small town, resort-like culture of the valley. It's Tag who's waffling. After almost eight years of marriage, he's allowed himself to drift away into a make-believe world. He has no one to blame but himself.

"I'm sorry," he apologizes to the photograph. It won't be that easy in person.

Tag downs the last bit of water in the bottle. He tosses it in the trash can under his desk. He rises from his desk, flips off his office light, and leaves. He's not sure what comes next.

FIFTEEN

Mo's hoeing in his garden late this afternoon. Once a week, on the same day of the week, at the same time, which is right before dinner, he hoes in his garden. The weeds are threating to choke his Larry the cucumbers, Bob the tomatoes, and other garden vegetables. He has names for all of them. Also, he's repaired holes in the chicken wire fence surrounding the garden. He enjoys watching the chipmunks play, but not in his garden. It makes him angry when he finds Bobs with bites in them.

When he hoes in his garden, Mo follows the same routine. He starts with his Bobs and ends with his Larrys. He continually softly chants to himself a phrase he learned from his Veggie Tales tapes, "Faith…plant seed, love…make grow." It's become prayer-like, and it motivates him to hoe.

He's reached the spot where he always takes a break from his hoeing. He stands from his stooped position. His massive hands are propped on the wooden end of the hoe as he stretches his back. At the far end of the garden, he spies a thin black snake sliding between his heads of lettuce toward the chicken wire.

"Git, snake! No…like. Git!" He won't say the bad words his daddy says. Mama wouldn't like it.

He knows from his picture books this snake isn't the kind that hurts you. He wants it out of his garden anyway, even if it's harmless. He watches it slide through a hole in the chicken wire and disappear into some tall weeds at the edge of the woods.

His daddy wouldn't let it escape. He'd chop it up with the hoe, laughing and saying bad words while he did it. Mo would have to stick his fingers in his ears. That's what his mama would want. Even though the snake wouldn't hurt nobody, his daddy likes to do mean things. It makes Mo sad.

Mo remembers the time his daddy got angry at an ole stray dog. Daddy wouldn't let Mo have a pet dog. He said a dog's too expensive. That dog weren't doing nobody no harm.

He was just hungry. He was so thin Mo could count his ribs just by looking at him. Mama taught him to count to ten. That ole dog just kept coming around the house looking for food. Daddy said "shoo," but that ole dog didn't shoo, so daddy shot him. Mo buried that ole dog back behind the collapsed work shed.

Mama taught Mo to be kind. He tried hard to please his mama. Sometimes, when she wasn't around, he'd become very anxious. He'd get scared. When he got scared, he couldn't control himself. He'd start tearing things up, and sometimes when he'd get really scared, he'd hit other children. It hurt them. When that happened, he couldn't be around them anymore. That made him sad. He didn't like hurting them, but he couldn't help himself. His mama would get really mad at him. He didn't like his mama mad at him. She told him it was wrong to hit people. God and Jesus wouldn't like it. She said they loved him, and he didn't want to disappoint them. He didn't want to disappoint her. He knew she loved him, too. He needed to be kind to others, and that included animals, except for the ones which might try to hurt him. She pointed out the bad ones in his picture books. She told him to remember these bad animals and to stay away from them, but if he couldn't, then he had her permission to hurt them so they wouldn't hurt him or anyone else. This wouldn't make her, or God, or Jesus, angry.

Since his mama and Billy went to live with God and Jesus, it's rare that he's around others without his daddy. As long as his daddy's around, he doesn't get anxious, so he doesn't hurt anybody. He knows if he did, his daddy would get mad and start saying bad words. His mama wouldn't like him hearing those bad words.

He's sorry he made his daddy mad today. He just wanted to watch the children play. He remembers playing on that same playground, but most of the time he had to play by himself. He just wants to be kind. That's what his mama wanted. He wanted to be kind to the children today. Also, he wanted them to be kind to him. He wants friends. He's happy he made a new friend today, May-Z. She was kind to him.

Mo pulls the clover bracelet from his overalls' pocket. He holds it up to his nose and sniffs. He smiles. He likes his new friend.

He's sorry he made the lady mad, too. He would never hurt May-Z. He never wants to hurt anyone or anything. Mama told him to be kind. He hopes he gets to see May-Z again real soon. He'll pray for her tonight, like mama, Bob, and Larry told him. He'll even pray for his daddy.

Even though mama's with God and Jesus, and not around anymore to remind him to be kind, Larry, Bob, and all their friends remind him to be kind when he watches his videos. He's glad he has friends like Larry and Bob...and now May-Z.

Mo gets back to work. He needs to finish his hoeing before dinner. Mr. Jimmy's been checking on him. He knows how long it takes Mo to finish his chores. He knows Mo's routine calls for dinner after he finishes hoeing. He needs to have it ready, or Mo could become frustrated and destructive. Mr. Jimmy's reheating the Spam and macaroni from a meal earlier this week. He mixes them in a pan on the stove. He'll also have some butterbeans and fresh sliced tomatoes from the garden. He'll give Mo a couple of slices of bread he bought from the Dollar General this morning so Mo can use it to sop up the remains on his plate.

Mr. Jimmy almost has it ready when he sees Mo headed toward the back door. He hollers out the back screen door, "Hey boy, go on and wash up for dinner. It'll be ready when your through."

Mo walks over to the hose pipe next to the back door. He uses it to water his garden when it's needed, and to wash up when he's been working. He turns the spigot. The water's cold when it rushes from the end of the hose pipe. Mo grabs the furrowed, stained, hard, shriveled cake of soap resting on the windowsill. He soaps his hands and then rinses them. Then he scrubs his arms, face, bristled head, and neck with the soap. He raises the hose pipe and lets the chilly water rinse the soapy remnants away. He turns off the water and grabs the stiff, dirty, ratty towel hanging on a wire his daddy put up to hold it. A rust stain bisects the towel where the wire has rusted from supporting a damp towel. The cloth on the towel is initially stiff and rough against his skin. It's been weeks since it's been washed. The towel softens when it becomes damp from him drying off. Mo flips his ratty towel over the wire and enters the house through the screen door. The rusty spring on the door creaks before the door slams behind Mo. The scratchy country music blaring from the old clock radio resting on the kitchen counter absorbs the sound of the slam in the room.

"Sit down, boy, and eat up. Tomorrow we got a busy day. We're gonna be helpin' the Smelly brothers clear some brush on their farm. It's gonna be damn hard work. You'll need all your strength boy."

Mo's too hungry to stick his fingers in his ears. Mama wouldn't like him hearing daddy's bad words, though.

Mr. Jimmy sets Mo's plate in front of him. Suddenly, Mr. Jimmy recognizes the familiar saucy lyrics and raucous rhythm of the song *Trashy Women* by Confederate Railroad. He twitches and jerks an awkward dance. Mo smiles at his father's funny wiggling.

Mr. Jimmy grabs the spoon he used to scoop the reheated mix of spam and macaroni. It still has remnants of the gooey mix stuck to it as he sings into his pretend microphone. "Too much lipstick and uh too much rouge! ...hum, hum, hum, hum, hum, hum...I like my women just a little on the... trashy side."

Mo laughs!

"How 'bout it boy! You like yer women just a little on the trashy side?"

Mo's clapping now as Mr. Jimmy continues to gyrate. He doesn't understand his daddy's question.

"I guess not boy. Yer never gonna know a woman in that way. Never mind then! Well come on boy! Get up and dance!"

Mr. Jimmy grabs Mo's hand and pulls coaxing him to stand while he gyrates.

"Come on boy, like this! You can do it!"

Mo stands while guffawing and stiffly wiggles while his daddy claps and dances in a circle around him.

"That's it boy! That's it!"

As the song wanes, Mo and his dad continue laughing and dancing.

SIXTEEN

"Rat snake?" Jase is incredulous.

"Yes, rat snake," Liesl repeats.

"It doesn't look like a rat."

"Jase is stupid! Jase is stupid!" Maize needles while laughing.

Jase is embarrassed and crushed by his sister's unkind words.

"Hey! We don't talk that way about Jase or anyone else young lady!" Liesl scolds. "You apologize to your brother, right now! If I ever hear you say that again, you'll be punished. Do you understand me?"

"Yes mam." Now it's Maize's turn to be embarrassed and crushed.

"Now apologize!"

After a pause of a few seconds, "I'm sorry," Maize offers softly and insincerely.

Embolden by his mother coming to his defense, Jase smiles and sticks his tongue out at Maize.

"Jase stuck his tongue out at me!" Maize shouts trying to deflect her blame.

"Young man, that's not nice either. Apologize."

"Sa-ree," Jase's crushed again.

"Okay, I think that's enough reading your snake book tonight," Liesl closes the book. Her skin crawls every time she looks at the pictures of the snakes, but if it'll prevent Jase from mistakenly grabbing a poisonous snake, she'll stomach it. "Y'all watch TV while I get dinner ready." Maize hops on the couch where Liesl was sitting. Jase scoots away from her. Liesl finds one of their favorite shows. It'll distract them until dinner.

"Oh! I almost forgot," Liesl remembers there was something she needed to tell them. "Jenny Jean's going to be back in town for a couple weeks between her semesters. She wants to take y'all up to the alpine meadow for a picnic. Does that sound like fun!"

"Yeah!" is the collective scream from her children as they jump on the couch.

"Don't jump on the couch! You might fall and hurt yourselves." They stop, but the joy is obvious as they twist and clap their hands.

"I love JJ!" Jase shouts.

"Me too!" Maize chimes in. "I wish she could live with us!"

"I thought you'd be excited. She said she misses y'all. She's sorry she couldn't babysit this summer like she did last year, but she needed to go to school."

"I'm going to draw her a picture of a scary dinosaur," Jase roars.

"I'm sure she'll like that. The scarier the better!" Liesl laughs.

"I'm going to draw her a picture of some pretty flowers," Maize sweetly adds.

"Oh, I know she'll like that. After dinner y'all can draw your pictures. Now settle down and watch TV until dinner's ready."

Tag's house is less than ten minutes from his office. It's taken him thirty minutes to drive home. He's been driving around running his meeting, or was it more of a rendezvous, with Suzy through his mind. His prevailing emotions are guilt, fear, regret, and embarrassment. He finds it strange he feels this way since nothing happened with Suzy today. He's convicted himself of having an affair with Suzy even though it was all fantasy. He's fearful of how Liesl will react if she finds out about Suzy and their aborted child, and how embarrassing it will be for her and their family. He's even more fearful if Liesl discovers he has feelings for Suzy. He now realizes the resolution of this dilemma is going to cause some serious emotional pain...perhaps for everyone. Tag takes a deep breath, chides himself to act normal, and opens the kitchen door off the driveway to enter his home.

"Hey everybody! I'm home!"

"Daddy!" Maize and Jase shout. They hop off the couch and run into kitchen. Both grab a leg and begin climbing on him.

"Hey now! I'm not a jungle gym," Tag leans down and kisses them on the top of their heads. Now that he knows there was a chance they might not have been born, he feels more affectionate and protective of them.

"Walk daddy!" Maize hollers.

"Yeah, walk daddy!" Jase smiles.

Both Maize and Jase have wrapped themselves around a leg and are each sitting on a shoe. Tag struggles into a stiff legged walk dragging a different child with each step. Maize and Jase giggle. Liesl leans in with a brief kiss on his lips.

"So, you had drinks at your new client meeting, huh?"

Tag's frustrated he didn't totally rid himself of the Ole Pappy taint. "Yeah, we had a drink."

"How'd it go?"

"Fine," Tag doesn't really want to encourage any discussion of his meeting with Suzy because he'll have to lie. He doesn't want to lie to Liesl. He doesn't think he'll be very convincing in his emotional state. Quickly changing the subject, "Alright kids, hop off. You're gonna make me pull a muscle."

"Aw dad," Jase moans. They both climb off and head toward the couch.

Turning to Liesl, Tag asks, "And how was your day?"

"Nothing serious, thank goodness. Just some summer colds, poison ivy, aches and pains, and sore throats. Speaking of sore throats, I treated one of Jase's classmates from his daycare. Her mother said she saw you today on the boardwalk," Tag's pulse quickens. "She said some attractive woman gave you a hug. She thought it might be your sister. I told her you didn't have a sister. What was that all about?" Liesl's intently watching for some non-verbal clues.

Fortunately for Tag, he'd already planned what he would say if anyone had seen him and Suzy on the boardwalk. Tag, trying to act nonchalant answers without looking at Liesl, "Oh that was someone I knew from high school who was back in town. We hadn't seen each other since then." Tag opens the oven door. "Hey, what's for dinner? It smells good!"

"Pigs in a blanket."

"Well, they smell good."

"Based on what you told me today when Maize and I called, I wasn't sure when you were going to be home. I thought this would be easy to reheat if you were late."

"I like pigs in a blanket. They look like they're almost ready. I'll go change and be right back. Do you want me to grab the kids when I come back?"

"Yeah, as soon as these bake beans heat up, we're ready to eat."

"Great!" Tag leaves the kitchen hoping he pulled it off. Technically, he tells himself, he didn't lie. Suzy is someone who he knew when he was in high school, and he hasn't seen her since then. At least not in person. Of course, saying the Super Bowl is just a football game really doesn't do justice to the gravity of the event and all that has occurred up until the game. There is so much more about this woman he knew in high school that he's not ready, if ever, to discuss with Liesl.

As Liesl stirs the baked beans, she's a little perplexed by Tag's response. It was almost too casual. Oddly, she's comforted in knowing that if he were having an affair, there's no way he would show any public affection for anyone to see. With that said, she just has a funny feeling there's more to this than just a reacquaintance with a high school classmate. She's not ready to dismiss it yet. It's not Tag's personality to encourage or receive hugs from women in public, or at least she hasn't seen it very often.

SEVENTEEN

Just from looking at it from the street, you wouldn't think this small, austere shop was the news and gossip center for Pocket Watch Valley. It's an old, one-story, red brick building, which at one time was painted white, but now appears almost whitewashed as more red brick bleeds through than is covered by the faded and peeling white paint. It's located a block off the town square. There aren't any windows on the sides or back of the building, but there's a grand picture window which stretches across the front of the building. A large, weathered, black awning shields the picture window preventing the sun's rays from blinding those inside. "Magnolia's" is written in hot pink across the picture window in big, clumsy script. Below "Magnolia's," printed crudely in smaller block black letters, is the phrase "A Tonsorial Parlor for Those Who Want to Look Their Best." Located to the right of the picture window is the door to the building. On either side of the door are half barrels of planted pink geraniums. There's an amateurish attempt at what's supposed to be a painting of a magnolia blossom on the window of the door. Posters announcing various community events, some of which occurred a few months ago, are taped to and lined up inside along the bottom of the grand picture window so those passing by on the street can read them.

Upon entering the building, one is immediately immersed into a whirlpool of noise. Buzzing shears, snipping scissors, roaring, hand-held blow dryers, running water, whirring cone-shaped hair dryers, music chosen by the owner based on her mood for the day blaring from scratchy speakers, humming fluorescent lights, and the constant cacophony of whispers, shouts, laughs, and endless chatter of the customers and employees all mixing to create this loud, swirling buzz. The only time the voices are quiet and measured are when a man enters the building. The air reeks of hairspray, shampoos, cleaning solution, the hot electrical smell from heated dryers, snack foods, coffee, and drifting clouds of conflicting, pungent aromas from clashing perfumes and chemicals. The effects of the noise and smells can be dizzying for the uninitiated.

Visitors will spot six chairs in the middle of the room in two rows of three each. They would face each other if not separated by small cabinets supporting large, narrow mirrors facing each chair. An industrial strength extension cord extends from the back of the room feeding a strip of plugs which provides power for each chair/cabinet combination. The extension cord is covered by a ratty rug to prevent people from tripping over it when headed to the bathroom or office/supply room in the back of the building. Colorful abstract prints decorate the exposed brick walls. There's a flat screen TV on each wall tuned to the channels the owner prefers. Today, the TVs are silently broadcasting cooking shows. Also, scattered about the room are robust plants and colorful flowers. But, the most dominant feature of the building is unseen. It's the charismatic personality of the owner, Magnolia Winter-Blossom. Her colorful, revealing outfits and boisterous personality create a lively and fun atmosphere. Her customers feel special and welcome… unless they're the subject of speculation and rumor. They talk freely and glowingly about themselves and their families, and skeptically and horribly about others. Separating the truth from pure speculation is never attempted. The juicier the better. News gleaned from Magnolia's advances at lightning speed throughout the community.

Liesl enters the building for her regular hair appointment.

"Well, hey darlin'! Looks like you've arrived just in time," Magnolia trumpet's while eyeing Liesl's hair. Her comments are never measured. "Have a seat over here Doc," Magnolia points with her scissors at the middle chair on the right side. "I'll be right with ya."

There's a strong aroma of pungent perfume when Liesl takes her seat. She can't determine whether it's from someone near her or the chair's previous occupant. The din, combined with the intermittent roaring of the blowing of hair dryers, makes it difficult to eavesdrop. In the few minutes she's been waiting, she's heard snippets of a conversation from the woman in the chair next to her about the new casino. She hasn't gathered if the woman is for or against it. She's learned that Honey and Rex Rock, a couple Liesl doesn't know, are swingers. At least this person has it on good authority they are. Liesl shudders at what people may say about her in Magnolia's.

What's intriguing her is a conversation which Magnolia is finishing with a customer who's leaving. It's about some rumored model or movie star in town. She'll ask Magnolia.

"Alright Doc, same as usual?" Magnolia asks as she steps to Liesl's chair, places a sheet over her clothes, and snaps it behind her neck.

"Yeah, that would be great."

"I talked to your husband the other day about our city council meetin.' He says he's gonna vote for the casino. Do you believe he's tellin' the truth?" Magnolia asks as she cuts.

"Yeah. I'm fairly certain he is. He thinks it's best for the community."

"Good! I need to be able to count on his vote. I'm working on gettin' the third vote. I hear your...

Thanks, hun, for comin' in today," Magnolia hollers at Gladys Singer as she leaves. "Now remember, tell your husband to use zinc oxide, witch hazel, and cold packs for his hemorrhoids. Works every time, right Doc? If not, he might have to drop'm and lean over for Doc to take a look!" Magnolia laughs.

Liesl's a little stunned by the open discussion of Jesse's health issue. "Should work," Liesl stammers. It's all she can think of to say sbout this common self-treatment for hemorrhoids.

Gladys waves and offers an embarrassed smile while glancing at Liesl, "Sure will." She disappears from the building.

"Let's see, where was I? Oh yeah, I hear your preacher's plannin' to gather a group of Bible thumpers to surround city hall durin' our meetin' to pray against us votin' for the casino. I've asked Tag to try to stop it. Do you know if he has?"

"I don't know. He hasn't mentioned it."

"Well, if he don't, I'll put the fear of God in that preacher to stop him," Magnolia laughs.

"Hopefully, it won't happen."

"I told your husband that he needs to let me cut his hair. What do ya think?"

Magnolia's large breasts brush against Liesl as she cuts her hair. As Magnolia moves in front of her, very little is left to the imagination as to what those massive breasts look like. Liesl can't avoid staring straight at Magnolia's cleavage bulging from her tight, low-cut top. There's no damn way she's going to let Magnolia cut Tag's hair. They already have too chummy of a relationship for Liesl, even though she's certain it's all in fun."

"Well, I don't know. He seems to be very happy with the barber he has. I'm not sure you can get him to change."

"That hedge trimmer of his don't know nothin' 'bout how to cut his hair! Send'm over here one time, and he'll never go back!"

That's what scares Liesl. Changing the subject, Liesl asks, "I heard you talking to your previous customer about some model or movie actress in town. What's going on?"

"I don't know nothin.' Bein' on city council, you'd think I'd know if some photo shoot or movie was bein' made in town. I don't know who she is, but my shop's been a buzzin' all day 'bout it. Seems this lady, and I may be using the term loosely, she's probably about your age, was turnin' heads on the boardwalk at sunset last night. Seems her powder blue top was so tight it 'peared as if it were painted on. They that saw her said there was nothin' left to the imagination, if you know what I mean," Magnolia chuckles. "Her short white shorts were really short shorts. They said the bottom of her cheeks were visible. Of course, some of what young women wear as swimwear is just as revealing, if maybe not more, but they said there was something special 'bout this lady. She was stunningly gorgeous and moved gracefully with an air of confidence. Women were coverin' their kids' eyes and punchin' their husbands' arms fussin' at them to turn away. No one's ever seen her before. She didn't seem to fit our normal Glides, pardon my use of that term. That's why they thought she might be some model or movie star. Tag hasn't said anythin' to you about this lady, has he?"

"No. He hasn't mentioned anyone being here for a photo shoot or movie."

97

"Hey Ethel," Magnolia hollers at the customer about to leave, "don't forget to tell your daughter that it's fine for her to put up on our bulletin board her number for babysittin' jobs. I know she's a responsible young lady. I always enjoy havin' her in one of my chairs."

"Thanks Magnolia!" Ethel beams.

Liesl didn't notice the interruption. She was lost in her thoughts wondering if this same mystery woman strolling on the boardwalk displaying her assets might be the same woman that Karen saw hug her husband. Also, who did Tag meet with last night when he had a drink? Tag having a drink with a client is rare, but not unheard of. Her curiosity's prodding her to know for sure. Again, he's been acting a little strange towards her. She needs to watch him more closely.

EIGHTEEN

"Mr. Jimmy, that boy of yer'n has the strength of two or more fellas. How'd he get so strong?" Bobcat Smelly asks prior to taking a bite of his banana, peanut butter, and mayonnaise sandwich.

Now Bobcat's not his given name. It's Lucious. The "Bobcat" nickname was hung on him when he was a teenager based on the way he would fight. He's proud of earning that reputation and prefers his nickname.

His brother, Toad, isn't thrilled about his nickname. He's a short, heavy fellow. His round head seems to sit right on the top of his shoulders. As he's aged, rolls of fat now bulge between his head and shoulders accentuating his appearance as a toad. His real name's Egbert. He doesn't like that name either, so he'll reluctantly answer to both. The Smelly brothers' parents did them no favors when it came to names.

Mo's chosen to sit on a log in the shade away from the men while he eats his three Spam and tomato sandwiches for lunch. He's fascinated by ants scurrying around their anthill. Also, he sits alone because he knows his daddy and these men will be saying bad words. His mama doesn't want him hearing bad words.

"His mama's genetics gave the boy his size and I gave him his strength," Mr. Jimmy chuckles while digging a Vienna sausage out of the can with the blade of his pocket knife. "Plus, I keep the boy active. It's good for him. The doctors say in his condition he needs to stay active."

"What's wrong with the boy, Mr. Jimmy?" Toad croaks before wolfing down his second pineapple, cheese, and mayonnaise sandwich.

"The boy's touched in the head. Happened at birth. Just my bad luck. He can do some things, but not much. Normally he's calm like a mill pond, but you get the boy off his'n schedule, and he erupts like that Pompei volcano they talk about in the Bible. It plum scares me to death when he goes off. He damn well nearly kilt me once. If he gets a goin', I gotta get outta his way and find a way to calm the boy."

"Damn, Mr. Jimmy! That's rough. Does the boy talk?" Bobcat asks.

"Yeah, he can talk. Not much, though. Not like us. Sometimes it's hard to understand him. I've gotten use to his talkin', so most of the time I can figure out what he's sayin'. I don't really want him talkin' to many folks, though. I'm afraid they might set him off."

"Well, he's strong as two mules! There's no damn way Toad and I could've pulled up some of the saplings that your boy done did. He's more nimble and just as strong as a bobcat tractor," Bobcat laughs. "Course, I'm a better-looking bobcat than that ole tractor," Bobcat grins.

"Ain't," Toad croaks after swigging his PBR.

Bobcat's eyes narrow.

Mr. Jimmy laughs, "Fellows, there ain't none of us gonna win any beauty contests!" They all chuckle. Mo quickly glances at them and then returns to watching the ants. He inadvertently dropped a crumb of bread, and he's fascinated at how the ants are pushing it to their mound.

"Mr. Jimmy, I hear tell you had a son that was a football star, but he passed, may he rest in peace. Sorry fer yer loss. What's his name?" Bobcat asks.

Mr. Jimmy glances up at the clouds and rubs his lips with his right thumb and index finger as he gathers his thoughts and tries to calm his emotions. Looking back at Bobcat and Toad, "His'n name is Billy Ray. That boy was one helluva an athlete. He was faster than a sun beam and quicker than Toad's burps!" They all laugh. Again, Mo glances at them but returns to his ants and their struggle to move the crumb. "He won so many races I lost count. Like his brother over there," Mr. Jimmy nods toward Mo, "he was big, but not as big as that one, but bigger than most of the boys his'n age in this here valley. Once they put a football in his hands, no one could tackle him, or catch him!

We had colleges all over the country after my boy. I'm talkin' about the big SEC, ACC, and Big Ten schools. They

100

wanted my boy, but he weren't going for free. They was gonna have to pay us to have my boy go to their school."

"Ain't that illegal Mr. Jimmy?" Toad again croaks as he polishes off another PBR.

"It ain't illegal, it was just against their rules. Hell, I know'd of stories where families were getting lotsa money. By damn, it was the Quick's turn at the trough! It was gonna buy us some respect and hopefully there'd be some left over to take care of that boy," Mr. Jimmy nods toward Mo, "when his momma and I passed. But, he done up and died on me. Hell, he was kilt!"

"What happened Mr. Jimmy?" Bobcat interrupts.

"Like I said, he was kilt! The cops said it was a boatin' accident. To hell it was!" Mr. Jimmy raises his voice. Mo hears him and sticks his fingers in his ears. "He was kilt by God! Oh Mr. Tag Ryder done it. They was ridin' in a boat in the lake over there," My Jimmy gestures in the general direction of the lake. "My boy was being dragged behind the boat that Mr. Tag Ryder was drivin.' Mr. Tag Ryder was tryin' to impress some of them damn Glide girls. I'm sure he wanted to snuggle up with one. Well by damn, he was a flirtin' and run my boy into a dock! Messed him up bad. Ole Doc Flowers said there was nothin' could be done to save my boy. He was gone! And the cops did nothin' to hold Mr. Tag Ryder accountable. He walked. I couldn't get the DA to do nothin' and I couldn't get no attorney to sue 'em. They all said it was an accident. It weren't by damn! Mr. Tag Ryder, that high falutin' land man, is responsible! Now that he's on the city council, he ain't never gonna be held accountable!

When my boy died, all our dreams went with him. He was gonna be our meal ticket. Hell, his mama died of a broken heart soon, thereafter, leavin' me with that retard over there," again, Mr. Jimmy nods toward Mo. "We've just been hangin' on financially. Fortunately, that boy's strong and helps us earn extra money like today, which we 'preciate, but we could've lived like kings if my boy hadn't been kilt." Mr. Jimmy's eyes narrow, "Even though the law ain't gonna do nothin' 'bout it, by damn, I will! One day Mr. Tag Ryder's gonna feel my wrath for what he done to my boy and my family. Like the Good Book says, an eye for an eye…an eye for an eye."

Bobcat wishes he hadn't asked the question. He and Toad are stunned by Mr. Jimmy's anger and vitriol. The tension from Mr. Jimmy's rant has created an uneasiness among them.

Suddenly, Mr. Jimmy shouts at Mo, "Boy! Let's get back to work now. Lunch is over with. We're burnin' daylight!"

Bobcat and Toad rise in silence. They don't want to ask any more questions.

"Toad, give me one of dem PBRs." Mr. Jimmy orders more than asks. "I need somethin' to calm me."

"Take as many as you'd like Mr. Jimmy. I don't need more than the two I've already had since I'm a workin'".

"'Preciate that." Mr. Jimmy grabs one, wrenches off the cap, and takes his familiar seat on the log where he's been watching them work all morning. As he takes a swig, he's still emotional. He continues to stew over how he's going to get his revenge.

NINETEEN

"Tag, is everything alright? Ronette asks.

"Sure. Sure. Why do you ask?"

"You seem to be a little jumpy today. Out of sorts. I just want to make sure you and your family are fine. After all, I depend upon you for my income."

"Oh yeah, everything's fine. I'm sorry I've caused you concern. Just having an off day, I guess." As Tag walks away from Ronette, he's disappointed his anxiety's evident. Fortunately, his dad's out of town or he might really be quizzing Tag.

Sliding into his desk chair, he's been on pins and needles all day. He's been afraid that Suzy was going to march into his office and cause a scene by demanding an answer. Ronette would then know everything. That would be a nightmare situation. He used to adore Suzy's bold persona because of the pleasure he received, but now he's afraid of it.

Being late in the day, he wonders why Suzy hasn't tried to contact him. After all, she's only two floors away. At least he thinks so. His mood briefly changes when he wonders if last night was too embarrassing for her and she's left town. Although, he remembers, he did hear from multiple sources about the gorgeous woman strutting on the boardwalk last night. From the description of this mysterious woman, he's certain it was Suzy. Her actions don't seem to be those of someone embarrassed. If she's left, he's not so sure how he feels about her disappearing again. He still has deep cravings for her. "Damn it! Why does life have to be so hard?" he mutters to himself.

He's still somewhat in shock over his aborted child. He can't decide whether to be angry, sad, or grateful. In any event, he's filled with guilt over it, even though it wasn't his decision. He places his elbows on his desk and drops his head in his hands. He's struggling to make sense of what he's learned.

"Damn!" The loud ring of his cell phone startles him from his thoughts. Anxiously he peers at its screen. He's fairly certain it's not Suzy since they didn't exchange cell numbers last night, but of course his number is on his business website. His heart skips a beat when he recognizes the number. It's Sheriff Justice. He quickly prays nothing's happened to his family as he fumbles to answer the call.

"Is my family okay?" Tag blurts nervously.

"Sure! As far as I know. Calm down. I'm not calling about them."

"That's a relief," Tag's heart beat slows. "What's up?"

"I've got an uncomfortable situation I need your help with. It's the Jester brothers. I'm over here at their farm with the demolition crew. They were supposed to have vacated the property yesterday. The demolition crew showed up this afternoon to get started, but the boys were still here. They've barricaded themselves in their home. In fact, when the crew approached their home, the boys fired shots at them. No one was hurt, and I think they were probably just warning shots, but it scared the crap out of these guys. Doug came out to talk to the Jesters, but they won't budge. He called me to evict them, but of course I need to get a court order first. Doug asked if I would at least try to talk to them.

The Jesters let me walk up to the house to talk to them. They wouldn't let me in, though. I had to holler at them while they remained locked in the house. Doug's right, they aren't budging. Says they want to break the sale. Doug says no way. The brothers said they want to talk to you. I know this is last minute and an imposition, but could you come out here and try to talk some sense into them? They apologized for shooting their guns, but they said they didn't know what else to do to prevent the bulldozer from leveling their home. I believe you won't be in any danger. How 'bout it, can you drive over here now?"

"Sure. I'm not surprised that they're causing a problem."

"Why's that?"

"They recently came to see me. They also told me they wanted out of the contract. I told them they would have to talk to their attorney, but I also told them I didn't think Doug and his investors would be willing to do that. I tried to convince them

104

that selling their land was a brilliant decision on their part. Obviously, it didn't work. I guess I'm not as good at reversing sales as I am at creating them," Tag nervously chuckles. "I'll be there in a few minutes. I'm sorry this is tying you up when you could be doing more important things."

"Not a problem. That's what I'm here for. Hopefully, this will result in an easy and peaceful solution. I like those. Thanks for coming."

"I'll see you in a few minutes."

Tag's thankful and relieved his family's alright. He's also glad he has a reason to leave the office. It should take his mind off Suzy, at least for a little while.

Tag stops by Ronette's desk on the way out, "Your secret admirers are causing trouble out on their farm. Sheriff Justice just called and asked me to come out and talk some sense into them. Wanna come?" Tag smiles. He already knows her answer.

"Let me see…No! I'm good here. Whatever you do, don't bring them back!" They both laugh.

"I won't. I probably won't be back before you leave, so just lock up. If for some reason someone needs me and calls the office instead of my cell, just text me."

"Will do."

Tag's more relaxed as he leaves the office, but he quickly scans his surroundings while walking to his car to ensure that Suzy isn't lurking, although part of him desperately wishes she were.

As Tag pulls out of his parking place, he quickly dials Liesl's cell.

"Hey, is everything alright?" she answers.

"Yeah. Yeah. Just wanted to let you know I might be a little late getting home again tonight, but I should be there by dinner."

Liesl's immediately suspicious. "Why's that?"

"The Jester brothers are causing a problem with the developers. Sheriff Justice called me to come out and talk some sense into them. Hopefully, it won't take long, but if it does, I wanted you to know."

"Okay, thanks. I've got to get back to my patient."

"Love ya," Tag forces.

"Yeah, me too."

The call's ending seemed awkward to Tag. He was hoping to sound sincere. He believes he did. She didn't respond as she normally does. She didn't sound sincere. She seemed distant. Does she know about Suzy's feelings for him and his for her? How could she? His anxiety spikes.

TWENTY

Tag turns off the paved county road on to the dirt road leading to the Jesters' house. For a quarter of a mile the Jesters own the fields which border the county road. The dirt road bisects these fields. The uneven depressions in the undulating dirt road cause his car to uncomfortably bounce. He slows. His tires kick up a rooster tail of dust. Portions of the dust cling to his car's chassis, while the rest of it swirls and scatters until it gently settles along the road and on the bordering foliage. Even though he knows the way, he follows the fresh ruts of the heavy equipment.

Around a bend he slows dramatically. The sheriff's large truck and the heavy demolition equipment block the road. He parks behind the sheriff's truck. Before he exits his car, he spots Sheriff Justice through his windshield headed toward him. The sheriff's mirrored aviator sunglasses briefly catch the sun's rays at just the right angle causing them to briefly flash at Tag. This merely adds to the sheriff's commanding appearance if his immaculate uniform wasn't enough.

Sheriff Bill Justice is an imposing figure. At 6'4" and built like an NFL middle linebacker, he doesn't have to command respect. He automatically gets it. His deep voice is enough to intimidate you. He's a former Navy SEAL marksman. He proudly claimed his military heritage in his campaign ads. That experience alone was enough to persuade the voters to support him for the job. His last name didn't hurt either.

"Hey sheriff," Tag offers as he steps from his car and slams the door.

"Thanks for coming!" They shake hands when they meet at the front of his car. Tag was mentally prepared for his crushing grip. "Nothing's changed since we last talked. Please step over to my truck for a minute."

Sheriff Justice reaches into his truck and removes a small plastic box with a clip on it. Extending from the box is a wire. There appears to be a white button-shaped disc at the end of the wire. "I want you to wear a wire while you're in the house. I'll be listening to what's said."

Tag suddenly appreciates the gravity of the situation, and it's making him nervous, "I'm not sure I want to do that. Won't that be dangerous?"

"Nah! Not at all. The worst that can happen is they make you take it off. They said they only want to talk to you."

"Are you sure?"

"Yep, nothing to worry about. Now, untuck your shirt and let me attach this battery pack to your belt. I'm going to lower it down your back inside your shirt."

Even if he protests, he knows he can't change Sheriff Justice's mind. He's going to have to trust him. Tag untucks his shirt. Sheriff Justice steps behind him and gently lowers the battery pack inside Tag's shirt. It's cold as it bumps against his skin. It makes him flinch. Once it reaches his belt line, Sheriff Justice reaches up under Tag's shirttail, grabs it, and clips it to Tag's belt with the battery pack snug between his skin and the waist of his pants.

Sheriff Justice drops the wire so that it falls between Tag's back and shirt. It exits from his shirt and hangs to the ground. Sheriff Justice grabs the unconnected end of the wire. With it in his hand, he reaches under Tag's shirt and wraps his arm around Tag's ribs. This invasion of Tag's personal privacy creates an awkward discomfort. "Tag, please grab this from me and hold it." Tag reaches his arm under his shirt and grabs the wire. "Thanks! Now, hold on to it." Sheriff Justice lets go of it, removes his arm from under Tag's shirt, and steps in front of Tag. Sheriff Justice unbuttons Tag's shirt and takes the wire from Tag. He grabs the white button-shaped disc and threads it up through the open button hole.

"Now tuck in your shirt." Tag complies. Sheriff Justice fiddles with the white button-shaped disc until it fits tight like a button. He then grabs a strip of adhesive tape, reaches in the gap in the shirt between the buttons, and attaches the tape inside

Tag's shirt so it holds what Tag has now determined to be a microphone in place in the button hole.

"Tag, after I place this earphone in my ear, say something."

Tag waits until Sheriff Justice has the earphone in place, "Testing. One. Two. Three."

Sheriff Justice gives him a thumbs up. He removes his earpiece and places it in his pocket. "Now follow me and I'll let the Jesters know you're here. I'll be able to hear everything that's said."

Tag stretches and twists his waist to ensure the wire isn't restricting him and it doesn't come loose. He's pleased when it doesn't. He trusts the sheriff, but he doesn't want to deal with this awkward issue if it's detected by the Jesters.

He lines up behind the sheriff and they squeeze past the sheriff's truck along the edge of the narrow dirt road. Tag spots a BMW parked in front of the sheriff's truck. He didn't notice it until now. He knows it's Dumpy Doug's BMW because Dumpy Doug's waddling straight for him. His face is beet red, probably from anger and frustration. As they meet, Tag notices streaks of sweat on Dumpy Doug's face.

"Sorry Doug." They shake hands.

"Not your fault Tag. I just appreciate your help. I sure hope you can talk some sense into those hayseeds. This is costing me money! I can't afford too much of a delay. This project has a tight time table since the equipment and workers must travel from an hour away. The bank isn't going to be very forgiving on our loan payments because these geezers, who we paid a very fair price for their property, are now trying to back out. Work some magic, please!"

"I'm no magician, but I'll do my best. Were you aware they've been talking about backing out of the sale?"

"Yeah," Doug wipes the sweat from his brow with his shirt sleeve. It exposes the polished gold wristband of his watch which reflects the rays of the setting sun. "I told them no way. A deal's a deal. As I said, I told them they received a fair price for their land. They should be very happy."

"Yeah, I told'm the same thing. Unfortunately, they have seller's remorse. Rare, but not unheard of. Usually, I see it more on the buyer's side."

"Yeah, whatever it is, I ain't breaking the sale. Time has expired. They need to get out!"

"I completely understand. We're on the same side."

"Fellas," Sheriff Justice interrupts, "y'all can discuss this later. Tag come on. Let's get this settled."

Tag follows the sheriff as they weave past the heavy equipment. Doug's waddling closely behind them. As they squeeze past the last piece of equipment, the area opens into a sizable clearing where the house rests. Pickups are parked haphazardly around the clearing near its entrance to the dirt road. Their owners and passengers are milling around by the trucks and equipment. All eyes turn to Tag as he steps out from behind the sheriff.

The house is rather simple, and it hasn't aged well as it approaches its one hundredth birthday. It's constructed of clapboard and covered in whitewash. Whitewash was probably applied multiple times over the years, but not in the last decade...or two. Three large chestnut trees provide generous shade. The architect's plan for the new development is to preserve these magnificent trees. The front lawn, framed by a poorly patched, weathered, wooden picket fence, contains islands of grass and weeds, but it's primarily hardpan. Most of the soil's washed away. A gravel walkway, peppered with tufts of weeds, leads to the steps of a covered front porch. This sagging porch must be crossed to enter the house. Some of its boards are warped and rotting. Two worn, wooden rockers, with sun-faded seat cushions, rest on the porch. Also, a wooden, slatted swing, covered in faded whitewash, hangs from rusty chain-link at one end of the porch. Covering the second floor is a steep gabled roof. A brick chimney extends above the sagging roof line. Two dormer windows protrude from the roof. Tag knows Homer and Virgil's room is located on this tiny second floor. The last time Tag was in the home, he was surprised to learn that they still sleep in twin beds in the room they grew up in.

Surrounding the home, extending to the county road, and bordered by dense woods on the other three sides, are fields

110

which primarily lay fallow. A large vegetable garden grows close to the home where it can be watered by a sprinkler connected by a hose to a spigot near the back door. Cows roam in the fallow fields. The Jesters rent their fields to a local rancher for grazing. Dumpty Doug hasn't attempted to evict the cows yet. He may soon, though, as a gust of wind bearing their stench instantly reminds those milling around the clearing that cows are near.

Sheriff Justice grabs a bullhorn which was resting on the hood of a pickup. With such a booming voice, Tag wonders why he needs it. "Homer. Virgil," the sheriff's voice reverberates. "I've got Tag with me." Sheriff Justice lowers the bullhorn and turns toward Tag, "Stand up here by me and raise your hand." Tag walks up beside Sheriff Justice and offers an awkward brief wave toward the house. Sheriff Justice again raises the bullhorn to his lips, "You asked to meet with him. Is it okay for him to come on in?" Now that Tag's experiencing this tense situation, he's become more anxious. He wonders what he can do to diffuse this situation.

After what seemed to be a lengthy pause, a breathy voice hollers, "Send'm in sheriff."

"Will do!" Sheriff Justice lowers the bullhorn and turns toward Tag. "Head on in. I'll be listening to everything that's said. You'll also be my eyes. If possible, stealthily describe what you see. It'll help me understand what I'm facing. If you're uncomfortable doing that, no problem. You'll be fine. Leave when you feel you need to. Whatever you do, don't make any promises. Just tell them you'll see what you can do. Got it?"

"Got it." Tag notices two deputies have arrived on the scene and are quickly approaching Sheriff Justice.

Tag takes a deep breath to calm his nerves. As he walks toward the house, his eyes quickly dart trying to assess the situation. He's also looking for the brothers…and their gun barrels. As he steps on to the covered porch, the front door swings open. Tag strolls into the home, and the door closes behind him.

What Tag sees once inside accelerates his anxiety. Each of the brothers is caring a shotgun. There are four more shotguns resting on the sofa cushions. A sturdy carboard box containing boxes of shotgun shells, two of which are open, rests on the coffee table.. Aside from the arsenal, what mostly concerns Tag is that the normally stoic brothers are obviously anxious and agitated.

Hoping to break the tension, and comply with Sheriff Justice's request, Tag clears his throat and speaks, "Homer and Virgil, I'm here at your request. Whatever's upsetting you can be resolved without violence. There's no need for you to have six shotguns. And why do you have all this ammunition? Nobody wants to hurt either of you. I'm sure you don't want to hurt anyone else either. How can I help?"

"We told you we wanted to break the sale," Homer barks. "We meant it! This is our home, and we ain't giving it up!"

"Yeah!" Virgil jumps in. "You tricked us into selling our home!"

"Now fellas," Tag's forcing himself to stay as calm as possible, "I didn't trick you into selling your home. I merely approached you about an offer I had received from developers who wanted to buy your land. A very generous offer I might add. You're the ones who made the decision, and again, it was the right decision."

"Naw," Virgil protests, "you tricked us! You filled our heads with big dollars. Money we'd never dreamed of before. You told us we'd be rich. Could do whatever we wanted to! It was tempting and confusing. We didn't know what we was doing. Before we had time to think about it, you'd shoved a piece a paper in front of us and we signed it not knowing what we'd done."

Anger's now competing with Tag's anxiety, "You know that's not true. We fully discussed the ramifications of the sale. You both met with Ned Scales. He fully explained to you what documents he needed you to sign and the purpose of those documents before you signed them. We both made sure you understood what you were agreeing to." Homer and Virgil are pacing about the small living room gesturing with their guns which has Tag on edge. "Would you mind putting down the guns? They're making me nervous."

"Good!" Virgil shouts. "Hell no we ain't putting down our guns! We ain't letting anyone take our house!"

"But it's not your house anymore, you…"

112

"Shut up!" Virgil shouts again. This time he points the barrel of the shotgun at Tag. "This is our house! We ain't leaving!"

Tag's anxiety spikes. His mouth's dry. Looking to diffuse the anger Tag asks, "May we sit down and talk about this calmly, and may I have a glass of water?'

This seems to ramp down the tension in the room for the moment, "Virgil, go get Tag some water." Homer looks back at Tag, "I'm sorry. We should've offered you something to drink when you came in our home like your pretty secretary does for us at your office." Virgil storms off to the kitchen.

Homer removes the shotguns from the sofa and places them on the coffee table. Homer gestures, "Have a seat on the sofa."

Tag sits. Virgil reenters the room with a glass of water and hands it to Tag. He takes a drink while Virgil and Homer sit across from him in matching faux leather recliners, generously patched with duct tape. They each lay the shotgun they're carrying across their armrests. Even though Homer's seemed to calm, Virgil's still fuming.

"Thanks," Tag offers while setting his unfinished glass of water on the floor. "Fellas, we talked about this a few days ago. I told you that you needed to go talk to an attorney about breaking the sale. Did you do that?

"Yep," Homer answers. "He checked and said they didn't want to do that."

"That's what I thought he'd tell you. I'm sorry you're not happy, but I didn't trick you into selling your home and land. I still think you made the right decision."

"Stop saying that!" Virgil screams leaning forward in his chair. "We didn't make the right decision! Maybe you feel you didn't trick us, and the law might be on your side, but you know you were pushing us hard to sell our land, filling our heads up with a lot of glitter that frankly was just nonsense."

Tag briefly wonders if there's some truth in Virgil's statement. He was pushing hard to make the sale. Was he blinded by the size of his commission? Did he push too hard and too fast? He doesn't think so.

"You got six million dollars for this land. I mean, come on! Most folks would be doing cartwheels! It was a good price. As we've discussed, due to your ages, there was a high probability that if these developers hadn't come along, you might've been forced to sell the house and land at a much, much lower price if either or both of you developed health problems." Tag's not going to say it was the right decision anymore.

"You may be right, but we're willing to take that chance," Homer glances at Virgil before continuing. Virgil nods in assent. "This is all we've ever known. We've lived here our entire lives. We were born in this house, and we've decided we want to die in this house." A tear meanders through one of the deep crevasses in Homer's face. "Our blood, sweat, and tears are deep in this dirt. Our mama and daddy, and kinfolk, are buried out back by the fence line. All our special memories were made in this house and on this land. This is our home. Our world. We ain't leaving. No amount of money can change our minds." Virgil's now leaking tears, too. Simultaneously they wipe their eyes.

"What do you want me to do?"

"Get us back our land," Virgil answers.

"I don't think I can. I'm happy to try again, but I know the developers have already spent a lot of money. What are you going to do if I can't convince them to sell it back to you?"

Immediately there's an uncomfortable pause. "We thought about taking you hostage," Homer bluntly states without a smile, "but we decided not to."

Tag's stunned. He's thankful Sheriff Justice heard that. "You're kidding right?"

"Naw, we sure did," Virgil adds, "but that ain't right, even if you did trick us. You got a wife and kids you need to care for."

Tag takes another swig of water to calm his nerves. He again places the glass on the floor. "I appreciate that. So, seriously, what are you going to do?"

"I guess everyone'll have to find out," Virgil cuts his eyes toward Homer.

"I hope you're not considering violence. Neither you nor anyone else needs to get hurt." Tag's position on the couch allows him to see through a window the group of people standing out front. Their sudden movement catches his eyes when he sees the deputies directing the throng back down the road out of sight. Tag's thinking it's time for him to leave.

"We'll do what we need to do to defend our home. We ain't leaving," Homer's looking more agitated now than he was a few minutes ago.

"Please fellas," Tag pleads. "Violence is not the answer. You could get killed! You might end up killing someone else! Even if you don't, you might end up in prison for the rest of your lives. Don't do this!"

"That's for us to worry about," Virgil responds, "not you."

"Not if you hurt someone else!"

They just stare at Tag and say nothing.

Tag has an idea, "Okay, let me go talk to them again. Let me see what I can work out. What if I can get them to agree to move your home to a corner of the property for you to live in the rest of your lives, or build you a new home in the corner? Would that interest you?"

"Naw," they simultaneously answer.

Deflated, Tag rises from the sofa, "Okay, you want it all back, as is, right?"

"Yep," they respond simultaneously as they look up at him.

"I'll see what I can do." Tag weaves past the Jesters toward the door. Virgil and Homer stand and say nothing as he leaves.

As Tag bounds off the steps on to the gravel walk, there isn't another person in sight. Only the pickups and heavy equipment. When he entered the home, he assumed the Jesters would eventually recognize that their quest was futile, and they would give in. Now he's not so sure this situation will be resolved without violence.

"Tag. Over here," Sheriff Justice waves from behind a bulldozer. Tag walks toward him. When Tag steps behind the bulldozer, the only people he sees besides Sheriff Justice are the deputies. Everyone else is out of sight.

115

"Tag you did a good job. I appreciate your effort. Nice 'Hail Mary' at the end. I'm sorry it didn't work. You can take off the wire now."

Tag reaches under his shirt, peels off the adhesive tape, pulls the microphone through his button hole, unhooks the battery pack from behind his back, pulls it out, and hands it all to Sheriff Justice. "Sheriff they seem to be prepared for a long siege based on the arsenal I saw. I'm sorry."

"Yeah, I was disappointed to hear you mention that, but appreciate you letting me know. How'd they appear?"

"I'll be honest, I've never seen them this agitated or hyped up. Usually, they're pretty bland. I didn't see any alcohol or drugs, but it wouldn't surprise me if some stimulant is flowing through their veins based on how different they were."

"That's helpful."

"So, what happens now?"

"I'm going to try one more time. If it doesn't work, I'll call the DA. I think we'll have to go through the eviction process. Technically, they're now trespassing if what Doug's telling me's true. The DA will need to look at the documents. I've already called Ned Scales and asked him to scan copies of the sales documents to the DA for him to review.

Since they're armed, and they've already fired their guns, possibly at individuals, I may have the authority to act. You witnessed their arsenal, which leads me to believe they're prepared to use it. I can't allow that to happen. I've got everyone out of sight. I don't want them to become unsuspecting targets. I'll let the DA tell me what to do on this one. Let's walk back and talk to Doug one more time."

As they weave past the trucks and equipment, Tag notices that the sun's beginning to quickly drop toward the mountain ridges. He's sure Sheriff Justice wants to resolve this before it's dark.

They find Doug sitting in his BMW. It's idling. Doug's enjoying the air conditioning. They can hear someone talking, but Doug's lips aren't moving. Obviously, he's using his Bluetooth to make a telephone call.

Sheriff Justice raps on his window with his knuckle. Doug holds up his finger and mouth's "one second."

116

After a few seconds, Sheriff Justice raps again. Harder this time. When Doug glances at him, Sheriff Justice forcibly says, "Now Mr. Shaw!"

"Gotta go. Call you later," they hear Doug utter. He turns off his BMW and struggles out of his car. "So, did you convince them Tag?"

"Sorry, but no," Tag averts his eyes to the ground.

"So, what happens now sheriff? I want them off my land!"

"Hold your horses there Doug. I need to ask you one more time, are you willing to compromise at all?"

"Hell no!"

"Okay. Let me try one more time. If it doesn't work, I'll call the DA. I'm not really sure what he'll want me to do. Don't expect a quick solution, though."

"Damn it, sheriff! This is costing me money!"

"Mr. Shaw, I'm sorry about that, but I didn't create this situation. You did."

"How so?" Doug's indignant.

"You shouldn't have allowed them to stay after you closed on the sale. Now shut up and let me do my job! If I can convince them to leave, will you and your investors agree not to press any criminal charges or file a civil suit?"

Doug responds meekly, "Yes sir."

Sheriff Justice turns and storms away.

After a few seconds, Tag and Doug hear Sheriff Justice again on the bullhorn, "Homer and Virgil. Tag did as you asked. He asked if the new owners would reconsider. They won't. Now, I need for you to come on out. If you'll do that for me, there won't be any charges or lawsuits filed against you. We'll act like this never happened. What do you say?" he lowers the bullhorn in anticipation of an answer.

Tag creeps behind one of the pickups to watch the events unfold. Others are doing the same while trying to remain out of sight. He observes Sheriff Justice peering around the blade of the bulldozer toward the house. Aside from a few birds chirping, the random moos of cows, and the wind gusting through the tall grass bordering the fields and chestnut trees, there's not another sound.

Five minutes pass.

"Homer and Virgil, I need an answer."

No response.

Suddenly, two shots ring out!

Tag hits the ground. His heart's racing. Looking underneath the pickup, he observes Sheriff Justice crouched behind the blade of the bulldozer with his pistol in his hand. Glancing around, he notices everyone else has hit the ground. After a few seconds, some have risen to a crouched position and are waddling behind the trucks and equipment down the road. Tag isn't moving. He feels he's now a part of this drama. He also believes he's safe laying on the ground behind the wheel of the pickup.

Tag observes Sheriff Justice remove his cell from his pocket and dial a number. He can't quite hear the conversation. After a few minutes, he does hear Sheriff Justice say prior to hanging up, "Yes sir. We can handle it. I'll let you know when it's resolved." After hanging up, he waves at the deputies to come to him. While darting behind the trucks and heavy equipment they creep over to him. Again, Tag can't hear the conversation, but he sees Sheriff Justice motion toward the fields on either side of the road. The deputies nod and creep back toward the dirt road. Once they're a few feet down the road out of sight from the house, the deputies split up and disappear into the fields on either side of the road. Tag's curious, but he knows he can't move from his position toward Sheriff Justice. He can only retreat down the road.

Tag checks the clock on his cell. It's been ten minutes since the deputies disappeared. Nothing's happened. Sheriff Justice is still peering around the blade of the bulldozer. No additional shots fired. No movement in the house. The sun has now dropped below the mountain ridge. Shadows are quickly growing around the home.

Suddenly, Tag notices Sheriff Justice grab his cell. He's frozen as if he's reading a text. He hurriedly responds to this message, crams his cell in his pocket, and again removes his pistol from its holster. He adjusts his position from being in a crouch to a sprinter's position. Tag senses something's about to happen. His heartbeat accelerates.

118

BOOM! BOOM!

Tag jerks at the sound of two successive loud explosions. He's certain they've come from inside the home. His heart's now racing. Sheriff Justice is poised for action. A mist oozes from inside the home. It dissipates quickly. A gust of wind blows a remnant towards Tag. He smells a hint of vinegar followed immediately by a slight burning sensation in his eyes and nasal passage. Tag quickly retreats down the road, looking over his shoulder as he moves. He's met by the demolition workers creeping toward him curious about the explosions. They stop and, maybe foolishly, all stand to watch the action unfold. Sheriff Justice is still in position. He has a cloth over his nose and mouth as he continues to peer intently over the blade of the bulldozer.

After a few minutes, whatever was oozing from the home has stopped. Sheriff Justice is now standing, seemingly unconcerned about any additional danger. The front door suddenly opens! There's an audible gasp among the spectators. Stepping from the door is one of the deputies. His nose and mouth are covered by a gaiter and he's wearing goggles. He motions to Sheriff Justice and disappears back into the home. Sheriff Justice places a pair of goggles on and jogs toward the house while still covering his nose and mouth with a cloth. He's holstered his pistol.

Tag and his fellow onlookers intently watch the home. There's no movement of any kind. After a couple of minutes Sheriff Justice emerges from the home walking in their direction. After clearing the picket fence, he rips off his goggles and lowers the cloth. He stops when he reaches Tag and the group of curious men.

"Gentlemen, the situation has been resolved in a most unfortunate manner. The two elderly gentlemen are dead." There's an audible gasp from the group. "The explosions did not kill them. That was merely tear gas the deputies tossed into the home to try to drive them out without incident. When the elderly gentlemen did not emerge from the house, my deputies entered to assess the situation. They did not find the gentlemen in the downstairs portion of the house, so they climbed to the second story. There they found the gentlemen in their beds, deceased, from self-inflicted gunshot wounds." The crowd again gasps.

119

Most are shaking their heads. Many look to the ground. "Mr. Shaw?" Doug looks up with a stunned look on his face. "We will need to investigate and clean for the next twenty-four hours. You may not like this, but I'm requiring that you hire movers to clean out their personal effects. Also, you need to find a place to store them until their next of kin or beneficiaries claim them. You'll be reimbursed by their estates. Can you take care of that?

"Yes sir. I'll make those arrangements tomorrow. Just let me know when they can start."

"I will. Thank you. Now if the rest of you will leave so our investigators can have room to work, I'd appreciate it."

Tag's stunned. He realizes he was the last person to see them alive. He's nauseous as he worries over whether there was anything more he could have done to prevent this situation.

"Tag," Sheriff Justice interrupts his thoughts, "please get in your car and move it as soon as my deputies remove their cruiser from behind you. I need to get everyone out of here as quickly as possible. Again, I appreciate your help. This wasn't your fault."

Tag turns without saying a word.

"Tag, are you alright?"

"Yeah, I'll be fine," he answers glancing back over his shoulder.

"Hey! Again, it's not your fault. Okay?"

"Yeah. Yeah. I hear you," as Tag shuffles to his car.

He climbs in and starts the engine so the air conditioner will circulate cool air. He's still stunned. He feels he should be crying, but he's not. This disturbs him. While he waits for the deputies, he instinctively removes his cell from his pocket. There's a text from an unknown number. He opens it. "It's been 24 hrs. We need to talk. Call me at this number."

"Just great," he mutters. Tag looks away from the text, closes his eyes, and rubs them with his right thumb and middle finger.

TWENTY-ONE

Liesl's anxious. Her heart rate accelerates when Tag's car pulls in their driveway. Her emotions have battled all day about her perception of Tag's aloofness toward her, this mysterious woman who was seen hugging him, the woman seen on the boardwalk last night, and more importantly, whether the boardwalk strutter and the hugger are the same woman, and if so, is Tag having an affair with her.

After leaving Magnolia's, she was determined to confront him this evening. Almost brazen about it. As the day shortened, she softened. She's concerned she's stirring up trouble where none exists.

She confronted him about the hugger last night. He said it was someone from high school. He didn't offer anything else. Was he too cavalier? Do high school friends who haven't seen each other in years normally hug? Not based on her experience...but it's possible. Was there more than just a friendship in high school...and possibly now?

Is she always going to be suspicious of his activities and parse everything he tells her? She doesn't want to be one of those wives.

She's now reluctant to confront him, but she also doesn't want to be a fool. She loves him, but she won't stay if he disrespects her by having an affair. She should demand respect and fidelity. Afterall, they're married. There are rules associated with being married. In his defense, he hasn't shown interest in any other woman since they've been married. Why would he now?

Why is a simple hug bothering her so much? Why can't she just accept his answer and move on?

Liesl tries to calm herself before Tag walks in. She can't. She doesn't have a plan. She's unsure of what she'll do. Anxiety reigns.

Tag didn't call Suzy. He struggled with whether to call her on his drive home, but he's too stunned over the Jesters to have a coherent conversation with her, or really anyone. His emotions are shot. His energy's zapped. He doesn't even know what he'd say to her, even though he knows what he should say. Even if he wanted to call her, it's too late now. Liesl's watching him from the kitchen window. She seemed cold when they talked this afternoon. He's paranoid she's suspicious of him. He turns off the engine and exits his car.

Tag opens the kitchen door. He briefly hesitates when he sees Liesl. She appears tense and anxious as she looks at him with her arms folded across her chest.

Liesl's shocked by Tag's appearance. His clothes are disheveled, and his hair's unkempt as if he's been running his fingers through it. He looks shaken. He looks dazed.

Simultaneously they blurt, "What's wrong?"

"You first," Liesl anxiously defers to Tag since she has no plan.

"The Jesters are dead. They committed suicide."

"What!" Liesl's shocked. Confusion and empathy now prevail over anxiety. Her mouth's agape. She instinctively utters, "Why?" She's uncrossed her arms and now slowly shakes her head.

"I don't really know why, but I believe they did it because they didn't want to leave their home." Tag gently closes the kitchen door behind him.

"That's crazy! I'm sorry, I shouldn't have said that," Liesl apologizes.

"No, you're right, that is crazy. Do you know what's even crazier? I was the last person to see them alive." Tag's doleful eyes and somber attitude depict the depth of his sorrow.

They move closer.

Liesl embraces him. Tag's comforted by her compassion. He's still bothered he hasn't cried over their deaths.

"Do you want to talk about it?" Liesl whispers in his ear.

"Yeah, I think I do," Tag answers as they separate.

They face each other while holding hands.

"You told me this afternoon that the sheriff had asked for your help with them. What happened?"

"Well, when I got there, it was a pretty tense situation. When the crew the developers hired to demolish the home arrived this afternoon, the Jesters were still inside. They supposedly fired shots to keep the crew away."

"Did they shoot anyone?"

"No, the sheriff said he thought they were just warning shots."

"Why was the demolition crew there if the Jesters were still there?

"The Jesters were supposed to move out yesterday, but they didn't. The crew was surprised they were still in the home. The sheriff said they wanted to talk to me. I knew they had second thoughts. They had recently come by my office wanting to rescind the contract."

"Didn't you tell me they received six million dollars for their land?"

"Yeah, you and I would have sold in a heartbeat."

"And raced to the bank with the check!"

"You're right about that. Well, they didn't feel that way. I think at their ages they'd decided they were content without the money. It was the familiarity of where they lived which brought them contentment. In fact, they told me this afternoon, since they'd lived there all their lives, they'd decided this is where they wanted to live the rest of their lives. I had no clue they were contemplating ending the rest of their lives today! It never crossed my mind." Tag tightly squeezes Liesl's hands, lowers his eyes from hers, and drops his head. "They told me I tricked them into selling."

Liesl recognizes their accusation has crushed Tag. "Look at me," Liesl states defiantly as her righthand lifts Tag's chin so he must stare into her beautiful eyes. Eyes which have brought him immense pleasure over their years together. "You did nothing wrong. They're adults. When Doug approached you about buying their land, you merely approached them with the idea. They jumped at it is what I remember you telling me. You told me you made sure they discussed it with an attorney. I believe you told me this same attorney handled the closing. I think their attorney would have stopped the closing if he felt anything nefarious occurred. I can understand why you're upset. Anyone would be if they were with someone who ultimately committed suicide minutes later. You didn't cause their suicides. This is NOT your fault."

He's heard this before. Once again, people die tragically around Tag, and once again, he's told it's not his fault.

Tag is overcome by Liesl's passion in defending him and her compassion for him. Why is he even considering Suzy! This is all just crazy! He takes a deep, calming breath, "Thank you. I appreciate your kind words, but I still have this nagging feeling I could have prevented this tragedy. I don't believe I tricked them, but did I push them too hard to agree to the sale because I was focused on the size of the commission? I don't think so, but it's eating at me anyway. I've got to resolve that issue in my own mind.

It also bothers me that I haven't cried about their deaths. I should be upset about them. Why aren't I? Is there something wrong with me?"

"No, you're fine. You're probably just still in shock. I mean this just happened. The tears may flow later, but even if they don't, please don't let this upset you any further. This is not your fault."

"I hear you. Thanks! I love you."

"I love you, too."

They softly kiss.

"Where are the kids?" he softly asks.

"I believe they're upstairs playing. Are you alright if I have pizza delivered tonight for dinner?"

"Oh yeah! You know how to cheer a guy up!" Tag forces a smile.

"I thought that might help," Liesl grins.

Tag removes his wallet, keys, checkbook, and phone from his pockets. He lays them on the kitchen counter by a plug which contains his charger. He plugs the charger into his cell. "I'm going to take a shower before dinner. Is that alright with you."

"Oh sure! That should help you relax."

"Thanks," Tag turns to leave the kitchen, but stops, "I'm sorry. I think you had something to tell me when I came in. What is it?"

Liesl's heartbeat accelerates. It wouldn't be right to talk to him about this mystery woman at this time. Her brain's scrambling for something to say, "Uh...uh...," she's quickly thinks of something, "Jenny Jean wants to take Maize and Jase up to the alpine meadow for a picnic. I'm a little anxious about it, but I want to know what you think."

"Hummm. I think it'll be alright. She's been very responsible in the past. Of course, college can sometimes encourage irresponsibility. Unless you see something in her that bothers you, I'm fine with it. Since the Forest Service built that road a few years ago to within a half a mile of the meadow, it should be an easy, short walk for the kids. Let's just make sure she does it on a day when there aren't storms in the forecast. Lightning's what scares me."

"Yeah, I think it'll be fine, too. I wanted to make sure you're in agreement. For some reason it's just been nagging me since she asked"

"I am. I shouldn't be long." Tag turns and leaves the kitchen.

Liesl turns her attention to Tag's cell. She's sure what's on his phone will either confirm or dispel her suspicions. She knows his code. It would be easy for her to look. She picks it up, and then quickly sets it down again. She paces while staring at his cell. She's conflicted. "Damn," she mutters. Finally, curiosity and her desire to resolve this issue prevails. She picks up his cell and enters his code. The cell lights up with all his aps glaring.

She checks his recent calls. His most recent call is the one to her this afternoon. She quickly scans through his calls for the last three days. There are some numbers she doesn't recognize, so she quickly decides it's a waste of time to figure out if any of these numbers are from the woman without dialing all of them. She notices he doesn't have any recent voice mails.

She flips over to check his texts. His most recent text was this afternoon from someone stating this person hadn't heard from him in twenty-four hours and they need to talk. Probably a real estate offer. She continues to scan through the texts. There are no smoking guns from what she reads.

Next, she checks his emails. The most recent ones are junk emails. As she scans through them nothing causes her concern.

She sets his phone down. She's somewhat relieved, but she knows there's the possibility he could have deleted a message from this woman. She flushes that thought. She's decided there's nothing for her to worry about. She's slightly embarrassed and frustrated she allowed herself to become so worked up over a public hug on the boardwalk. She's always trusted him. She's decided there's no reason not to trust him now. She relaxes.

Liesl fishes her phone from her purse, pulls up her contacts, and finds the one for the pizza restaurant. She snickers to herself. She bets most people don't have a pizza restaurant on speed dial.

TWENTY-TWO

Tag closes the door to his office. He must get this call behind him. He needs to return Suzy's text message before she shows up in his office. Ronette would easily notice that something wasn't right. That would cause her to become suspicious. He can't take that chance.

He hopes 8:30 isn't too early to call Suzy. He can't wait much longer, though. The stress is killing him. He takes a deep breath and dials.

"Well hello love!" Suzy cheerfully answers. "I knew you'd eventually call. I could tell you still had a fire for me when we were together."

God how he hates her brash nature now! He used to crave it. He's decided to ignore her remark, "I'm sorry I didn't call you yesterday. I don't know if you've heard the horrible news, but two elderly gentlemen committed suicide late yesterday. They were my clients. In fact, I was the last one to see them alive. It was very upsetting. I just didn't feel like talking to anyone. Again, I apologize."

"I didn't know. That's just awful...horrible! Love, I'm so sorry! How can I help you?"

Again, Tag ignores her pet name for him, "There's nothing you can do. Thanks anyway." He wonders why he's being so nice. "In your text, you said it had been twenty-four hours. So, what were you expecting to hear from me yesterday?"

"That you had decided to run away with me, silly!" she laughs.

"Suzy, our meeting was very uncomfortable for me. I mean...I mean...you dropped a bombshell on me! To find out we almost had a kid was shocking. I'm sorry you've had to live with this burden all these years, but at least you'd gotten used to it. The other night was my first time to learn of our child. I didn't know what to say. I didn't know what to do. I had to get out of there. I needed to think, to absorb this. I apologize for leaving so abruptly, but I just couldn't stay."

"No, I understand. If there had been an easier way for me to tell you, I would've done so. I hope you understand it was also emotionally hard for me to tell you."

"I do, and I'm sorry if I was insensitive toward you. I frankly didn't know what to do."

"So, what about us?"

Tag pauses to gather his thoughts. He wants to make sure he communicates this clearly. He's planned his response, "There is no us. There was us, but that was almost half our lives ago. That time was an awakening for me. You helped transition me to manhood. I will always fondly look back on our time together, but the hurt from your abandonment was painful and disruptive. I struggled with it as I searched for you to learn why you abandoned me. Based on your revelation the other night, I now understand some of why you did. I eventually moved on. I found someone else." For some reason he can't say Liesl's name to Suzy. "I now have a family and responsibilities. I can't leave them. I won't leave them. There isn't an us today."

"But there can be an us! I know you still love me. It was obvious when we were together. I can understand why you're hesitant to leave your family, but if I'm your true love, as you're mine, then you'll never be happy until we're together.

If it's your children you're reluctant to leave, I have enough money to buy custody from their mother. Since I can't have children, and you love yours, I will learn to love them, too. They'll enjoy the best of everything, schools, toys, clothes, vacations, you name it!

You know you love me! Admit it to yourself! We can tackle these problems together. Yeah, there'll be some short term hurt, but that'll pass quickly and be overshadowed by the years of joy we'll share. Why don't you come on up and we'll discuss this in person? This is hard to talk about over the telephone."

Tag's afraid there's some truth in what Suzy said, but her statement that she would "buy custody from their mother" frightens Tag. How could she be so callous toward Liesl! Liesl would never give up these kids for any amount of money! He knew from their summer together that Suzy was always focused

128

on what Suzy wanted, and she usually got it. Her extraordinary financial success has emboldened her even more than when she was as a teenager. Yes, he still has feelings for her, but are those feelings for the Suzy he knew fifteen years ago? Who is Suzy now? After her upsetting statement, he's not so sure he'll like the new Suzy. If he chooses Suzy, he might eventually become collateral damage.

He loves Liesl. It's monotony and his provocative memories of his passionate times with Suzy which are threatening his relationship with Liesl. Suzy's callous statement has stained those memories. She's quickly shoving him back to Liesl.

"Suzy, if I were to come up to your room, I think we both know what might happen. I'm not going to do that. I love my wife."

"Okay, I thought this might be difficult, but I'm not giving up. You better get used to me. I plan to be around. I want you to show me the most expensive lake houses."

"I can't represent you. You need to talk to someone else."

There's a pause, "I'm not sure that's a good idea."

"Why isn't it?"

"They might ask me why I'm interested in purchasing a home on Pocket Watch Lake. Are you sure you want me to tell them?"

Tag's heart races, "You wouldn't do that?"

"I wouldn't want to, but who knows?"

Tag isn't only frightened by Suzy's comment, he's also angry. Very angry! "Are you trying to blackmail me? So, we had a fling when we were in high school, and you got pregnant. I'm sorry! You had an abortion. I'm sorry! I didn't even know any of this until the other night. You've got nothing on me! Who you tell is going to think you're either desperate or demented!"

"Oh, I can spice it up. Make it real juicy. Then it's a question of who the voters, your clients, your friends, and your family believe. But, let's don't fight lover. You know what I want. Don't make this hard. You just need to follow your gut. You and I both know what you crave. Give in!"

"Screw you!" Tag abruptly hangs up.

129

He's fuming while scared to death. He can't believe he allowed his memories of Suzy to come between he and Liesl. He's almost as angry with himself as he is with Suzy. He can't see them together again. He prays it's not too late to save his marriage. He knows he needs to tell Liesl, but how?

"Hey Mags!" Tag answers recognizing her telephone number.

"You still miss me hun?"

"Always."

"Is this a good time for me to bring the casino boys by?"

"Sure."

"Great! I'll be there in a few."

"See you then."

Tag's cell pings as he hangs up. It's a text from Suzy. She's called him numerous times today since their conversation this morning. He hasn't answered any of them. Also, he knows she's left two voice mails, to which he's yet to listen.

He's concerned what the text may say, but he opens it anyway. He snickers when he realizes at least a text can't argue with him. "I'm SO SORRY about this morning. :(Was out of line. Way out of line!!!!!!!!!!! Don't know what got into me? I'd never do that to you!!!!!!!!!!!!!! Please forgive me!!!!!!!!!!! Let's talk love!!!!!!!!!!! :) :)"

This text doesn't change his feelings from this morning. He's uncertain whether she's sincere or trying to deceive him. He deletes her text.

Right now, he's anxious about the city council meeting tomorrow night. He can't let Suzy distract him from this important decision affecting the future of the citizens of the valley.

As instructed by Mags, he did talk to Pastor Honeycutt. Tag thought he made a logical and impassioned argument. He explained to Pastor Honeycutt that he clearly respects his position and understands his concerns, even though they disagree. He explained that having a group of people encircling the building would be intimidating to those citizens who want to attend the meeting to truly understand both sides. He encouraged Pastor Honeycutt to attend the meeting and state his case. Tag

130

tried to make the case that holding a prayer meeting at the church prior to the council meeting would be heard by God just as clearly as one held while encircling the building. He asked Pastor Honeycutt to please let the citizens attend without feeling awkward or intimidated.

Pastor Honeycutt quietly listened to Tag's plea. He was non-committal on canceling the prayer circle. Tag didn't attend church last Sunday to avoid being a distraction. At this moment, he hasn't heard whether the prayer circle's been canceled tomorrow night. Many members of the congregation have told them they don't plan to participate in a prayer circle. They're also reluctant to attend the meeting if Pastor Honeycutt is outside encouraging people to pray against the casino.

Tag's anxious to see the casino's presentation this afternoon. It will give him the opportunity to be better prepared for any questions which might arise during the meeting tomorrow night when it's presented to the voters. Also, if he identifies any gaps or errors in the presentation this afternoon, perhaps they'll have time to make last minute changes. Finally, to impress the citizens of Rock Slide, Mags and he can coach those presenting on how to make the presentation more effective.

"Hey Tag," it's Ronette on the phone. "Mrs. Winter-Blossom is here with the gentlemen from the casino."

In the background, Tag hears a familiar roar, "It's Magnolia hun! By the way, who does your hair? Lord, they need to be imprisoned!"

Tag suppresses a laugh, "Thanks! I'll be right there."

TWENTY-THREE

On summer days when the sun creeps toward the horizon, the majestic red oaks shading the Ryder's backyard provide intermittent shade to all its parts. Some parts receive longer periods of shade. In these shady areas, it's been a constant challenge to grow grass. Tag and Liesl have recently surrendered growing grass in these perpetually bare spots and instead have converted them to oases of rhododendron, azaleas, and mountain laurel, except for one area. This area is reserved for Maize, Jase, and their friends. A swing set, slide, and playhouse all purchased on line and frustratingly constructed, due to missing screws, from complicated kits of metal and plastic dominate this area. Decorative pea gravel has been sprinkled unevenly across the surface of the play area to provide foundation and cushion. Unfortunately, the pea gravel tends to spread into the grass creating a hazard when Tag mows the lawn. A crack in one of the kitchen window panes serves as a reminder of the amount of force generated when a whirling metal blade catches a pebble.

Maize and Jase are enjoying a gorgeous afternoon under a cobalt blue, cloudless sky in their backyard. Maize's hosting a tea party in the playhouse for her barbies. She painstakingly set the rickety dolls' table for her party. In the middle of the table there's a small, pink plastic pitcher of cool water filled from the hose. Small, pink plastic plates are placed at each end of the table and stacked with recently pulled rye grass, plucked dandelions, and picked clover. Her statuesque barbies are in various states of dress, and undress, while posed around the table. Maize's entertaining them with lively conversation. Periodically she changes her inflection to speak for one of her mute guests.

Jase isn't invited to the party. Boys aren't allowed. He's stretched out prone in one of their swings. His stomach rests in the U-shaped stirrup. He's pretending he's flying over plastic dinosaurs he's placed in the pea gravel. He'll run forward until

132

his feet leave the ground. While his legs are raised, his momentum swings him back and forth until he slows to the point where he'll drop his feet again and repeat the process. As he flies, he imitates the supposed sounds of clashing dinosaurs. He also scraps his hands across the pea gravel, scooping some up, which he drops as bombs over the unsuspecting herd. He squeals with delight when one topples.

"Hey kids," Liesl hollers from the backdoor she's cracked open. "Come on in. Let's pack for your adventure with Jenny Jean tomorrow. You're leaving early in the morning, so let's get it done now."

Jace carpet bombs his dinosaurs with the remaining pea gravel in his hands, drops anchor with his feet, and bolts from the swing toward the house. "I'm gonna win!" he shouts over his shoulder toward Maize who hasn't left the playhouse yet.

"Boys!" she exclaims to her guests. She shouts, "I don't care!" from inside the house, even though she hates to lose to her brother. As Jace reaches his mom, Maize exits the playhouse. She slowly saunters toward the door to show Jase she wasn't racing. By now, Jase and her mom have disappeared into the house.

After Maize steps through the backdoor into the house, she finds Jase and her mom in the kitchen. Jase is standing on a chair at the sink washing his hands. Her mom's placed a loaf of bread on the counter and is removing a jar of grape jelly from the refrigerator.

"Hey Maize, grab the peanut butter from the pantry," Liesl instructs. "We're gonna make your sandwiches for tomorrow. Also, wash your hands when Jase is through."

Maize grabs the jar of creamy peanut butter and places it on the counter next to the jar of grape jelly.

"Thanks sweetie!" Liesl offers while grabbing a knife from the drawer.

Jace jumps down from the chair and pulls it to the counter where Liesl's making the sandwiches. As Maize stands on her tip toes to wash her hands, Jace climbs into the chair, "I wanna do it!"

"Hey, I need your help picking out the snacks. Will you grab what you want to take with you on your adventure?" Liesl knows there'll be peanut butter and jelly all over her counter if Jace tries to make a sandwich. She glances at Maize as she's drying her hands on a dishcloth, "Maize, you pick out what you want, too. Also, y'all pick out something you think Jenny Jean will like."

"It's JJ mom," Maize corrects in a haughty tone.

"Okay, pick out something for JJ."

Liesl makes six peanut butter and jelly sandwiches, two for each of her children and two for JJ just in case she doesn't bring enough to eat.

Jace has stacked boxes of Goldfish crackers, Vanilla Wafers, and Fruit Rollups on the counter. Maize's still working on her selection. She's only placed a package of Oreos on the counter.

"Jace, grab some of those Capri Suns from the refrigerator."

Jase grabs the Capri Suns and drops them on the counter. Then he climbs back on the chair. He helps his mother and sister pack their insulated lunch boxes, first with the Capri Suns, then the snacks, which are packed in baggies, and finally the sandwiches, which are also packed in baggies.

After the lunch boxes are zipped closed, Liesl places them in the refrigerator. She also places three bottled waters next to them. She wants them to take these bottles of water in case the Capri Suns aren't enough. "Alright, we'll put these in your backpacks tomorrow. Go up to your rooms and put in your backpacks what you want to take with you on your adventure. Don't put too much in them. You don't want them to be too heavy. Bring'em down to me when you're finished."

Both kids sprint for the stairs.

"I'm gonna beat you!" Maize hollers.

"No, you're not!"

Liesl hears them bounding up the stairs.

"Alright," Liesl yells up the stairs after fifteen minutes. "Finish packing and bring down your backpacks so I can see what's in them." After a few seconds of silence, "Maize! Jase! Did you hear me?"

"Yes!" Jase screams.

"Yes what?

"Yes mam."

"That's more like it. Maize?"

"Coming mama!"

Maize bounds down the stairs with her backpack on. "Alright, let's see what you're taking on your adventure." As Liesl unzips Maize's backpack, Jase comes hopping down the stairs dragging his backpack and a small aluminum canteen.

Liesl digs in Maize's backpack. She finds Maize's favorite brown teddy bear, one half-naked Barbie, a pad of paper, her package of felt tip markers, a strip of colorful bead stickers, plastic sunglasses, three Elsa band aids, plastic scissors, and a plastic compass. Liesl removes the Barbie, "So why are you taking her?" she asks Maize.

"I don't know," Maize shrugs her shoulders.

"How 'bout we leave her here?"

"Mom! Please? JJ and I may want to play with her." Maize pleads.

"Okay, I guess she can go, but only if we can fit your lunch box in your backpack. Also, I want you to take your raincoat in case it's windy and rainy in the meadow. Go get it and bring it to me."

Maize bounds up the stairs.

"Okay young man," Liesl turns to Jase, "let me see what you've packed." Liesl's slightly anxious as she opens his backpack. You never know what Jase has in mind. While carefully rummaging she finds a plastic knife, his Dino Blaster toy pistol which whirs and lights up when the trigger's pulled, his toy light saber which hums, a Power Ranger, a plastic flashlight, a faux coonskin cap, toothbrush, toothpaste, dinosaur pajamas, a small plastic toy car, and three plastic toy dinosaurs: T-Rex, triceratops, and stegosaurus.

Liesl removes the pajamas, toothbrush, and toothpaste. She hands them to Jase, "Take these back upstairs. You're not spending the night. Y'all are just going for a picnic."

"Okay mom!"

"What was that?"

"Yes mam," Jace utters softly hiding his embarrassment as he slowly ascends the stairs carrying the items.

"Jase?"

"Yes mam," he stops and turns.

"Good!"

Jase smiles.

Liesl holds up the small aluminum canteen. "Are you sure you want to take this?"

"Yes mam. I want to look like a real hiker!" Jase smiles wider.

"Okay," Liesl laughs, "Just don't fill it up until you leave tomorrow. I don't want you spilling it in the house."

"Yes mam," Jase turns and bounds up the stairs.

"Hold on young man. There's no reason to take your Dino Blaster pistol, light saber, and Power Ranger. Come get these, too."

"Oh mom! I gotta take those to kill bears, lions, bad guys, aliens, and monsters!"

"I don't think you'll have to worry about killing anything, but how about you just take your Dino Blaster pistol?"

"Okay," Jase responds dejectedly.

Liesl drops the Dino Blaster pistol into his backpack and hands him the other items to take to his room, "Oh, and grab your raincoat, too, in case it rains."

With his arms full, Jase slowly, and dejectedly, climbs the stairs. Liesl can't help but chuckle.

TWENTY-FOUR

Tag's having a difficult time this morning focusing while reviewing the copy of the presentation he received yesterday at his meeting with representatives of the casino. He's disturbed he didn't tell Liesl about Suzy last night. He justified it by convincing himself that her reaction to the shocking news might distract him from being focused on the meeting tonight. He can't risk that happening. Although, he's now convinced that's a flimsy excuse. It was primarily "cold feet" which prevented him from telling her. He knows he must tell her soon, especially before she hears it from another source. He shudders to think how she'd react.

"Tonight. Yes tonight," he mutters. He'll tell her tonight…or maybe…tomorrow night. Especially if it's a long, stressful meeting, or if he's too tired.

Since he didn't respond to any of Suzy's flurry of attempts to contact him yesterday, he's anxious she's going to become more aggressive today. She's already left him a voicemail this morning, which he's ignored. He can't have her distracting him either. He's concerned she might show up in his office. He's convinced himself seeing her again would be a mistake. Her tantalizing beauty and his passionate memories of their intimate moments threaten to again ignite his desires. Fanning those flames might start a fire he can't put out.

He hasn't heard if she's hired another real estate agent. He's beginning to believe her desire to purchase a home on the lake is a ruse. He's convinced she's using it to tempt him to choose her. He must persuade her that she's wasting her time. He's struggling with how to do that since she's so headstrong.

Ronette's knock on his open office door interrupts his thoughts.

"Tag, there're two men here to see you. Something about a new car."

"A new car? I'm not looking to buy anything new right now. Just tell them I'm too busy to talk. They can leave their contact information."

Ronette's confused, "Uh…they said they're here to de-liv-er your new car."

"What?" now they're both confused. "I haven't bought a new car. They're mistaken." Tag rises from behind his desk. "I'll go talk to them." He scoots past Ronette.

"Hi! I'm Tag Ryder. How may I help you gentlemen?" Tag asks as he strides into the reception area with his hand extended to greet them.

"Yes sir, Mr. Ryder. I'm Dusty Corbin," he introduces himself as he shakes Tag's hand, "and this here's Don Peterson," he nods to the fellow with him. "We got your new car outside. It sho is pretty!" Dusty smiles. "I just need you to step outside and inspect it. If you're satisfied with its condition, then all I need is your signature on this piece of paper and its yours!" He holds up the document for Tag to see.

"I'm sorry, but there's some mistake. I haven't bought a new car."

Now it's Dusty's turn to be confused. He hesitates. There's a puzzling look on his face. He glances at the document and asks without looking up, "Are you Mr. Tag Ryder?"

"Yes I am."

"And is this Ryder Real Estate?"

"Yes, it is."

"Well, this release I have," he waves the document," says I'm to deliver this car to you at this location, but you say it's not yours?"

"That's right. I haven't bought a new car."

"How 'bout yer wife?"

"No. If she had, she'd told me. Now my dad works here, too, but he's out of town. His name's not Tag, though."

"Well, this sho is strange. Don, you ever had this happen before?" Dusty glances at his associate.

"Nope."

"Well, Mr. Ryder, I really don't know what to do. We drove this car all the way up from Pineville," Tag's emotions leap, "this morning to deliver it to you just as this paper says."

138

He waves the document again. "I don't know how our back office could've messed this up so bad. Why don't you go outside and look at while I call my boss, maybe it'll jog your memory," Dusty suggests while removing his cell phone from his pocket. Tag doesn't respond. "Mr. Ryder?"

"Sure. Sure." Tag wasn't focused on what Dusty was saying once he heard the name "Pineville." His thoughts distracted him. He's certain he now knows what's happening. Suzy's trying to buy his love. His mind's scrambling for solutions. Anger and anxiety simultaneously build. If Liesl hears about this, he'll be put in a very difficult position explaining it. What may be even worse, though, is there may be suspicion that he's taken a bribe, or the casino owners have offered him a bribe. In either bribe scenario, he must deal with ethical and legal problems which carry fines and imprisonment if he can't prove he's innocent.

Tag steps outside followed by Ronette and Don while Dusty calls his boss.

"Wow!" Ronette exclaims.

A brand spanking new, light gray Range Rover rests in a parking spot in front of the office. It seems to sparkle like a polished cut diamond as its immaculate sheen reflects the bright sunshine.

"Tag," Ronette chuckles, "if you don't want it, I'll take it!" She slowly walks around the beautifully engineered machine admiring it from every angle.

"It's not mine or yours. It needs to go back. They've made a big mistake."

"Mr. Ryder," Dusty hollers as he steps outside with his cell phone next to his ear, "my boss pulled the documentation and says this is yer car. It was bought and paid for by..."

"Let me talk to your boss," Tag interrupts Dusty afraid he's about to reveal to Ronette what Tag suspects. Dusty hands Tag his cell.

"Hello, this is Tag Ryder. Who am I speaking with?"

"Hello Mr. Ryder, this is Carl Huffstutler, the sales manager for Pineville Luxury Motors. I understand from my associate that you say this isn't your car. Our records reflect that this car was purchased from our dealership with instructions to deliver it to you."

Tag steps back into the empty office suite. Ronette is still outside admiring the Range Rover. "Can you tell me who purchased the car?"

"I'm sorry Mr. Ryder, without permission from the purchaser, I can't."

"Why not, if you say it's my car?"

"I'm sorry Mr. Ryder. It's our policy. I'm happy to contact the purchaser and seek her permission. Would you like me to do that?"

Tag's now sure it was Suzy since he said "her." "No, that's fine, but I'm not accepting it."

There's an uncomfortable pause. "I understand Mr. Ryder. Hand the phone back to my associate and I'll instruct him to bring it back."

"What do you understand?"

"I'm not sure I need to answer that question. We'll void the sale."

"What you understand is wrong! Do you understand me?"

"Mr. Ryder, there's no need to get angry. There's nothing else to be said. Hand the phone back to my associate. I apologize for the discomfort we've caused."

"Again, what you understand is wrong!"

"Please Mr. Ryder. Hand the phone back to my associate."

Tag complies. He listens to Dusty's end of the conversation, "Uh huh...Oh!..." Dusty glances as Tag with a sly smile. "I understand...Yes sir...Yes sir...Okay, bye." He ends the call and hollers, "Hey Don. We're taking it back. No need to follow me unless you want to."

"Gotcha!" Don marches toward a pickup parked a few spaces down.

"Sorry Mr. Ryder," Dusty says nervously. "We'll pretend this never happened." Dusty opens the door of the Range Rover, climbs in, cranks the motor, and pulls away.

"Wow, again," Ronette marvels. "Wish it were yours. What'd they tell you."

"It was a mistake," Tag storms off to his office and shuts his door.

Ronette knows something's not right. She won't push him about it, but she's sure curious enough to stealthily snoop.

Tag removes his cell from his pocket. He finds Suzy's most recent voice mail and listens.

"Hey love! Again, I'm sorry. I hope my surprise this morning shows you how deeply sorry I am and how much I want us to be together. Please call me love, or better yet, come see me. Tata for now! Love you!"

Tag's fuming! He wants her gone from Rock Slide, immediately! He quickly decides that he can't call her from his office. He's afraid he'd raise his voice resulting in Ronette hearing him. He's concerned she's now suspecting something anyway, probably a bribe from the casino owners.

Tag tries to act calm when he leaves his office. "Ronette, I'm going out for some air," Tag hollers down the hall before walking out the backdoor onto the boardwalk. "I'll be back in a few minutes."

He's torn as to who he needs to call first. Suzy to let her have it, or the city attorney to report this attempted gift. To stay out of trouble with the law, as an elected official, he knows he needs to report this, otherwise he might end up in jail. He hates to have to tell the city attorney about his relationship with Suzy before he tells Liesl. Unfortunately, he believes the law dictates that he must immediately report this to the city attorney, especially before he tells anyone else.

TWENTY-FIVE

The drive to Wildflower Meadow has been filled with silly songs, "I spy with my little eye" games, imaginary dinosaur sightings, curious questions, and waves of laughter. It's been months since Maize and Jase have seen Jenny Jean Jenkins, their favorite babysitter of all time. There's a lot to catch up on.

Maize and Jase were so excited to see her, they sat on the front stoop of their home eagerly awaiting her arrival. When they realized it was her Jeep Cherokee pulling into the driveway, they sprinted across the lawn. Like two excited puppies, they bounced with joy outside her car door. After shutting her door, Jenny Jean quickly squatted with her arms wide while bracing herself for a group hug. The force of the kids leaping into her arms was uneven. It knocked her off balance. They rolled together in the grass laughing with excitement.

Jenny Jean, or "JJ" to Maize and Jase, is home for a few days from college. She took extra courses this summer to have a lighter course load next spring. She walked on the softball team as a non-scholarship freshman catcher last fall at her college. She survived all the cuts to make the team. She played sparingly this past spring, but the coach told her she was pleased with her progress and if she keeps improving, she'll earn more playing time, and possibly some scholarship money. When Liesl helped put the car seats in JJ's jeep, she couldn't help but notice how much thicker JJ was now than last summer when JJ babysat for them four days a week.

As the jeep climbs the steep, uneven Park Service-road, Maize giggles prior to posing a question, "JJ? What has four wheels and flies?"

Glancing in her rearview mirror, JJ answers, "My jeep!"

"No! A garbage truck!" Maize and Jase scream in unison. Both kids laugh hysterically.

"Oh!" JJ joins the laughter.

"Hey JJ, uh, uh, why did the chicken cross the road?" Jase queries.

"I know that one! To get to the other side!"

Disappointed, Jase scrambles for a different answer. He was hoping to fool JJ, "Uh...uh... no, he wanted to see a T-Rex!" Jase laughs wildly.

JJ's puzzled by his nonsensical answer, but snickers anyway so as not to hurt Jase's feelings.

"That's stupid," Maize deadpans.

"That's not nice!" Jase counters.

"Yeah Maize," JJ agrees quickly glancing in her rearview mirror. She's reluctant to remove her eyes from the narrow potholed road in fear of having an accident. "Let's be nice."

"Sa-rcc!"

When JJ's jeep bounces around the next bend, she slows it to a stop. Fluorescent orange cones loosely connected by bright yellow crime tape block the road. A crude sign reads, "Closed for Repairs." JJ had no idea the road to the alpine meadow was closed, but she can understand why. The bumpy ride to this point could destroy a car's shocks if it steered into a deep pothole. Snow, ice, freezing temperatures, torrential rain, and heavy usage can easily erode a road in these mountains.

"What's wrong?" Maize asks seeing JJ's concerned look reflected in the rearview mirror.

"The road's closed. They're fixing it. We can't drive up to the meadow."

"Oh no!" Maize sighs.

"I wanna go!" Jase hollers.

"We can't. I'm sorry. We'll have to do something else. Afterall we can't waste your picnic lunches! Is there some other place you want to go?"

"I wanna go to the meadow," Jase whines.

"Me, too!" Maize adds. "I promised my mama I would bring her flowers."

"Me, too!" Jase agrees.

"I'm sorry, but…" suddenly, JJ remembers there's another way. It means a hike of over a mile to the meadow. She's not sure they can do it, though. "There's another way for us to get there, but it means we'll have a long walk. Do y'all want to try it? It'll be an adventure!"

"Yeah!" is the enthusiastic response from the back seat.

"We'll have to hike up the mountain on a trail. It may be tiring, but since we're in no hurry, we can rest when you're tired. I have y'all all day."

"We can do it JJ!" Maize shouts.

"Yeah!" Jase agrees.

"Okay then! We'll try it."

The road is blocked just after a scenic overlook. JJ assumes this spot was chosen to allow people to easily turn around. She steers into the scenic overlook turnout and turns down the mountain road again.

On her way up the mountain she passed the turn which leads to a parking lot providing access to various hiking trails. It's not too far from the scenic overlook. There are maps in a kiosk at the lot showing the various trails through the mountains. These maps include distances and estimates of hiking times. They're also rated for difficulty. Unfortunately, the Park Service isn't prompt in replacing the maps once the supply's exhausted, but JJ knows the right trail to take anyway. She's walked it many times with her family, even as a child. She can't remember if she was as young as Jase when she hiked it her first time. The trail's not easy, and some places can be hazardous if you're not paying attention, but she'll be careful with Maize and Jase. She's never heard of anyone getting hurt on the trail, but she knows not every incident is reported.

JJ's excited to be taking the trail. She wasn't sure when she was going to find time today to get in her workout, but this hike should be all she needs. She's trying to stay in shape to get a jump on next season. She knows how hard her parents work to pay her college tuition. If she can earn even a partial scholarship it will help them greatly with their finances.

JJ turns her jeep onto the gravel road leading to the parking lot where the hiking trails are located. The thick overstudy makes it appear as if they're entering a dimly lit tunnel.

After a couple hundred feet of jarring bounces, they reach the clearing which cradles the gravel parking lot. Her jeep is the only vehicle in the lot. JJ parks and unbuckles the kids from their car seats. They bounce with excitement as JJ opens her tailgate to retrieve the backpacks.

"Whoa! These are heavy. We may have to remove some items before we set out on our hike."

"Please, no JJ!" Maize pleads.

"Yeah," Jase agrees.

"Okay, I'll take some stuff out of mine and move some of your items to mine. If they're too heavy for you, we can move some more items to my pack later."

That seems to satisfy them. They skip around the lot while JJ culls items from her backpack. She moves some of their items into her backpack. She snickers at the items they've chose to bring on their hike. It reminds her of the dolls she wanted to bring with her when she hiked as a young girl. At the time she thought it was important that her dolls shared in the fun, too.

"Either of you need to go the bathroom before we take off?"

Maize and Jase glance at the Port O Potty.

"Yucky!"

"Yeah, yucky!"

"Okay, but don't say I didn't warn you."

JJ helps each child strap on a backpack. Neither child stoops signaling the backpack is too heavy. That's a good sign. Of course, they're not walking up hill yet. She left room in her backpack to pack more items from their backpacks if they become too heavy for the children.

JJ slides her backpack on and hurriedly walks to the kiosk. As she suspected, no maps. Not surprising since it's late summer. Also, that's a great sign reflecting there's probably been many hikers this year. The businesses in Rock Slide thrive when there are more tourists.

Three trails lead from the parking lot. The far left one is marked "Alpine Meadow." She knew this was the right trail without needing the sign since she's hiked it many times before.

145

"Okay kids, are you ready for our adventure?"

"Yes!" They scream in unison.

"Alright! I'll lead the way. Maize, you follow me. You're in charge of the songs on our hike."

Maize grins.

"Jase, I want you bringing up the rear watching for dinosaurs. Can you do that?"

Jase puffs out his tiny chest, "I'll beat 'um up!"

"Good, then let's go! Y'all follow close behind. If you get tired, let me know."

They quickly disappear from the parking lot into the dark forest.

TWENTY-SIX

Franklin Howard's experiencing more anxiety than normal before a city council meeting. In his twenty-seven years as city attorney for Rock Slide, aside from the approval of Sunday alcohol sales, he's never had a more controversial issue to advise upon than the approval of a casino. It's by far the most complicated. Based on his informal poll, he's certain most of the residents are supportive of the casino, but the minority are very vocal in their resistance. He's concerned about the formation of the prayer circle outside the building. He's hoping they won't show up, but if they do, he's familiarized himself with the law to ensure the city doesn't violate any laws in how it's addressed.

Franklin's spent hours researching and learning the new law regarding the establishment and regulation of casinos in the state. He's also talked to city attorneys from other states he's met through professional association who've previously, and successfully, dealt with this issue. He feels he's prepared, but it's the unknown which is causing his anxiety. As he likes to remind his clients, it's the bullet you don't see which eventually get you. That keeps his clients up at night, and has kept his family fed.

The ring of his telephone interrupts his review of his notes for tonight's meeting.

"Hello."

"Franklin, this is Tag. I need to talk with you. Do you have a few minutes?"

Franklin senses from Tag's tone of voice this can't be good, "Sure, go ahead and talk. I'm just reviewing my notes for tonight's meeting. Are you calling about the meeting?"

"Well…kind of. I need to come see you as opposed to discussing it over the phone."

"Okay," Franklin rocks back in his chair, "when would you like to come?"

"How about now? I'm standing outside your office."

"Now's good," Franklin chuckles. "Come on in." Almost before he can hang up his telephone, the door opens and in walks Tag. Distress is etched in Tag's face as he closes the door behind him. "Have a seat. This must be serious for you to be standing outside my door."

"Unfortunately, it is."

They shake hands and take their respective seats. The known and unknown have immediately created an uneasy tension in the room.

It's still awkward for Tag to call him Franklin. Until Tag was elected to the city council, he'd been Mr. Howard for Tag's entire life. Tag's parents and the Howards have been friends for as long as Tag can remember. Franklin was very helpful in ensuring that no spurious criminal charges were brought against Tag when Billy died. For that, the Ryders, and Tag, are eternally grateful.

"So, what brings you here?" Franklin asks. His antique desk chair squeaks when he leans back.

As Tag gathers his thoughts and fights embarrassment, he's still intimidated by Franklin's piercing stare. That stare has made Tag uncomfortable since he was a child. It's as if he's reading his mind and knows his thoughts before he expresses them. Behind those aging eyes resides a mind packed with wisdom and knowledge. Tag likens him to the Gandalf character from the *Lord of the Rings* trilogy. Franklin's snow-white hair and creased facial lines enhance the image.

"I've got an issue you need to be aware of because, even though it's not, it might be deemed to be a breach of ethics or a violation of the law in my position as an elected public servant."

"Please tell me more. Do you mind if I take notes?"

"No."

"Thank you," Franklin's chair squeaks as he rocks forward to grab a legal pad and pen.

"Do you remember when Billy Ray Quick died?"

"How could I forget that most unfortunate accident."

Tag appreciates Franklin's continued defense of Tag, "If you'll remember there were four girls in the boat with us."

148

"Yes. I read their statements. Their consistent rendition of the facts of the accident is one of the primary reasons I concluded there was no evidence of any criminal action on your part."

"Which I really appreciated."

"Just doing my job."

"Well, due to the horrible events of that day, one of the girls and I became very close. I mean very, very close. If you know what I mean?" Tag slightly flushes.

"I believe I do, go on."

"In fact, we believed we were in love. Unfortunately, within a few months after that crazy summer, she quit responding to me. I was devastated. I eventually learned that my immediate attraction to her never allowed me to properly grieve the loss of Billy, and when she dropped me, I tumbled into a deep hole of despair due to having lost both important relationships so close in time."

Franklin's wondering how this has anything to do with an ethical issue or illegal activity. His chair squeaks again when he leans back. No need to take notes yet.

"It took me a few years of wandering in the wilderness to come to grips with my losses and move beyond them. I often wondered what happened to her, but I quit looking for her after I met Liesl.

Well, a few days ago she shows up out of the blue here in Rock Slide. I was stunned to say the least. She said she wanted me to help her buy a home on the lake. I wasn't sure I wanted to help her due to the pain she caused me, but I agreed to meet with her.

When we met," Tag pauses. He wants to suppress his emotions, but it's becoming difficult. "When we met to review properties," Tag averts his eyes to the floor, "she told me she had an abortion. She insinuated the child was mine." Tag rakes his sleeve across his eyes and then raises them so he's now again peering at Franklin. He believes Franklin's cold blue tired eyes are slightly wider than they were before. Other than that, he notices no empathy or any other change in Franklin's demeaner. He's sure he must've surprised Franklin. He senses he's being

149

judged, although it's too late for him to care. He's already convicted himself of his teenage transgression.

"If that news wasn't enough to upset me, she also told me the reason she returned to Rock Slide," Tag again averts his eyes, "was because she still loved me and wants us to get back together." Tag isn't going to reveal his thoughts about her.

As Tag glances back at Franklin, this time he's met with a question, "What did you tell her?"

"I told her I had a family, which she already knew, but she didn't care! She said she had made so much money on Wall Street that neither of us would ever have to work again. In fact, she said that if it was important for me to have Maize and Jase, she'd offer Liesl enough money in a divorce to, in essence, buy custody of the kids!"

Franklin's repulsed by this insensitive remark! His chair loudly squeaks as he slowly leans forward, "What'd you say?"

"I was shocked! Angry! I let her have it and hung up the phone."

"So, what did Liesel say?"

Tag again averts his eyes and sheepishly answers, "I haven't told her."

Tag hears Franklin's chair squeak again. When he glances back at Franklin, he's leaning back in his chair in pensive thought.

The silent pause feels eternal.

"Are you thinking about getting back with this girl?"

"No!" Tag hopes his denial's convincing.

"Well, I think you need to level with Liesl."

"I know, I know, it's just very uncomfortable, at least to me it is, to tell your wife that you almost had a child with another woman. I know it was before we met and all that, but it still feels like in some way I've cheated on her. There's now this horrible secret which if she knew about, could affect our relationship. I'm struggling with how to tell her and when the best time is to tell her. I hope you'll keep this confidential. I know this would also upset my parents and possibly affect our relationship."

"Of course, I'll keep it confidential, but if you're looking for advice, I suggest you go ahead and tell them before they find out from someone else. I think you're jumping to some hasty conclusions on how they'd react. After all, it was years ago. Yes, there may be disappointment, but it sounds to me like the abortion wasn't your decision, if you think that's what'll upset them. So, help me understand where you perceive there's a legal issue here which affects your position as an elected official? I don't see anything yet, unless of course there's more to the story."

"There is."

"I was afraid of that," Franklin's chair again squeaks as he leans forward to finally take notes.

"Even though I've made it clear to her that I'm not leaving Liesl, she keeps trying to convince me. Well today she took it to another level. She gave me a new Range Rover.

"A new Range Rover?" Franklin's dumbfounded.

"Yep!"

"What did you do?"

"I refused to take delivery from the dealership. I told them to take it back."

"You need to tell Liesl about this before she finds out. Did anyone see this delivery take place?"

"Ronette's the only one I know for sure who saw it, but there could have been others. Fortunately, dad, and mom, are out of town."

"So, what did Ronette say?"

"That I should keep it, and if I don't want it, she'll take it."

Franklin chuckles, "Who wouldn't, but in all seriousness, what do you believe she thinks?"

"I'm not really sure, but I didn't want her to know about the woman, so I may have led her to believe it was a bribe from the owners of the casino."

"So, that's why you're here. You want me to cover up this gift by reporting it as a bribe."

"No, I'm going to come clean with Liesl...soon. I'll also let Ronette know, but I felt I needed to report this intended gift to you so that you would know the facts in case it was to come to light. The timing of this is awful. It can easily look to someone like a bribe, which is why I came to see you. I want to ensure that

151

there are no issues which could result in a fine and/or imprisonment."

"You did the right thing," Franklin's chair squeaks again as he leans back. "Are you sure it came from this woman?"

"Reasonably sure. I talked to the dealership on the phone. and their representative gave me some excuse about not being able to reveal who purchased the car, but he did say 'she' which leads me to believe it's her…and oh, she left me a voice mail this morning about a gift."

"Yeah, I agree. If it were a bribe, I don't think it would have been so public. A car would be too easy to check. It probably would have been cash. By the way, is there any chance she works for the owners of the casino? Has she mentioned the casino to you?"

Tag pauses, "That's a good question. I don't think so. She hasn't mentioned the casino to me."

"I just want to make sure we've thought of everything. Again, I don't think a bribe would be so public."

"Is she still in Rock Slide?"

"As far as I know. I haven't seen her since our meeting, but I understand she's been seen by others walking on the boardwalk."

"How do they know who she is?"

"As far as I know they don't, but the rumor mill has run rampant on a beautiful stranger walking on the boardwalk. I'm positive it's her."

"Oh yeah. I've heard about this beautiful stranger. Effie told me she was the talk of Magnolia's when she went in to have her hair done the other day. I haven't seen her."

"So, what happens now?"

Franklin grabs a legal pad and hands it to Tag, "I want you to write down what you told me. All the details. I'll need her name and the name of the car dealership. I'll check with the dealership regarding the car and check on her to ensure she has no connections to the casino. Assuming everything checks out, I'll just file this away and hope it's never needed. It'll remain confidential. I do think you need to tell Liesl as soon as possible. I understand the conversation will be difficult, but it'll be worse later, and even worse if she finds out from someone else. I won't tell your parents. Up to you if you want to tell them. If you do, and they say something to me about it, I'll act surprised, unless of course you tell them I know. If so, please let me know before you talk to them, okay?"

"I will. Thanks for your advice and help. I feel much better after our conversation."

"You'll even feel better after you tell Liesl. Now go ahead and write down your story before you forget it. I'll continue reviewing my notes for tonight."

TWENTY-SEVEN

Mo sits quietly cross-legged in the shade under the branches of a large sugar maple. Under its thick overstory, he's found a soft grassy spot in what's otherwise mostly barren dirt patches peppered with exposed, tangled roots. The cool, swirling mountain breezes are comforting, but they don't help his demeanor. He's troubled.

Mo's been watching a nest of purple finches in a neighboring sugar maple for the past few days. He was alerted to their presence by the chirping of the new-born birds. He's enjoyed watching the mama and daddy bird feed the babies. He laughed when he watched the babies crane their necks while chirping loudly to attract a parent's attention for food.

He's seen birds do this before, but he's keenly interested in these birds because they're purple finches. His mama taught him about purple finches. She said the daddy's the one that's purple. This daddy's purple just like the one his mama showed him. He remembers his mama telling him that they're special because there aren't many of them left. Kinda like him she said. God made them special, like God made him special. Special always needs to watch out for special his mama told him. That's why he's watching them so intently.

The past two days, all the baby birds have been learning to fly, except one. That one seems to rest quietly in the nest as the others test their wings. What's troubling Mo is that they all flew off this morning, except this baby bird, and they haven't come back. Mo occasionally hears the baby bird chirp, but his mama and daddy don't come back with food. He's worried they've abandoned the baby. Mo remembers the hurt when his mama went to live with God and Jesus. It made him cry. He's hurting again. He's struggling not to cry.

Earlier, he sneaked into his house when his daddy was outside on the front porch whittling, drinking his beers, and listening to his music. He pinched a small piece of white bread off the sandwich prepared for his lunch in the refrigerator and hid it in his pocket. His daddy might say bad words if his daddy knew he was feeding a bird. His daddy doesn't like birds.

Not only is Mo troubled, but he's also antsy. He can't wait any longer. Larry and Bob told him that, "Loving means lending a hand." His mama wants him to love the purple finches because their special, like him. His hand can help the baby bird. That's why he pinched a piece of white bread off his sandwich.

Mo glances around the yard. He doesn't see any finches, and he doesn't see his daddy. His daddy wouldn't like it if he caught him feeding the baby bird. He might say bad words his mama doesn't want him to hear.

Mo rises and awkwardly creeps toward the bird's nest. Fortunately, it's about the height of his shoulders off the ground. When he reaches the nest, he peers at the scrawny bird. Mo's immediately overcome with sadness. The bird is all alone. At least Mo has his daddy. The bird's not moving as it lays in the nest. Mo reaches up and gently nudges it with his finger. It wiggles and begins to chirp.

Mo smiles. He reaches into his overalls' pocket and removes the crumbs of bread. He pinches a few crumbs between his right thumb and index finger. He holds it above the baby bird's beak. He nudges the bird with his left index finger. It chirps again. Mo sprinkles the crumbs in its mouth. The baby bird cranes its neck for more as it loudly chirps. Mo again reaches in his pocket and drops a few more crumbs in its mouth. The baby bird stops chirping. For the first time Mo notices its tiny beady black eyes focused on him. He smiles.

Mo creeps from the nest and again takes his seat under the sugar maple. He plans to continue to watch until his daddy hollers at him to come in for lunch. He has a new friend. He likes his new friend. He'll call him Orville. He'll take care of Orville until he flies away. Orville's special, just like him.

TWENTY-EIGHT

"Hickory dickory dock. The mouse went up the clock," in unison they sing as they climb the hiking trail to the alpine meadow. JJ believes the silly songs they've sung on their hike have helped distract Maize and Jase from the difficulty of the climb.

"The clock struck three," they sing. She's taken rest breaks every ten minutes. Even though the kids aren't breathing hard, beads of perspiration cover their faces.

"Hey, watch that root!" JJ points hoping to prevent Maize and Jase from tripping over it. The drama from a skinned elbow or bruised knee would ruin the day. Also, of more concern are a few steep drop-offs as the trail winds up the mountain. She's very careful with Maize and Jase when they encounter one.

"Dong. Dong. Dong," JJ imitates the chimes. JJ knows how much they like Airheads candy from their time together last summer. She stuck some in her backpack this morning for them. At each rest break, she gives them each an Airhead and promises them another one at the next rest break as an enticement to keep going.

"The mouse went down." She's also forced them to take sips of water from the bottles Liesl placed in their backpacks.

"Hickory dickory dock." Having climbed this trail many times, JJ knows they're getting close to the meadow. It can't come soon enough.

"Hickory dickery..."

"I want to sing something else," Jase interrupts. "I'm tired of that song."

"Okay, like what Jase?" JJ asks glancing over her shoulder.

"I don't know."

"We don't have to sing anything."

"But I want to sing!" Maize whines.

"Well, what do y'all want to sing?"

"A song about dinosaurs!" Jase quickly responds.

"Yuck! Not me!" Maize complains with a pinched face.

The trail bends to the right to avoid a drop-off on the left. JJ stops to allow them to pass by her on her right, away from the drop-off. But, first she removes her backpack and places it where she wants them to go.

"Alright, y'all walk by me," she points the way, "and wait for me right up there by my backpack." JJ points to her backpack a few feet above her on the path past a large boulder which marks the end of the drop off.

Maize stops to adjust her pack. Jase bumps into her.

"Stop it!" she hollers and pushes Jase away.

Jase stumbles backwards. JJ's terrified, convinced he's about to lose his balance. She reaches out to grab him. When she pivots, her spin loosens the rocks under her right foot causing her to slip. Trying to avoid landing on Maize, she twists. This causes her left foot to come off the ground, too. JJ lands hard between the children on her right side on the uneven, sloping rocky path. She tucks hoping to avoid knocking Jase down as she skids toward him. Her tuck shifts the direction of her momentum. She's now sliding to her left over the embankment. She quickly untucks and wildly flails for roots, stumps, branches, rocks, anything to stop her from sliding down the steep slope. The few items she grabs slip through her fingers. Suddenly, and surreally, she's careening down the slope away from the children. Maize and Jase stare in horror.

While sliding feet first, JJ rolls to her back. Fear prevents her racing thoughts from organizing. Her survival instincts instantly predominate. She winces at the pain caused by the battering of the uneven granite rocks as she skips over them. She strains to keep her head raised to prevent slamming it against the rocks she's skidding over. Suddenly, her left foot crashes into the trunk of an evergreen tree growing on the steep slope. The searing pain is instantaneous as her leg awkwardly collapses. It rotates her body causing her to now slide sideways. Almost immediately her ribs crash into the trunk of another evergreen which is a few feet further down the slope. It knocks the air from her lungs and intensifies her pain.

157

Maize and Jase foolishly dash to the edge of the trail to witness JJ's frightening fall. They see her pinwheel off the evergreen and disappear. The foliage is too thick to see past these hairy trees.

The force of the impact has flipped JJ's body one hundred-eight degrees. She's now sliding on her opposite side and gasping for air. The blur of her rapid slide doesn't prevent her from seeing she's about to slam into a large rock outcropping. She braces for impact. Her only thought is to cover her head. Her body slams into the outcropping. She bounces off it. Fortunately, pinballing off the evergreens slowed her slide just enough so that the outcropping catches her on her rebound and doesn't flip her further down the slope. Her slide has violently stopped. She's now pinned against the rocky outcropping about thirty feet below the trail. She doesn't know that, though. The force of her head hitting the rocks, even cushioned by her arms, has knocked her out.

Suddenly, Maize and Jase no longer hear JJ sliding down the hillside.

"JJ!" Maize screams. "Where are you?"

Silence.

"JJ! Answer me!" Maize hysterically screams.

The silence is interrupted by Jase's crying. This causes Maize to cry. They both scream for JJ to respond, but even if JJ answered, their bawling more than likely would prevent them from hearing her.

After about ten minutes the crying stops.

"Did she die?" Jase asks while wiping away his tears.

"I don't know. How should I know?"

"She's dead, 'cause she's not answering."

"I said I don't know!"

"I don't want her to be dead."

"Me either."

"What will her mama and daddy say?"

"I think they'll be sad."

"Will they be mad at us?"

"I don't know."

"Will mama and daddy be mad at us?

"Maybe."

"I'm scared."

"Me, too."

Jase stares over the edge of the drop-off, "I don't want to look for her."

"Neither do I."

"I don't want to see a dead person."

"Me either!"

"What if she's just hurt?"

"Then why doesn't she answer?"

"I don't know."

After a pause, Jase asks, "Will the bears eat her."

"I don't know."

"Do you think she's a ghost?"

"I don't know."

"Do you think she's a nice ghost or a bad ghost?"

"She's a nice ghost," Maize hopes.

"Yeah, she wouldn't hurt us."

"I don't want to see her ghost, even if it's nice."

"Me either!"

After another silent pause, Jase asks, "Do you think her ghost will try to find us?"

"I don't know! How should I know?"

"Do you think her ghost will look scary?"

"I don't know!"

"I'm afraid of ghosts."

"Me, too."

Both children fearfully scan their surroundings.

"I don't think we should stay here," Maize says.

"Why?"

"Do you want to see her ghost?"

"No. It would scare me."

"Then we should leave. Let's go find mama and daddy."

"Okay, but what if they're mad?"

"Maybe we can hide from them until they're not mad anymore."

"Yeah! Which way do we go?"

"That's so silly! We have to go down the mountain."

Maize and Jase turn to follow the hiking trail back down the mountain.

Maize and Jase are puzzled. They've reached a junction in the trail. They didn't notice the various trails converging as they climbed the mountain with JJ. They were singing and following JJ.

"What do they say?" Jase asks pointing at the signs.

This past year in kindergarten, Maize learned the alphabet and some sight words. Mrs. Matthews encouraged her to sound out the letters in the words she couldn't read. Sounding out the letters might allow her to read the word. She's struggling with reading the words on the two signs, though. Only one word is a sight word. The other words are unfamiliar.

Maize pronounces the letters on one sign, "T-R-A-I-L-H-E-A-D P-A-R-K-I-N-G L-O-T."

"What do those spell?" Jase asks.

"I don't know." Maize sounds out the letters, "Tee-Are-A-IL something," she stammers in frustration.

"What does that mean?"

"I don't know!" she barks at Jase. She can instantly tell she's hurt his feelings. "Let me try the other one."

Maize pronounces the letters on the other sign, "F-O-L-L-O-W T-O T-H-U-N-D-E-R F-A-L-L-S."

"How about that one?" Jase hesitantly asks.

"I know the middle word is 'to.' I learned that word this year." Maize sounds out the letters, "Fuh-Oh-Luh-Luh-Oh,"

"Follow?" Jase interrupts

"Yeah, 'follow'," although Maize's not sure, but it sounds like it, "to. Yeah, we need to go this way."

"I'm glad you can read. I can't wait to read!" Jase chirps as they march down the trail convinced they're almost home.

TWENTY-NINE

Tag's not sure he's made a smart decision as he stands outside the door of Suzy's rental unit, but frankly, he doesn't care. Anger's controlling his actions. It's time to end their relationship.

"Suzy, we need to talk," he shouts pounding on the door. As opposed to the last time he was here, he no longer cares if he draws attention.

The door opens. Once again, Tag's dumbfounded. She's not dressed provocatively as she was before, but her beauty's still breath-taking. Her growing smile's inviting. He quickly suppresses his urge to pivot from his reason for being here.

Suzy's smile quickly disappears. It's obvious Tag's angry. She realizes he's not here for the reason she hoped.

"I apologize for just showing up, but we need to talk. May I come in?" Tag sternly pleads.

"Sure, please do. You're always welcome."

Tag storms in without a "thank you" and paces while Suzy closes the door.

"Would you like something to drink?"

"No!" Tag barks.

"I'm sorry. I didn't mean to offended you," Suzy meekly mutters.

"I'm sorry. My response was rude. I apologize, but frankly I'm really pissed off at you right now!"

Suzy's anxiety spikes. This isn't at all what she was expecting. "Would you like to have a seat?" she timidly asks.

"No thank you. I'm too upset to sit."

"May I have a seat?"

"Sure! Sure!"

Suzy sits in the chair closest to the bedroom. She needs a place to quickly escape to if Tag becomes aggressive. When she sits, she crosses her flawless, enticing legs. Her short skirt ensures he has a tantalizing view.

Tag doesn't notice she's barefooted. His eyes haven't dropped below her calves. "Stop it!" he scolds himself out loud.

"Stop what?" Suzy's confused.

"I'm sorry. You have me flustered. Why do you have to be so beautiful?" Frustratingly, Tag's inner thoughts spill.

"I'm not sure how to respond to that." Suzy calms. She realizes he's the one confused.

"You don't need to respond. It's a fact. A fact that has me really confused right now. Suzy, you could have any man you want, why me?" Tag's now fully off script from what he planned to say to her.

"I think I've already told you. I love you."

"But you don't even know me! Sure, you knew me when we were young lovers, but I've changed."

"How so?"

Tag pauses to search for a response. He's frustrated he can't think of an example, "I don't know, but I'm sure I've changed. You may not like how I've changed."

"You'll grow on me," she chuckles.

Tag senses, just as he did when he was here last, that Suzy's experienced at this game, and he'll fail if he debates her.

"Suzy, you need to leave Rock Slide."

"Why?"

"Because I said so!" she's frustrated Tag again.

"Well, who made you king?" Suzy glibly responds.

"Boy, you sure frustrate me! You need to leave because I'm not leaving my wife and kids. That's it. Pure and simple. You're wasting your time."

"Does your wife know you're here?"

"What's that got to do with you leaving?"

"Does she know you're here?"

Tag pauses searching for the right answer to her question.

"She doesn't know, does she?"

"Again, it doesn't matter if she knows or doesn't know."

"I think it does. I think I still have a chance." Suzy unfolds and rises from her chair.

"Damn it, Suzy! Why do you make me so confused?" Tag places his hands on his head in frustration.

"Because you still care for me," Suzy steps toward Tag.

"Stop!" Tag commands as he extends his arms in a halting manner. "It doesn't matter Suzy if I still have feeling for you. I've made my decision. I'm not leaving my wife and family. You can't buy me, and you can't buy my kids!"

"What does that mean?"

"That Range Rover you tried to give to me today."

"Did you like it? I guessed at the color."

"I couldn't accept your gift, and you know it!"

"Well, you can't fault a girl for trying," she grins.

"Uh!!!"

"Okay, I guess that was a little too obvious, but it's an example of the lifestyle we could enjoy based on my wealth."

"I don't want that lifestyle."

"You don't?"

"Well, yes, it would be nice to have that lifestyle, but I've made my decision, and it doesn't include you or your lifestyle."

"What did you mean by saying 'you can't buy my kids'?"

"When we talked over the phone, you said you would pay my wife enough money so we could have custody of my kids."

"I wasn't trying to 'buy your kids,' I simply wanted you to know that I would be willing to help in any way possible for you to have custody of your kids if that was important to you."

"They are EXTREMELY important to me, but they are also important to their mother. I would never do that to her, and I won't have to do that to her, because I'm not divorcing her for you."

"Why can't you say her name to me?"

"What?"

"Why can't you say your wife's name to me?"

"I can!"

"Then why don't you?"

"What are trying to get at?"

"I think you saying her name to me is uncomfortable for you. It's like you're keeping her separate from our relationship, almost like you're hiding our relationship from her. She doesn't know about our past, does she? You haven't told her about our

163

aborted child, have you? She doesn't know I exist, does she? You can tell me all you want you've decided you're not leaving your wife and kids, but even though your head made that choice, your heart hasn't."

Tag's speechless. Suzy's pretty much nailed it. She's right. Even though he's angry with her, he still has a deep, unresolved, burning desire for her. This keeps him from telling Liesl about Suzy. He's afraid Liesl will sense his desire for Suzy when he tells her. He's concerned Franklin's already sensed it.

"I'm right, aren't I?" Suzy interrupts the tense pause.

"That's ridiculous!" He won't confirm she's right.

"How so?"

"It just is."

Suzy laughs.

Tag quickly changes the subject, "Are you working for the casino operators?"

"Huh?"

"The casino operators. Are you working for them?"

"What are you talking about?"

"Are you in Rock Slide at their request to try to entice me to vote for their casino?"

"I don't have a clue what you're talking about. Are you accusing me of doing something illegal?"

"I hope not, but if your gift of the Range Rover was an enticement for me to vote for the casino it would be illegal."

"That's insulting! I can't believe you would think that I would do something like that!" Suzy's indigent and upset.

"It could get both of us in a lot of trouble if you did."

"I think it's time for you to leave! I would never stoop that low, especially if I loved someone like I love you. Right now, though, you've really hurt me." Suzy's eyes dampen.

She's reeling him in. Tag might say, or do, something he'll regret if he attempts to comfort her. She invited him to leave. He'll leave.

"I'm sorry I've upset you, but as a city councilman hopefully you understand the issues I might face due to the timing of your gift. With a town meeting tonight to discuss the casino, it looks very suspicious. I've already had to tell the city attorney about your gift."

"I don't give a rats ass about your meeting or casino, but for you to accuse me of doing something underhanded, especially illegal, is cruel and hurtful. Get out!" Tears roll down her cheeks as her nostril's flair in anger.

"I will, but you need to consider doing the same."

"Get out!"

Tag quickly exits. Suzy sobs as she slams the door behind him.

He's disappointed as he stands in the hall. He's not sure he accomplished anything. Perhaps, though, her perception of his accusation will motivate her to leave Rock Slide and never contact him again. He doubts it, though. His frustration hasn't subsided as he walks to the stairwell. He believes Suzy won today's match. Jousting with her is fruitless.

THIRTY

It's mid-afternoon. Rain's coming. The stiff breezes swirling through the overstudy of the ancient, immense white oaks, red oaks, and sugar maples, which predominate the vast mountain forest, cause their branches to creak and collide. Sometimes the violent collisions cause weak branches to snap and noisily fall. They splinter with a thunderous crash against the granite outcroppings. For the skittish preschool hikers, this ignites fears of monstrous creatures bounding from the forest to devour them. They quicken their pace as they anxiously scan the thick understory for these frightening beasts. So far, so good.

"I'm tired, and hungry," Jase whines, "is it lunch time yet?"

"I don't know, but I'm hungry, too." Maize slows. "I don't see anything scary, do you?"

"Me either," Jase carefully scans in all directions.

"Wanna have a picnic on that rock?" Maize points to a flat boulder a few yards down the path.

"Yeah, I'm really hungry."

They hurry the boulder and climb on. There's enough room for them to sit and enjoy their meals. They take seats at the opposite ends of the rock facing each other. They remove their backpacks and unzip them. They each remove one of their two Capri Suns and their lunch boxes.

After unzipping their lunch boxes, they quickly scan the variety of choices. Each removes one of the three peanut butter and jelly sandwiches. Jase removes his Goldfish crackers. Maize removes her Oreos.

As they unwrap their meals, Jase poses a curious question, "Are we close to home?"

"I think so, but I don't know," Maize answers before biting into her sandwich.

They sit silently while they eat. Sticky jelly and creamy peanut butter ooze from their sandwiches. Maize wipes her fingers on the rock to remove the goo while Jase licks his fingers.

"May I have some of your Goldfish," Maize asks.

Jase peers at his bag, "Only two."

"How 'bout four?"

Jase pauses, and then with a smile, "Okay." He takes another bite of his sandwich.

Maize wipes her fingers again on the rock and then fingers four Goldfish from Jase's baggie.

A brisk breeze swirls. The empty sandwich baggies float off the rock and drift on to the decaying leaves. Suddenly, a large limb crashes through the canopy and explodes when it hits the rocks. They freeze and stare in the direction of the loud, frightening noise, fearful that a monster is about to rush upon them. They relax when there's no further sound and, more importantly, no voracious monster rushes from the forest.

"What's that?" Jase is uneasy.

"I don't know. I don't like it."

"Me either."

"Do you think it's a monster?"

"What kind?"

After a pause, "I don't know. What kinda monsters live here?"

"I don't know," Maize shrugs her shoulders while finishing her sandwich.

"Do mean monsters live here?"

Maize swallows, "Probably."

"If one shows up, I'm gonna kill it," Jase boldly proclaims.

"How are you gonna kill it? You're just a little boy."

Jase ponders for a moment. Suddenly, his eyes sparkle, "With rocks, like David!"

"You don't have a slingshot!"

"I'll throw them," Jase defiantly claims. He looks around. "Just watch!" He slides off the rock and digs under the decaying leaves for rocks. He uncovers four he can dig from the soil. He places them on the boulder where Maize continues to sit. He grabs one with his right hand and wildly throws it into the forest. "See!"

"That wouldn't kill a monster!"

"Yes, it would!"

"No, it wouldn't!"

"Yes, it would!"

"You can't even hit that tree!" Maize points to the trunk of a large sugar maple about twenty feet away.

Jase picks up one of the three remaining rocks on the boulder. He flings it toward the tree. He misses.

"See! I told you," Maize laughs.

Jase seethes. He snatches another rock and stares at the tree. He remembers the times when he and his daddy threw the ball in their backyard. His daddy told him to aim at what you're throwing at and act like you're trying to touch it with your fingers when you let go of the ball. He takes aim and lets the rock go. Smack! It hits the tree.

"See! See! I can do it!" he excitedly exclaims.

Maize ignores him. She's suddenly saddened by what's not in her backpack. "Hey, I forgot, JJ put my Barbie in her backpack!"

Jase hops back up on the boulder and looks in his backpack. "I forgot she took my canteen. I wanna go get it."

"Do you wanna see her ghost?"

"No!"

"Me either. We'll let mama and daddy get them."

"Yeah, that's a good idea."

"What's in your backpack?" Maize asks.

Jase rummages around in his pack. "I forgot this!" he removes his coonskin cap and places it on his head. He beams! "I'm now a real hunter!"

Maize laughs, "You look funny!"

Jase makes a funny face and laughs while moving his head from side-to-side. He digs deeper in his backpack and removes his Dino Blaster. He squeezes the trigger. It flashes colorful lights and makes an awful, loud whirring sound.

Maize places her hands over her ears, "Stop that!"

Jase stops squeezing the trigger. Maize removes her hands from her ears. He presses the trigger again and laughs. Maize reaches out and snatches it away for him.

"I'm gonna break it if you do it again!"

"I'm sorry. I won't," he timidly replies.

She hands it back and he sets it on the rock. He again rummages in his backpack. "I have a knife, car, flashlight, and my dinosaurs." He whips out his tiny T-Rex and roars.

Maize's not paying attention to the roar. She's poking in her backpack. Suddenly, she swiftly removes her hand. "I forgot I had this!" she exclaims. She's holding a small, plastic compass.

"What's that?"

"A compass," Maize answers excitedly.

"What does it do?"

"It shows the way home!"

"Really!"

"Yeah!"

"How do you know which way to go?"

"Look!"

Jase peers at the round object in her hand and notices an arrow vibrating.

"We just need to follow the arrow!"

"Wow! I'm glad you found that!"

"Yuck! Ants!" Maize exclaims while scrambling off the rock. She furiously wipes the legs of her jeans and stomps her feet.

Jase glances at the boulder. There's a stream of ants marching in a jagged line on the boulder. The ants in front of the line are climbing over the dropped crumbs and the area where Maize wiped her hands on the rock. Jase grabs his Dino Blaster, drops it in his backpack, and scrambles off the boulder.

They quickly grab and throw their baggies of uneaten Goldfish and Oreos back in their lunchboxes and zip them. They yank their backpacks off the boulder, stuff their lunchboxes into them, zip their backpacks, and place them on their backs. Jase is still wearing the coonskin cap.

They stand close and peer at the arrow on the compass. It's pointing into the forest.

"That way?" Jase hesitantly asks.

"That's what it says."

"Are you sure?" Jase anxiously stares at the thick understudy. He can't see very far past the trail into this tangled barrier of foliage.

"Yeah. I learned about this." At least she thinks she remembers that's what this means. She's also anxious about trekking through the thick forest, but if it means getting home faster, she's willing to do it.

Jase trusts his sister. "Okay."

They grab their Capri Suns and suck the last drops of juice. They toss the empty containers to the ground and plunge into the forest. They're eager to get home.

THIRTY-ONE

Liesl's medical training tells her she's in the midst of a panic attack. Her breathing's shallow and rapid. She's lightheaded. Her heart's racing. She's becoming nauseated, but that could also be due to the speed she's driving as she descends the mountain on its winding roads. She's certain she shouldn't be driving a car. She should probably pull over and try to calm herself, but she's convinced every second is critical. She can't find her children, and it'll be dark soon.

Aside from the looming darkness, the clouds are growing darker and creeping lower. They'll soon blanket the mountain. Rain's in the forecast. A gentle, soft drizzle. Praise God the forecast isn't predicting a lightning enhanced deluge! She can't imagine her children, alone, in a frightening thunderstorm. She can't imagine her children alone, period. She's consumed with crushing fear, worried they're lost in the mountains. It's difficult for her to grasp that she doesn't know where her children are at all! That fact is undeniable, though. She must find them, quickly.

Tag and she agreed that Jenny Jean could take them to the alpine meadow. How stupid could they have been to trust their children to a nineteen-year-old! But, then again, she took them numerous places last summer without incident, but, of course, never to the mountains.

It's both comforting and concerning that she can't find Jenny Jean either. She prays that Jenny Jean's with her children. Marge Jenkins didn't sound too concerned when Liesl talked to her about ninety minutes ago. Marge said she would call her daughter, too. Liesl's calls, voice mails, and texts to Jenny Jean have gone unanswered. Cell service is spotty in the mountains, so to some degree that's understandable, but Jenny Jean shouldn't still be in the mountains. At the latest, she should have been back with the children by mid-afternoon.

It was Marge's call an hour ago which caused Liesl to jump in her car and drive to the alpine meadow. Marge sounded more worried. She hadn't been able to reach Jenny Jean either. Marge said she also called some of Jenny Jean's friends. They hadn't heard from her. Liesl hasn't heard back from Marge since their last call, but again, cell service is spotty in the mountains.

Liesl's panicked state heightened when she found the road to the alpine meadow closed for repairs. They didn't make it to the alpine meadow unless they hiked. Jenny Jean's car wasn't parked along the road where it was blocked, so if they hiked to the meadow, they must've taken another route. Since Liesl isn't a hiker, she isn't aware of other routes to the alpine meadow. Liesl's praying that Jenny Jean decided to choose another activity when she saw the road blocked. Hopefully, a much safer activity where both her cellphone and car are experiencing problems simultaneously. If so, then it's just a matter of time until Liesl hears from her. Liesl's anxiously anticipating that news.

Liesl's been reluctant to call Tag. She knows how important tonight's meeting is to him and the community. To cause him to panic wouldn't be fair if the children aren't in danger and show up soon. She knows she must call him if soon isn't very soon. If their children are lost in these mountains, she needs to alert the authorities before nightfall. If they're lost, she's trying not to consider how far they might wander and what dangers they might face if the search doesn't begin soon.

Suddenly, a pickup truck winding up the mountain toward her begins to flash its lights and slow. Liesl slows her car. The truck pulls up next to her. They both stop with their drivers' side windows facing each other. Liesl recognizes Jeff Jenkins, Jenny Jean's father, when he lowers his window. Marge is frantically waving at Liesl from the passenger's seat. She didn't tell Marge she was going to look for her children. Liesl's concerned this isn't good news. She lowers her window. Concern is heavily etched in their faces.

Above the idling engines, Liesl strains to hear Marge's panicked question, "Did you see Jenny Jean or her car?"

"No, I didn't. The road's blocked for repairs. I don't think they went to the alpine meadow unless there's another way."

"What? I'm gonna skin that girl alive when I see her! She knows she should've let both of us know if their plans changed."

"Yeah, I would've thought the same." Liesl's measuring her comments so the Jenkins aren't offended by something she might angrily say about their daughter. "Is there another route to the alpine meadow that Jenny Jean might have taken?"

After a brief pause, Jeff chimes in, "Yeah, there's another way. We hiked it a few times when she was younger. I'm sure she remembers it. It hasn't been too many years ago since we last hiked it. We'll go check."

"I'll follow you. Which way?"

Jeff points, "It's straight up this road, and then there's a turn off. You passed it on your way down."

"Gotcha! Let me turn around." Liesl drives forward, performs a U-turn, and pulls in behind the truck. They drive ahead.

Now that Liesl's again facing up the mountain, she's unsettled by how fast the weather's changed from just minutes ago. The clouds are swiftly settling. The soupy layer has now obscured the ridge tops.

Due to density of the clouds, it's becoming harder to clearly see the Jenkins' truck the higher she climbs the mountain. She flips on her wipers to remove a light mist suddenly coating her windshield. Both vehicles slow in the soupy mix as they creep higher.

The truck's right taillight begins to flash red signaling a turn. Liesl slows and turns behind the truck. They're soon bouncing along an uneven road. The encompassing clouds thicken making it difficult to see beyond the foliage along the rough mountain road. The eerie setting enhances Liesl's concern.

Suddenly, the truck's rear lights flash red. It's come to an abrupt stop. The occupants quickly exit and disappear into the mist. Liesl slams her car into park and exits. She jogs alongside the truck. Once she reaches the front of the truck her heart leaps. Illuminated through the swirling mist in the beams of the truck is Jenny Jean's jeep. Jeff and Marge are tugging on the handles and peering in the windows.

When Liesl arrives at Jenny Jean's jeep, Marge is frantic. Marge's fear is obvious, as is her panicked state. Liesl appreciates her fear, but she's not sympathetic, her children are also missing.

The frightened parents scream their children's names in hopes there'll be a response. They pause and listen intently. Hearing nothing, they repeat their desperate cries over and over. The accumulating mist feels as if it's absorbing their desperate pleas and blocking their children's responses.

"I'm going after them!" Jeff announces as he runs to his truck. He removes a flashlight and flips it on. The mist swirls and reflects in its bouncing beam as he runs toward where he believes he remembers the trail is located.

"I not sure that's a good idea," Marge cautions. "I don't need you lost, too!"

"I'll be fine," Jeff counters as the beam of his flashlight sweeps the fringe of the forest searching for the trail.

"You're having a hard enough time finding the trail in this pea soup! There's no telling what you'll encounter once you leave this clearing," Marge argues.

"Hopefully, the children," he smartly replies.

"Hey, I don't need your smart-ass attitude!" Marge screams.

"I don't need your lip, either! Do you wanna find the children or not?"

"Hey!" Liesl interrupts. "You're arguing isn't helping the situation!"

"You're right," Jeff calms while still sweeping the forest with the beam of the flashlight.

"Yeah, I'm sorry. My emotions got the best of me," Marge apologizes

"No need to apologize, but we need to think clearly," Liesl redirects the conversation.

"Found it!" Jeff interrupts as his beam lights the first few yards of the trail. "I'm going Marge. I can't just sit here and do nothing. I'll be careful. You wait here." Jeff and his beam of light quickly disappear into the dense forest and fog.

Liesl and Marge stand quietly illuminated by the truck's headlights. Their shadows reflect off the dense fog giving the impression they're not alone. It prods Liesl into concluding they may not be able to find their children by themselves. It's time to call Tag.

"Let me call Tag and get him to alert the authorities."

Marge nods. She's softly crying.

Liesl's thankful her cell connected as she listens to Tag's phone ring. She's frustrated when it rolls to his voicemail. She tries again with the same result.

"Marge, will you be fine if I go get Tag and we alert the authorities?"

"Yes, please do," Marge wipes a tear.

"I'll be back as quick as I can."

"Alright."

Liesl jogs back to her car. She hears Marge shrieking the names of the children again in hopes they'll answer. Liesl's praying Marge's successful, but if not, she prays Jeff's successful and finds them all safe on the trail.

THIRTY-TWO

Maize and Jase wail. They slump to the ground in the swiftly enveloping cloud and misting rain. Directly in front of them looms a sheer, granite rock wall. Due to the ever-thickening fog, they can't see the top of the wall or either end of it. Solid granite rises in front of them like an impenetrable fortress, preventing them from reaching the safety of their home.

It's difficult to distinguish tears from rain droplets on their wet, cherubic faces. They were already damp from the misting rain before they began to cry. As instructed by their mother many times, they removed their raincoats from their backpacks and put them on when it began to rain. Their hot pink and fire engine red color raincoats are a sharp contrast to the gray, green and brown shades of their surrounding environment. Maize's saturated hair is slick and plastered to her head. Jase's hair, aside from its fringe, is dry due to his coonskin cap. Fortunately, the raincoats have kept their clothes dry, except for their lower pants legs and sneakers. Also, Jase's coonskin cap is saturated. Their shoulders bounce as they sob.

They cry out of fear. Fear of the forest. Fear of the unknown. Fear of being lost. Fear of the creeping fog. Fear of the looming darkness. Fear of imaginary beasts and ghosts. Fear of being an evening meal for some frightening creature. Fear of punishment from their parents.

They cry out of sheer exhaustion. They're worn out. They've dragged their heavy backpacks up and down slopes. Their emotions are raw. They're thirsty. They were hot and sweaty, but now they're chilled. They're bone tired. They're very sleepy.

They cry out of frustration. Frustrated they can't find their home. Frustrated their parents aren't here. Frustrated JJ died. Frustrated it's raining. Frustrated this rock wall looms in front of them. Frustrated the tiny, vibrating arrow hasn't led them home. Frustrated with each other as they've bickered as they've wandered up and down the mountain.

"I wanna go home!" Jase screams between sobs.

Maize doesn't respond. Exhaustion is slowing her tears. She wipes away tears with the sleeve of her raincoat and glances at her compass. The arrow's wiggling. It points directly at the granite wall. She's trying to think of what to do next, but her mind is muddled.

"When are we going to get home!" Jase screams again. His tears are also subsiding.

"I don't know," Maize whispers.

"What?"

"I don't know!" Maize screams in frustration.

"I thought the arrow on your compass was leading us home?"

"It is!" Maize responds defiantly

"Then why aren't we there?" Jase shouts

"Shut up! Can't you see that big rock?" she points ahead at the granite wall.

"Is our house on the other side of it?"

"I...don't...know!" Maize shouts.

Jase is too tired to be upset by his sister yelling at him. They rest silently on their knees listening to the pitter-patter of the rain.

"I'm sorry," Maize utters glancing at her brother.

"Okay."

The only sound they hear is the constant pitter-patter of the rain striking their raincoats.

"I'm tired," Jase utters.

"Me too."

Maize's teary eyes dart to and fro searching the rock wall for a passage. None exists in the limited area she can scan through the thickening fog. She has spotted a wide crevice in the wall which runs horizontally. She's worried it's a bear cave and that a snarling, ravenous bear is about to leap out to devour them.

"Jase, can I see your flashlight?"

"Why?"

"I want to shine it in that cave," she points to the opening.

"Well...okay...but give it back!"

"I will."

Jase unzips his backpack, rummages around, and removes his flashlight. He hands it to Maize. She flips it on with great apprehension and shines it toward the crevice. The beam illuminates the space. Maize's relieved when she sees it's shallow…and doesn't shelter a scary bear.

"Hey, let's climb in there and wait for the rain to stop. We can rest for a while."

"Okay."

They struggle to their feet and creep to the crevice. When they get close, Maize shines the light in the opening again to ensure there aren't any snakes, spiders, or bats. Seeing none, Maize hands the flashlight to her brother. He drops it in his backpack and zips it. Then they both climb up and over the stack of rocks at the base of the crevice and crawl in.

There's just enough room in the crevice for them to sit up. They instantly feel better being out of the rain in their cozy, dry cubbyhole.

They remove their backpacks and unzip them. They each grab their water bottles their mother packed and enjoy refreshing swigs. They position their backpacks to act as cushions for them to lean against. Since they're chilled, they don't remove their raincoats. Their plastic raincoats squeak as they squirm into comfortable sitting positions. Once settled, they sit quietly and stare bleary eyed at the falling rain, scanning the forest for any movement. They're anxious about what they might see, but too worn out to worry. They're also too tired to talk. The constant pitter-patter of the rain is calming. Soon, they're fast asleep.

THIRTY-THREE

Tag's anxious as the city council chamber fills. The clashing of voices of those taking their seats mixes to cause an ever increasing, undulating wave of irritating noise as the room fills. It enhances his anxiety.

The primary reason for his anxiety is the Range Rover which Suzy attempted to deliver to him this morning. If anyone saw it, and questions it tonight, he's afraid his lie of it being delivered to an improper address will not be convincing. This will cause unwarranted suspicion. Even if he tells the truth, Tag believes the truth sounds more like a lie than the lie he'll tell. It'll create even more suspicion and expose him and his family to unwarranted speculation. Plus, he hasn't told Liesl about his prior relationship with Suzy. If she learns about his relationship with Suzy in an open city council meeting it will cause her to be deeply embarrassed and become livid. It might create irreparable damage to their marriage. He's praying it won't come up.

In the hour prior to the meeting, he reviewed the draft of the casino's presentation many times. He sequestered himself in his office in total silence. To ensure he wouldn't be distracted, he turned off his cell, shut down his computer, and unplugged his land line. He wanted to be prepared to answer any questions from the crowd. To help with his answers, he's made notes on a legal pad of some of the key issues.

He was delighted it was misting rain when he left his office to walk to city hall. He was relieved when he arrived and didn't see his pastor or others gathering in the rain to encircle city hall. He isn't sure if the prayer circle is still on, but if so, the rain should severely affect participation in the circle. He hopes it's been canceled so that it won't intimidate those who want to attend the meeting. Also, he doesn't want to confront his pastor and fellow church members.

As he scans the dais, all the city council members are in their seats except for Magnolia. She's huddled with the casino representative at their table in front of the dais. She's chairing the meeting tonight. She's facing the crowd as she leans over while in private discussion with the casino's representatives. Tag snickers when he notices some of the men in the crowd craning their necks to get an enticing view of Magnolia's robust breasts. This helps relieve some of his anxiety.

While continuing to scan the room, Tag nods at Franklin Howard when they make eye contact. As city attorney, he's in his designated spot in the council room. He has a thick file resting in front of him on his desk. He's nervously rolling his pen in his fingers. Tag briefly considers walking over to him to ask how he should answer the question about the Range Rover if it comes up tonight, but he quickly decides not to ask. He's worried he won't get the advice he wants. He'll go with the lie and deal with the consequences later. He's confident, based on his meeting with Franklin, that he hasn't violated the law. If it's later discovered he lied, he'll just resign from the city council. His family's privacy is more important to him than serving on the city council.

Standing along the back wall, by the entrance to the room, he spots Sheriff Justice and a couple of his deputies. He assumes they're here to ensure the meeting is civil and doesn't become violent. Tag watches as they closely eye each person when they enter the room. He's sure they're making mental notes and identifying those who they need to watch.

Suddenly, Tag's overcome by an uneasy feeling. He's spotted Pastor Honeycutt in the crowd. He's glaring at Tag. Tag recognizes some of the others sitting near Pastor Honeycutt as being individuals who've angrily railed against the casino. Immediately, the seriousness of this meeting hits home with Tag.

He's pleased Pastor Honeycutt isn't leading a prayer meeting outside. Rightfully so, he assumes Pastor Honeycutt and his supporters are attending the meeting to verbally oppose a casino being built in the valley even though this may result in the meeting becoming heated. Tag's glad Sheriff Justice and some of his deputies are in attendance.

Tag's been concerned whether he'll ever feel comfortable again in his church if he votes for the casino. So far, he's been comforted by knowing many in the congregation have privately told him they support the casino. He fears his relationship with Pastor Honeycutt will change. He hopes to remain a member of his church. It's the church he grew up in. He's been a member much longer than Pastor Honeycutt.

Magnolia's now taken her seat. She glances at the clock. She picks up the gavel and hammers it down three times on a square block of wood. As the noise reverberates throughout the packed room, the attendees become quiet.

Magnolia positions her mouth in front of her microphone and speaks while staring at the back of the room, "All ya'll standin' in the back, there's some empty seats down front."

There's fidgeting and uncomfortable glances from the standing attendees, but no one moves to take a seat.

"Come on down. We ain't gonna bite!"

A nervous laughter rises from the attendees. A few brave souls quickly make their way down the aisle and find a seat.

"That's better. Some of you men might want to offer some of these ladies still standin' your seats."

Immediately, the men seated rise and awkwardly glance around the room at the women standing. Through multiple eye contacts, a series of nods, pointing, and movement all women who want a seat now have one. Those men abandoning their seats have now replaced the ladies along the wall.

"Don't ya love it ladies!" Magnolia smiles. Once again laughter fills the room.

"A'right, A'right, calm down now. We need to start the meetin'." She puts on her reading glasses and looks down at a sheet of paper on her desk, "I, Magnolia Winter-Blossom, council woman for the City of Rock Slide, do declare that this special council meetin' is now in session." She picks up her gavel and once again hammers it down. She continues to read, "The purpose of tonight's meetin' is to..."

"Excuse me Madame Chairperson."

All eyes shift to a lectern which has been placed at the end of the aisle in front of the audience facing the dais. It is where people will be encouraged to make comments after the casino's presentation so they can be heard by everyone in the room. Hovering at the lectern, and hunched over the microphone, is a tall, thin young man wearing a suit which appears to be too small. The sleeves of the suit jacket creep up his forearms. He tightly grips the lectern. His blond hair is closely cropped and neatly combed. He's nervously shifting weight from leg to leg as he stands, but his facial expression is serious.

It's very rare, but Magnolia's speechless as she stares at him with her mouth agape.

"I'm sorry to interrupt…"

Now it's Magnolia's turn to interrupt as she quickly gathers her wits, "Well you sure have interrupted me young man! Just who are you and why are you interruptin' me?"

"Madame Chairperson, I'm an attorney licensed to practice law in this state. I've been hired by some concerned citizens to represent them at this meeting tonight."

"Who hired ya?" Magnolia interrupts.

The young attorney pulls stapled sheets of paper from a file resting on the lectern. "Their names appear on my engagement letter," he answers while holding up the stapled sheets of paper. "They're all registered voters of the City of Rock Slide. Would you like to have this copy of my engagement letter for your records revealing the names of those who hired me?"

Magnolia points to Franklin Howard, "Give it to him. He's our city's attorney."

The young man walks to Franklin and hands him a copy of the engagement letter. He returns to the lectern while Franklin quickly peruses the document. Franklin looks up from the document and leans toward his microphone, "Madame Chairperson, I recognize many of the names on this document as being registered voters of the City of Rock Slide. This gentleman," Franklin glances at the document again, "Phillip J. Lincoln, has the authority to represent these registered voters before this council."

"Mr. Lincoln, welcome to our meetin' tonight," Magnolia states derisively. "We've reserved time at the end of the presentation for remarks. You can make your remarks at that time. Until then, I suggest you take your seat again, unless of

course one the ladies still standin' has decided she wants to sit."
Nervous laughter fills the room. The young man flushes.

"I'm sorry Madame Chairperson, but my remarks are
warranted at this time," he boldly states.

Magnolia leans in closer to her microphone, "Mr.
Lincoln, I won't allow you to disrespect this council. You'll wait
your turn like the rest of the good citizens of Rock Slide. If you
don't yield, I'll have you removed from this meetin'!" She
glances at Sheriff Justice. She's not sure she has that authority,
but if not, she's hoping her bluff works. Sheriff Justice stands
statuesque in the back of the room.

The tension in the room is palpable as Mr. Phillip J.
Lincoln and Mrs. Magnolia Winter-Blossom stare at each other.

Gradually a smirk appears on the young attorney's face,
"If you do, Madame Chairperson, my clients will file suit."

An immediate buzz emanates from those in attendance.

Magnolia's frustrated and infuriated. She glances at
Franklin. She believes his demeanor is reflecting concern about
her stated authority. She knows he can't comment unless she
requests. She's concerned what Franklin might say. She quickly
decides the best way to diffuse this situation is to allow Mr.
Lincoln to speak his peace, even though she believes he should
wait until the casino has made their presentation. The last thing
she wants to do is cause the city to be sued because of her
actions. That could cost her in the next election. She likes having
power in the city.

"Okay, Mr. Franklin. I'm in a generous mood tonight.
Even though you're buttin' ahead of all the good citizens of Rock
Slide, I'll let you have your say now. I'm not sure how relevant
it'll be since you ain't heard the presentation."

"Thank you, Madame Chairperson, but my comments are
very relevant at this time. My clients believe tonight's special
session of the city council violates city law because proper notice
wasn't provided by state law. They request that the meeting be
rescheduled after proper notice has been provided to the good
citizens of Rock Slide."

A smattering of boos, which swiftly grow in number and
intensity, rise in the room.

"Excuse me!" Magnolia utters glancing at Franklin.

Liesl can't find a parking place, so she slams her car into park and leaves it in the middle of the street outside city hall. She can't see the sun due to the low hanging clouds and rain, but she knows it'll be dark in a matter of minutes. She can no longer hold back her tears as she sprints from her car and up the steps of city hall. Immediately all eyes of those standing in the lobby listening to the events occurring in the city council meeting turn to her when she bursts through the outside door. She's crying hysterically. She pushes through the crowd and rushes into the room.

"Tag! Tag! I can't find them! They're lost! They're lost!" she screams hysterically as she sprints down the aisle toward him.

The standing room only crowd is aghast while watching her run.

Tag's never seen Liesl like this. He's stunned and horrified. He knows something awful has happened. His mind races as she throws herself against the dais in front of him. His microphone is live.

"I can't find the children!" she wails uncontrollably. "They're somewhere in the mountains. Help me, please help me!" Aside from Liesl's wailing, there's not another sound in the room. The crowd heard everything she said over his microphone.

Tag jumps from his seat and quickly hurries to Liesl. She turns to the crowd and pleads, "Please, oh please, won't you help us find our children." She collapses to the floor in hysterics when Tag reaches her.

Suddenly, a loud *thwack* jars the crowd.

"This meetin's adjourned!" Magnolia screams releasing her gavel.

THIRTY-FOUR

"Cough, cough...cough!"

The rain pooling in Jenny Jean's mouth awakens her. She gags, quickly turns her head, and regurgitates the rainwater. The drowning sensation shocked her body into survival mode and her brain into consciousness. The shooting pain she experienced as she coughed also helped awaken her, but now that she's conscious, it's excruciating!

Her head throbs. Her arm throbs. Her side throbs. Her leg throbs. She's quickly finding any movement ignites horrific pain.

She's immediately concerned when she opens her eyes. Either the last vestiges of light are fading or, much worse, she's losing her eyesight. She reasons it's the former and not the latter since she can still recognize shapes.

As the cobwebs begin to dissipate, she racks her brain to remember why she's hurting. Her memories of what happened quickly push through the throbbing pain. She remembers her sensation of panic while sliding down the mountain. The sharp pain caused by crashing into trees. Her covering her head with her arms. Then, nothing, until now.

As the light completely fades and darkness prevails, she realizes she's lying against a rock on a steep slope. Suddenly, fear grips her. She's trapped!

"Oh my God!" she hoarsely whispers. Maize! Jase! Where are they? Are they okay?

Weakly she cries out, "Maize! Jase! Ugh!!!" The pain's horrific! She's not sure she can do that again. She believes her voice is too weak to be heard anyway. Strangely, knowing she doesn't need to yell again because they won't be able to hear is comforting. She can avoid that pain.

Even though she's comforted by not having to yell again, she's panicked over where they are and how she's going to escape. Her panic ignites her tears. She fights to suppress them believing the pain will be awful if she sobs. She's also trying to listen for any sign of Maize and Jase. All she hears is the pitter patter of the rain as it strikes the trees and the decaying leaves covering the ground.

Her panic grows. She fears she might be dying. She has no clue how badly she's hurt. She just knows there's persistent pain, especially when she moves. Even breathing deeply causes horrific pain. She's forcing herself to take only short, shallow breaths to avoid the pain.

She doesn't know if she's bleeding. Even if she is, she can't see it in the dark. Plus, she's convinced the rain will disguise her bleeding. She's soaked, therefore trying to force herself to feel for damp spots on her clothes signaling she might be bleeding is a waste of time. She needs light to be able to tell the difference.

She doesn't have light because it's now dark, but also because her cell phone is in her backpack, and her backpack is somewhere above her on the trail. She thought placing her cell phone in her backpack would prevent her from losing it as she hiked. She quickly decides if she survives this ordeal, she'll always have her cell phone in her pocket when she's hiking. It would be her lifesaver if she currently had it, assuming it didn't get damaged in the fall.

The rain's slowing, but there's a new concern. She's chilled. Now that it's dark, the temperature's plunging. Being wet exacerbates her problem. She has no way to block the cold. She's frightened of the cold. It'll cause her to shiver uncontrollably. She fears the pain will be unbearable! She wonders if it could cause hypothermia.

Suddenly, her eyes catch sight of a bouncing beam of light in the trees above her. The mist swirls and dances in its beacon as it randomly and swiftly darts through the treetops.

Jeff Jenkins is cold, wet, and out of breath, but adrenaline fuels his effort to trek the dark and slippery trail shrouded in fog. He must find his daughter. She's somewhere on this mountain. Finding her quickly may be extremely important. He believes she won't be too far from the trail. He doesn't accept she's lost. She has too much experience hiking these mountains to become lost.

186

He senses she's hurt, or she would be home by now. He believes she's alive, simply because he refuses to accept the alternative.

He scolds himself for letting himself get this much out of shape. He used to easily climb these trails. He realizes advancing age, a growing waistline, and inactivity has caught up with him. He's promised God as he's climbed that he'll get in better shape if God will allow him to find his daughter alive. He continues to shine his flashlight from side-to-side into the forest looking for any clues which may reveal her location.

As the flashlight's beam swings back-and-forth along the trail, he briefly catches sight of something out of place in the forest. He fixes the beam on the object on the trail above him. It's a backpack!

He rushes to the backpack and picks it up. It's similar to one Jenny Jean owns. He unzips it and points the beam inside. He recognizes some of the contents. It's hers!

"Hallelujah!" he shouts for joy. "Jenny Jean! Jenny Jean! It's dad. Where are you?" he screams into the shrouded, misty darkness. He freezes listening for a response.

Jenny Jean's heart leaps! She recognizes her father's voice. "Dad!" rolls weakly from her lips. The pain's excruciating. She takes a deep breath to try it with more force, "Da..ugh!" The pain's more than she can take.

Jeff's frustrated. All he hears is the pitter patter of the rain on the leaves.

"Jenny Jean! Jenny Jean! Please answer me?" he screams.

She can't. She just can't. The pain's too much. Her eyes fill with tears.

Jeff slowly swings the flashlight to his left. What he doesn't see frightens him. He doesn't see earth and rocks, just tree trunks and limbs. As he lowers the beam he's troubled by the steepness of the slope. It drops off into an abyss which is deeper than the beam of his flashlight. He swings the beam across the angled slope looking for any sign of his daughter.

Through her tears Jenny Jean sees the beam of the flashlight pointed in her direction. Its light is filtered by the thick evergreens above her, but pinpoint diffused streams of light penetrate the hairy branches and sweep across her. Fighting through intense pain she struggles, raising her free arm attempting to wave. Once again, she forces "Dad!" from her lips, only to collapse in severe pain.

Seeing nothing below, Jeff swings the beam to the edge of the trail above the dark abyss. He's horrified by what he sees. Leaves are scrapped away from a portion of the edge of the path. Also, small foliage is either dislodged, bent, or snapped. Leaves are stripped from some of the foliage. He shines the beam down the slope below this portion of the path. Again, he sees damaged foliage and leaves which appear to have been displaced. It looks like something large tumbled down the slope. Evergreens block him from seeing very far, but he notices some of their branches are snapped.

"Jenny Jean! Jenny Jean!" He desperately screams.

Again, Jenny Jean sees the pinpoint streams of light. This time they're not sweeping. She attempts to take a deep breath to answer her father's calls, but she can't. The pain's too great. Tears continue to flow.

Jeff believes someone has fallen down this slope. He prays it's not his daughter, but he's sure it is, simply because her backpack is here. He's frightened and panicked he hasn't heard a response to his calls. He refuses to believe she's dead. He'll try calling one more time.

"Jenny Jean! Jenny Jean! Answer me! Are you hurt? Please darlin' give me some signal you're okay?"

He waits and listens. Again, no response.

Jeff quickly decides attempting to climb down this slippery slope would be a huge mistake. It greatly frustrates him that he can't. He removes his cell from his pocket to call for help. His attempts to call 911 are futile. He has no service.

He recognizes he has no choice. He must go get help. It tears at his soul to leave his possibly injured daughter alone again, but getting help is his best chance to save her.

He decides to leave Jenny Jean's backpack on the trail as a marker for where to look. Time is of the essence. He turns, and as fast as he can in these slippery conditions, he takes off down the trail he just climbed.

Jenny Jean's panic spikes when she sees the beam quickly disappear. Her father was so close to her, yet she couldn't signal him. She doesn't want to die! For him to be so close to saving her is devastating. She doesn't understand why he's leaving her alone in her condition. He should have helped her.

Tears flow more freely now. Frustration, fear, abandonment, and pain have smashed the wall of bravery she constructed. She sobs uncontrollably. The pain's intense. She faints.

THIRTY-FIVE

Liesl believes she should be embarrassed by her hysterical reaction in front of so many people, and also for interrupting the city council meeting, but frankly, she doesn't care. She'll apologize later. Her babies are lost. Finding them is all that matters.

Tag quickly moved her to a nearby office so their family drama would unfold in private. Once she found Tag and begged for help from the town, she gained control of her ability to think and speak coherently.

Joining them in the cramped office are Sheriff Justice and Mayor Lamar Freeman. As Tag held her hand, and she wiped away tears with her free hand, she related the terrifying events which unfolded the last few hours.

Pursuant to his request, Liesl provided Sheriff Justice with Marge Jenkins' cell number so he can call her to see if her daughter and the children have been found. He punches her number into his cell phone and waits for her to answer.

"Mrs. Jenkins, Sheriff Bill Justice here. Liesl Ryder told us about her children and your daughter. Have they been located?"

Even though Sheriff Justice is holding his cell phone closely to his ear, everyone in the room can hear Marge's voice. Her words are unrecognizable, but it's clear she's frantic.

"Uh huh......Uh huh......Yes mam......Just stay put, we'll be there with help soon. When your husband shows back up, please tell him I said to wait right there and not to go looking for them again. I'm bringing help right away......Yes mam.......You're welcome. I'm on my way."

As soon as Sheriff Justice hangs up, Magnolia barges into the office, "I got a bunch people in that big room who're itchin' to help! What do we need to do to get started?"

190

"You tell'em to hold their horses," Sheriff Justice booms. "We don't need a bunch a people going off half-cocked and stumbling 'round in the rain in those mountains, or we're going to have a much worse situation on our hands. I'll be out there in just a minute to let 'em know how they can help."

"Gotcha!" Magnolia nods and leaves the room.

"Hold on Magnolia," Mayor Freeman hollers, "I'm coming with you to help keep them calm." Before leaving, he turns to Liesl, Tag, and Sheriff Justice, "Please know the full resources of the city are behind you. We'll do whatever we need to do to find your kids."

"Thanks," Liesl and Tag offer simultaneously.

He nods as he exits, closing the door behind him.

Sheriff Justice turns toward Liesl and Tag, "As much as you can, I need for ya'll to try to calm down. The chances are excellent that we're gonna find them real soon and they're gonna be just fine."

Sheriff Justice's attempt to calm them falls on deaf ears. Tag's still in shock over this sudden, horrific news about his children, and Liesl's been unable to suppress her fears since she finally accepted her children are lost.

"I'm gonna contact Smokey Bear, the head of the local Forest Service," he notices the queer look on their faces, "his real name's Alex Bear, but everyone calls him Smokey. Since this is government land, it's his jurisdiction, but he'll use us to help. He knows these mountains better than anyone. He'll activate his SAR crew, search-and-rescue, to help. They're experienced in finding people.

Now, I'm not gonna pull any punches here, but there's not a lot he, or I, can do in the dark. These mountains are too treacherous to be sending people out in the dark. Especially in the rain, and I'm sure since it's been raining it's also very foggy up there. We'll search tonight along that trail they were on and in the alpine meadow, but we can't do much more. As soon as it's light, if we haven't found them, we'll blanket these mountains with people. As you heard from Magnolia, they're a lot of people in that room who want to help. As soon as we finish talking, I'm going out there and ask them to assemble at six in the morning in the park across from city hall. We'll divide them into teams and assign them areas to search based on what we learn tonight. They'll be in place at first light.

This is gonna be a long night for all of us, especially you. Let's hope tomorrow isn't a long day.

As for both of you, again I need you to try your best to remain calm so you can think clearly and answer questions. Smokey has a motor home. Liesl, he'll park it in the clearing where you found the Jenkins girl's car. That'll be our command center and where I need both of you to be. When you get there, Smokey will tell you what to expect and what he needs from you.

Liesl, can you find your way back to the clearing?" she nods. "Good. I'm gonna have one of my deputies take ya'll home. You need to pack any medicines you take, a change of clothes, or anything else you think each of you might need health wise. Also, and this is important, I want you to grab some of your children's dirty clothes. Not washed but dirty clothes. We need these for the search dogs.

Now, I'm gonna once again level with you, with this rain, I'm not sure how helpful the search dogs are gonna be. The rain may wash away their scent. We're gonna try them anyway."

Liesl and Tag jump when there's a knock on the door. Sheriff Justice, obviously disturbed by the interruption, cracks it open. Liesl and Tag can't see who's at the door.

"Excuse me sheriff, but Magnolia said the Ryders are in this office. My name's Bobby Honeycutt. I'm the pastor of their church. Would it be alright if I spoke to them?"

"Sheriff! Please let him in," Liesl pleads.

"Preacher, you heard the lady." Sheriff Justice swings the door open. "Come on in. Let me finish with them first before you talk to them."

"That's fine. I'm sorry to interrupt." Pastor Honeycutt nods to them and stands in front of the door after Sheriff Justice shuts it.

Liesl's delighted that he's joined them. She knows God loves her children. She believes He's watching over them. She strongly believes in the power of prayer. Tag does too, but Pastor Honeycutt's presence makes him uncomfortable.

"Let's see. Where was I. Oh yeah. Aside from the dirty clothes, please pack some clean clothes for your kids. We'll need

192

them when we find them. Make sure some of them are winter clothes. They might be pretty cold being out in the rain with the temperature dropping into the fifties tonight. Also, bring any medicines they regularly take.

Liesl and Tag, I need for you to write down for me what they were wearing so we can identify them." Sheriff Justice intentionally doesn't expand on why. "If they took anything with them, I need a detailed list of what they took. This could be really helpful in pinpointing their location if we find random items in the forest.

Okay, I've told you a lot. When you meet with Smokey, he'll have questions and information to share with you. What questions do you have?"

Tag and Liesl's emotions were racing as they listened. They tried to be attentive, but their minds were distracted and clouded. They hope they can remember what they need to do.

"Sheriff," Tag asks, "what's your experience in finding people lost in these mountains?"

Sheriff Justice measures his response, "Pretty good. Trust me, we're going to do everything possible to find your kids. I feel good about it. How 'bout you preacher?"

Caught off guard, he clumsily stammers, "Uh…yeah. I do." Not a ringing endorsement.

"Alright, I'm gonna get a deputy to drive you. I'll be right back."

Sheriff Justice leaves. Immediately, Liesl senses there's tension.

"Tag, what was happening in that other room earlier isn't important now," Pastor Honeycutt begins. "All that matters right now, at this very moment, is reuniting you with Maize and Jase. I'm here to let you know our church is here to help in any way possible. I've already asked some of our members who were with me tonight to get the word out. As a reminder, our church is not the building, it's the people. A people who loves your family, just as I do." Tag's eyes moisten. "We're going to beg, plead, and implore God through constant prayer to keep your children safe and to reunite your family as soon as possible. He will provide."

Tag feels the tension dissipate while he weeps. A warming-sensation envelopes him as his weeping becomes a sob. Liesl's not sure she's ever seen her husband cry this hard. She hugs him, and also weeps. Pastor Honeycutt walks over and lays his hands on them. He prays loudly in order to be heard over the wailing of the parents. He too weeps.

THIRTY-SIX

Alex "Smokey" Bear steps from the custom, government-owned motor home into the clearing's muddy parking lot. The down, water-proof jacket he's wearing hides his wiry physic. His well-worn Forest Service baseball cap is pulled down tightly on his balding head to keep it dry and warm. It also signals to everyone he's the person in charge of the search. Fortunately, it's rare in his career he's had to deal with lost hikers, but each situation carries enough stress to threaten to send this forty-three-year-old ranger to an early grave.

Attempting to relieve the tension, he energetically greets Sheriff Justice, who's been feigning control of the base camp for the past thirty minutes, "Damn Bill, that was one helluva drive up here in this fog! I thought I was headed over a cliff at any moment. Why can't people get lost on bright, sunny, comfortable days?" there's an uneasy smile while reaching out his hand to Sheriff Justice.

"If it were easy, we wouldn't need you." Sheriff Justice returns the smile while firmly shaking Smokey's hand. Intentionally dissipating any sense of levity, he seriously adds, "I appreciate you coming out in this mess. We got some devasted parents to deal with."

"Yeah. I can only imagine. This has to be a parent's worst nightmare."

"As soon as your SAR crew got here, they took off up the trail," Sheriff Justice reports while pointing in the direction of the trail. Flood lights illuminated by portable generators have shoved away the darkness in areas of the clearing allowing them to see the entrance to the trail. "The Jenkins went with them. Mr. Jenkins said he had to go to show your crew where he found his daughter's backpack. I tried to convince Mrs. Jenkins to stay behind, but she wouldn't hear of it. I was afraid she'd slow them down. I sent a deputy to walk with her so your crew could quickly move up the trail, although I heard Mr. Jenkins appeared to be pretty winded from his first assent so I'm not sure how fast they're moving. The deputy I sent has experience dealing with the parents of victims, so he may be an important participant."

"Yeah, it's hard to keep parents away from a rescue effort. I clearly understand myself why they want to be there. I'd be that way if any of my kids were lost or hurt. The challenge is to keep them from getting in the way. Your decision to send a deputy should prevent that from happening."

Sheriff Justice is dreading the answer to his next question, "So," he pauses, "do you think this is a rescue or a recovery effort?"

"I'm praying it's a rescue effort, but Mr. Jenkins' description isn't encouraging. Sadly, the facts are leading me to believe we're facing a tragedy. He finds his daughter's backpack on the trail. He calls her name but receives no answer. He finds where it appears someone fell down the mountain. It sounds to me like the two kids may have fallen off the mountain, and then the young lady removed her backpack to climb down to find them. Then, something tragic happened to her. I'm praying I'm wrong."

"Me, too," Sheriff Justice hangs his head.

"Are the Ryders here yet?"

"No, but they should be here any minute."

The flood lights and headlights of the numerous vehicles now crammed into the small parking lot illuminate the misty, chilly drizzle as it sweeps and swirls.

"Bill, it's cold, and wet, out here," Smokey shivers. "Let's go into the motor home. I have something important to discuss with you before they arrive."

They climb into the motor home and close the door. The welcomed warmth of their cozy surroundings doesn't bring any emotional relief for its new occupants.

"Have a seat." Sheriff Justice plops onto the stiff couch. "I'm leaning toward not telling the Ryders about what Mr. Jenkins found. We don't know for sure if their kids went over the cliff. In fact, we don't know if the Jenkins' daughter did either, but of course, the Jenkins are already aware that it appears something happened. To alarm the Ryders without any evidence

196

at this point seems to be premature and could torment them for no reason. There's already going to be enough emotional swings for them in this process without creating this one yet. Your thoughts? Do you know them?"

Sheriff Justice pauses to consider Smokey's position on not telling the Ryders. He's been wondering the same thing since he received the panicked call from Mr. Jenkins after he left Tag and Liesl.

"Yeah. I know 'em. He's on the city council of Rock Slide. He recently did me a huge favor, which unfortunately didn't end well. Not for him, but for others. She's more or less the town doctor.

I really don't know what's right. Normally I'm a straight shooter. I believe in being transparent. But, if based on your experience, you believe in keeping 'em in the dark for the moment is the best course of action, then I support your decision. I agree it doesn't seem fair to take them through a lot of stress if its unwarranted, and if their kids are already..." he pauses, "you know what I mean. Creating false hope doesn't seem to be fair to them."

"I think it's best right now. We should know something soon from my SAR team which went up with the Jenkins."

"What happens if they ask where the Jenkins are?"

"Good question. I'll handle that. If not telling them becomes an issue later, I think it's best that they be mad at me and not you. They need to have confidence in their sheriff."

"Thanks."

They're interrupted by a knock on the door. Smokey opens it.

A young deputy stands quivering in the rain, "Sorry to bother you sir, but will you tell Sheriff Justice the Ryders are here?"

"I heard you Jack," Sheriff Justice calls while rising from the couch "I'm on my way." He turns to Smokey before leaving, "I'll go get 'em. Are you ready to talk to 'em?"

"Yeah. Bring them in."

Smokey paces while alone in the motor home. He's always anxious before he meets the family of lost hikers. It can be very emotional. Their fear and pain are upsetting. All he can do is reassure them that he and his team are doing all they can to find their loved ones. This one has him rattled before he's even met the parents. He's never had to search for children this young. Based on experience and training, he knows they're much more vulnerable to injury and death than school age children. If they're still alive, he knows his team needs to find them quickly. He tries to shove from his brain the thought that these kids are dead. He takes a deep breath when he hears the knock on the door.

"Come in."

Sheriff Justice climbs in followed by Liesl and Tag. Smokey immediately reads the distress etched in their faces. Their eyes are bloodshot. They're carrying a suitcase and a stuffed plastic bag. He tells himself this'll be tough.

After introductions, Smokey asks them to sit. They perch on the edge of the couch holding hands.

"Any news?" Tag hurriedly and anxiously asks.

"Nothing yet on your kids." He glances at Sheriff Justice who stares back emotionless.

"What are you doing to find them!" Liesl passionately demands.

"Tonight, we're searching along the trail we believe they hiked today. We're also going to search in the alpine meadow. It may be too foggy to effectively search in the meadow, or even along the trail, but we'll do our best without putting the lives of our team in danger.

If we don't find them tonight, the forecast for tomorrow is sunny and clear. We'll then blanket the mountains with searchers, but I want to caution you, there's thousands of acres to comb in these mountains and the surrounding foothills, most of which is uninhabited. I understand from my phone call with Sheriff Justice your Rock Slide neighbors will be gathering at six in the morning to help. We'll need all of them to cover this area as quickly as possible, assuming we don't find your children tonight.

What did you bring?"

Liesl holds up the plastic bag, "These are Maize and Jase's dirty clothes. Sheriff Justice said you would need them for the dogs."

"Great!" Smokey takes the bag. "I'll put those up here." He reaches above the sink, opens a cabinet, and stuffs them in. "I want to keep them away from any additional contamination until the dogs arrive. They'll be here in the morning. This rain may make it difficult for the dogs to be effective, but if they can find your children's scents, they'll work quickly to locate them. Sometimes the old-fashioned way is the best way.

And the suitcase, what's in there?"

"Just some of our stuff and some clean clothes for Maize and Jase." Tag answers glancing at it.

"Good, ya'll hang on to that. Do your children take any medication on a daily basis?"

"No," Tag and Liesl answer simultaneously.

"Great! Your daughter Maize, was she in first grade last year?"

"No," Liesl answers, "she starts first grade in a few weeks."

Tag's curious, "Why do you ask?"

"Are you familiar with the Hug a Tree program?"

"No."

"Neither am I," Liesl adds.

"I'm not surprised. Most parents aren't until they have a first grader. They began teaching it in our area schools to first graders ten years ago. It's a program which was started about forty years ago in California after a nine-year-old boy became..." he quickly stops himself from telling them the boy was dead when they found him. "It teaches kids how to keep from getting lost, what to do if they become lost, how to protect themselves from the environment, and how to help people find them. Simply put, they're taught to immediately hug a tree and stay there no matter what until an adult finds them. If kids don't wander, there's a good chance they'll be found pretty quickly."

"So, Maize would learn about it..."

"Will! Will learn about it!" Liesl loudly interrupts Tag.

"I'm sorry, will learn about it this coming school year?"

"Yes. I'm sorry it hasn't been pushed down to kindergarten. Perhaps it needs to be."

"Damn right!" Liesl shouts.

There's a tense pause as Liesl fumes. Tag silently condemns himself for not knowing he needed to teach this to his children.

"Have you taught them anything about what to do if they're lost in the woods?" Smokey asks with trepidation.

"No, we haven't," Tag answers. "We're not into hiking and there's no woods around our home. We never," he glances at Liesl," dreamed this would be an issue for us. Rarely do we ever let them out of our sight without competent adult supervision. We thought Jenny Jean Jenkins fit that description since she kept our kids all last summer without an incident. She probably does, but we were foolish to let her take Maize and Jase into the mountains without another adult." Tag drops his head.

"Listen, don't beat yourselves up. Based on your experience with her, I think any other parent would have done the same. She may have them sheltered somewhere right now."

"I've been praying for that," Liesl adds softly.

"Are your kids comfortable around strangers?"

Liesl and Tag glance at each other. They're puzzled. They're not exactly sure how to answer that question. They both sense there's an awful reason for the question.

Tag's heart's racing. He notices Liesl's eyes welling with tears. He's hesitant to ask but he needs clarification, "Do you think they've been abducted?"

"No, but that's always a possibility. We don't rule out anything. With that said, I think there's an infinitesimal chance that happened. We're not treating it as an abduction."

"Nor are we," Sheriff Justice adds.

"I asked that question because the Forest Service has found in many situations young children don't respond to searchers. These are strangers hollering their names. Most kids have been taught to stay away from strangers. They're taught strangers are dangerous. Kids should be taught 'stranger danger,' but it can hinder us in searching for them. Lost kids will hide from searchers as opposed to respond to them. There are cases where rescuers were within a few feet of lost children and never saw them. That's why I asked that question. How do you think they'll react to searchers calling their names?"

There's a tense pause before they answer. Tag and Liesl are now feeling overwhelmed. Smokey's question enhances their fears and escalates their panic. They sense Maize and Jase will hide as opposed to respond to searchers.

Smokey, reading their tension, senses he knows their answer. He doesn't wait for it. He offers a solution which he hopes will cause Maize and Jase to positively respond to the searchers, and calm Liesl and Tag.

"To encourage them to respond to the searchers, we're going to record both of you. We'll give you a script to read. Basically, we'll record you pleading with your kids to respond positively to the searchers. You'll be letting your kids know they're not in trouble, these people are their friends, they're here to bring them home, they won't hurt them, and to please call for them to help you or go to them if you can. We'll text your message to a person on each team of searchers. We'll ask that person to download your message on their cell. We'll give these people a mini speaker to carry with them which will broadcast your recording for your children to hear. It can easily be heard as far away as one hundred feet. We believe your children will positively respond to your voices."

Tag and Liesl are relieved to learn of Smokey's plan. They both wipe tears from their eyes.

"I'm going to make some coffee. There are sodas in the refrigerator. I have some food for you to snack on if you're hungry. If needed, we'll take care of ordering any meals. Feel free to use the bathroom, and if you need to sleep, there's a bed through that door." Smokey points at a closed door. "I hope you won't be here long, but while you are, it will be extremely helpful to us if you'll stay in here. That way we'll know where you are if we need you."

Tag interrupts, "But we want to go search for Maize and Jase!"

"I understand you feel you need to be doing something to find your children, but the best thing you can do is to wait here. If we need you, we'll probably need you quickly. We don't want to be having to look for you or wait for you. That could result in critical delays. Do you understand?"

They nod.

"Good, what questions do you have?"

"Please find our babies!" Liesl pleads.

"We're doing all we can Mrs. Ryder."

"Please call me Liesl."

"Okay." Smokey fights back tears. He reaches for the kitchen counter and picks up two hand held radios. "I want you to keep this one," he hands one to Liesl, "and I'll have the other one." He flips it on and attaches it to his belt. "We'll be the only people on these radios. You can call me on it at any time if you have questions or think of something I need to know. Also, please turn yours on so I can reach out to you when I need you. They have fresh batteries, so we're good there."

"Thank you," Liesl whispers.

"You're welcome. Now Sheriff Justice and I are going to go check on the search and the location of our teams. I'll give you an update once I have one."

"Thanks for all your help, Smokey. We're praying y'all find them quickly," Tag offers.

"You're welcome."

Smokey and Sheriff Justice exit the motor home. Liesl and Tag hold hands and pray.

"Zipping his jacket while standing in the drizzle, Smokey asks Sheriff Justice, "So, how do you think it went?"

"Better than I would have thought since they didn't ask you about the Jenkins girl."

"Yeah, we should get some news on her soon." Smokey shivers as he stares into the darkness.

THIRTY-SEVEN

"There it is!" Jeff Jenkins exclaims. Bright lights from multiple headlamps secured to climbing helmets swing and lock on Jenny Jean's backpack.

"Right here! Right here is where it looks like someone slid off the trail!" The headlamps of the SAR team members swing again and spotlight Jeff anxiously pointing at the spot where the dirt, rocks, decaying leaves, and foliage appear to be disturbed. The SAR team quickly illuminates the steep slope. The bushy evergreens, some with broken limbs near their roots, block seeing very far. Fortunately, the rain has now changed to a heavy mist.

Stan Irons rubs his unshaven chin as he peers down the slope. He then closely examines the disturbed area next to the trail. Even though Stan's only been doing search-and-rescue for the Forest Service for about five years, he's the team leader. He agrees it appears someone might have fallen off the trail.

Stan swings his head uphill to light the area across the trail. He's satisfied with the size of the white oaks growing near its edge. They'll support a man rappelling.

"Okay fellows," Stan barks to the other three members of his team. "Jimmy and Bob, the three of us are going to rappel down the slope to check it out. Sid, you wait up here with Mr. Jenkins."

All four SAR team members drop their forty-pound backpacks. The team members, except Sid, remove their nylon climbing ropes. They each unwind their ropes and secure them to separate white oaks. Sid helps each team member secure his rope to a tree and attach his harness. While the team members prepare to rappel, Sid opens the pack of chemical light sticks which will be deployed to help illuminate the climbers' descent. He then removes his climbing rope and securely attaches it to a white oak. It'll be used to lower or raise items based on the needs of the rappelling team.

While the SAR team prepares, Jeff nervously paces and yells his daughter's name. He stops when his wife and the deputy arrive.

"Have they found her?" Marge hopefully pleads seeing the SAR team preparing for their descent.

"No, but look here?" Jeff warily points to the area of the trail which shows disturbance. "It looks like something slid off the mountain here."

Marge fearfully raises her hands to her mouth. Her eyes dampen. She interlocks her fingers and presses her hands together. She squeezes her eyes shut and quickly prays to God for her daughter and the Ryder children's safety.

Jeff interrupts her prayer, "Over there's her backpack."

Marge peeks to see Jeff pointing at her daughter's lonely backpack resting on the trail.

While sliding on his heavy climbing gloves, Stan provides last minute instructions to the SAR team. Then swiftly they disappear over the edge of the trail. The others step to the edge and watch in anticipation. They follow the lights from the headlamps randomly swinging across the slope as the climbers descend along the slide path. The dancing beams in the mist create an eerie glow.

When the team reaches the evergreens, Stan examines the broken branches. He can immediately tell they're fresh breaks by the condition of the wood, sticky sap, and pungent aroma. He and his team snap more branches as they fight through the thick evergreen barrier.

Once they reach the other side of the evergreens, and look downhill, their lights sweep across Jenny Jean wedged against the rocks. She's not moving. They quickly scramble to her. Stan grabs her wrist. He's elated when he feels a pulse.

"We've found her!" Stan hollers up the slope. "She's alive!"

Jeff and Marge hug. Tears softly stream down their cheeks.

"Lower light sticks!" Stan hollers.

Sid quickly places some in a small pack, attaches it to carabiner, and then attaches the carabiner to a loop in his rope.

While the rope is being lowered, Stan grabs one of the broken evergreen branches which slid down the slope. He places the broken end under Jenny Jean's nose. Being so close to her nose, the pungent aroma causes Jenny Jean to rouse. She coughs and squirms. The SAR team notices her face pinch as if in pain. She emits a breathy, "Ughh!"

"Jenny Jean! Jenny Jean! This is Stan Irons of search-and-rescue. Can you hear me?"

Jenny Jean wonders where this strange voice is coming from as she awakens. Her eyes flutter open, only to quickly squeeze shut again due to the blinding bright light. Her brain leaps to a horrific thought. Fearing she's dead, she panics. Her eyelids pop open revealing darting, fearful eyes.

"Guys, swing your light from her eyes!" Stan commands. "Jenny Jean, can you hear me? This is Stan Irons from search-and-rescue."

Her confusion dissipates. As her eyes adjust from being blinded by the stark bright light, she sees the dark shapes of three men hovering over her. She doesn't know them, but they know her. She's saved, thank God! Her sight blurs as her eyes well with tears.

"Jenny Jean, do you understand me?"

"Yes," she whispers trying not to sob fearful of the pain it will cause.

"Are you hurting?"

"Yes," she whispers again.

"Where do you hurt?"

"All over."

"Can you move?"

"Yes."

"Show me."

Jenny Jean breaths deeply. Tears of joy now mix with tears from pain. She raises her free arm, wiggles her fingers, and bends her free leg. She releases a guttural, "Ow!," and is still again.

"Fantastic!" Stan's excited and relieved she can move. "Okay, we're gonna get you outta here. It may take a while, but it's gonna happen. You're gonna be alright."

Jenny Jean cries harder. Her sobs bring more unwelcomed severe pain. She moans.

Jenny Jean's pain is obvious to the men. Stan hollers up the slope, "Mr. and Mrs. Jenkins, your daughter's gonna be fine, but she's in a lot of pain. Is there any reason why we can't give her a morphine shot?"

The Jenkins glance at each other quizzically and shrug their shoulders.

"Give her the shot!" Jeff hollers back. Marge nods her approval.

"Sid," Stan yells again up the slope, "tell base camp to send paramedics. Also, tell base camp to bring up a portable generator, extension cords, and floodlights so we can make it look like day down here."

"Will do!" Sid hollers and removes his two-way radio.

Stan removes the syringe from his pack and the vial of morphine. Jimmy and Bob shine their headlamps on him so he can see to prepare the shot. He then injects Jenny Jean.

"Hey guys, get the light sticks out of the pack," Stan points at the pack Sid lowered, "and place them around her so we can see better."

Suddenly, Jenny Jean feels a warming sensation. It's as if she's being immersed into a warm bath. Her pain is sweeping away. Also, their faces are now recognizable due to the light emitted from the light sticks.

Stan notices a semblance of a smile on Jenny Jean's face as she relaxes. "Jenny Jean, I just gave you a shot of morphine. It should deaden your pain for a while. We're getting the paramedics up here to check you out before we can move you. Do you understand?"

"Yes," she murmurs as her tears subside.

"May I ask you some questions?"

Jenny Jean doesn't know who this man is that took away her pain, but she'd do anything for him. "Yes."

"Did you fall trying to save the children?"

"Yes."

"Were you able to communicate with them before you started to go after them?"

"What?" she's confused.

"Were you able to talk to them? Call out to them and get a response before climbing down after them?"

"Did they fall? Are they alright?" her confusion erupts in fear.

"So, they didn't fall?"

"Not before me."

"Do you know if they fell?"

"I don't know. Are they alright?"

"We don't know. We haven't found them. We thought you might have fallen going after them."

"No."

"Jimmy, come over here." Jimmy moves next to Stan. "Jenny Jean this is Jimmy Ball. He's going to sit here with you while I do something else. Is that okay? I'll be back in a few minutes.

"Hi, Jenny Jean," Jimmy smiles.

"Yes."

Stan scoots away toward Bob and whispers, "Let's rappel down the slope a little further to see if we can find any evidence of the kids' falling."

Bob and Stan climb away from the rock holding Jenny Jean. They peer down the slope. Their headlamps don't reveal any bodies in the area they can see. Before rappelling, Stan grabs some light sticks, bends them to break the interior glass so the chemicals mix to emit light, and then tosses them down the slope. Bob and Stan carefully watch looking for any sign of the children as the sticks bounce and roll down the mountain. The sticks randomly stop at various intervals creating small areas of glowing light on the dark slope.

Bob and Stan rappel a few feet at a the time down the exposed rock. They periodically stop to sweep their light over that area of the slope to search for the missing children. They're encouraged when there's no sign of them or any disturbance on the slope.

After about fifty feet, the slope ends in a gully which is quickly funneling rainwater into the darkness down the mountain. Bob and Stan briefly look around. They're relieved when there's no evidence of the children.

Stan removes his two-way radio from his buttoned pants pocket.

"Smokey, this is Stan. Pick up. Over." Stan relaxes as he awaits Smokey's response.

"I'm here Stan. Over."

"Smokey, did Sid tell you we found the girl alive? Over."

"Yes. Over."

"She's in a lot of pain, but she's alert. I don't think she has a head injury. I need to talk to the paramedics when they show up. Over."

"Sid told me. They're on their way. Also, I just sent some guys with the portal generator. Over."

"Great! We need to bathe the area in light. Bob and I just rappelled to the bottom of the slope. No sign of the kids. I don't think they fell down the slope. I'm gonna send Bob and Jimmy to the meadow to search for them. Sid and I will stay with the girl until the paramedics arrive. Are you good with that? Over."

"Yeah, but tell them to wait until the guys bringing the generator get there. Those guys can go with them and help with the search. Over."

"Good idea. Will do. Over."

"Anything else? Over."

"No, that's it. Over."

"Great job! Are the parents of the girl and the deputy there? Over'"

"As far as I know. I left them up on the trail before we rappelled. Over."

"Okay. Thanks! I'll check in with you later. Over and out."

Stan peers up the steep slope. He chuckles as he glances at Bob, "Now the hard part."

THIRTY-EIGHT

The black bear slowly lumbers among the towering hardwoods and granite boulders in the dark, misty forest. The old sow's guided by her keen sense of smell when she forages. It's always been more reliable than her eyesight, even though her night vision is excellent.

She's on a mission. Food. The delicious food which she associates with the smell of the strange, colorful creatures who walk on two legs.

She gently sways from side-to-side with each massive, plodding step. Her powerful muscles and jet-black fur ripple. Fine water droplets from the heavy mist coat her thick fur causing it to appear luminescent during brief periods of moon shine. Occasionally she pauses, rising on her haunches and lifting her muzzle high to confirm she's on the correct path. Each pause signals she's closer.

She's passed food she normally eats for the possibility of a tantalizing meal. Experience tells her it'll be worth it. Experience also tells her to be careful. These strange, colorful creatures who walk on two legs can be unpredictable. Her moans and snorts are a testament to her nervousness. Her nervousness doesn't stop her, though. Again, she knows the scent of these creatures means there's delicious food nearby. The closer she gets, she can smell the food, too

Her encounters with these odd creatures have not been dangerous. Most of the time they quickly abandon their delicious food and disappear. Though, there have been times when these creatures pelted her with objects, but her expressive defiance and loud roar caused them to quickly disappear. Her only frustration is the shells surrounding the food. They can be difficult to penetrate. The extra work is worth it, though, once her taste buds are excited by what her meaty tongue scoops.

Maize's eyes pop open. The darkness immediately frightens her. Suddenly, there's a strange sound which intensifies her fear. She sits up and peers into the darkness, but she doesn't see anything even after her eyes adjust to the dim light. Her hands feel for Jase. When her fingers find him, she grabs and shakes him violently.

"Wake up. Wake up, Jase. There's something out there," she frantically whispers.

"What? What?" Jase groggily responds. "Why did you wake me?" he's irked as he pushes to a sitting position. When he realizes he can't see her, he reaches out in panic in the cloaking darkness. "Maize!"

"Ouch!" Maize utters when his right hand smacks her cheek. "I'm right here." She grabs his arms and pushes them down. "Be quiet. I heard something."

They sit silently and peer into the darkness. There's a lighter shade of darkness outside their cubbyhole, but not enough light to enable them to see more than a few feet. Briefly a gap opens in the clouds allowing moon shine to illuminate the area, but they only see dark shapes of foliage and rocks in the pale light before shifting clouds cloak it again.

Then they hear something. The sound of a breaking branch. Then a thud and the scraping of wet leaves and earth. A deep moan and snorting sound cause them to grab each other.

"JJ's ghost!" Jase fearfully blurts.

"Hush!" That never crossed Maize's mind. She doesn't believe JJ's ghost would hurt them because they loved her. But, then again, does a ghost love?

"I'm scared! Make it go away!" Jase whispers.

"How do I do that?" Maize whispers in frustration. "I'm scared, too."

Another moan. It seems closer this time. Jase shuffles behind Maize.

"Do something!" Jase whispers in a quivering voice.

Suddenly, there's another gap in the clouds. The moon shine illuminates the landscape. They see a large shimmering figure ambling toward them. Then it disappears in the darkness as clouds cloak the moon shine again.

Maize's hair stands on end. Her breathing's choppy. Jase hugs her harder.

"What was that?" Jase asks with a panicked tone.

"Hush! We need to be quiet. Maybe it won't find us."

They scoot as far back in the crevice as they can. Their hearts are racing. They want to run away, but they can't make themselves do it. They're afraid they're about to be eaten by some horrible, evil creature.

The sounds are now closer.

"I'm gonna shoot it," Jase whispers.

"With what?"

"My Dino Blaster."

"It's not real."

"Yes, it is, just watch!" Jase fumbles with his backpack and removes the toy gun.

"It doesn't shoot real bullets!"

"It shoots an invisible ray. Watch! Do you still have my flashlight?"

Maize reaches in the pocket of her raincoat and removes it. "Yes."

"Shine it on it, so I can see where it is to shoot it."

"It's not a real gun! You're gonna give us away!"

"I'm gonna shoot it! Give me the flashlight!"

"No!"

"Give it to me! It's mine!"

"No!"

Quickly Jase is on her. It catches her off guard. She's knocked over and hits her head on the rock. "Stop Jase! That hurt!"

He's pinned her. She's lying in an awkward position that doesn't allow her enough leverage to push him off. Jase feels along her arm until he touches the flashlight.

"Get off me! You're hurting me! I'm gonna tell mom and dad!"

Jase digs his fingernails into her arm.

"Ouch!"

She releases her grip on the flashlight. He fumbles for it, finds it, grabs it, and flips it on. The crevice is immediately bathed in light. He shines it's beam where he dropped his Dino

211

Blaster. He grabs it with his other hand. Before Maize can push herself up and grab the flashlight, he swings its beam outside the crevice. As the beam pierces the darkness, it quickly lands on the bear. It's massive and frightening in the narrow beam. Its huge eyes reflect a frightening glow from ten feet away. Maize and Jase scream!

The bear's blinded by the sudden bright light. She roars in frustration. Maize and Jase scream again in horror. Jase points his Dino Blaster at the bear and squeezes the trigger. The gun whirs a high pitch pulsating, loud noise while flashing colorful lights. Jase keeps pumping the trigger. The sound and light appear to be never ending.

The old sow's confused and frightened by the horrible, unfamiliar sound and mysterious lights. She whimpers, turns, and quickly scampers away. Jase keeps pumping the trigger even when the bear's no longer visible in the flashlight's beam.

They both stare in disbelief at the beam of light. Mist swirls in its glow. Jase continues to pump the trigger. Maize can see in the gun's flashing light that Jase is wide-eyed.

"Hey! Stop it! It's gone."

Jase continues to pump the trigger.

"Stop it!" Maize yells. She grabs the muzzle of the gun and pushes it down.

Jase rotates the beam of the flashlight so that it's shining off the roof of the crevice illuminating the area. As opposed to being happy about his accomplishment, his eyes fill with tears. He sobs uncontrollably. Maize wants to hit him for hurting her, but she can't make herself do it while he's crying.

"I want mama and daddy!" Jase wails.

Suddenly, Maize's can't prevent herself from crying. Quickly she explodes into a guttural wail. She wraps her arms around her little brother. They hug tightly as they wail. They're terrified. They want to go home.

THIRTY-NINE

"Ow!" Tag utters arousing from his fitful nap. His neck throbs with a sharp pain due to sleeping in an awkward position. He rubs it. The pain slowly subsides.

He stretches his arms, rubs his eyes with his palms, and yawns. He peeks between the slats in the blinds hanging in the RV's window and notices it's still dark outside. It depresses and frightens him. His children are alone and shrouded by the dark night. He offers a silent prayer to God desperately pleading for their protection and they'll be found soon.

He removes his cell from his pants pocket. His glance at its bright screen reveals that it's 4:22 am. It'll still be dark for a few more agonizing hours. He slides it quietly back in his pocket.

Inches away, Liesl sleeps soundly in a chair. He doesn't want to wake her. She'll need all the sleep she can get. He's glad Smokey convinced them to take some of his sleep-aids. He knew Smokey was right when he told them he needs them alert today as they widen the search.

Tag's frustrated by his helplessness. His instincts as a father tell him he needs to be combing the mountains for his children, even if it's extremely dangerous in the dark. His primary, undeniable job as a father is to provide for and protect his family. He's convinced he's failed.

He's haunted by his decision. If he had just said "no" to Jenny Jean's request to take them to the meadow. Even though he frets over his decision, every time he reviews the facts, he believes his initial decision wasn't flawed. Last summer Jenny Jean had free reign with Maize and Jase. There were no issues. She's hiked these mountains her entire life with her family with no incidents. He keeps telling himself it was a freak accident. That still doesn't bring him peace. Why didn't he know about the Hug a Tree program? He could have prepared them for what to do if they became lost, even if it scared them. He knows, if he

213

had just said "no" to Jenny Jean, they would all be sleeping safely in their beds. He aches for their touch. He's reluctant to think about how Maize and Jase are reacting to being lost. It's uncomfortable. He senses they're alive. It's that mysterious connection which links parents and children when their separated which spawns this belief.

It's been hours since Jenny Jean was carried down from the mountain. He's thankful she's alive, but secretly he's furious at her for not protecting his children. He trusted her with his two greatest treasures, and she blew it! He knows he needs to get past the frustration and not blame her, but right now he can't. Her inability to offer any help on what happened to them has enhanced his frustration. He's embarrassed he allowed his frustration to boil over in anger when browbeating her as she was rushed to the ambulance. He hopes the Jenkins will forgive him. He's fortunate Smokey and Chief Justice restrained Mr. Jenkins from taking him apart. He'll apologize later.

The team searching the meadow came up empty. They did surprise a young couple enjoying themselves in the warming hut on the crest of the meadow. After the embarrassed couple quickly dressed, they told the tickled team they arrived at the hut a few hours before sunset and hadn't seen anyone else, including children. They did say they would be on the lookout for them. Tag normally would have laughed with the team as they shared the awkward story. Under different circumstances he might have enjoyed their banter, but not now. Not while his children are lost.

After this team reported their findings, which was a few minutes before midnight, Smokey concluded there was nothing else to be done tonight. It was too dangerous. According to him, the mountains are treacherous enough during the daylight, but to be roaming at night in a wet forest shrouded in dense fog was untenable. He halted the search until daylight. The forecast calls for a clear day after the fog burns off. Aside from leaving two deputies outside the trailer, they were all going home to sleep for a few hours. Smokey said dawn will begin around 6:20 am. He'll be back no later than 6:30 am with his team.

His decision to stop was devasting for Tag and Liesl. After the search was halted, they helped the search-and-rescue team develop a plan for where to search the next day. That plan was dictated by Tag and Liesl's answer to an important question. Smokey wanted to know if Tag and Liesl thought Maize and Jase would stick to obvious hiking trails or strike out through the forest. Tag and Liesl agreed they believed their children would stay on the trails. They thought they would be too frightened to do otherwise. At sunlight, Smokey will send searchers along the spiderweb of trails which crisscross the mountain. They stretch for miles. They're hopeful they'll find them wandering along a trail. If not, the search will become significantly more complicated and worrisome. The bloodhounds will be here by then to help. That'll increase the chances of them being found even if much of their scent has been washed away by the rain.

Tag watches Liesl sleep. She rests peacefully. He envies her. He wishes he could protect her from the emotional pain she'll experience as soon as she awakens. He snickers when she emits a loud snore. They've laughed about her denying she would do anything so vulgar as to snore. For some reason it embarrasses her. Tag loves to playfully tease her about it. She'll feint anger, but his teasing always ends with her grinning.

While staring at her, he fills with shame. He deeply regrets letting his fantasies about Suzy affect his reality with Liesl. His farcical affair caused him to question his marriage. How immature! How ridiculous! How stupid! How embarrassing! It's time he grew up. It's time he became a man. He needs to become the best version of him he can be. He believes it starts with truly loving Liesl.

Liesl's splayed awkwardly in the chair while she sleeps. His eyes absorb her soft features It's been a while since he really, really looked at her. She's slightly fuller than when they first dated, but she still turns men's heads. Her skin is delicate and flawless. His memories of gently caressing her and their tender kisses are titillating. Even though askew as she sleeps, her hair is still soft and natural. He used to love the feel of its texture as his fingers entangled in it when he passionately kissed her. Her lips, slightly parted with spittle pooling in one corner, are still voluptuous. He craves their press against his. Her eyes, hidden behind their lids, have always signaled her true unspoken feelings. He loves their sparkle when she laughs and is

215

discomforted by their glare when angry. It's seeing her wedding ring, snug on her finger, which causes his eyes to mist. Her ring, a visible signal to the world of her love for him, has made him emotional. He's tempted to remove his wedding band. He feels he's unworthy of her love. He won't though. He'll now wear it proudly as her husband and work to ensure he's worthy.

Tag wipes his misty eyes with his shirttail. He believes Suzy may be more physically attractive, and she's certainly wealthier, but she falls short of all other comparisons to Liesl. Tag knows Liesl's beauty is more than skin deep. She radiates beauty unseen by the naked eye. It envelopes her like an aura. It's beauty which can only be experienced. Her compassion and kindness are unrivaled. She's more loved in Rock Slide than he is, even though he grew up here. Her smile melts away fear. Her laugh generates joy. Her words offer peace of mind. Her presence brings delight. Her relationship with her children is magical. She loves them unconditionally and they adore her. She fulfills their every need.

Tag smiles. He rises quietly from his chair, leans toward her, and softly kisses her forehead. She stirs and emits a loud snore. His smile widens, but only briefly. Sobering reality slaps him again. Their children are lost. They must find them. He sits, bows his head, and prays.

FORTY

The suffocating darkness slowly surrenders to a gray pea soup. Maize and Jase peer anxiously from the dark crevice. In the emerging dawn, bleak and dim shapes appear fuzzy and distorted in the heavy fog. They're still fearful the terrifying bear, or some other hideous beast, will charge snarling and howling from the mist to devour them. Tears no longer flow. They're cried out. They shiver due to the cool, damp dawn and the effect of fear run amok. They desperately want to be home with their mama and daddy.

Gradually the mist thins. Shapes and colors are more familiar. They now see deeper into the dense forest. There are no visible, hungry creatures lingering to eat them for breakfast, but just in case, Jase's Dino Blaster rests in his lap. The chirping birds, which they watch dart among the foliage searching for their morning meals, bring familiarity and a lessening of their anxiety. They relax.

"I'm hungry," Jase moans.

"Me, too."

They grab their backpacks and remove their lunch boxes. Each removes one their two remaining peanut butter and jelly sandwiches. Once removed from the baggies, they discover their sandwiches are soggy and sticky. They wolf them down while keeping a wary eye on the forest. Peanut butter and jelly sandwiches have never tasted so good. Once they're finished, they lick their fingers not wanting to waste any of the satisfying food. Maize grabs the few Oreos she didn't eat yesterday.

"Hey, do you still have some Goldfish left?"

Jase peers into lunch box. "Yep."

"I'll give you two of my Oreos for six of your Goldfish."

Jase ponders it for a brief second. "Okay."

They remove the Oreos and Goldfish. They scatter them on the rough boulder in front of them. Quickly they devour them.

Maize reaches into her backpack and removes her bottled water. Jase does the same. They unscrew the caps and sit quietly while drinking.

"Do you think it's gone?" Jase warily asks.

Maize peers into the forest. "I think so."

"Good. My Dino Blaster scared it off." Jase picks it up and points it into the forest.

"Don't shoot again!"

"Why?"

"It might hear it and come look for us."

"Do you really think so?"

"Maybe."

Jase ponders the thought for a few seconds. He then stuffs the gun in his backpack.

"Are mama and daddy looking for us?" Jase asks.

"Yes."

They sit silently staring into the forest. The mist is dissipating. Sunbeams now break through the thick canopy and create bright, warm, golden shafts of light.

"Should we stay here?" Jase wonders.

"I'm not! I wanna go home!"

"But what if mama and daddy come and we miss them?"

Maize doesn't answer. She considers her brother's question. Suddenly, she has an idea. She reaches into her backpack and removes her notebook and pens.

"I'll leave them a message. That way they'll know where we're going."

"Good idea!" Jase smiles.

Maize flips open the notebook and removes her red pen. She crudely scribbles their names and draws an arrow. She smiles and shows it to Jase.

"What does it say?"

"Maize and Jase went this way."

"Which way?"

"See the arrow."

"Oh yeah. I see."

"I'll leave it here." She rips the page from the notebook and places the paper on the boulder. "That way they'll know where we're going."

"Where are we going?"

"Home!" Maize's exasperated with her brother's questions. "We're going home. Don't you wanna go home?"

"Yeah," Jase meekly replies afraid of upsetting his sister any further.

"Put your stuff in your backpack and let's go."

"Okay."

They both grab their lunch boxes, zip them shut, and cram them in their backpacks. Once again, they check the forest. Seeing nothing, they climb out of the crevice onto the damp, thick, decaying leaves. Maize removes her raincoat. Jase does the same. They wad them up and cram them into their backpacks. Jase also removes his coonskin cap and crams it in his backpack. They grab their bottled waters, drink the remaining contents, and drop the empty bottles on the ground. Maize checks to make sure her message for her parents still rests on the boulder. It does.

"Let's go!" Maize orders.

"Which way?" Jase asks sheepishly

"Remember, home's on the other side of this big rock mountain." They both peer up the steep rock. "We gotta go around it."

"Which way?"

Maize looks in both directions. She can't see the end of the rock either way. "Which way do you wanna go?"

Jase swells with pride. His big sister wants him to choose. He ponders his choices for a few seconds. Then points, "Let's go this way."

"No, we're gonna go this way," Maize points in the opposite direction.

Jase, crushed by his sister's deception, still falls in line behind her when she marches off weaving among the boulders and trees along the edge of the rock mountain.

FORTY-ONE

Tag and Liesl fight to suppress their emotions. They need to appear strong. Inside, though, they're a horrible mess. They're terrified! Tears finally flowed when they learned there were 338 of their fellow Rock Sliders milling at dawn on the lawn of the courthouse park anxious to help with the search. They're overwhelmed by the out pouring of love from their community.

Since daylight, the base camp in the crowded mountain parking lot has been a beehive of activity. Smokey's been in constant motion. He and his search-and-rescue team have been pouring over trail maps and topography maps. They've divided the mountains into eight sectors. Members of the search-and-rescue team will be responsible for leading the search in a sector. Also, they'll each be joined by twenty-five of the volunteers. Hiking trails will be searched first. If that's unsuccessful, they'll fan out through the forest using a grid pattern. Depending upon the terrain, the goal will be to have twenty-six people fanning through the forest in a horizontal line with each searcher separated from the other by twenty-five yards. This will allow each team to cover one-third of a mile at a time.

The remaining 138 volunteers will be used for other services, such as gathering and supplying food and water for the search teams, notifying all those living on the boundaries of the mountains to be on the lookout for the children, providing relief for tired volunteers, and helping the Sheriff's Office with assigned tasks. Magnolia Winter-Blossom demanded that she be allowed to lead these efforts. No one challenged her.

While the searching volunteers were divided, instructed on their roles, and told their personal safety was a priority, Tag and Liesl recorded their impassioned plea to their children. They made it clear in their message that these people weren't mean and weren't going to hurt them. They were going to bring them home. Their heartfelt plea was electronically sent to each search-

and-rescue team leader. These leaders were supplied with a small, wireless, powerful speaker which allows them to blast the message through the forest as they search. Experience employing this tactic has shown that lost children will immediately respond to verbal recordings of their parents, and if instructed to do so, will approach anyone they see in the forest.

Tag rubs his forehead as he stands on an uneven bump of piled pea gravel. He's partially surrounded by shallow, irregular-shaped puddles of rainwater. Some of the puddles have recently been churned into quagmires of thick, sticky, chocolate-colored muck due to the constant trampling of busy feet. People hurry gingerly through the parking lot trying to avoid the gooey traps. Fortunately, above the thick canopy, the sky is now cobalt blue. The fog has dissipated. There's no rain in the immediate forecast.

Tag's thanked God for this clear day. Not because of the lack of rain, but because it will improve the ability of the search teams to find his children. He still has faith they're alive. He remembers from his bible studies that Hebrews 11:1 defines faith as "being sure of what you hope for and certain of what you can't see." He now fully understands the meaning of the New Testament definition of "faith". He periodically repeats it to himself. It comforts him

Truthfully, he's enjoying his moment of solitude. It allows him to clear his mind, although he's finding it impossible not to worry.

Liesl stepped into the trailer to make the difficult call to her parents about their grandchildren. She wanted to do it by herself. She thought Tag's presence might be distracting. She was afraid it might confuse and anger her if he was interrupting her with instructions on what to and not to tell her parents.

Tag's not upset by being excluded. He wants to avoid any situations which may create additional stress. He's already extremely agitated he's not allowed to do anything except wait. He feels he should be doing something, but logically he understands Smokey's need to have him nearby so they'll be able to act swiftly. He wishes he could quell his anxiety.

He made the difficult call to his parents earlier. It was gut wrenching to tell them such devastating news. He called his

221

father rather that his mother. He thought he would be less likely to cry talking to his father than his mother. Unfortunately, his father put her on the phone so Tag could repeat to her what he told him. It was easier having told his father first, but he still couldn't avoid becoming emotional. They said they would leave immediately from their vacation. He thanked them, told him he loved them, and said he hopes he can turn their car around with good news before they get here.

A sunbeam strikes his face causing him to squint. As opposed to turning his head, he closes his eyes and lifts his face toward the sun. The beam bathes his entire face. Its warmth is comforting. He senses God's signaling him He's in control, and He loves Maize and Jase.

"Tag, I'm so sorry. I'm here to help."

Tag's momentary peace dissolves into panic. His heartbeat spikes. He doesn't need this additional stress, but it's arrived. His eyes pop open and confirm his fear. Suzy stands facing him.

Suzy hugs him. He's speechless. He's confused. Liesl's only a few yards away in the trailer and Suzy has her arms around him. He senses not only is Liesl watching them, but so is everyone else.

Instincts take over. He aggressively breaks free. "Why are you here?" he angrily and loudly demands. Suzy initially appears shocked, then her eyes narrow.

"Well, I was here to help, but I'm not so sure now! That was extremely rude of you! I'm not going to be treated like that!" Suzy yells back.

"Fine! I don't need your help. Get outta here!" Tag's now screaming.

Now all eyes are on them due to the uncomfortable nature of this encounter. Smokey suddenly appears stepping between them.

"Hey, you two, please calm down. What's this all about? Also, who are you?" Smokey asks eyeing Suzy.

"She's a former friend..."

"Former friend?" Suzy defiantly interrupts.

"Yeah! You heard me. Former friend!" Tag's veins in his neck bulge.

"Stop it!" Smokey shouts. "We don't need this. Miss, you're going to have to leave."

"Who the hell are you telling me I have to leave?" Suzy's crossed her arms. She glares at Smokey.

"I'm in charge of this operation. What I say goes. So please leave."

"Fine!" Suzy throws her arms up. She turns to march off, and delivers a parting shot, "I thought you might need a fleet of drones to help with the search, but I guess not."

Suddenly, Liesl's by Tag's side. His panic level rises.

"Hold on there!" Smokey pleads. "What's this about drones?"

"Yeah, when I heard about the missing kids, I did a little research. I found that drones sure can come in handy in helping find missing people in rough terrain. I thought you could use some, but I guess not," Suzy smugly replies as she walks away.

"Whoa there!" Smokey quickly jogs toward her and steps in front of her blocking her path. "Can you quickly get us drones?"

Suzy pushes by him, "Yeah, at no charge to you, but again, I guess you don't need them."

Smokey grabs her arm, "Yes, drones would be very helpful to our search. Will you reconsider?"

Suzy jerks her arm free from Smokey's grasp, "Only if he asks me?" She nods her head toward Tag.

"Who is she?" Liesl asks. Tag can easily see Liesl's confused. He can't answer.

Smokey turns toward Tag, "The drones would be tremendous help and allow us to search the mountains much faster," he implores.

"Who is she?" Liesl's request is firmer.

Tag's head's spinning. Liesl and Suzy stand facing each other. His worst nightmare. His past and present have collided. He wants to flee, but he knows he can't. Liesl doesn't know Suzy's recently been his fantasy. Someone with whom he's recently enjoyed an emotional affair. With whom he almost actually had a baby. But more importantly, Suzy's been tempting Tag to leave Liesl for her. He's certain Suzy's guessed who Liesl is. He's frozen in fear. He doesn't know what he should do. The silence is tense and awkward.

Liesl breaks the ice. "Hi, I'm Liesl, Tag's wife," she sticks her hand out and walks toward Suzy.

"I'm Suzy," they lightly shake hands and warily eye each other.

Tag's eyes widen.

"I apologize for my husband. I'm not sure what's gotten into him," Liesl shoots Tag an ugly glare, "but if Smokey says we need drones to find my children, then I hope you'll overlook my husband rudeness and reconsider. I desperately need to find my children."

Suzy's anger melts, but not her resolve, "You got 'em, but only if he asks." Again, Suzy nods in the direction of Tag.

All eyes turn to Tag. Liesl and Smokey's eyes beg for an affirmative answer. Suzy's smug appearance radiates a "gotcha" grin.

Tag knows he has no choice. Not to ask would be stupid. It might prevent them from finding his children alive. He's also very sure he's about to have a difficult discussion with Liesl.

"I apologize Suzy. Yes, we could use your help. Your offer of drones is very much appreciated. I hope you'll reconsider."

"They're yours," Suzy responds flippantly.

"Great! Great!" Smokey's relieved and delighted.

"Thank you," Liesl offers gratefully. She glares at Tag, "Tag, don't you have something to say?"

"Yes, thank you."

"Sure."

"Suzy, please come with me. Let's discuss your access to drones for our search," Smokey points toward his command center. They walk off together.

"Come inside. I need you to tell me who this person is," Liesl glares while nudging Tag in his back toward the trailer.

"So, who is this Suzy?" Their knees almost touch as they sit across from each other in the cramped trailer. Tag feels as if the space is closing in on him. He takes a deep breath to calm himself. He's thought about how to have this conversation

224

numerous times over the past few days, but he never decided exactly how. Now he's forced to have it under circumstances he feared. It's obvious Liesl's upset. Her eyes are narrow and piercing. Her nostrils are flared. Her lips are pinched. Her arms and legs are crossed. She taps her toes on the cheap, tacky carpet. She waits anxiously for his response.

"Do you remember a few days ago you asked me about the woman who hugged me on the boardwalk? It's her."

"Go on."

"As I told you, she was someone I knew from high school."

"Come on, Tag! This is ridiculous!" Liesl throws up her hands. "Cut to the chase!"

"Okay, okay! I'm getting there." Tag leans forward. He wrings his hands. Liesl's heartbeat accelerates.

"I met her the day Billy died. It was her parents' boat I was driving when Billy had his accident. It was just as emotionally and mentally scarring for her as it was for me. We uniquely shared something horrible that no one should witness. Strangely, this tragedy created an intimate bond between us." Tag averts his eyes to the floor. "We fell in love, fell in infatuation, or fell in whatever you wanna call it!" Tag throws his arms up in frustration. "We had a desire to always be together. She was my first love." Tag pauses. He glances up at her.

The silence threatens. Uneasiness swells in Liesl. She's uncomfortable. There's something coming she doesn't want to hear, but she must hear it, "I need the truth. How much did you 'love' her?"

"Is that important now?" Tag's frustration spills as he leans back. "You've never told me the intimate details of all your past loves!"

"None of my past 'loves' have ever shown up in our present. If so, I would tell you. Answer my question!"

Tag bows his head and stares absentmindedly at the cheap carpet while leaning forward. He's frightened. He's afraid he might lose Liesl. He's stunned as to how ironic it is that only a few hours ago he recommitted his love for her as she slept. He'll parse his words carefully. He doesn't want to mess this up. He looks up into her eyes, which glare at him with a mixture of anger and fear.

"You're right. I'll tell you, but I want you to understand that this is the past, not the present. You're my wife, and I love you very much." He grabs her hand. She pulls it away.

"We were young. We were care free. I thought we were deeply in love. For the first time in our young lives, we were exploring something…um, wildly and wickedly enjoyable." Liesl's eyes widen. Her discomfort deepens. "It was an incredibly confusing, horrible, exciting, and memorable summer. One that affected me for a few years. Then everything crashed.

She lived in Pineville. Yep, the town where we met. My only reason in attending that college was to find her.

She quit communicating with me in the early fall of my senior year of high school. I mean just stopped! I got no 'Dear John' communication. It was just cold turkey. I never heard from her again, until she showed up, out of the blue, a few days ago.

I was devastated by her…her…I guess you would call it, for lack of a better description, callous unresponsiveness. When you combined that with the death of my best friend, I was an emotional wreck. Then my parents unwittingly added to my stress by keeping close tabs on me at all times. I couldn't do anything without their intense scrutiny"

"Why was that?" Liesl unwittingly asks.

"They thought Mr. Jimmy was going to kill me. He blamed me for Billy's death. I'm sure he still does. As you know, I try to avoid him."

"I've noticed. That explains why you have no relationship with Billy's family." Liesl's surprised she's making this conversational. She assumes it's a way to deflect her anxiety.

"Yeah. Well, I was a mess when I graduated. As you know, I didn't go to college right away. I was still struggling with losing Billy and with Suzy breaking my heart. I hit the road to 'find myself' as they say. All I found was life on the road doing menial jobs for room and board wasn't the life I wanted. I enrolled in Pineville hoping to find Suzy and rekindle our relationship. I didn't though," Tag looks directly into Liesl's eyes. "I found something better. Something I never dreamed of. I found you."

Liesl's heart's racing. That's sweet, and she senses he's sincere and has been truthful, but she believes there's more that's unsaid based on the events of today. "Yeah, yeah, but you're not telling me everything. I need to know about your relationship with her today. Why would she offer to supply drones for the search after y'all not seeing each other for all these years, and why are you so upset with her?" Again, Liesl folds her arms across her chest.

Tag quickly runs his hurriedly, crafted response through his brain. His pause prior to answering makes Liesl suspicious he won't be telling the truth.

"Excellent questions. I'm not sure why she's offering the drones. From what she's told me, she's worth a whole lot of money, so the drones are pocket change to her."

"How much is she worth?" Liesl's curiosity gets the best of her.

"She told me, her net worth's in the low nine figures, but I have no proof."

Liesl's eyes widen.

"I can only assume she's trying to make up for hurting me in the past. When she surprised me on the boardwalk, she said she wanted my help purchasing a lake house, but she also said it was time to tell me why she disappeared. She said she owed it to me."

"So, did she tell you?" Liesl interrupts.

"Yes, she did."

"What did she say?"

"She said her parents stopped her from having a relationship with me. They thought our relationship was, I guess you would say, unhealthy for her. They were probably right. We were too young to be doing what we were doing."

Liesl isn't going to ask what he means by that. She thinks she knows but doesn't want to hear him say it. Her mental picture of them together is disturbing. She changes the subject to focus on the second part of her question, "So why are you still so upset with her after all these years?"

"She hurt me! I don't want her around! I don't want her around you or our kids!"

"I've never seen you act the way you did toward anyone like you did toward her. You seem to still be carrying a lot of emotion." Liesl pauses and asks the uncomfortable question, "Do you still love her?"

"No! It's you I love! Not her! Yeah, I'll admit in the past I thought I loved her very much. We talked about getting married out of high school."

"Married!" Liesl's dumfounded.

"Yeah, we were young and dumb. Thank God it didn't happen! We were too young to have a family."

"What do you mean by that?"

Tag drops his head and squeezes his eyes shut. He's inadvertently stepped in it. No avoiding telling Liesl now. In a way, he's relieved he's about to tell her. He's hated keeping this secret from her. He's been afraid how she'd react.

Seeing his reaction to her question, Liesl's anxiety spikes..

"What I'm about to tell you, I just learned a couple of nights ago." It's obvious to Liesl he's struggling. His voice is cracking. "This is difficult for me to say. My emotions are scattered about it, which has upset me. I learned... I learned...that Suzy...was pregnant with my child... and aborted it."

Liesl gasps and reflectively places her hands over her mouth.

"I swear...I swear...I had no idea until the other night!" Tag frantically scrambles seeing Liesl's shocked reaction. "It scared me to death! I might have never met you, fell in love, and had Maize and Jase if she had made a different decision. Y'all are the most important three people in my life! I can't imagine life without y'all! But, I also feel overwhelming remorse about this aborted child. My child! A child I never knew. A child who never had the opportunity to live and enjoy life. It breaks my heart that neither I nor Suzy seem to care about this lost life." Tears now stream down his cheeks. "It made me angry that I wasn't asked to participate in this important decision. I should have. It was my child! But then again, I'm thankful that I wasn't asked, because it might have changed my life. This is difficult. I'm very conflicted over how I should feel. Obviously, her reappearance, and this stunning knowledge of an aborted child, has reopened an emotional wound which I thought was healed. It's erupted in anger.

Also, I think I reacted the way I did toward her was because I was afraid. Afraid she was going to disrupt my life with you and our children. Afraid of what you might think of me if you found out. Now, not only have I lost that child, but I may be on the verge of losing…" Suddenly he's bawling. Gasping for breath as he weeps uncontrollably. He can't speak. His head's in his hands. His body heaves from the sobbing.

Liesl's stunned. She's never seen him this upset. She softly weeps, too. Her world has been turned upside down…but then suddenly…she realizes… has it really? What's changed other than this shocking news? It shouldn't be a threat to her future. This all happened prior to her having a relationship with Tag. He didn't cheat on her. Although, doubt is creeping into her head. It's horrible news, and she understands why he didn't want to tell her. Would she have kept it a secret from Tag if she had an abortion? She believes she probably would.

This is too much for Liesl to process with the stress of her own children missing. She knows she…and him, must stay strong for their children. They can't be having their relationship appear strained while encouraging others to find their children. She struggles for words.

She places her hands on his cheeks and lifts his head from his hands. His eyes open as he continues to sob. She kisses his forehead. His sobbing slows. His blurred vision clears. He sees her tear-stained cheeks. "I'm sorry," she utters. "Wipe your tears and let's find our children." Liesl stands and leaves the trailer. Tag's not quite sure what to make of her reaction, he believes they're still together, at least for now. He just couldn't make himself tell her that Suzy's trying to destroy their marriage.

FORTY-TWO

Mr. Jimmy's head throbs. Once again, passing out from drinking a six-pack of rock-gut beers was his method for coaxing a night's sleep. The earsplitting, uneven honking of a car's horn has interrupted his alcohol induced rest. It's startled him. It's also intensified his headache.

"Damn it! What the hell's going on!"

He struggles off the couch, wobbles when he stands, and grabs the back of a chair to steady himself. He staggers to the front door and jerks it open. The bottom of the door rakes across the top of his bare right foot.

"Crap!" he screams in pain. He hobbles through the door. The bright sunshine exacerbates the throbbing pain in his head. His foot stings from the raw scrape. He squints in the direction of the ear-piercing noise. He's not in a good mood.

Mo stands on the deeply rutted, partially graveled driveway. His back is to Mr. Jimmy. He too is cautiously peering in the direction of the noise.

As Mr. Jimmy's bloodshot eyes adjust to the harsh sunlight and focus, he spots an idling, old pickup truck parked in front of his gate. It's the source of this horrific noise which has rudely interrupted his sleep.

"Quit blowin' that damned horn you son-of-a-bitch!" he screams while waving his arms frantically. The noise stops.

Mo jerks and looks back at his dad. He presses his hands to his ears. He quickly steps aside as Mr. Jimmy hobbles barefoot past him toward the gate.

Mr. Jimmy's feet quickly are covered in mud. He must choose his steps wisely to keep from slipping and stepping on something which might induce pain on the bottom of his feet. The scrape on the top of his right foot still burns.

"God damn it! What do ya mean by makin' all this racket?" he hollers as he nears the gate. Two strangers, a young man and young woman, step out of the cab. She's holding a piece a paper in her hand.

"You got no right bein' up here makin' all this noise! That boy," he points at Mo who's slinking away, "is a retard. If you upset him, there'll be hell to pay!" he threatens them as he approaches the gate.

"Sorry mister, we meant no harm," the young man answers. "My name's Roscoe and this here's Wilma," he points at the young woman.

"Hidy," Wilma squeaks.

"We're here on official sheriffin' business," Roscoe boasts.

Mr. Jimmy's anxiety spikes. "What fer?"

"Wilma, hand'm that flyer."

Wilma cautiously approaches the metal gate. It's a long metal pole attached at one end to a metal fence post and secured at the other end by a combination lock on a metal chain. The chain's wrapped around another metal post. Holding the flyer, she reaches over the top of the gate. Mr. Jimmy hobbles up to the gate and snatches it from her. She jerks her arm back and hurriedly stumbles away from the gate.

"Mister, see the pictures of the kids on the flyer?" Mr. Jimmy looks at the flyer and notices the beaming faces of two young children, a boy, and a girl. "Those kids are missin' in these here mountains." Roscoe sweeps his arm while pointing at the mountains. "There's a bunch people lookin' for 'em. The sheriff asked us to pass out a copy of that flyer, which your holdin' in your hand, to everybody that lives next to the mountains. If you see 'em. He wants you to call that number on there right away. You got that mister?"

Mr. Jimmy glances at the flyer again. The number boldly appears. Hard to miss it. Suddenly, his heart leaps when he reads the names of the children.

"Are these here Tag Ryder's kids?" he asks squinting at them.

"Yes sir mister! Do you know 'em?"

"Heard of 'em. Feel sorry for the family. I know what it's like to lose a kid," Mr. Jimmy's trying to suppress a grin. "I'll definitely be on the lookout for 'em. Now y'all run along and finish yer sheriffin'.'' He waves them off while turning his back. He can no longer suppress his grin.

"Thanks mister," Roscoe hollers as he and Wilma climb back in the cab and drive away.

Suddenly, Mr. Jimmy's head no longer aches. He's not fretting over the pain in his foot as he hurriedly hobbles back to his house. After all these years his time for revenge has finally come.

"Hey boy!" Mr. Jimmy hollers at Mo. "Lower yer hands. I need ya to hear me good." Mo drops his hands. "I got an important job fer ya. Come on over here."

Mr. Jimmy climbs up the rickety, weather-beaten steps on to his front porch. He leaves a trail of muddy footprints to his favorite rocker. He grabs an old weather-beaten chair and drags it next to his rocker. Mo still stands in the mud in the yard.

"Boy, come on up here and sit. I got somethin' to show ya." Mr. Jimmy drops in his rocker. Mo plods up the steps. He leaves massive, muddy boot tracks alongside Mr. Jimmy's muddy, bare footprints. Mo eases in the chair and stares at his dad.

"Boy, did you git yer cereal this mornin'?"

Mo nods.

"Good! So proud of ya fer doin' that!"

Mo grins.

"Boy, there's kids lost in these here mountains. There's people lookin' fer 'em, but they don't know these mountains like yer'un does. I need fer ya to go find 'em. Can ya do that fer me?"

Mo smiles and nods his head enthusiastically.

"Good! Good! Proud of ya son!"

Mo's smile widens. It's rare he hears his dad call him son and tell him he's proud of him.

"Here, I wantcha to look at these here pictures." Mr. Jimmy shows Mo the flier with Maize and Jase's pictures.

Mo touches Maize's picture, "May-z."

Mr. Jimmy's stunned! "Boy, who taught you to read?"

Mo has a troubled look on his face.

"What's this say?" Mr. Jimmy asks pointing at Maize's name below her picture.

Mo appears confused while staring at the jumbled letters.

232

Mr. Jimmy points at Jase's name. "Can you read this 'un?"

Mo's confused face seems to be contorting into frustration. That's a trigger Mr. Jimmy doesn't want pulled. Mo may become destructive.

"A'ight boy. Calm down. I ain't gonna ask ya anymore what this says, but do ya know her?"

Mo relaxes. He touches Maize's picture again. "Friend."

Mr. Jimmy's perplexed how Mo knows her, but he's not going to ask in fear it'll cause Mo to become frustrated, and ultimately destructive.

"Well, she needs yer help. She's lost in these here mountains." Mr. Jimmy points at Jase's picture. "This is her brother. Ya know like Billy. He's lost, too. I need ya to go find 'em and bring 'em rite cher. Can ya do that fer me?"

Mo grins and nods. "Find May-z…and Billy."

"Good boy! His name's Jase, not Billy."

Mo appears confused.

Mr. Jimmy touches Jase's picture. "Jase. His name's Jase," Mr. Jimmy slowly enunciates. He touches Maize's picture. "Maize." Then he touches Jase's picture again. "Jase. Can you say 'Jase'?"

"Jaysss."

"Good! Good! Jase…and Maize. I need ya to find 'em and bring 'em rite cher. Can you do that?"

Mo nods enthusiastically, "Find." He grins.

"A'ight! Let me make yer lunch. Carry it with ya. I'm gonna give you that old clock that'll ring when it's time fer ya to eat. You just stick it in yer pocket like before, got it?"

Mo smiles and nods. Mr. Jimmy came up with a way to let Mo know when it was time for lunch when he wasn't around. He has a small, wind-up alarm clock he sets to go off at noon. He worked with Mo to make him comfortable with its screeching, sudden noise, and he showed him how to push down a button to make it stop. He's also demonstrated to Mo that the noise will eventually stop if he can't find the button to press. Mr. Jimmy only needs to set it to ring for Mo's lunch, because he knows Mo will come home when it's time for dinner. He's often wondered how Mo knows when it's time to come home for dinner.

233

"A'ight." Mr. Jimmy rises from his chair. "Follow me into the kitchen and I'll make yer lunch. I'll pack ya some of them 'Niller Wafers. I know how much ya like 'em."

Mo giggles and awkwardly claps his hands.

FORTY-THREE

"Quit crying Jase!" Maize screams. Maize's scolding only makes him cry harder. His cries echo off the large granite rocks which surround them as they follow what's normally a dry stream bed. Last night's rain has filled it with rushing, tumbling water.

"What's wrong with you?"

"I'm...I'm," Jase sobs, "tired! Can...can...we stop?" he sniffles.

Maize's also tired. They've been walking, or more like wandering, for almost four hours, weaving up and down the slopes trying to find their home. They've climbed over and around granite rock outcroppings, squeezed through thick, tangled, wild rhododendron, and stumbled over unseen obstacles in the thick carpet of decaying leaves. Maize used one of her Elsa band-aids to patch a scrape on her arm when she tripped and skinned herself on a rough rock. She was proud of herself for not crying, even though she wanted to. Being brave for her brother is important to her. He placed the band-aid on her wound.

Every unfamiliar sound creates waves of anxiety causing them to freeze until they realize they're safe. Maize's also afraid for another reason. She's afraid to tell her brother the compass leading them home is broken. She's decided not to tell him. She removed it from her pocket before they left the crevice this morning, only to find it's plastic cover broken and the slender, metal arrow unattached. She remembered from the previous day that it was pointing through the rocks toward their home. She's not sure if they're still going in that direction.

"Okay, Okay. We'll stop. I'm hungry anyway."

They find a flat rock bordering the stream and climb on it. Jase's dirty face is streaked with tears. He rubs his eyes and cheeks with his palms to dry them. The dirt smears on his face in irregular shapes. He's still sniffling as he calms from his exhausted outburst.

"What do you have to eat?" Maize asks as she unzips her backpack and removes her lunch box. She digs a Capri Sun from the bottom of her pack. Jase does the same.

"I have Vanilla Wafers, Fruit Rollups, and one more peanut butter and jelly sandwich."

"Me, too."

"Is it lunch time?" Jase asks.

"I dunno, but I'm hungry anyway."

"Me, too!"

They unwrap their sandwiches. They're too soggy and sticky to remove from their baggies. They leave the sandwiches in the baggies, tear off pieces, and stuff the pieces into their mouths. When their through, they rake their fingers along the inside of their baggies. They scrape the remaining contents of the baggies on to their fingers and lick them. They hop off the rock and stick their hands into the rushing water to remove the sticky residue of the peanut butter and jelly. Then they wipe their wet hands on the rock and their pants to dry them. They both scramble back on the rock.

Maize pokes a hole with the straw into the Capri Sun and sucks the sweet juice. Jase mimics her. Jase reaches into his lunchbox and removes his baggie containing the Vanilla Wafers.

"Don't eat those yet," Maize cautions. "Then you won't have anything for a snack later. I'm not going to give you any of mine!"

"Okay," he pitifully responds as he removes his hand from the baggie and places the Vanilla Wafers in his lunchbox. "How about a Fruit Rollup?"

"How many do you have?"

Jase peers into his lunchbox, "Two."

"Eat just one, okay?"

"Okay," Jase answers eagerly tearing the paper away from his snack.

They sit quietly and survey their surroundings. Nothing but tall trees, bushy plants, and lots of rocks as far as they can see. The water rushing down the slope generates a soothing sound allowing them to relax for a few minutes while they finish drinking their Capri Suns.

"When are we gettin' home," Jase breaks the silence.

"I dunno. Maybe soon."

"Is this still the right way?"

"Of course!" Maize's defiant.

"I'm sorry," Jase whispers.

Again, they sit in silence. Maize's anxious. She's not sure where they are, but at least they're walking downhill.

Since they left JJ, Maize and Jase have wandered eight miles away from her. They're now on private property. There aren't any more hiking trails to stumble across.

"Do you think mama and daddy are still looking for us?" Jase asks.

"Yeah."

"Maybe they found your note!"

"Maybe so, but I doubt it."

"Why?"

Maize shrugs her shoulders and stares at the stream.

Jase stares down the slope into the forest. A strong gust of wind rushes through the forest. The cool breeze is welcoming. The tree limbs sway and creak. The leaves dance causing the sunlight to flicker. Suddenly, Jase notices something he didn't see before. He stands on the rock, narrowing his eyes attempting to peer deeper into the forest. The wind swirls again. The tree limbs bend. He does see something!

"A treehouse! Look a treehouse!" he screams.

Maize scrambles into a standing position next to her brother. She stares in the direction he's pointing. She can't see anything. The wind gusts again, and as the tree limbs bend, she sees it. It is a treehouse!

"Let's go look at it!" Jase gleefully hollers.

"Yeah!"

They hastily stuff their lunchboxes into their backpacks, throw them over their shoulders, and jump off the rock. They splash across the stream and scurry down the slope.

They're excited when they reach the old, abandoned deer stand. They don't know why there's a treehouse in the forest, but they feel like they're now almost home. Old two-by-fours are nailed in their centers to the trunk of an old white oak in a rising horizontal row. Each board is separated by about a foot. Maize counts ten of them. Next to the eighth highest two-by-four is a small wooden platform. The boards creating the narrow platform are nailed to separate thick tree branches. The wood for the steps and platform is heavily water stained. Its color is a blend varying from smokey gray, charcoal gray, and black. White mold grows on parts of the wood. The sawed edges are pot-marked with indentions and deterioration from rot. Maize and Jase don't care, though. They've asked their daddy to build them a treehouse. He's told them their too young. Now they get to climb into one.

"Me first!" Jase demands. "I saw it first, so I get to climb it first."

"Okay, but hurry up!" Maize concedes.

Jase reaches up and grabs the third two-by-four and steps on the first one. They swivel and wiggle. He's anxious. He reaches for the fourth one, pulls himself up, and steps up on to the second one. He repeats this process as he slowly and carefully climbs the tree. The higher he climbs the more anxious he becomes as each board's unsteady under his weight. When he reaches the seventh one, he looks down. He's overcome with a fear of falling. He freezes, afraid to climb higher. He whimpers.

"What's wrong?" Maize asks looking up at him.

"I'm...I'm...scared."

"Of what?"

"Falling!"

"I'll catch you."

"Promise?"

"Yeah. You're almost there. Keep going!"

Jase looks down again at his sister. She's standing under him. He'll have to trust she'll catch him. He looks up. He carefully reaches up to the eighth board and slowly steps up to the sixth one. His fear briefly spurts when they swivel, but he relaxes when he realizes they'll hold.

"You're almost there," Maize encourages.

He looks to his left and can see the top of the platform. He reaches up and grabs the ninth board and steps ups to the seventh. He then reaches for the tenth board and steps up to the eighth board. The boards wiggle. He carefully steps on to the platform and let's go of the tenth board. The platform slightly sags, but it holds. He turns around and faces the forest. He's excited now. The view's amazing!

"That was easy! Come on up," he hollers down at Maize. She looks so small below him. He wonders if this is how dinosaurs see the world.

Maize grabs the boards and climbs. As the boards wiggle, she too becomes anxious. She loves to climb, though. She quickly scampers up the boards on to the platform. Jase is sitting with his legs hanging off the platform. Maize sits next to him. The platform sags further but holds.

"Can we see our house?" Jase asks excitedly.

"I don't think so." Maize peers into the distance anyway.

"I like being up here. Do you think daddy will build us a treehouse?"

"Maybe one day, but I hope it's not like this one. This one's too small and rickety. I want one that's big, has walls, and a roof."

"Yeah, and a kitchen and a TV!"

They laugh!

"Maybe even a bathroom!" Jase adds laughingly. "Then we could live in it!"

"That'd be fun! I could have tea parties for my dolls…"

"…and I could shoot dinosaurs…and aliens!"

They continue laughing about their make-believe treehouse. It's a momentary distraction from their fear of not being home. Unfortunately, their peace is short lived. Suddenly, there's a new concern.

Four scrawny dog-like creatures appear around the rock they were just on. They're sniffing the rock and licking it. One of them snaps at another. They momentarily growl at each other and then continue sniffing. They march around and over the rock alternating their long, narrow snouts from the ground to above their heads. They all look alike. Their fur is a mix of white, brown, black, and tan, except underneath it is mostly white. They have big, pointy, perky, triangle-shaped ears, and a bushy tail like a raccoon.

"What kinda dogs are those?" Jase whispers.

"I dunno."

"They look mean."

"Yeah. Sshh. Sit still. Maybe they'll leave."

They watch the dog-like creatures continue to sniff and march around the rock. Then one of them sniffs by the stream. He laps some of the running water. Soon, all four of them are sniffing by the stream and lapping water. Two bumps into each other, bare their teeth, and growl. Again, their snouts alternate from the ground to the air.

One wades across the stream and sniffs on the other side. The others follow. Soon, they're following the route Maize and Jase took to the tree. Maize and Jase sit silently watching them come closer. Quickly, they reach the base of the tree. Maize and Jase are glad dogs can't climb trees. They're safe, for now, but frightened of these strange dog-like creatures.

The dog-like creatures' stalk around the tree. Maize and Jase can now smell their gamey scent. It's not long before the coyotes see them and yip, bark, howl, and growl. Maize and Jase weep in fear. The coyotes sense their fear and become more agitated. Soon, there are more of them, including pups. They also scamper to the tree. Some lay in the leaves, watching each other... and Maize and Jase, while others march below the tree and yap.

Maize and Jase cry harder. Their wailing mixes with the excited sounds of the coyotes. This concoction of strange noise is frightfully eerie as it cascades through the forest. Fear's consumed Maize and Jase. They know they're trapped, and there's nothing they can do about it. Bloodcurdling shouts of "Mama!," "Daddy!," "I wanna go home!," and "Come get us!" erupt from their mouths periodically interrupting their crying. If anyone else is near, they should be heard, even above the din of the coyotes.

FORTY-FOUR

It's been almost two hours since Stan Irons' group started their search along the trail to Thunder Falls. The searchers were hastily trained on how to look for signs of humans in the forest, so they've deliberately crept along attentively practicing what they learned. They've fanned out on either side of the trail with each searcher only separated by a few feet. The search has progressed slowly due to the challenging terrain and thick foliage. False alarms have also slowed their progress. Previous hikers didn't heed the Park Service's request to leave the park pristine. Random pieces of trash were found along the trail. This brought the search to a halt as each item was carefully examined. So far, due to the level of deterioration of each piece of trash found, none of it was left by Maize or Jase

Stan blasts the message recorded by Liesl and Tag every ten minutes. When it was initially played, many searchers were seen wiping away silent tears. The anguish in the parents' voices was heartbreaking. The first few times it was played, there was also a palpable level of excitement among the team when the message ended. They froze, hoping to spot the children running toward them from the forest. Unfortunately, now it's become somewhat monotonous. It's also having a depressing effect on the search team. The team's excitement has waned. Now the team doesn't even stop searching when the recording's played. They continue plodding forward kicking up dead leaves and peering under foliage for any evidence.

Stan's relieved that Jenny Jean will be alright. When he arrived at the command center this morning, he learned she doesn't have any life-threatening injuries. She has a broken ankle, a couple of cracked ribs, a nasty hematoma on her head, and cuts and abrasions. She should be home from the hospital by tomorrow.

He's glad he squeezed in five hours of sleep, but lack of a full night's rest and the stress of looking for the children is catching up with him. Very soon he plans to guzzle the energy drink he stuck in his pocket. That should carry him past dark, which is only about four or five hours away. They won't be searching in the dark. At least he doesn't think so. At this pace, it's probably another hour until they reach the falls. Then, if his team hasn't found the children, they'll fan out in the woods and search for another two hours. He knows he must allocate enough time for them to return along the trail to the command center before it's too dark to see.

Stan walks a few feet ahead of the group along the trail. Unfortunately, last night's rain has washed away any sign of footprints. There's a chance, though, the children might have crossed or jumped on the trail after last night's rain. If he finds any footprints, it'll be easy to tell if they've been left by children due to their small sizes.

Even though the trail dead ends at the gorge overlooking Thunder Falls, he's confident the kids would be too frightened to go near the cliff. He does worry in the dark they might become disoriented, but he refuses to consider that scenario. The thunderous sound of the water cascading through the gorge should be enough warning to let them know they're near the falls. But of course, sometimes children are too curious.

Approaching a large, flat rock beside the trail, something shiny amongst the dead leaves catches Stan's eyes. As he approaches the object, he discovers there are two of them. They appear to be made of aluminum. They're reflecting the sun's rays. They're colorful and rectangular shaped, maybe three by five inches in size. The closer he gets he notices there's writing and pictures on them. Standing over them he sees slender red straws protruding from the objects. He quickly recognizes they're empty containers of Capri Suns.

Stan leans over and picks them up. He quickly brushes away the ants crawling on the containers. The searchers near him crowd around. The others continue looking.

Based on their condition, the Capri Suns appear as if they've recently been discarded. Prior to picking them up, he noticed small amounts of water pooled on the concave indentions

242

in the containers. This makes him believe they were discarded prior to last night's rain. Also, the presence of the ants is evidence they were recently discarded. Perhaps, they were left by the children.

Stan grabs from his belt his handheld radio provided to him for communication with the command center. "Smokey, come in."

"Yeah Stan, go ahead."

"I've found two empty Capri Suns in the leaves right off the trail to Thunder Falls. I don't know if the kids dropped them, but based on their condition they appear to have been recently discarded. Could you check with the parents to see if perhaps the kids had Capri Suns?"

"Will do."

"What da ya think, Stan? Could these be the kids?" one of the searchers asks.

"Yeah, what do you think?" another chimes in.

"Could be, but I don't know if the kids had these with them. We'll see what the parents say. While we're waiting, y'all keep searching. I'll let you know."

As the crowd around Stan disperses to continue their search, Stan continues to examine the empty Capri Sun containers. He offers a quick prayer hoping the kids left them.

"Hey Stan! Come look at this?" one of the searchers excitedly hollers. Stan drops the empty Capri Sun containers on the rock and hurries over to her, as do other searchers. "Look," she's pointing at the ground. As everyone crowds around, Stan sees what looks like a small empty baggie. Because it's clear, it could've easily been missed. He picks it up and dumps out the water which had pooled in it. He immediately notices a faint smell of peanut butter as he raises it close to his face for examination. There are tiny smears of a brown sticky substance clinging to the interior of the bag. He also notices a few tiny smears of a purple substance.

"Stan, come in," screeches from his radio. He hands the baggie to the searcher who spotted it.

"Yeah Smokey, I'm here."

"I've got some anxious parents with me. Yeah, the mom packed Capri Suns in their lunch boxes. Can you tell what flavors they are?"

"Hold on." Stan hurries back to the rock where he dropped the Capri Sun containers. He reads the labels over the radio. "Smokey, ones a fruit punch and the other one's a…lemonade."

"I've got some real excited parents with me! The mom says she packed the fruit punch for the boy and the lemonade for the girl. Great job! Where did you find them?"

"By a large rock next to the trail to the Thunder Falls. We're probably about a couple of miles or so from the falls."

"Thanks." Stan notices a tinge of concern in Smokey's voice. "Do you have any thoughts on whether they were left today or yesterday?"

"I believe yesterday. Water was pooled on the indentions in the Capri Suns, which was probably from last night's rain."

"Makes sense. Keep your team searching along the trail. Also spread them out wider in the search area. Make sure you're playing the recording every ten minutes. I'll redirect some other teams over to help you. Got it?"

"Yes sir! Will do! Hey, one more question, will you ask the parents if their kids might have also had peanut butter and jelly sandwiches?"

"Yeah, why do you ask?"

"One of my searchers found an empty baggie which appears to have some remnants of peanut butter and jelly in it."

"Hold on. Let me check." There's a pause. Stan waits. "Yep, they had peanut butter and jelly sandwiches!"

"Thanks, I guess that's just further confirmation."

"Yep! Again, great job!!

"Thanks!"

Stan attaches his radio to his belt. There's now a raucous excitement among the searchers. Some of them high five each other. "Gather round!" he hollers. "We have confirmation from the parents that these were probably left by the kids." He's holding up the Capri Sun containers and baggie for everyone to see. A loud cheer erupts from the group. Stan smiles. "Simmer down. We still haven't found them, but at least we know they

244

were here at one point. Alright, we're going to change how we're looking."

With that Stan provides instructions on the new way they're going to search. He immediately sends two fit twenty somethings sprinting ahead on the trail to get to the falls quickly in case the kids are near it. As they sprint ahead, they whoop and holler with excitement. The remaining members of the team cheer them on.

FORTY-FIVE

Tag's emotions are tangled: he's excited Maize and Jase survived whatever caused Jenny Jean to fall; astounded that evidence of their presence in the mountains was found so far away from Jenny Jean; confused as to what made them take this route; and still worried something may happen to them. His belief they're alive hasn't waned, but the stress of not knowing where they are is suffocating. There will be no peace until they're found. He's not going to wait any longer to become more active in their search.

Smokey and his close team of advisors are scrutinizing the map of the sector where the evidence was found. He's sent a runner to his command trailer to gather more detailed topographical maps of this area and the surrounding areas. They believe the topography may drive the possible routes the kids may take. It allows the search to become more strategic. The newly delivered drones will have the greatest impact on their search.

Suzy's recently returned to the command center. She left earlier to fetch the drones. Smokey was elated when Suzy told him she would supply drones for the search. He learned she recently was the lead investment banker in taking a company public which manufactures drones. She's still close to their management team, and she's a shareholder. She offered to purchase drones from this company for the search. She hastily arranged a conference call with the CEO and Smokey. They agreed on the type of drones needed for the search. Smokey determined they needed four of them. The CEO graciously donated them to the county in exchange for testimonials. Smokey quickly agreed to this condition even though he didn't have the authority. He'll beg for forgiveness later as opposed to asking for permission now. With time of the essence, he's in no mood to play politics.

Suzy chartered a jet to bring the drones to the nearest landing strip. The CEO sent one of his experts on the charter, at no charge, to quickly train the people flying the drones. Tag and Liesl were watching them practice flying the drones until Stan called. Both are uncomfortable Suzy was one of the people selected to fly a drone. She demanded it. Her reasoning was simple, and persuasive. They wouldn't have the drones without her and no one else was already trained to fly one. Smokey had no choice other than to allow her.

Every male at the command center periodically glances at Suzy while she practices flying her drone, but for reasons other than assessing her flying skills.

"Smokey," Tag interrupts the planning for the new search pattern, "I'm going to look for my children. I can't wait around here and do nothing any longer. Liesl and I talked about it. She'll wait here in case you need one of us close by, but we decided that I'm going. We feel strongly that one of us needs to be there when they're found."

The stern inflection in Tag's voice, combined with his serious demeanor, easily signals to Smokey that Tag's determined. Reasoning with Tag to remain here is probably a wasted effort, but he'll try anyway.

"Tag, I understand how badly you and Liesl want to find your children. We're trying to do that as quickly as possible. Sure, there's very good evidence that your kids were on the trail to Thunder Falls, but it looks like that evidence may be almost twenty-four hours old. They could have wandered a long way from there since then. Afterall, I think we're all surprised how far they roamed from where we found the Jenkins' girl. It might turn out that we're searching the wrong area. If we need to quickly pivot to a new area, you wouldn't be able to participate."

"I don't care. I'm going to look for them. Liesl's here if you need one of us. Now, I need you to show me the right trails to take to get to that team."

"I wish you'd reconsider, but I can't make you stay. Will you at least wait a few minutes? The people with the bloodhounds are about ten minutes away. Also, it appears that those learning to fly the drones are close to being ready. I'm going to send one of them with the dogs."

"Suzy's not going with me!" Tag interrupts.

"I didn't say she was! I'm sending her somewhere else. But, if you'll wait a few minutes for the bloodhounds to get here, I'll send you with them and with one of the drones. Will you at least do that?"

"Yeah, I'll wait," Tag reluctantly agrees, "but it better not take long!"

"It won't, I promise. Will you get some of your kids' dirty clothes for the bloodhounds? They'll need to be trained on their scent."

"Yeah."

Suddenly, Tag and Smokey find themselves surrounded by the new drone pilots, including Suzy. Tag walks away.

"Smokey, right?" Fred Stone, the company expert asks.

"Yeah."

"I've taught them what I know. I'm impressed with how quickly they've learned. You can now deploy them." Fred glances at his watch. "The pilots said they'll need to leave in about two and a half hours from now. Some regulation they said. So, I'll wait here another hour and a half in case someone needs help, but I'll have to go by then." He hands Smokey a card. "On this card is the number of our twenty-four hour a day call service center if someone needs help after I'm gone. My number's also on there, so feel free to call me for help, but it'll have to be after I land. It's about a two-hour flight. I sure hope these drones help you find the kids quickly. There's no better equipment on the market to help you find them."

"Thanks Fred." They shake hands. "You have no idea…well I guess you really do," Smokey chuckles, "how helpful this will be today and in the future. Suzy, thank you again for making this happen!"

Suzy nods.

"My pleasure," Fred smiles. "I'll get out of your way now. Do you mind if I sit in one of those camp chairs?" Fred points at a group of chairs haphazardly arranged in the trail parking lot.

"No that's fine. If we need them for any reason, I'll let you know."

"Thanks." Fred walks away.

248

"Suzy," Smokey redirects his attention. "You really don't have the proper clothes to be hiking in these mountains." He glances down at her flats. "I want you to go down to the base of the mountains and search the borders of the park and the contiguous private property. I'm gonna give you a map of where I want you to fly your drone. I need you to keep flying it in that area until I tell you to stop, or it gets too dark. Are you willing to do that?"

"Sure," she nods.

"Great, I know these drones have the capability to see in the dark, but I'm not gonna ask you to fly yours at night. I'll get these guys to fly theirs tonight," he nods toward the other newly trained drone pilots. "If we don't find the kids before tomorrow morning, can you help us tomorrow?'

"Yeah, I can help."

"Fantastic! Hopefully, we'll find them today and we won't need you tomorrow. I'll let you know. Also, again, I can't thank you enough for your wonderful gift of these drones. They're gonna make a huge difference today... and in the future."

"You're welcome, but really they're a gift from the company."

"Hey, you're the one who made it happen! Also, I'm sure the cost of chartering the plane to get them here is infinitely more expensive than these four drones."

"My pleasure. I can afford it. I'm blessed to have the money to do it."

Smokey smiles. He's noticed she's blessed in so many ways. "Okay, come over here and I'll go over the map to show you where I want you to fly your drone. If anyone bothers you, I'm gonna give you a card to show them which shows you're authorized on my behalf to do what you're doing and where you're doing it. Do you want me to send anyone with you for protection?"

"No, I can take care of myself," Suzy grins.

I bet you can Smokey thinks to himself as they walk to the table covered in colorful maps.

FORTY-SIX

The arrival of the bloodhounds amped up the excitement, and the noise, in the base camp. Tag and Liesl hope these sad looking, smelly, howling...and suddenly beautiful... dogs will find their children. If they do, they've agreed they'll get a dog for Maize and Jase. Maize and Jase have been begging for a dog, but Tag and Liesl believed they were too young for one. They now muse about how ironic it would be if it turns out what they didn't want their children to have might be what saves them.

"Liesl and Tag," Smokey strides over to them. He's accompanied by a middle-aged man of normal height with an athletic physique. The man's wearing khaki hunting pants and a hunter green, short sleeve knit shirt which accentuates his physique. His hiking boots are well worn. A navy-blue baseball cap is pulled down tightly on his head. The cap and shirt have written on them "Tracking USA, Dogs Just Wanna Have Fun!" arranged in a pattern as an emblem. The man's salt-and-pepper hair curls up under the edges of his cap. His salt-and pepper-beard is neatly trimmed. His eyes hide behind reflective sun glasses. He has a backpack slung over his left shoulder. "I want you to meet Rodney Roberts. He's the owner of these dogs and will be tracking with them today."

"Howdy folks! You can call me Rodney, Rod, or my friends call me R Squared. I'm very sorry about your kids, but these dogs here are two of my best. They'll find...I believe it's Maize and Jase?"

"That's right," Tag answers.

"Love the names! They'll find Maize and Jase. Meet Petunia and Skunk." Rodney reaches down and pets the dogs while holding their leashes. "Go ahead. They won't bite."

Liesl and Tag also pet the dogs. The dogs crane their necks, wag their tails, pant, and slobber on Tag and Liesl's hands.

"Rodney, thanks for your help. We can't tell you how much we appreciate it." Tag glances at Liesl.

"Yeah, thank you," Liesl reinforces while wiping her hands on her pants.

"Hey, my pleasure! We aim to be a blessing, don't we?" Rodney coos, squats, and rubs the dogs' heads. "We'll find 'em," he adds standing.

Tag's afraid to ask his question, but he will. It's worried him. It's been burning a hole in his soul too long to keep it suppressed any longer, "Rodney, as you can see, we had rain last night. Will that affect your dogs' ability to track?"

"Heck no! Actually, it'll improve it."

"Really?" Tag's relieved since he's been led to believe it would.

"Yeah, really. Rain makes the scent rise so it's easier for the dogs to track. You'd think that dry, hot weather would be best, but it's not. Moist weather is better, as long as it's not a downpour. A heavy rain can disperse the scent causing the dogs to become confused because the scent's all spread out, but the rain y'all had last night's perfect since I understand it was a gentle rain. It should be a good day for tracking! It would've been better if we had been able to track this morning, but we should be fine this afternoon. Right dogs?" Rodney reaches down and scratches under their necks. The dogs' tails wag faster.

"That's amazing!" Liesl interrupts.

"Yeah, these are amazing animals," Rodney continues to scratch them. "Aren't you?" he lovingly coos at the dogs. "They can smell almost one-hundred thousand times better than a human. They can smell something that's miles away and track a scent for almost two weeks."

"I had no idea they could do that. Did you have to train them to do that?" Tag asks.

"Naw, God made 'em this way. God gave us the opposable thumb and He gave them their keen sense of smell. It's hard to explain exactly how it all works. It has to do with their olfactory system. You know, how they smell. I guess the only thing that a human might be able to relate to is if I blindfolded you, then had you pick a jelly bean from a bowl of 'em, and taste it, you could probably identify the flavor without

251

seeing the jelly bean just by its taste. Well, their smell is like that, except on steroids. You couldn't find another jelly bean like the one you tasted by smelling. You'd have to taste all of them in the bowl to find one like the one you tasted. They can find similar jelly beans like the one you tasted all the way down in Rock Slide from here just by their smell! Tracking your kids' scent should be a piece a cake for ole Petunia and Skunk.

Now, Smokey said you got some of your kids' dirty clothes. I need to borrow them for a minute. I need to make sure Petunia and Skunk know what they're tracking. I'm gonna have Petunia track Maize and Skunk track Jase. Hopefully, their tracks don't veer off from each other, but in case they do, I've got each dog tracking a separate child. There's only one of me, though, so if that happens, we'll have to figure out how we'll split up. I'm guessing the tracks won't veer too much. Usually lost people stay together, unless..." Rodney stops. He realizes he's about to say something he shouldn't. There's an awkward pause.

"I'll go get the clothes," Liesl interrupts. Her eyes moisten. "I'll be right back." She turns and jogs toward the trailer.

Suzy's watched Tag out of the corner of her eye when the search-and-rescue team member reviewed the map with her of the area where she is to fly her drone. When Liesl jogs away, Suzy hustles over to the men.

"Tag, I'm going to be searching at the bottom of the mountains with the drone." Rodney raises his sunglasses to get a better look at Suzy. "If I see anything, I'll call you, okay?"

"Sure," he answers perturbed by her presence.

"It's going to be alright. We'll find them," she adds before walking away.

Tag forces a grin.

Suzy's convinced herself that Tag's merely acting rudely toward her to put up a false front so Liesl can't tell how much Tag really loves her. After seeing Liesl, she's confident there's no way he would prefer Liesl over her. She's much prettier than Liesl, and she's confident she's imminently wealthier. She can give Tag more than Liesl ever imagined. Suzy believes if she can help find his children, Tag will be so grateful that he'll choose her. They're cute kids, she can stomach living with them for a few years if it means getting Tag. Once their old enough, she'll ship them off to boarding school. She's confident she can entice him to agree. She has her ways. Also, she believes if his children don't survive this ordeal, her chances are even better that she can pull him away from Liesl. She knows he'll want to start a new life. Hanging around with that hag, Liesl, will remind him daily of the pain of losing his children. It'll destroy their marriage. At least this'll be one marriage Suzy hasn't destroyed all on her own.

Her grin widens when she reaches her car. She knows the men watching her walk to her car enjoyed the show.

As he ascends the step grade of the trail, Tag's disappointed he's let himself get out of shape. Too much entertaining clients and prospects he guesses, but deep down he knows it's primarily due to just being too lazy. Once this ordeal is over, and his family's reunited, he's decided to take better care of himself. Exercise will become a priority. Right now, though, this hike's killing him!

Once the bloodhounds caught the scent of Maize and Jase, they've hurriedly dragged Rodney along the hiking trail which winds up and down the mountain toward Thunder Falls. Tag wondered if he was the only one struggling to keep up, but the young search-and-rescue worker is also having a hard time, but of course he's carrying the case which holds the drone. Tag's only carrying unwanted pounds.

Suddenly, the bloodhounds stop. Their noses are pressed to the ground. They appear to be franticly searching.

"What's wrong?" Tag's worried.

"They've temporarily lost the scent. They'll find it in a minute. Back up, I'm gonna walk them back to pick up the scent again and then have them search in a wider arc."

Tag backs up and steps up on to a large, flat rock beside the trail. He watches Rodney work the dogs in an arc as he coaxes them backwards. When they reach the rock Tag's standing on, both dogs climb on to rock. They busily smell and howl. Tag hops off. Rodney pulls the dogs off the rock. He drags them so they're working the area downhill from the rock. The dogs continue to busily sniff in the leaves in a haphazard pattern. They've stopped howling. Rodney drags the dogs to the uphill side of the trail across from the rock. The dogs are no longer haphazard in their pattern of sniffing. They're pulling Rodney toward the forest above the trail. They've also started howling again.

"It looks like your kids left the trail here and struck out into the forest," Rodney yells above the din of the dogs. "Are you willing to follow them?"

Tag's confused. Why would Maize and Jase leave the trail? That doesn't make sense to him. He'd convinced himself they would be too scared to strike out into the forest. His anxiety spikes. He's worried something may have scared them. Was something chasing them? More importantly, was this something that could hurt them?

"Yeah, let's go!" Tag yells.

"Hey…uh…what's your name?" Rodney asks the guy carrying the drone.

"Brian."

"Brian, call Smokey on your radio. Tell him if the team searching this sector hasn't found the kids or any evidence of them, to redirect some of them to this rock." Rodney nods at the rock while holding back the howling dogs. "Once they get here, they need to follow the trail we're about to cut through the woods. I've got some fluorescent tape we'll leave as markers on trees so they can follow us. Got it?"

"Yes sir Mr. Rodney." Brian removes his radio and calls Smokey.

"Tag," Rodney asks. "Reach into my backpack. You'll find a roll of fluorescent pink tape. Remove it. Also, there're some scissors. I want you constantly cutting about a foot of tape as we track. Every twenty-five yards or so slap a strip of it on a tree so the searchers will be able to follow us. Can you do that?"

"Yes, I can!" Tag unzips the backpack and removes the items Rodney requested.

"Great! Now go ahead and cut the first strip and place it on the rock pointed in the direction we're about to go. Cut two smaller pieces and place them at forty-five-degree angles on either side of the end of the strip on the rock closest to me so that it forms an arrow pointed in this direction." Rodney nods up hill. "Brian, did you talk to Smokey?"

"Yes sir Mr. Rodney."

"How 'bout dropping the mister."

"Yes sir,"

"Tag, hurry up. I can't hold these dogs back much longer!"

Tag nods, quickly peels the tape, cuts the strips, and forms an arrow with the pieces pointing toward Rodney and the dogs.

"Okay, I'm done. Let's go!"

Rodney immediately eases his restraint. The dogs leap forward, howling, as they begin their ascent. Their heads are down and their snouts hover above the floor of the forest. They plow a trail through the damp, dead leaves as they climb. Tag and Brian fall in behind Rodney and the dogs.

FORTY-SEVEN

Maize and Jase are worn out. They're also cried out. No tears remain. Their cheeks are rosy and sting from their frequent rubbing away of tears. Their noses drip. They're hoarse from shouting for help. That doesn't stop them, though. They continue to shout, but less frequently. Their shouts are weaker. Their throats hurt. It made them thirsty. They drank their last Capri Suns.

When they removed their lunchboxes from their backpacks to retrieve their Capri Suns, something awful happened. Maize's teddy bear accidently fell from her backpack to the ground. The coyotes quickly leaped upon it. One of them grabbed the teddy bear's head with its teeth and lifted it from the ground. Another one immediately grabbed a leg of the teddy bear with its teeth. A vicious, snarling tug-of-war ensued. Maize screamed in horror when the teddy bear's leg tore off. Soon stuffing was spread across the forest floor as the coyotes fought over the teddy bear's severed limbs. Sadness and rage roared in Maize as she wept. She was inconsolable. Maize's pain made Jase weep. They huddled closely weeping until exhaustion stemmed their tears.

Maize and Jase possess unconscious incompetence of time. Due to their ages, they're unaware of how it works, and they don't possess the knowledge to track it. Their concept of time is based on when routine daily events occur. They know when it's dark they go to bed. When there's light outside, they can get up, unless their parents tell them it's too early and to go back to bed. They also know they go to school soon after awakening, except when their parents stay home. Their parents and teachers tell them when it's time to eat. Their mother turns on the TV when their favorite TV shows are on. Experience, though, has taught them to be able to judge when the day begins moving closer to night. They've noticed from their perch the

256

shadows of the trees creeping longer. A sign to them that the light's getting closer to becoming swallowed by the dark. They wonder why their mommy and daddy haven't come to get them.

"Do you think they heard us?" Jase wearily asks.

"I dunno."

"I think so."

"Why?" Maize curiously looks at him.

"Aren't we close to home?"

"I think so."

"Then they had to hear us!"

Maize's voice rises, "Then where are they?"

Jase ponders Maize's frustrated question for a few seconds. He shrugs his shoulders. They sit in silence and stare at the coyotes below. They're entertained by pups frolicking in the leaves.

"Maybe they're nice dogs." Jase wonders aloud.

"I'm scared of 'em."

"Me, too."

They sit silently and continue watching the pups. They notice the mommy and daddy coyotes are watching them. Frequently, one of the coyotes in the group will stir up the rest of them. They'll yap and howl for a few minutes, and then become quiet. It's happening now. It scares Maize and Jase.

"I don't like that," Maize states with a deadpan expression when the noise ceases.

"Me either."

Maize scoots closer to her brother and grabs his hand. She glances at his tear-streaked, raw-cheeks, dirty face. He forces a grin. His grin's comforting. She grins. No words are spoken. They continue to watch the coyotes below.

"Momma! Daddy! Come get us!" Maize suddenly screams in desperation.

"Yeah! We wanna go home!" Jase's voice cracks while screaming.

The coyotes stand, stir, and glare hungrily at them while pacing below. Some of them yap nervously. Maize and Jase sit quietly and listen longingly for their parents' response. Nothing…just like every other time. They scan the forest hoping to see them.

257

"I'm tired." Jase interrupts the silence after a few minutes.

"Me too."

"Do you think momma and daddy will come before its dark?"

Maize shrugs her shoulders. "I hope so."

They lean against the trunk of the tree. Their backpacks provide a soft, lumpy cushion for their backs and heads. They squirm to find comfort. Their eyelids are heavy. They struggle to stay awake.

Suddenly, a horrible, loud, blood-curdling scream startles them! It startles the coyotes, too. The scream's unceasing and undulating. The coyotes are immediately alert and skittish. Crashing through the forest is a huge man. A giant of a man! He's screaming as he lumbers. His movement is oafish. He's awkwardly brandishing a huge tree limb. Maize and Jase are frozen in fear. The coyotes aren't. The pack is spilling away as quickly as possible in the opposite direction from the lumbering man and his frightening screams. A rear guard protects the pups as the pack skedaddles.

The man's wearing faded blue overalls and a white t-shirt. As he comes closer, they notice the shape of his head is unusual. It's longer than normal. It's also shaved. His ears are huge. There's something unusual about his eyes, too.

Maize's fear swiftly changes to curiosity. This man's familiar. She glances at Jase. He's terrified. He's clawing at the trunk of the tree as if he's trying to climb it. His eyes are filling with tears. Maize glances back at the man. A wave of comfort overcomes her. She recognizes the man.

Maize again glances at Jase and yells excitedly, "Jase! Jase! It's Mo! He's nice! I promise, he's nice! He won't hurt us." Maize again focuses on the man and pleads, "You won't hurt us will you Mo? He won't hurt us Jase!"

Mo reaches the tree. The coyotes have disappeared. He looks up at Maize and Jase. Maize's smiling. Jase is now hiding behind her.

"Mo won't hurt us, will you Mo?" Maize excitedly repeats.

Suddenly, appearing on Mo's distorted face is a huge smile. He utters in a deep voice, "May-Z. Friend." He reaches into his pocket and removes the wilted clover chain Maize gave him a few days ago. He holds it high on a crooked finger.

"My bracelet!" Maize screams in delight. "You still have it!" Mo's smile grows wider. Jase watches this unfold while peeking from behind Maize's back. He's comforted by his sister's excitement, but still leery of this giant with the scary face.

Mo's expression changes. "Down," Mo utters while motioning with his arm. "Home," he points in the direction from which he came.

"Jase! Mo's gonna take us home! He's gonna take us home!"

"Home," Mo smiles again at them.

"What...what about...the mean dogs?" Jase asks still cautious about leaving the tree stand with this strange man.

"Ky-oats. Scare...away. No hurt." Mo answers.

"What'd he say?" Jase's puzzled.

Maize ignores his question. She's already climbed onto the two-by-fours to make her way down. Mo reaches out to steady her as she quickly climbs down. When she reaches the ground, she hugs his leg. He stoops. She hugs him around his neck. He softly returns her hug. He's beaming.

"Come on down Jase! Mo's gonna take us home!" Maize hollers as she releases her hug.

Jase's reticent, but he's comforted by his sister's excitement and she appears unafraid. Also, the giant hasn't eaten her. He slowly rises and steps onto the first two-by-four. As he carefully descends, suddenly, the two-by-four he steps onto loosens and turns ninety degrees. His legs slide off. He clings to the two-by-four above him while his legs dangle and kick for traction. His grip loosens. "Help!" he fearfully screams. Immediately he's lifted up and pulled away from the tree. He's gently placed on to the ground. He turns. He's looking straight up at the giant, whose smiling at him. His tension releases. "Thank you," he shyly utters.

"See, I told you he was nice," Maize taunts.

Maize's tiny hand subtly grasps Mo's pinky. It's soft against his calloused skin. A long-absent warmth surges reminding him how much he's missed the gentleness of a soft touch. His smile widens as he casts his eyes downward at Maize. She's beaming a smile back at him.

"Nice," Mo softly repeats. He points with his other hand, "Home."

FORTY-EIGHT

Adrenaline pushes Tag forward. He's tired, but he's not about to stop. He must find his children soon. He's thanked God numerous times for the dogs finding their scents and tracking them. Since he knows where they've been, the task of finding his children doesn't seem as overwhelming as it was last night. Now it's a matter of finding where they are. The search area has narrowed. He believes it's just a matter of time. He's a bundle of nerves.

Time, though, is becoming his enemy. All searching will halt when it's dark. Smokey's cautioned the mountains are too dangerous in the dark. Earlier Tag checked his cell phone for the time. His battery was dead. He forgot to charge his phone. Tag, though, possesses conscious competence regarding time. Determining the approximate time is automatic to him due to his knowledge and experience. Based on earlier checks of time, he knows there's not much daylight left.

He needs to find his children before they're forced to spend another night in a dark, forbidding forest. Just as it's dangerous for the searchers in the dark, he's concerned it's even more dangerous for his children due to their young ages and immaturity. He finds it amazing and encouraging they've made it this far. That fills him with hope.

He still senses they're alive. That belief's comforting. It keeps pushing him forward. He's confident he'll find them because he's following a trail they've trekked. As opposed to before, when he was passively waiting at base camp, he now feels he's doing what a father should do since he's actively searching for his children.

Every so often he screams their names praying for a reaction. So far...nothing. He won't give up. At least until it's dark. He's thought about continuing his search in the dark, but he knows he'll become a distraction if he's lost or injured. As hard as it might be, he must trust Smokey and stand down when it's dark.

In the distance, Tag spots an imposing wall of natural granite. The dogs are headed straight for it. Quickly they reach the wall. At the base of the wall the dogs howl and circle randomly as if confused. When Tag reaches them, he notices they're also stepping over two empty, plastic water bottles.

"Move dogs!" Rodney shouts while tugging them away from the empty bottles.

Tag reaches down and picks one of them up. It's not muddy, it's not caked with flecks of dead leaves, nor does it have any water in it. The paper labels are loose but not dirty. Based on the bottle's condition, Tag believes it's recently been discarded.

"What do ya think Rodney?" Tag asks excitedly.

"Looks like it's recently been left here to me."

"I agree."

"Do you know if your kids had bottled water?"

"According to my wife they did. She packed some in their backpacks." Suddenly, Tag's emotions spike when he recognizes the label, "And this is the brand we buy!"

"Looks like the dogs are on the right trail! Aren't you Petunia and Skunk?" Rodney reaches into his pocket and feeds a snack to each dog. "Good dogs! Good dogs!"

In the wall in front of them is a crevice. Tag peers into the crevice and spies a piece of paper. He crawls onto the rocks and reaches into the crevice to grab the paper. When he snatches it, he climbs down and stands staring at the paper. Tears fill his eyes. Awkwardly written in red are "Maize" and "Jase." There's also a drawing of an arrow.

"They were here." Tag shows the paper to Rodney while wiping away tears with the back of his other hand. Brian curiously peers over Rodney's shoulder and reads the names.

"Which way was the arrow pointing?" Brian asks.

"I didn't notice," Tag answers. "I'm not sure Maize understood she needed it to point in the direction they were headed. She's never had a good sense of direction."

"Don't get discouraged," Rodney interrupts. "This is a wonderful sign they're alive and we're on the right track. Unfortunately," Rodney looks at his watch, "we're out of time.

As much as this may hurt, we need to start heading back. Even leaving now, I'm not sure we're gonna make it before nightfall."

"How about a few more minutes?" Tag pleads. "Can the dogs tell which way they went?"

"Sure they can, but we need to wait until tomorrow. Smokey's orders. Also, for our safety and the safety of the dogs." It's clear to Rodney that Tag's disheartened. "Uh...Brian, yes Brian. I'm gonna water the dogs and let them rest for a few minutes. Why don't you fly that contraption over this rock wall and see what you can see? Possibly they're on the other side of it."

"Will do!"

"Before you get started, hand your hand-held radio to Tag. Tag you call Smokey and let him know what we've found."

Tag grins. Brian removes the radio from its holster and hands it to Tag.

"Just press this button and talk," Brian instructs.

Tag raises the radio to his mouth and presses the button, "Smokey, this is Tag Ryder. Come in please."

The crackle of static is interrupted, "Tag, this is Smokey. I gotcha. What's up?"

"The dogs have tracked Maize and Jase to a crevice in a large granite wall. We found empty water bottles outside the crevice and a paper inside the crevice where Maize printed their names. They were here!"

"Fantastic! Any idea of how close you might be to them?"

"No, but there was no water pooling in the bottles, so I'm thinking that they must have left them today, otherwise some of the rain from last night would have collected in the bottles."

"Great detective work! Sounds reasonable to me."

"Tell him I'm texting him our location," Rodney interrupts.

"Rodney says he's texting you our location."

"Tell R squared I appreciate it. It'll help further narrow the search. Tag sorry to disappoint you, but I was just about to call in all the search teams for the night. It'll be dark soon and we can't take any chances. Again, I'm sorry."

"I understand. We don't want anyone to get hurt looking for Maize and Jase. We're gonna send the drone up for a quick look while Rodney gives the dogs some water and rests them for a few minutes."

"I pray you'll spot them."

"Thanks. All prayers are appreciated. I've been doing that constantly. I'll now be praying for God to protect them another night. Is Liesl around?"

"No, she's in the trailer, do you want me to get her?"

"No, just tell her what we found. Tell her I'm sure they made it through last night and I know God will protect them another night. Oh…and tell her I love her."

"Will do. I hope to hear good news from you soon, but if not, I'll see you in a little while. Be careful on your way back. It's easy to get hurt in the dark."

"Thanks! Over and out."

Tag watches as Brian carefully navigates the drone to avoid the overhanging tree limbs.

Rodney's bothered by the secret he's keeping from Tag. To tell Tag, though, will create additional stress. Stress which may not be warranted. But, based on his experience as a tracker, he knows a bear has been here. The evidence is fresh. It worries him. He knows a bear won't stop in the dark. He prays it's not tracking the kids.

FORTY-NINE

Suzy's frustrated. She doesn't like searching by herself. She's always craved being the center of attention, especially around men. They've never disappointed her.

She understood why Smokey banished her to searching along the public roads at the edge of the mountains. She wasn't dressed appropriately for hiking up and down the steep slopes. If the children aren't found before morning, she's decided to buy appropriate hiking clothes when the outdoor gear store in Rock Slide opens. Then she'll join the search in the mountains. Her entire career in investment banking involved working on a team. Working alone is for the birds. Her only reason in doing it this time is to impress Tag.

It's extremely boring to drive a mile, park, unload the drone, fly it, concentrate on the viewfinder, which only shows tree after tree after tree, land it, load it back in the car, and then repeat the process a mile down the road. If she didn't love Tag, she would've quit by now. Day dreaming has stemmed her monotony. She's fantasized about sipping a glass of wine while relaxing in a bubble bath of warm water. Of course, in her fantasy she's added Tag to her tub. Since the sun has dropped behind the mountains, she knows soon her fantasy will become reality, except without Tag. One day, she's sure, he'll join her. Men have never been able to resist her when she sets her mind on them.

"Whoa!" she suddenly exclaims. Something's caught her eye as the drone hurriedly passed over the forest. She reverses its course.

"Oh…my…God!" she mutters. On the screen she's watching a large man in overalls walking along a deeply rutted, old logging road. Walking on either side of him are two children. The large man appears to be carrying backpacks, but she's not sure. The children appear to about the age of Tag's children. The

265

taller child appears to be a girl and the smaller child appears to be a boy. She's not sure if it's Tag's children. She's only seen their pictures on the flyer. The drone is too far away to clearly see their faces. Also, based on their movement, the children don't seem to be forced to be with this hulking man. They seem to be comfortable walking beside him, even though his gait is clumsy and awkward. In fact, it looks like the girl is animated and having a conversation with the large oafish man. The boy is skipping. The children and man don't seem to match, though. The man's dressed plainly in overalls and what appears to be a t-shirt, while the children seem to be dressed in coordinated clothes from a nice children's shop. Maybe they're wearing hand-me-downs purchased at a thrift store or the clothes were given to them by a charity.

Suzy's confused as she carefully flies the drone to keep these three individuals in her viewfinder. She's not sure what she should do. Should she try to confront them? What if it's simply a father and his children coming home from a day in the woods? But then again, what if it IS Tag's children? She would a hero to Tag. Surely, this would help sway him to choose her.

Suzy glances away from the viewfinder. She scans the horizon to spot the drone. She can't see it. There's a ridge containing tall hardwoods between her and the drone. She steers the drone higher. Suddenly, off in the distance, it appears as a tiny speck on the horizon above the trees hovering in a position which is northeast of her. She now has an idea of where they are, but she knows she can't climb the ridge fast enough to catch them.

"What should I do?" she exclaims. Her worrying is causing her to become frantic. "Calm down," she scolds herself. "Think. Think." She implements breathing exercises she learned to stay calm when it appeared deals were on the verge of collapsing.

"Aha!" she shouts. She'll make sure it's them before deciding what to do next. She'll drop the drone as low as she can hoping they'll see it. When they look up, she'll be able to tell whether it's them.

The drone still hovers high above them. She navigates it above and along the rough road in the direction they're traveling.

She's trying to spot a clearing where she can lower the drone. Quickly a clearing comes into view. Surprisingly, she finds the clearing is an unkempt yard next to a shabby home. As she maneuvers the drone to scan the area, she also spots a large garden and sees where the home's rutted driveway empties into the road she's on.

Quickly she steers the drone over the three walkers to ensure they're headed toward the home. She then again steers the drone over the clearing and lowers it to about fifty feet above where the trio will emerge from the logging road into the clearing. She's glued to the viewfinder in anticipation as she watches for them to emerge. Nervous energy and excitement surge as she believes she's about to find the missing children. Tag will be so grateful! She licks her lips.

The trio appear on the rutted road headed toward the drone. As they come closer her excitement rises. She's not one hundred percent sure these are Tag's children, but they sure look like them. Suddenly, the trio stops when they step into the clearing. They look up at the drone. She believes it must be them now that she can clearly see their faces. She quickly steers the drone away. Why are they with this strange man? Are they in danger? She's decided to sneak up on them to get a better look. It'll be dark soon. That'll provide cover for her covert operation.

She's bothered by the face of the large man. She was focused on the children's faces, so she didn't concentrate on his face. It was a quick glance at his face. It appeared to be distorted, but it was a quick impression. It's made her uncomfortable, but not afraid since the children don't seem to be afraid of him. Again, she needs to get a better look.

Mr. Jimmy rises from his chair under the covered porch when he spots Mo and the children ambling across the weed infested lawn. Even though he sent Mo to find the missing children, he's surprised he did. He's also surprised they came with Mo. Usually, children run away in fear of Mo. He now knows Mo was right when he said he recognized Maize. Mr. Jimmy's confused how this relationship developed, but his confusion can't dampen his glee or hide his hideous smile.

"Well, what ya got there boy?" Mr. Jimmy hollers as he steps off the porch into the waning light.

Mo smiles, "I...did...good."

"Yes sir re, ya did good boy! Proud a ya!"

Mo's grin widens. Maize and Jase ease behind Mo, wary of this wiry, unkempt, rough old man. His demeanor frightens them.

"Hey young'uns." Mr. Jimmy stoops. "Is Mr. Tag Ryder yo daddy?" They nod their heads.

"Good. Good." He stands. "I know he and yo mama are missin' y'all. I'm sure they've been worried sick. Y'all hungry?"

Again, they nod their heads, this time more vigorously.

"Boy, I got yer supper on the stove. There's plenty for dem, too. Go on in da house and eat. I'll be in shortly."

Mo, still smiling, nods his head. He smiles at Maize and Jase, "Come." When Mo leads the children into the house, they take a wide berth when they pass Mr. Jimmy.

Suzy peers through the gate from behind the trunk of a large, old, gnarled red oak growing beside the road. It's large enough to conceal her body. Daylight is rapidly disappearing. She doesn't spot anyone in the yard. Her plan is to creep as close to the house as possible, hopefully without being seen, to get a good look at the children.

It's been a while since she's experienced this much nervous anticipation. The thrill of the deal always excited her. The chance it could crater at the last minute created a burst of adrenaline which was captivating. She never felt more alive living on the edge of success or failure, especially when millions of dollars of compensation were on the line. She was an adrenaline junky, at least that's her layman's term for her diagnosis while in therapy. It's what led to her drug abuse. When she didn't have deals, she used the drugs to artificially create the thrill. She's worked hard to avoid being swallowed by the rush again. She's crumbling, though. Her pursuit of Tag is evidence. She's fully surrendered to the rush as she creeps through the woods closer to the home.

It's now dark enough for her to easily see what's happening inside the home due to the inside lights illuminating its contents and activities. The rain from last night has dampened the leaves enough to keep her footsteps muffled as she tiptoes from tree to tree. Her heart's racing. She's loving it! Inwardly she's convincing herself she'll avoid the drugs this time.

She's stealthily slinked along the edge of the woods around the side of the house, straining to look through each window for the children. When she's made her way to the back of the house, she suddenly spots them through a screen door. They're sitting at a table eating with the large, oafish man. She quickly checks her surroundings to see if she can spot anyone outside. It's clear. She takes a deep breath and darts from the cover of the trees into the yard. It's exhilarating! She reaches an outside wall and presses her body against it attempting not to be seen. She slowly edges along the wall toward the screen door. She can hear the voices of those eating at the table.

When she reaches the edge of the house next to the stairs leading up to the small back porch she squats. She waddles along the edge of the raised back porch keeping her head below the floor. She's glad she's maintained her exercise routine. When she reaches the steps, she slowly raises her head so she can peer into the home.

Her heart leaps for joy! It's Tag's daughter! No doubt. She can't see the boy's face because his back's to her. She's certain, though, it must be Tag's son.

Suzy quickly lowers her head, waddles back to the wall, stands, creeps along the edge of the wall, and then darts back to the cover of the woods. When she reaches the woods, she pauses to scan the area to see if she was spotted. Seeing no one, she relaxes, although her heart's still racing.

Suzy carefully creeps deeper into the woods. It's hard for her to see where she's going in the darkness. The light streaming from the home's windows projects enough of a glow to allow her to distinguish shapes in the woods so she can navigate without injury. When she can no longer see the home, she stops and removes her cell phone from her pocket. It frightens her when she realizes she never placed it in silent mode while sneaking up to the house. She's thankful she didn't receive a random text message, email, or call which would have given her away.

Her face is bathed in light from her cell phone as she scrolls though her contacts for Tag. She presses "call" when she finds his contact and places the phone to her ear. It rolls to his voicemail.

"Tag, this is Suzy," she whispers. "I've found your children! They're in a home off…crap! I don't know the name of the road! The name on the mailbox is Quick, though. I'll call you back in a minute with the name of the road."

Suzy terminates the call and swipes her screen looking for her maps ap. Suddenly, something uncomfortable is pressing against her back.

"Hold it right there lady." Suzy's immediately overcome with fear. "I want ya to close that phone and hold it above yer head. I'm gonna take it from ya. The barrel of my shotgun pressed against yer back what's give me the rite to do it. Also, yer trespassin' on my land."

"I'm sorry, mister, I…"

"I didn't say ya could talk! Not a word. Now hold it up."

Suzy raises the phone above her head and begins to turn.

"No mam! Don't ya turn. My barrel's just fine pressed against yer back."

Suzy freezes. Her heart races. She's having difficulty implementing her breathing exercise to calm herself. Her phone's quickly snatched from her raised hand.

"I bet yer the one flyin' that contraption over my property just a little while ago. I don't 'preciate that neither."

"Mister, I…"

"Lady! What part of don't talk don't you understand? Now, shut yer trap! You ought not be trespassin' on other people's land. That's a crime. We don't take kindly to criminals 'round here. Now I gotta hold ya until the sheriff gets here."

Suzy relaxes when she learns her fate. She knows the sheriff will straighten all this out and he'll be thankful she found the missing children, even if she did have to trespass. Again, she's confident in her persuasive powers with…

The strike to the back of Suzy's head from the butt of Mr. Jimmy's shotgun sends her crashing to the ground. She's out cold.

270

FIFTY

The bright, exposed light bulb dangling from a wire over the kitchen table creates moving shadows as it gently swings in the breeze from wind blowing through the screen door. Its harsh light illuminates the three new friends, who momentarily are silent as they hastily devour their crude meal. The meat tastes strange to Maize and Jase, but they're too hungry to complain. They're so hungry they fail to notice cockroaches scurrying along the edge of the baseboard over the peeling linoleum floor searching for fallen crumbs. The concoction of rice and Spam, with sides of field peas, tomatoes, and cornbread, are filling.

"Good?" Mo breaks the silence. Both children nod in agreement. Mo smiles. "I grow...in...garden," he proudly points to his plate. The children briefly glance at him and then continue their feast.

"Burp!" unexpectantly rushes from Jase's mouth. "'cuse me," he hastily apologizes while flushing with embarrassment.

Maize giggles. Her shoulders bounce as she tries to suppress her glee.

Mo smiles, then he forces from his gut a loud belch.

Maize now laughs uncontrollably. Jase joins her. Mo guffaws.

Suddenly, they all jump as the slamming screen door startles them. Mr. Jimmy's wide eyed. He frightens Maize and Jase. Their laughing stops. Uncomfortable silence reigns.

Mr. Jimmy's face contorts to a sleazy smile, "I spoke to yer daddy. He's gonna come getcha tomorrow. Mo, you take'm to yer room. Watch yer videos. Then y'all go to bed. I'll clean up."

"Why isn't he coming to pick us up now?" Jase softly protests.

"Yeah?" Maize agrees.

"He didn't say. Now do as I say!" he sneers.

Fear rises in Maize and Jase causing their appetites to ebb. They quickly scamper from their chairs and cower behind Mo. Tears well.

Mo's empathetic. At times he too fears his father. He's also experiencing a feeling normally reserved for his plant and animal friends. He felt this same feeling earlier in the day when he saw Maize and her brother trapped by the coyotes. He senses his new friends need his protection. His fear of his father and need to protect his new friends confuses him.

Mr. Jimmy quickly recognizes in Mo's facial expressions and movements that he's confused. He knows he must quickly diffuse him before he triggers, or Mo will become uncontrollable. "I'm sorry to snap at y'all. Yer daddy said he loved ya, but he just couldn't make it tonight. He'll be here tomorrow, I guarantee it!

Hey boy, grab that jar in the cabinet with the suckers. Why don't ya get one and one for each of these here young'uns. You can eat 'em in yer room. Would ya'll like a sucker?"

Maize and Jase nod. They still cower behind Mo. Mo smiles lessening Mr. Jimmy's concerns about Mo's possible agitation. Mo rises from the table and grabs the jar in the cabinet. He unscrews the top and lowers it so Maize and Jase can see what's inside. The siblings study the contents and then select the color of their choice. Mo then grabs his favorite, a red sucker. He again screws the lid on the jar and replaces it on the shelf in the cabinet. Mo knows it's a special treat when he's allowed to pick a sucker from the jar. Mo tears the paper from the sucker and crams it into his mouth. Maize and Jase follow suit.

"Come," Mo mumbles while twirling the sucker with his tongue. He leaves the kitchen with the children following him.

"Now please close the door to yer room," Mr. Jimmy hollers from the kitchen.

When they enter Mo's room, Mo flips on the overhead light. Just as in the kitchen, a single bulb hanging from a wire in the center of the ceiling starkly illuminates the room. White paint flakes from portions of the wall. A simple, single, unmade bed is shoved into the corner. Beside the bed is a bedside table. A large, ratty, stuffed chair is in the middle of the room. It faces the thickest TV Maize and Jase have ever seen. The TV rests on a small table which has an open shelf below the top of the table. On the shelf is large metal box. Smaller black, plastic boxes, all the same size, are neatly stacked next to the metal box on the shelf. Wires run from the back of the box to the back of the TV. A small chest of drawers stands against the wall next to the TV. Stacks of well-worn, thin, colorful books are haphazardly scattered on top of the chest of drawers. A well-worn, ratty throw rug is in the center of the room. Aside from the TV, what fascinates Maize and Jase the most are the many stuffed animals lying about the room and on the bed. The room also has an odor, like the smell of their grandparents' basement.

Mo closes the door and points to the chair. "Sit," he commands. Maize and Jase climb into the chair which faces the TV. They watch Mo turn on the TV. It emits a static sound as the picture pulsates a multitude of black, gray, and white dots. Mo also presses a button on the metal box. It illuminates. He presses another button on the metal box and up pops an open metal casing on top of the box. Mo reaches for one of the smaller black, plastic boxes. He opens it and removes another black, plastic box from inside it. He turns to Maize and Jase, and with a huge smile proclaims, "Larry…and…Bob." Maize and Jase are confused by his comment. Mo's disappointed they aren't smiling. He places this box in the open metal casing and pushes it down. It disappears into the metal box. He presses another button on the metal box. The static is silenced. The picture turns blue. Mo steps back clapping his hands in excitement. Suddenly a scratchy video appears. Mo hums to the music while clapping his hands. Maize and Jase are quickly introduced to world of "Veggie Tales." Something they've never seen before.

Mo excitedly waves his arms at them and cries, "Up! Up! Up!" Maize and Jase hurriedly climb from the chair. Mo plops down in the chair. Again, he waves his arms, but this time he cries, "Sit! Sit! Sit!" Maize and Jase climb onto his lap. Soon they're entranced by the singing, dancing, and hopping vegetables and fruits. Mo hums the songs as Maize and Jase watch the stories unfold.

Before the video is over, Maize and Jase are fast asleep. Mo gently places each of them in his bed and returns to his videos. Periodically he glances over at them, smiles, and softly whispers, "Love…friends."

While they watched the video, Mr. Jimmy was busy. He quickly cleared away the dishes and food. Then he left the house, but quickly returned struggling with Suzy's limp body. He hurriedly carried her into his room and closed the door. He left the room only once to retrieve a rope, a sharp knife, duct tape, and a bucket full of cold beers.

FIFTY-ONE

Tag's wrung out. He's running on empty. The emotional stress and strenuous hike have drained him. He needs rest to recharge. He's found a secluded spot in the woods just outside the border of base camp which isn't illuminated by the artificial lights. He sits in a camp chair, alone with his thoughts, hidden from view by the shroud of night. His light jacket keeps him warm in the cool mountain night air. He's bunched the collar, so his face is partially hidden. He doesn't want to be recognized.

He appreciates everyone's concern for his children, but their frequent expressions of compassion are no longer consoling. They've become convicting. They reinforce his failure as a father to protect his family. Here in the obscurity of the darkness and the cloak of an oversized jacket he's found an oasis of anonymity. Smokey and his team know where to find him if he's needed, but for the moment, he treasures his uninterrupted solitude.

When his parents arrived earlier in the evening, he put on a brave face. He needed to be strong. He knew his parents were hurting, after all Maize and Jase are their grandchildren and he's their son. It had been a long day on the road for them. They must've been tired. He feels guilty for fussing at them to go home to rest, but he thought the travel, the stress of sitting around worrying, trying to make small talk, and the spartan conditions at the base camp might cause one, or both, of them to incur a health problem. He can't manage an additional boulder added to his heaping pile at this time. There's really nothing for anyone to do anyway. The search has shut down for the night. They can come back in the morning.

He's glad Liesl's sleeping. It took coaxing and prescription drugs to do the trick, but she needs the rest. Understandably so, she's been at her wit's end. Her emotions are on edge. In addition to her children being lost, Tag knows her learning about his past relationship with Suzy has created even greater stress. Their conversations have been curt and emotionally charged. It was helpful for them to be away from each other this afternoon while Tag was searching. She seemed to be warmer toward him when he returned, but he knows it'll take some time for her to thaw. Saving his marriage will become his top priority after he finds his children.

Tag's finding it hard for him to slay his sleep monster. He's had to jerk his head up a few times to prevent from nodding off to sleep. Each attempt is becoming harder.

Suddenly, his thoughts are interrupted by singing. He shakes his head to ensure he's not dreaming. He recognizes the familiar song and softly sings along with the words:

"I once was lost but now I'm found, was blind, but now I see. 'Twas grace that taught my heart to fear and grace my fears relieved. How precious..."

Tears stream down his face. He can no longer sing the convicting verses of "*Amazing Grace*." His tears choke him. He heaves for air as he sobs. His emotional pain is almost unbearable.

Suddenly he understands the difference between happiness and pleasure. He realizes pleasure is fulfillment of a carnal, emotional, gnawing desire. It's an insatiable beast which claws at the soul wanting to be satisfied over and over again. It's powerfully addictive and may leave a sweeping wake of destruction. He knows it's devoured powerful kingdoms, successful companies, and loving families. Now it's trapped him. Convicting guilt is its antidote. Something he hadn't experienced until now.

He was bored. Unappreciative. He'd been consumed by a fantasy, wanting to relive the insatiable pleasure he enjoyed with Suzy. It was daring. It was exciting. It was wild and wicked. He was lost and blinded by his beguiling, passionate memories. He was lusting for what was fleeting and ignoring what was authentic. His craving was an escape from reality. His priorities were out of whack.

He now understands what real love looks like. It's not found in the lust for fleshly pleasures. That's fleeting. That's selfish. That's ultimately hurtful. It's revealed in the mundane.

276

It's reading a bedtime story when you're dog tired. It's wiping your toddler's nose. It's spending your savings on your family. It's punishing your child for his own good. It's doing without. It's being present. It's a belly laugh with good friends. It's a kiss on the cheek. It's praying for others. It's the warmth of a hug when you feel defeated. It's what carries you through the daily grind. It's amazement that your imperfections are ignored. It's what motivates you. It's what generates hope. It fuels confidence. It's special memories. It's sharing life's experiences. It casts the dreams of the future.

He's been enlightened to the truth. It's his loving relationship with his family which brings him true happiness and contentment. Now that there's a chance it's all possibly sliding away, it's more than he can bear. The stiff upper lip is gone. He's been rendered raw and naked.

He's filled with shame. He feels dirty. Unworthy of being a father and a husband. He's failed miserably. His children are lost. They must be frightened and hungry. What father allows that to happen? A horrible, selfish son-of-a-bitch! What kind of a man doesn't treasure a woman like Liesl? An egotistical, immoral idiot!

He wonders why it took the unsatisfying awkwardness of a fantasy coming to life and the devastating disappearance of his children to teach him this valuable life lesson. He took for granted what should have been prized and craved what was embarrassingly phony. He recognizes he has a lot to be thankful for. He continues to pray that he's able to recapture it. He promises his life will be different.

He's convinced Billy's behind this gut punch. Billy's now showing him the answer to his question from the other day. Billy's thrown him a life preserver. Tag's now desperately flailing to grab it before he drowns in his foolishness. He must save everything he loves before it all slides away.

Tag struggles from his chair and falls prostrate. Quickly he crumbles to the ground, sobbing uncontrollably as the singing voices continue beating his ears with the convicting verses. His fingers claw at the rocky earth as if trying to find anything to hold on to in case demons snatch him away to some horrible fate due to his ugly sins. In the enveloping dark, all alone, racked in deep, debilitating despair he bears his sins to God and asks for forgiveness. He prays like he's never prayed before.

Slowly a sense of calm wells, as if some wonderful, soothing drug has been injected into his body. It's warm and inviting, but more than anything it's a sense of profound love.

Tag pushes up on his knees. He wipes the tears and dirt from his face with the sleeve of his jacket. It leaves muddy streaks across his cheeks. He struggles to his feet. He summons all his strength and courage, and steps from the darkness into the light.

On the other side of base camp, he recognizes six members of his church's choir singing a Capella. A small gathering of people is positioned in a ragged semi-circle in a front of them. They've joined in the singing.

He suddenly spies Liesl with Pastor Honeycutt. The singing must have awakened her. He makes a beeline for her.

Liesl loses her balance when Tag wraps her with an unexpected hug. His python-like embrace steadies her. She's shocked by the thin streaks of muddy tears on his cheeks and his blood shot eyes. She's overcome with empathy as he continually repeats how sorry he is. She senses the apologies are for transgressions he hasn't admitted. Now is not the time to demand an accounting. It's a time for them to share a deep personal moment. Tears are the order of the occasion.

FIFTY-TWO

Mo awakens. He jerks his head up from its awkward position due to sleeping in his chair. He rubs his neck to relieve the soreness.

His TV blares a blank screen. His video ended hours ago. The flickering light bathes his bedroom in a soft glow. He turns his head to look at his bed. He smiles. He's comforted seeing Maize and Jase sleeping soundly huddled against each other. He fondly remembers when Billy would let him sleep with him. It was a special treat. He loved his brother. He misses him.

"New...friends," he softly utters while staring.

As the fog of sleep dissipates, he notices a noise. It's a strange, rhythmic sound. A sound he doesn't recall hearing at night before, and a sound he hasn't heard in a while. It reminds him of the noise created when Billy and he used to jump on their beds. Mama didn't like that. She threatened to switch them. That made him sad. He didn't want his mama to be upset. He needs to stop the noise. It'll make mama mad if he doesn't.

Mo rises from his chair and slowly lumbers across his bedroom trying not to rouse Maize and Jase. He carefully closes the door behind him when he enters the hall.

The sound he hears appears to be coming from his daddy's room. A wide, narrow beam of light shines from under his daddy's door creating a lighted pathway for Mo to follow. He briefly hesitates once he reaches his daddy's door. He's concerned about how his daddy might react to his presence, but he knows this sound makes his mama mad. He doesn't want his mama mad. He must stop it. Mo fumbles for the doorknob in the darkness. Once he grabs it, he turns the knob and pushes the door open.

Mo's immediately confused and uncomfortable. His daddy's bouncing on top of another person. He's never seen his daddy naked before. Mo flushes. The other person's naked, too.

Ropes bind the other person's ankles and wrists to the bed frame. Mo doesn't understand why. Nor does he know who this person is or why his daddy's bouncing on top of this person. Perhaps he might be able to recognize this person if a pillow case wasn't covering the head. Aside from the rhythmic squeaking of the bed, he now hears his daddy's soft, deep grunts and the muffled moans of the other person. Empty beer cans litter the floor.

Mo's anxiety gets the best of him. He stomps his feet and screams, "Mama…says… no!"

When his daddy jerks his head around, Mo's frightened. His daddy's eyes are pinched and glaring, and his jaw's firm. He's never seen his daddy this angry. Mo hurries from the room when his daddy shouts at him to get out. In his haste to leave the dark house, Mo runs into furniture, some of which is knocked over making horrific crashing noises as it skids across the floor banging into other furniture and the wall. Once in the yard, Mo rakes at his head with his fingers, shouts incoherently, and stomps.

Soon, his daddy staggers next to him wearing a ratty, dirty robe and carrying a hand full of suckers. "Hey boy, stop ya squalling! I got suckers fer ya. See here!" Mr. Jimmy slurs while raising his hand with the suckers.

Mo pauses, grabs a sucker, tears off the paper, and sticks it into his mouth. This soothes him.

"Sorry, I shouldn't yelled at cha like that, but you surprised me boy."

Mr. Jimmy wobbles as he stands. Mo smells the beer on his daddy's breath.

"Damn, ya wasn't 'posed to see that! Ya know what I were doing?"

Mo shakes his head. He no longer rakes at it. Raised streaks caused by his raking fingernails across the sides of his head glow red. He can't look at his daddy's face.

"I was getting ya a new baby brother!" Mr. Jimmy slyly smiles and snickers. "Don't ya want one?'

The edges of Mo's lips rise signaling a smile as he continues to suck. He nods his head.

"I thought so. It was 'posed to be a surprise. I sure was disappointed you saw me and ruint the surprise. That's why I yelled. Forgive me?"

Mo nods again, not sure of what all this means, but he does want a new brother. This excites him. He removes the sucker, "Name...Billy."

"Naw, we'll have to come up with 'nother name. You study on it and let me know, okay?"

Mo grins, then with a serious look asks, "When?"

"When what?"

"Brother."

"It'll be a while. You got plenty o' time. Now go on back to bed and get yer rest. We got a busy day tomorrow."

"No bed."

"Huh?"

"No bed...friends... in bed."

"Oh, okay, well then sleep where ya were."

Mo nods and turns back toward the house. He suddenly stops and turns back toward his daddy who's following him. He holds up one, meaty finger, "One," then a second thick finger "...two...mo'...suckers?"

Mr. Jimmy raises his hand which still contains suckers. Mo smiles and picks two. He then turns and hurries back into the house.

"Now, stay in yer room. Don't come out until I come get cha, okay?"

Mo nods.

"Alright, see ya in da mornin'."

Mr. Jimmy follows Mo into the house until he's in his room. Then he turns and staggers back to his room. As he steps into his room and closes the door, he notices Suzy thrashing on the bed. Her wrists and ankles bleed from where the rope has rubbed her raw. Also, her hands and feet are pale from where the tight rope has restricted the blood flow.

"A'ight pretty lady, one mo' time!" Mr. Jimmy snickers as he drops his robe to the ground'

Suzy briefly halts her thrashing when she hears his chilling words. She can't scream due to the wadded cloth crammed into her mouth which is taped shut. It's a struggle for her to breathe at all, especially with the hood over her head. His weight again on top of her adds to her difficulty of breathing. She summons through an adrenaline rush of fear and anger what remaining strength she has and bucks and thrashes hoping he'll fall off. Suddenly, once again, something sharp's causing discomfort against her throat.

"Pretty lady, as I tolt ya 'fore, if ya don't relax and enjoy this, I'm gonna slit yer throat. Got it?"

Suzy stops thrashing, and the sharp object's removed. She can no longer cry. His hands are rough against her soft skin. She trembles as he enjoys himself.

Mo stares from his chair at the suckers he's placed on the bedside table. He can barely make them out in the pale moonlight. He turned off his TV eliminating it's bright glow. It's uncomfortable trying to sleep with his fingers in his ears. The rhythmic sound coming from his daddy's room is distracting.

FIFTY-THREE

"Wake up boy." Mr. Jimmy whispers as he shakes Mo. "I need yer help. Don't wake the young'uns yet."

Mo squints at his daddy through heavy eyelids. It's still dark in his room. The sun's rays are just beginning to create identifiable shapes as it pierces the darkness. Mo rubs the sleep from his eyes, stretches, and yawns. He rolls his neck to relieve the stiffness caused by sleeping in an awkward position. Gingerly rising from his chair, he stretches again. A quick glance at his bed causes a smile. He's pleased to see his new friends are still sleeping. He clumsily tiptoes into the dark hall where his daddy waits.

"Close the door gently behind ya so as not to wake 'em, then come on to my room."

Mo obeys and then lumbers to his daddy's room. Upon entering the room, Mo's immediately uncomfortable, just as he was a few hours ago. He's never seen a naked body that's so different from his. He stands silently and stares trying to process what his eyes see. He knows this person must be hurting due to the raw, bloody areas around the wrists and ankles. The taut rope is soaked with blood. The pillow case is still over the head.

"Quit gawking boy, she's dead. She ain't gonna give pleasure no more, so don't get any of dem thoughts in yer head, if that's even possible," his daddy snickers.

Mo's emotionless. He believes he should be sad. That's how he felt when he learned Billy and his mama were dead. He wasn't allowed to see Billy or his mama, so this is the first dead person's he's ever seen. Having never seen a dead person, he's more afraid than sad.

"Boy, you ain't feelin' upset are ya?" Mo shakes his head. He can tell something's different about his daddy. He seems very jittery, which isn't like his daddy. He wonders if his daddy slept. His daddy's disheveled appearance, bloodshot eyes, and rank smell aren't abnormal, but his nervousness is very odd.

"Boy, I hate to disappoint ya, but ya ain't getting a new baby brother from this mama. She was defective, kinda like you. She up and died 'fore ya could get a new baby brother. We ain't gonna bury her with Billy and yer mama. We're gonna give her an Indian water burial. We're gonna haul her up to the top of Thunder Falls and drop her in. That's what she said she wanted 'fore she died. She don't want any of her kin knowin' 'bout it cause they'd been mean to her, so we gotta keep this a secret. Can ya do that boy?"

Mo's crushed. He was really wanting a new baby brother. Anger wells toward this strange mama who died before giving him his new brother.

Mr. Jimmy senses Mo's been triggered. He grabs the remaining suckers from last night off his dresser. "Here boy, take one of these?"

Mo grabs a sucker, tears the cellophane paper off, and crams it in his mouth. He soothes as he sucks.

Mr. Jimmy removes a heavy blanket from his closet and spreads it on the floor. He then takes the knife from his bedside table and saws through the ropes binding her wrists and ankles. Mo finishes his sucker while he watches his daddy. He twirls the empty stick like a toothpick with his tongue.

"Alright boy, go 'head, grab her ankles and I'll grab her arms. Let's put her on da blanket."

Mo hesitates when he reaches for her ankles. He's afraid the blood will get on his hands. He's never touched another person's blood.

"What's wrong boy?" Mr. Jimmy asks in frustration while stretched across her body holding her arms.

Mo shakes his head violently and backs up.

"Whatcha feared of boy?"

"No...touch."

"She's dead. She ain't gonna hurt ya!"

"Blood!" Mo exclaims as he points. "No...touch!"

"A'right boy," Mr. Jimmy barks in frustration. "I'll do it myself, jest like everything else round here. Move outta way!"

284

Mr. Jimmy drops her arms and steps toward Mo. He grabs Suzy's feet. He drags her off the bed. As he drags, the pillowcase scoots off her head. Suzy's body slams to the floor with a loud thwack. The sound of her head slamming on the floor reminds Mo of the time one of his watermelons rolled off the kitchen table and splattered when it struck the floor.

Mo's frightened when he sees her face. Her cheeks are abnormally puffy as if overly stuffed with food. Multiple pieces of duct tape cover her mouth. Her hair is matted and tangled. Her skin is pale and doughy. Blood pools around head where it slammed against the floor.

"Damn it boy! See what you made me do! Now we gotta clean up that mess of blood."

Mr. Jimmy struggles dragging Suzy's lifeless body on to the blanket. Once he has her in position, he wraps the blanket around her and rolls her up. Unfortunately, the blanket's not long enough. Her feet hang out.

"Boy, go get me a garbage bag."

Mo goes to the kitchen and retrieves a plastic garbage bag. When he returns, his daddy's holding a bloody towel.

"Hand me the bag."

Mo hands his daddy the bag. Mr. Jimmy crams the towel in it. He also crams clothes in the bag. He then bends over and stuffs Suzy's feet into the bag. Once he's pulled the bag up so it's even with the edge of the blanket, he takes the roll of duct tape from his bedside table and tapes the edge of the bag all around the edge of the blanket. He then uses strips of duct tape to seal the rolled blanket shut.

"Alright boy, ya got no choice on this, I need ya to carry her out on the back porch and lay her down. Then, go wake the young'uns."

Mo stoops and wraps his arms around the sealed blanket. It's heavy when he lifts. He struggles to his feet, balances the blanket on his shoulder, and leaves the room. As he weaves through the house, he wonders why some of the furniture is overturned. As he steps on to the back porch, the rising sun, still hidden from view, has painted the few wispy clouds in hues of purple and pink. Mo pauses for a few seconds to drink in the beauty. Then he tilts forward and slowly slides the rolled blanket off his shoulder. When he loses control of the heavy load, the blanket quickly drops on to the wooden porch. The blanket thuds on to the porch's weathered planks causing the porch to vibrate.

Mo hurriedly makes his way to his bedroom. He's excited to wake his new friends. Once he reaches his bed, he's confused. He's never intentionally awakened anyone before. He learned to be quiet and not wake his daddy when he's sleeping after drinking his beers. The few times he inadvertently awakened his daddy, it caused his daddy to unleash words his mama doesn't like. He doesn't want to do anything that would disappoint his mama.

Mo places his hands under his armpits. He flaps his arms, throws back his head, and forces a loud, guttural, "Cock-a-doodle-do!" He continues to repeat it. The children stir.

Maize's eyes drink in a hilarious sight as they crack open. Her new friend is oafishly strutting, flapping, and crowing like a rooster in the dawning light. Quickly she's giggling. As she sits up in the bed, she hears the familiar laugh of her brother. He's perched on his elbow while laying sideways behind her on the bed. Mo stops and smiles when he hears the laughter. His friends' laughing causes him to guffaw like a braying mule. This only makes the children laugh harder.

Mo's eyes catch sight of the suckers he left on the bedside table. He lumbers to the table, picks up the suckers, and while staring at the children proudly proclaims, "For...you."

Maize and Jase each grab a sucker. They both thank him while ripping off the cellophane and before cramming them in their mouths.

"'A'ight young'uns," Mr. Jimmy appears at the door. "I see Mo's done give y'all an early morning treat," he snickers. "Come on in the kitchen now. I done spread some peanut butter on white bread fer y'all to eat fer breakfast. Then we're all going on an early morning adventure 'fore yer daddy shows up to get cha." Mr. Jimmy disappears from the door.

Mr. Jimmy's disheveled appearance is frightening to the children. They're anxious to see their daddy.

"Hey, Mo?" Maize asks removing the sucker from her mouth. "Is your daddy mean?"

"Yeah," Jase mumbles while sucking.

286

Mo just stares at them.

"Is he mean?" Maize asks again.

"He…my daddy."

"But is he mean?"

Mo shrugs his shoulders.

"I wanna go home," Jase declares while chewing on the remnants of his sucker.

"He says daddy's getting us after the adventure." Maize reminds Jase while turning her head toward Mo, "What's the adventure?"

Mo shrugs his shoulders again.

"Y'all come on and eat!" Mr. Jimmy hollers from the kitchen. The inflection in his voice is stern. "We're burning daylight!"

FIFTY-FOUR

"Tag. Wake up," Liesl whispers softly while gently poking him. Tag doesn't budge. Liesl shakes him, "Tag! Wake...up!"

Drowsily Tag pops up from the cramped bed in the trailer. "I'm up! I'm...up!" he loudly proclaims while yawning and rubbing the sleep from his eyes.

"Did you plug your phone in?" Liesl asks.

"Huh?"

"Did you plug your cell phone in last night?" Liesl's firmer with her question.

When Tag's eyes focus, Liesl's standing in front of him with her hands on her hips. Tag squints adjusting to the harsh, bright lights in the trailer. A quick, narrow-eyed glance at the window reveals it's still dark outside.

"Yeah, yeah. It's somewhere over there on that counter," he points toward the counter containing the sink.

"Well, I don't see," Liesl lifts a wadded towel, "ah, here it is. Your parents called me. They said you didn't answer when they called you. I didn't think you'd plugged it in. I thought it might still be dead from yesterday. You must have the volume turned down since you didn't hear your parents call."

"Here. Hand it to me."

"Your parents," Liesl unplugs his phone, "are on the way." She hands it to him. "The sun's beginning to come up. The teams are about to head out toward the falls." Tag enters his password and his cell illuminates. "Are you going out with the dogs this morning?"

"Huh?" Tag's distracted by the number of texts and voice mails he sees as he blinks the cobwebs of sleep from his eyes.

"The dogs. Are you going out with them this morning?"

288

"Sure…sure."

"Well hurry up. That man's feeding them right now. I'll go let him know to wait," Liesl instructs while opening the trailer door to exit.

"Great! Thank you. Tell'm I'll be there in a minute."

Liesl closes the door behind her leaving Tag alone. Instinctively, Tag punches his voicemail app to listen to his messages as he yawns and stretches to awaken. He rises and grabs a bottled water from the small refrigerator. He then enters the small bathroom while still listening to his messages.

Upon exiting the bathroom, he freezes, not believing what he just heard. He frantically removes the phone from his ear and punches the replay on this message. He strains to listen intently to the whispering voice again. His hairs are on end and his heart's suddenly racing.

"Tag, this is Suzy. I've found your children! They're in a home off…crap! I don't know the name of the road! The name on the mailbox is Quick, though. I'll call you back in a minute with the name of the road."

Fear surges in Tag. He checks when the call was made. "Crap!" he shouts when he sees it was left yesterday evening, almost twelve hours ago! He's now more frightened for his children than he was when they were alone in the woods.

Tag bolts for the door and throws it open. He bellows for Sheriff Justice.

Tag's bloodcurdling bellows startle everyone milling in base camp. All eyes are on him as he stumbles down the stairs into the humid dawn. Quickly, Liesl rushes to him.

"What's wrong?"

"Our children are in terrible danger!" Tag's frantically scanning the faces focused on him. "We need Sheriff Justice, NOW!" Suzy's never seen Tag this frantic. It frightens her.

"Why? Why? What's happened?"

Tag pushes past her screaming for Sheriff Justice.

"Tag he's not here," Smokey instructs rushing up to him "Calm down, what's happened?"

"I need Sheriff Justice, RIGHT NOW!"

"I'll call him on my cell." Smokey punches in the number and switches the phone to speaker so he can hear the conversation. Those in the base camp meander close to learn what's happening.

"Hello," it's obvious from the tone of Sheriff Justice's voice that the call has awakened him.

"I need you to get to Jimmy Quick's house as soon as possible! My children are in danger!" Tag shouts.

"I'm sorry. Excuse me, but who's this?"

"This is Tag Ryder. My kids are at Jimmy Quick's house. I need you to get over there immediately. I'm afraid he's going to hurt them!"

Liesl gasps.

"I'm sorry. I just woke up. I'm trying to understand what's happening. How do you know your children are at the Quick home and why are they in danger?"

"I checked my voice mails and there's one from Suzy. The girl who bought the drones. She said she saw my children at the Quick house. You need to get over there now! They're in danger!"

"Again, why are they in danger?"

"Because Mr. Jimmy thinks I killed Billy. I didn't…at least not on purpose. He swore he'd get back at me. I'm afraid he's going to hurt my children!"

"I don't have a clue what you're talking about. Did you call… what's her name?"

"Suzy."

"I'm sorry, Suzy back?"

"No."

"When did she leave you the voice mail?"

"About twelve hours ago."

"Why are you just now calling me?"

"My cell was dead. I had to charge it. It charged why I slept. I just woke up,"

"That makes two of us."

"…and listened to my voicemails. That's when I heard the message. Can I explain all this later? Right now I need you to get to the Quick house. I'm headed that way as soon as we hang up!"

"Don't do anything stupid. I'll call a deputy to get over there and check things out. Text me this woman's number. I'll

290

call her. You don't call her. I need to have the conversation. I'll be at the Quick house as soon as I can. You don't do anything until my deputy gets there, and then you do exactly as he says. Understand?"

"Gotcha! Thanks sheriff! Hurry! I think something's happened to Suzy, too."

"Why do you say that?"

"In her voice mail she said she would call me back with the address of the home. I didn't receive that message."

"Once you text me her number, I'll call her. I'll call you right back once I talk to her. I wish I could convince you to wait, but I understand why you won't. If they were my kids, I'd do the same thing. Again, don't do anything without my deputy's approval."

"I won't."

Smokey speaks up as soon as the call ends, "Good luck. I'm not going with you. What I heard involves the law, that's not me. I'll hold everyone here. Let me know what you find and if I need to send out search crews."

"Thanks, Smokey, for all your help. I will," Tag responds while texting Suzy's number to Sheriff Justice."

"Yeah," adds Liesl.

Tag pats his pants leg to make sure he has his keys, "Let's go Liesl!"

FIFTY-FIVE

The load's becoming heavier for Mo as they walk the rutted, rocky, overgrown trail winding haphazardly up the mountain. He's constantly stopping and shifting his load from one shoulder to the other. The length and flexibility of his load makes it difficult to find a comfortable balancing point. His daddy said not to tell his new friends what he's carrying. He's ignored their pleas for information as they walk. His daddy leads the small group. Mo's next in line. His new friends lag behind.

Mr. Jimmy's a bundle of nerves. He's excited, anxious, scheming, troubled, and very much hungover. He sweats profusely. Slung over his shoulder is a cloth bag filled with melting ice and warming beer. Every so often he stops, retrieves a beer, and chugs another shot of courage. The cloth bag is drenched from the melting ice. It's cold and wet against his shirt. He doesn't care. Also, he'd probably be very worried if he'd seen the deputies at his house. Fortunately for him, they left about five minutes before the deputies arrived.

Maize and Jase are frustrated their daddy hasn't picked them up. They don't understand. Nor do they understand why their mama hasn't come to get them. They desperately want to see them and go home.

They're confused about this adventure. Mo won't tell them what he's carrying. They want to see what's rolled up in the blanket. They assume it has something to do with the adventure. They hope the adventure starts soon because they're getting hot and tired struggling up the trail. They're tired of being in the woods.

They're frightened of Mo's daddy. He looks mean. He growls at them to be patient when they ask about the adventure. He smells awful and looks scary. They don't like him dropping his empty cans on the trail. Littering is bad for nature. They keep their distance from him.

Mo stoops to pass under the limbs of a large red oak which have grown low over the crude path. As he passes under the limbs, one of them snags the plastic bag taped to the end of the blanket. The limb rips a gaping hole in the bag exposing Suzy's feet and bloody ankles. Maize and Jase scream in terror.

Mr. Jimmy whirls around. "Damn it boy! Can't ya do anythin' rite!" he hollers when he sees feet protruding from the ripped bag. Mo's confused not understanding what's happened.

Maize and Jase are frozen with fear while watching the feet and bloody ankles rake against the limbs as Mo nervously turns from side to side. The gouging from the sharp, stiff branches creates new, deep gashes in the ankles and feet. Fresh blood oozes.

"What's wrong with that person?" Maize screams.

"She's dead," Mr. Jimmy hollers scrambling past Mo toward the children. Maize and Jase backpedal, but they aren't quick enough to escape Mr. Jimmy. His calloused hands quickly clamp an arm of each child.

"Ow! That hurts!" Jase screams.

"Let go!" Maize demands as she squirms to escape his grip.

Their protests and attempts at escaping are to no avail. He has a tight grip.

Mr. Jimmy sneers, "Don't get no ideas 'bout runnin.' We're jest startin' ourn adventure."

"I wanna go home," Jase cries.

"Stop yer squalling boy!" Mr. Jimmy suddenly releases his grip on Jase's arm. He quickly slaps Jase across his face with the back of his hand. The blow knocks Jase off his feet. Jase explodes in pain induced tears. Mr. Jimmy reaches down, grabs Jase by his arm again, and jerks him close, "Shut yer trap boy or I'll wallop ya harder next time."

The awful smell of Mr. Jimmy's breath causes Jase to gasp and cough.

Maize's now crying, "Girl, ya want some o' that, too!" Mr. Jimmy hollers. She shakes her head while trying to suck in her sobs.

Mr. Jimmy turns to Mo, "Boy, set her down and grab those clothes I stuffed in the bottom of the bag."

Mo's perplexed. He doesn't understand why his daddy hurt his new friends. He knows hurting others is wrong, but he always does what his daddy says. Mama told him to always obey his daddy. He doesn't want to upset his mama, but he doesn't like that his daddy hurt his new friends.

Mo rolls the load off his shoulder and drops it in the tall weeds next to the path. The exposed feet and ankles extend over the rocky path. Mo carefully rips the bag from where it's taped to the carpet. He doesn't want to touch the body. He's frightened of it. He dumps the contents of the bag on to the ground. The children are horrified by the towel caked with damp blood. They want to run but Mr. Jimmy has a firm grip. They continue squirming trying to break free.

Blood oozing from the fresh scratches on the Suzy's feet and ankles drips on to the rocks. Gravity pulls the drips into slow, meandering, thin streams of blood which cascade down the rocks and puddle in the dirt on the path. Mr. Jimmy steps in some of the newly formed puddles of blood when he drags the children closer to the contents of the bag. The children struggle to avoid the bloody puddles.

"A'ight young 'un," looking at Jase. "I'm gonna let go of ya. If ya run, I'll hurt ya sis and then come hunt ya down and hurt ya. Don't move, got it!"

Jase sniffles while nodding his head. When Mr. Jimmy let's go, Jase rubs the throbbing, growing welt on his cheek.

Mr. Jimmy grabs Suzy's black spandex pants from the pile of clothes. He then stretches one of the legs, wraps it around Maize's wrists, and ties it in a knot so her tiny wrists are bound.

"Come o'er here boy," he growls at Jase. When Jase edges near, Mr. Jimmy takes the other pant leg and binds Jase's wrists. Mr. Jimmy then pulls on the crotch of the spandex pants. The children stumble forward. He's pleased they're tightly bound. He can now direct them wherever he wants to go.

Mr. Jimmy grabs Suzy's purse from the pile of jumbled clothes. He found the purse in her car when he hid the car in a thickly wooded remote section of his land. He removes the thin strap and knots one end of the strap around the spandex pants at the crotch. He'll hold the other end and use it to guide the children as they walk. While admiring his work, he grabs another beer from his crude sack and chugs it.

"A'ight," Mr. Jimmy pauses to wipe slobbered beer from his stubbled chin with the back of his hand, "it's time for ourn adventure! Yer the prisoners and I'm the law!" His laugh is sinister and laced with sarcasm. When he calms, he glares at Mo, "A'ight boy, pick 'er up again. The best is yet to come."

Mo stoops, cradles the blanket with Suzy's body, and lifts it onto his shoulder. While Mo's lifting the blanket, Mr. Jimmy rakes the remaining few pieces of clothes and bloody towel back into the ripped bag. He then knots the bag where it gathers at the top and tosses it over his shoulder to carry like a sack.

"Lemme git in front of ya with my prisoners," he snickers. When he pulls the purse strap and walks, the children lurch forward awkwardly. They scramble to stay upright and in step with Mr. Jimmy. As it stretches, the spandex pulls tightly around their wrists causing pain. Their hands tingle as the blood flow's restricted. Tears still stream down their faces, but they don't make a sound. They want to scream for their parents, but they're scared to death of what this evil man might do to them. They want to go home.

Mo stares into the anguished, tear-streaked faces of his new friends as they pass him. He can tell they're sad. He's confused.

They continue their trek up the mountain.

FIFTY-SIX

Dirt and gravel spray when Tag's car skids to a stop in front of the crude gate to the Quick property. He barely misses the parked county cruiser. After slamming the car into park, he and Liesl leap out. They hurry under the gate and race toward the house. After Sheriff Justice called Tag and told him Suzy didn't answer his calls, Tag's even more worried than he was earlier. Seeing the deputies standing outside the home without his children isn't helping.

"Are they alright?" Tag breathlessly pants upon reaching the children. "Are they alright?"

"Yes, where are my babies?" Liesl pleads arriving a split second later.

"They're not here," the older of the two deputies responds.

"What do you mean they're not here?" Tag's incredulous.

"I'm sorry Mr. and Mrs. Ryder, but they're not here. I think they were here, though."

The deputy's response generates a strange emotional mix of relief and fear. Tag needs to know more, "Why do you say that?"

"Here, follow me." The deputy turns and heads up the stairs of the porch. "Please don't touch anything inside without our permission since our crime lab might want to dust the house."

As soon as they enter the house, the smell's overwhelming. It's a rank concoction of mildew, mold, cooking grease, stale beer, and body odor. The smell immediately reminds Tag of his college days when he enjoyed wild parties in the dark, dingy basements of fraternity houses. He's concerned there was a scuffle when he sees the overturned furniture.

They follow the deputies into a bedroom decorated for a child. A huge, antique TV, a relic of a VHS player, and a large, ratty chair look out of place in this child's room.

"Do those look familiar?" the older deputy asks pointing at two dirty backpacks leaning against the wall.

"Oh my God, yes!" Liesl screams as she bursts into tears. Before she can grab the backpacks, the younger deputy grabs her.

"Sorry mam, but no one is allowed to touch them yet."

"But they're my children's!" she shouts.

"Sorry mam, sheriff's orders."

Tag, while wiping away his fresh tears with his palms, asks, "What else have you found..." he quickly reads the deputy's nametag through blurred vision, "Deputy Marks?"

"Knock, knock?" Sheriff Justice interrupts walking into the room. It's obvious by his appearance he skipped personal grooming this morning.

"Thanks Sheriff," Tag quickly speaks up, "for quickly responding to my call this morning,"

"Hey, that's my job!"

"...but my kids aren't here."

"He's right Sheriff," Deputy Marks speaks up. "When Deputy Cole and I arrived, the premises was vacant."

"How long ago was that?"

Deputy Marks glances at his watch, "About fifteen minutes ago."

"Any sign of their children?"

"Yes sir, the Ryders have identified those backpacks," pointing at the ones against the wall, "as belonging to their children."

"Yes, they're Maize and Jase's backpacks," Liesl interrupts.

"Sheriff, we need to find them, quickly!" Tag barks.

Behind Tag and Liesl's backs, Deputy Cole mouths only for Sheriff Justice to see, "We need to talk."

"Deputy Marks, take the Ryders outside to see if they might recognize anything of their children's in the yard. I'm gonna check the rest of the house with Deputy Cole."

"Yes, sir," Deputy Marks points at the door for the Ryders to lead the way, "After you."

When the Ryders leave the room, Deputy Cole whispers, "Follow me."

They walk down the short hall and enter another bedroom. It's in disarray. The bed's hastily made and there's junk stack everywhere, along with a few empty beer cans littering the floor.

"Step over there sheriff," he points at the bed, "and look closely at the corner of the bed where the covers are not completely pulled up." Sheriff Justice walks to the bed and peers at the spot where Deputy Cole is pointing. He notices a dark reddish-brown substance which has soaked the corner of the sheet. He leans in closer and whiffs a metallic smell.

"Blood?" he asks.

"Yes sir, that's what Deputy Marks and I thought."

"It looks fresh doesn't it."

"Yes sir. I didn't think the Ryders needed to see this."

"You're right," Sheriff Justice sighs. Suddenly, he notices something's been smeared on the floor next to the bed. He drops to his knees and looks closer. What he finds disturbs him. "This isn't good. I think someone tried to wipe up blood. If you look closely, you'll see the smearing is tinged in a reddish-brown." Sheriff Justice leans forward to support his weight with his hands and places his nose inches above the smeared substance. "It has the faint scent of blood, too," he adds scrambling to his feet. "Someone lost a lot of blood. Let's pray it isn't one of the kids. We'll need to get Charlie out here to get samples and document our findings."

"Yes sir," Deputy Cole turns to leave.

"Not yet though. Let's see if we can find a body first. I'll need to distract the Ryders while you and Deputy Marks perform a more thorough search of the area."

"Yes sir." Hesitantly, Deputy Cole interjects, "Sir, if I might add, unless the Quicks have another vehicle, which I've never seen them in, their old truck's still here. If the only vehicle they have is the old truck, then they must be on foot, unless someone else picked them up."

Sheriff Justice strokes his unshaven chin, "Good detective work." Deputy Cole grins. "Yeah," Sheriff Justice continues, "I've never seen the old man and his boy in anything other than that old rattle trap he drives. I've often wondered how he keeps it going. Anything else in the house you want me to see?"

"No sir."

"Let's step outside so I can intercept the Ryders before they might see something horrifying."

As they make their way down the hall, they're greeted by an excited Tag, "Quick, Sheriff, come outside! I think we know where they went!"

They hurriedly make their way outside and follow Tag around the house to outside the back porch. Deputy Marks and Liesl are slowly walking through an immense garden. They're carefully watching where they step.

"Look Sheriff," Tag's pointing to the ground outside the back porch. The ground's uneven and sparsely covered in a mix of grass and weeds. Most of the yard is bare dirt. Depressions in the earth are slightly muddy from the rain which fell two nights ago. As Sheriff Justice and Deputy Cole come near Tag, they notice Tag's pointing at one of the muddy depressions. Footsteps appear in the mud. It's obvious some of the footsteps were made by children.

"Do you see 'em?" Tag asks excitedly. His words are machine gunning from his lips, "Some of those footsteps were made by children. I'm betting they were made by Maize and Jase. They're alive Sheriff! They appear to be fresh since they haven't dried. Do you agree? They go off in the direction of the garden." Tag points. "Liesl and Deputy Marks have spotted some more. We need to go find my kids, now!"

Sheriff Justice squats and carefully touches the footsteps so as not to disturb them. They're fresh. The mud hasn't hardened. It's still wet. He takes note of the direction the toes are headed and follows imaginary steps with his eyes into the garden. It appears all the footsteps, even the ones made by adults, some of which are distorted having been stepped on by the children's prints, are headed in that direction.

"Yeah," Sheriff Justice stands, "I agree, those do appear to be children's prints, and they're fresh. I'm not aware of any kids living on this property. Let's go see what they've found," Sheriff Justice points at Liesl and Deputy Marks.

On their way to Liesl and Deputy Marks, they find more footprints in muddy patches. When they reach Liesl and Deputy Marks, they're standing at the edge of the garden. There's a few feet of overgrown lawn between the end of the garden and the beginning of the woods. It's obvious by the condition of the grass and weeds that someone has recently traipsed through it. The absence of morning dew in spots reveals the path.

"Clearly someone passed this way this morning," Sheriff Justice states the obvious. "Why, we don't know. It's not hunting season. From the tracks it looks like two adults and two children. Do you agree deputies?"

They nod their heads.

Sheriff Justice peers at spot in the woods where the footprints in the dew lead. He can't see very far into the woods due to the density of the foliage, but it's clear the prints lead to the beginning of a path. It's wider than a game trail. He believes it was made by humans over many years. Even though he knows the path heads toward the looming mountain in front of him, he pulls his cell phone from his pocket and punches the Google Earth ap.

"What are you doing Sheriff? We need to follow that path!" The frustration in Tag's voice is obvious.

300

"Hold your horses Tag!" Sheriff Justice responds without taking his eyes off his screen. "I'm just checking Google Earth to see what we might be facing. I know it gets pretty treacherous the higher we'll climb. In any event, the river will act as a natural barrier to keep whoever made the footprints from going too far away. Plus, walking with small children should slow them down." He closes the ap and dials, "Let me make a quick call."

"Hello," Smokey answers.

"Hey Smokey, this is Bill Justice."

"Hey Sheriff."

"Have you sent any of your search crews out this morning?"

"No, I've been waiting to hear if the children were at the Quick house."

"I'm here now, and it looks like they were here, but they've possibly headed back into the woods, maybe with Mr. Quick and his boy. We're going after them. The direction they're headed is up the mountain. If they're headed in the direction I think they are, the river should act as a natural barrier.

I want you to send a crew back to the gorge. It needs to only be your people, no volunteers. I want the two deputies I've left with you to go with them. I'm not sure what's going on, but Tag thinks there could be some danger involved, so just in case, I want them to have law enforcement with them. Can you do that for me?"

"Yes sir, right away!"

"Great, how long do you think it'll take them to get to the falls?

"Hard to say, but it'll take more than an hour, even if they hustle."

"Okay, thanks. Hopefully either they, or us, are close to finding the kids."

"That would be a blessing."

"Yep. Thanks for your help. We'll talk later. I doubt my cell's gonna work once I'm in the woods, but I've got my hand-held radio. Just buzz me on that if you need me, or your crew finds anything I need to know about."

"Will do. We'll talk later."

"Yeah." With that, Sheriff Justice terminates the call.

"Come on, let's go!" Tag shouts again in frustration as he and Liesl jog from the garden.

"Hold on a second!" Sheriff Justice shouts. "Liesl, I think you should stay here." Turning to Deputy Marks, "Will you stay with Liesl by your cruiser…"

"To hell with that!" Liesl interrupts, "I'm not about to stay behind! Those are my kids, too!"

"Liesl, I understand, but if Tag's right, it could be dangerous…"

"All the more reason I need to be there!"

"Plus, it may be a pretty rigorous trek."

"You won't have to worry about me. I can run all you gentlemen into the ground. I just hope you can keep up with me!"

"Tag, will you talk some sense into her?"

"Hey, I'm on her side."

"Okay…okay. I obviously can't keep you from coming with us. But, only on the condition that you do what I tell you to do at all times!"

"Will do!"

"That goes for you, too, Tag!"

"Got it! Now let's go!"

"Marks, you wait by the cruiser and don't let anyone in. You call me if anything happens you even think I need to know about."

"Yes sir."

"Cole, you're going with us. Tag, while we track 'em, I want you to fill me in on your history with the Quicks."

"Gladly."

As they make their way from the garden, Sheriff Justice's worried about where the lady is who called Tag last night to tell him she saw his children. He wonders why he can't get her on

302

the phone and why she hasn't tried to reach out to Tag again. He's wonders if it's her blood in that bedroom since it appears the children left the house this morning with two adults. He's afraid this isn't going to end well.

FIFTY-SEVEN

As the adventurers draw near the falls, the roaring sound of the boiling, rushing water cascading and crashing against the rocks, and reverberating off the steep walls of the gorge, increases with each step...as does Mr. Jimmy's anxiety. He'd dreamt about this day for many years, never sure if it would happen. When he learned Tag's children were lost in the mountains, he realized this was his best opportunity for revenge. His boy knew a section of the mountains better than anyone. If they had wandered into this section, the boy would find them. That's about the only thing the boy's good for, except hired out for heavy, grunt labor...and a monthly government check. Yesterday, he was giddy when the boy emerged from the woods with Tag's children. Finally, Tag will pay a painful price for killing Billy. An eye for an eye the Good Book says. He's justified in God's eyes.

He's amazed at how easy this is going to be. He can dispose of the children without anyone becoming suspicious. They'll be written off as more wayward, inexperienced hikers tragically swallowed by the mysterious mountains. There will be a funeral service attended by everyone in town dressed in their Sunday best. There'll be lots of bawling, lots of mournful singing, and lots of Bible verses repeated over two small, empty coffins. They'll be buried in the Rock Slide Cemetery, even though the coffins are empty. Everyone will thank their lucky stars that it isn't their kin. He'll rejoice watching Tag grieve. No one will ever know the children's real fate except him...and of course the boy, but he'll put the fear of God in the boy to keep his trap closed. Even if he does talk, no one will believe a halfwit like him anyway. He doesn't make much sense anyway when he talks, and he doesn't use many words. Plus, there won't be any evidence of anything the boy might say.

Yeah, it looked so easy, until he spied her tiptoeing from his house in last night's twilight. She was the fly in the ointment. He knew he didn't have a choice if his plan was going to work to perfection. He was going to have to dispose of her, too. But first, he was going to have his fun. It had been years since he'd been with a woman. He wasn't going to waste his opportunity, especially with one that attractive. The boy catching him satisfying his lustful urges was disturbing, but the boy didn't understand what was happening anyway since he doesn't know the ways of the world with women, and the boy bought the story. The story only a halfwit would believe.

"Pick up the pace young'uns! I'm tired o' draggin' yer asses up this here steep mountain. We're almost at the end of ourn adventure," he snickers while jerking the makeshift manacles.

Maize and Jase stumble forward, fortunate not to face plant on the jagged rocks serving as uneven stairs for their climb higher. It's been a struggle to keep pace with the older man's longer gait. They're scared to death. They're extremely emotional. Tear tracks appear as shiny streaks on their dirty, puffy cheeks when the sun's rays strike them at the right angles. They sniffle between breaths. They struggle to suppress tearful, emotional outbursts fearful of what this mean man might do to them if they did. Their hands are deathly pale and numb due to the constricting spandex.

The foliage is sparser and the ground rockier as they steadily march closer to the gorge. Only scrub pines, hardwoods, and clumps of weeds grow in the few crevices filled with wind-blown dirt. The trail is no longer apparent, but it doesn't matter. The thunderous sound of the water reverberating off the walls of the gorge acts as a homing beacon. This odd group can easily be spotted by anyone within fifty yards of them.

They're approaching the gorge below the point created by the Park Service for hikers to safely view the falls. No one ventures down to these rocks. The rising mist created by the crashing avalanche of water coats the rocks in this area making them slippery and dangerous to the unsuspecting tourist. Someone might fall and suffer a severe injury, made even worse by the difficulty of getting the injured help, or even far worse, someone might tumble into the gorge, never to be seen again. The crushing force of the surging water pinning the body against the jagged rocks will pulverize it and tear it apart. Due to this danger, the trail they've followed was abandoned years ago. Only senior citizens, like Mr. Jimmy, remember it.

Adrenaline's fueling Tag and Liesl's sprint up the rocky path. Branches and thorns pummel, scratch, and prick their clothes and skin, but it doesn't slow them. They panicked when they found blood on the trail. Every second they save may be critical in rescuing their children. They know they're headed in the right direction because they spot imprints of small shoes in muddy areas. They're fresh tracks or they would've been washed away by the rain from a couple of nights ago. If the blood they found is from their children, their wounds aren't bad enough to prevent them from walking. They continue to sense their children are alive, and that fuels their sprint.

Even though they promised, they've ignored Sheriff Justice's orders to slow down. He and Deputy Cole are close behind them. They're all sweating profusely and finding it difficult to catch their breaths' due to their frantic pace on this steep incline. Tag and Liesl won't slow, and Sheriff Justice and Deputy Cole can't slow, or they'll fall farther behind.

The sound's deafening a few yards from the edge of the gorge. The adventurers step gingerly on the slippery rocks hoping to avoid a painful fall. The mist from the gorge is cooling. It paints a thin coating on their skin, a welcome relief from a strenuous, hot, stressful hike.

Mr. Jimmy's felt steadily worse each step of the climb. The combination of beer on an empty stomach, no sleep, anxiety, and rising guilt have made him queasy and woozy. He senses he needs to end this adventure quickly before his conscience weighs on him…or he becomes incapable due to his impending illness. He'll never have a better opportunity. Plus, the children have seen too much.

The children's fear of the unknown is rampant. The thunderous noise created by the sheer power of this awesome volume of water is terrifying to them. Also, the rising mist from the churning falls creates fog-like conditions making for a spooky setting. If this mean man weren't dragging them, they'd be running in the opposite direction.

Mr. Jimmy pauses just before the edge of the gorge. After wiping away the mix of sweat and mist with his shirtsleeve, a crooked smile forms on his wrinkled, weather-beaten, unshaven face. He cups his hands to be heard over the roaring water and yells instructions to Mo, "Drop 'er here!" He then points down at the rocks near where he's standing.

Mo slides the blanket forward on his shoulder and tilts the long end down. The load quickly pinwheels off his shoulder and slams on to the rocks. The sound's swallowed by the roar of the water.

Mr. Jimmy leans in close to the children and sneers. He releases his grip on the purse strap attached to the spandex pants. He drops the bag containing Suzy's clothes and the blood-soaked towel, and he slides the damp bag slung over his shoulder to the ground next to it. "If ya run, I'll hurt ya when I catch ya. Understand?" he threatens inches away from their terrified faces. To them, his breath smells like garbage cans without their tops. Crinkling their noses, they hold their breaths, and quickly nod in agreement. "Good."

Mr. Jimmy steps to the rolled blanket and stoops over it. He tears and pulls at the duct tape which kept it sealed. After ripping off the last piece of tape, he grabs the edge of the blanket with both hands, braces himself, and then pulls it toward him while standing up causing the blanket to unroll. The harder he pulls as he steps backward, the easier it unrolls. Suddenly, Suzy's nude and scarred body rolls from the blanket on to the bare, slippery rocks. Mr. Jimmy steadies himself to keep from falling.

Maize and Jase gasp and scream! Their screams are swallowed by the thunderous roar of the falls. They instinctively step back in horror. Only fear of the mean man keeps them from fleeing.

Suzy's body lies face down. Her deep, bloody, raw scars around her wrists and ankles, the matted, blood-soaked hair on the back of her head, and the smeared blood across her back are grotesque. It's frightening and repulsive. Youthful curiosity prevents them from turning away, though. They've never seen a naked adult body.

"Hey boy!" Mo looks up from the body to see his father with cupped hands around his mouth staring at him. "I need ya to grab 'er legs and pick 'er up. I'll grab 'er arms. Once we lift 'er, we need to inch ourn way to the edge," he points to the edge of the gorge. "Then we're gonna swing 'er like we do when we're tossing a heavy sack a fertilizer on the back o' the truck, 'cept we're gonna let go so 'er body goes o'er the edge and drops in the water. That's what the injuns used to do when their kin died. This is what she said she wanted done with 'er body 'fore she up and died. Got it!"

Mo swings his head from side to side and mutters, "No…no…no."

Mr. Jimmy can't hear him over the noise from the falls, but he clearly can tell Mo's refusing to help. "Come on, boy! I need yer help!" he screams to be heard.

"No…no…no! No… touch! Blood!" Mo shouts while shaking his head faster and raising his hands.

Not wanting to trigger Mo any further, Mr. Jimmy resigns himself to having to do it himself. "A'ight! I'll do it myself! Get outta the way!"

Mr. Jimmy stoops, grabs Suzy's hands, lifts her arms, and drags her body while duck-walking backwards toward the edge of the gorge. He moves slowly, carefully placing each step, which isn't easy in his condition, so as not to slip and stumble into the gorge. Her body dips and bumps harshly as it snakes over the uneven, jagged rocks. Her breasts, hips, and thighs horribly scrape and gash resulting in red, raw abrasions and cuts leaving blood trails across the rocks

When he drops her arms, Suzy's body is perpendicular to the edge of the gorge. He carefully makes his way to her feet. He grabs her above her ankles, lifts her legs, and creeps toward the edge while shifting the position of her body. He drops her legs when her body's horizontal to the gorge and about five feet from the edge. He steps back to admire his work and assess his next step.

"Boy," Mr. Jimmy cups his hands around his mouth again, "go find me a long, sturdy stick." Mo scurries away. Mr. Jimmy steps back to his bag and snatches a beer. He needs another shot of courage. He's disappointed it's lukewarm. He quickly guzzles it and tosses the can into the gorge. He wipes the residue of the beer from his chin with the back of his hand and stares at Suzy's body for a few seconds while devising a plan.

He creeps to the body and harshly kicks at the mid-section. The soft skin easily absorbs the blows. The body merely rises and falls where it's kicked. Bruises suddenly appear on the body where the blows landed. He stands frustrated with his hands on his hips staring down at the body. That plan didn't work. Then he stoops over the body, inserts his arms underneath the torso, lifts, and pushes up on the body so it'll roll. His effort causes Suzy's body to roll up on its side. Then it quickly rolls on its back, a little closer to the edge.

The children now see the front of her body. They've been told to never show their private parts to others, so they're ashamed to see hers, but they're curious about her revealing features and don't turn away. They're startled by the multiple scrapes and cuts in her flesh and the fresh, oozing, smeared blood. They're terrified of her face. Before averting their eyes from her face, a quick glance revealed horribly distorted cheeks. Her mouth is covered by a strip of massive, smokey-gray duct tape. Her eyes protrude like a bug's eyes, but with a fearful, lifeless stare.

As Mr. Jimmy prepares to roll the body one more time closer to the edge, he pauses. He realizes the expensive rings on her fingers might fund a couple of years of expenses. He grabs a finger containing a ring and tugs. It doesn't budge. He stands, grabs her arm, and raises it. He places his shoe on her armpit and tugs harder. He twists and tugs her finger and hand, dislocating her arm from its socket in the process. Her tendons and muscles tear lose as he tugs harder. Still the ring doesn't budge. Frustrated, cuss words spew from his mouth. Fortunately, the roar from the falls absorbs them before they reach the ears of the children who can't avoid seeing this gruesome act.

Mr. Jimmy reaches into his pocket and removes a pocket knife. A sharp blade appears when he flips it opened. Quickly he begins the grisly task of severing her finger where it attaches to her hand. As he cuts and saws through muscle and tendon, blood covers the blade and drips to the ground. The children shriek in horror and stumble backward, frightened even more of what this mean man might do to them. Once he's completed his circular cut to the bone around the bottom of the finger, he grabs it, twists it, and wrenches it from side to side until the finger breaks from her hand. Her arm drops to the ground. Blood spills on the rocks from the open wound. He twists off the ring from the severed portion of her finger and shoves it into his pocket. He tosses the severed finger into the gorge. He repeats this process with her other ring bearing fingers. The children squeeze their eyes closed in terror. Once he's through, he wipes the knife's bloody blade and his bloody hands on the blanket. The children huddle in a fear a few feet away. Their faces are damp from their uncontrollable crying and the swirling mist.

Mr. Jimmy crams the pocket knife back in his pants pocket, stoops again, cradles Suzy's torso, lifts, and shoves. Her body rolls over again. This time it's face down, only a foot or so from the edge of the gorge.

Suddenly, Mo reappears carrying a thick tree branch as tall as him. Mr. Jimmy stands. He rakes his shirt sleeve across his face wiping away the coating of mist and sweat.

With both hands, and without a thank you, he jerks the branch away from Mo's grip. He places one end of the long branch against Suzy's body and shoves. Slowly her body scoots closer to the edge. He repositions the stick so it presses against other parts of her body and shoves each part closer to the edge. The jagged end of the stick creates gashes in her skin. More blood spills on to the rocks. Soon the weight of Suzy's body causes it to effortlessly slide when it reaches the slanted edge of the gorge. Without a sound, it rolls once again and disappears over the edge.

Carefully Mr. Jimmy leans forward and cranes his neck to watch, but it's too late, the body's disappeared in the swirling mist. The roar's too loud to hear the splash.

He drops the stick and turns. His eyes are narrow and piercing, while his visage is serious and determined. There's an angelic shine to his haggard face due to the fine coat of sweat and mist clinging to it, but it's deceiving. His heart has hardened and turned as black as a lump of coal from years of hate polluting it.

He's emboldened by having successfully disposed of Suzy's mutilated body. He'll not give his conscience time for rebuttal. He's determined to finish the adventure now and exact his revenge for Billy's death.

Mr. Jimmy once again removes the pocket knife from his pants pocket and flips open the blade. He quickly moves toward the children and grabs the spandex pants serving as their manacles. The children recoil in terror.

"Hold still young'uns or I'm liable to cut ya makin' ya bleed out like a stuck pig!" he barks. The children freeze. Terror's etched in their tiny, tear-streaked, dirty faces as they peer up at this evil man.

Mr. Jimmy quickly inserts the blade between Jace's skin and the fabric. He saws upward stretching the fabric until it cuts freeing Jace's hands. He quickly closes the blade and crams the knife in his pocket. He grabs the back of Jase's pants with one hand while his other hand wraps around Jase's neck. He lifts him and hurries toward the edge of the gorge. Jase violently wiggles and kicks trying to free himself from the grip of this mean man. The hand squeezing his throat causes intense pain and restricts his breathing. Jase is frustrated and confused as to why his hands have no feeling and can't help claw away the mean man's grip. Jase squeezes from his clamped throat a terror-filled, guttural, desperate, bloodcurdling scream. Maize tries to scream, but no sound erupts from her mouth. She's been robbed of her breath by the deep horror she's experiencing as she watches her brother's desperate fight for his life. She falls to her knees paralyzed with fear and gasps.

Suddenly, Mr. Jimmy slips due to the fine coat of mist and smeared blood on the rocks. He falls hard landing on his back. Jase lands on top of him. Mr. Jimmy's briefly stunned and in pain from the surprising blow. Jase flails on top of him, desperately trying to wiggle away, but it's difficult with his hands still numb.

Mr. Jimmy regains his composure in time to prevent Jase from escaping. He releases his hand around Jase's neck to use it to push himself back to his feet. When he does, Jase is ripped away from him by a powerful force. He looks up and sees Mo standing over him holding Jase cradled against his massive chest under his arm like a football.

"Damn it, boy! Give 'em back to me!" Mr. Jimmy screams while scrambling to his feet.

"Friend! No...hurt!" Mo protests swinging Jase away from his father when he grabs for him.

"Boy, I said give 'em back! His daddy kilt yer brother. Now it's ourn time to get revenge. Now give 'em back, or ya toss 'em o'er the edge." Mr. Jimmy screams so he'll be heard above the roar of the falls.

"No! Friend! Love!" Mo shouts back.

"Boy, I'm gonna take yer videos away and burn'em if you don't give 'em to me rite now!"

Mo's briefly confused by his dad's threat. Larry, Bob and all the video characters are his best friends. He doesn't want to lose them. He hesitates. This causes him to loosen his grip. Mr. Jimmy knocks Jase loose causing Jase to tumble to the ground at Mo's feet. Jase writhes and wails from the pain caused by the fall, and from the blood rushing back in his hands. It feels like a thousand pin pricks as his hands regain feeling.

Mr. Jimmy grabs for Jase. Mo regaining his resolve to protect his new friend, spins quickly. His massive arm inadvertently strikes his daddy with a hard blow in the middle of his daddy's back. The blow propels Mr. Jimmy toward the edge of the gorge.

Tag and Liesl sprint from the tree line with Sheriff Justice and Deputy Cole closely behind. Their hearts leap for joy when they see their children alive, but it instantly turns to panic when they see Mo strike his father in the back and knock him head first, over the edge of the gorge. They scream as they run, but they can't be heard by their children due to the roar of the falls. Maize's doubled over on her knees with her back to them. Jase is writhing at Mo's feet. Tag and Liesl fear their children are seriously injured as they dash forward.

Mo panics. He's confused. He doesn't understand what's happened. His daddy's disappeared over the edge of the gorge. He howls, "Bad! Bad! Bad!" while uncontrollably stomping his feet and raking his head with his fingers. Turning from the gorge he spots strangers running toward him. They look mean. Fearing they might hurt his new friends he leans over and grabs Jase's arm. He must protect him from these mean people. Suddenly, there's a burning, intense pain in his shoulder. He releases Jase's arm, quickly stands erect, and swings his opposite arm over to touch where the pain is located hoping to wipe it away. Instantly there's another horrible pain in his chest. It sucks his breath away. Then another one. Mo stumbles backwards.

Tag and Liesl notice Mo backpedaling and grabbing at his chest. There's a bewildered look on his face. Suddenly, Mo disappears over the edge of the gorge. Only their children remain.

They quickly reach their children. Their horrified by the amount of blood streaked across and puddled on the rocks. Maize's almost catatonic, but she quickly recovers and wails when she recognizes her parents. Tag scoops her up in his arms and moves her away from the gory scene. Liesl lifts Jase who's still writhing and crying. She hugs him. He suddenly recognizes her and screams, "Mama it hurts! It hurts!" She also hurries him away toward Tag and Maize. They collapse in a disheveled mass.

"Liesl, there's blood all over Jase and it's on you, too! Quick, check him!" Tag screams while loosening the spandex around Maize's wrists.

"Baby! Where does it hurt?" she frantically asks Jase while hurriedly pulling up his nasty clothes to check his skin for wounds.

"My hands! My hands! They sting!"

"Shake 'em baby! Tag, I don't see any wounds. Praise God, I don't see any wounds! I don't think the blood's his." Liesl gently rubs Jase's hands after checking him. He calms as the stinging subsides.

"Yes, thank you Jesus!" Tag holds Maize close and rocks her while crying tears of relief and joy. Liesl also weeps.

"Are they alright?" Sheriff Justice asks suddenly standing over them.

"Yeah, I think so," Tag tearfully answers. Liesl nods her head. She's too emotional to talk. When Maize complains her hands hurt, Tag rubs them to quicken the blood flow.

"Sheriff," Deputy Cole interrupts, "there's lots of blood over there. I looked over the edge. There's no way to get the bodies. I can't even see them."

"Yeah, I know. We'll need to check downstream over the next few days to see if they float up, but I doubt they will. The most we can hope for is body parts, and I don't really hope to find those either.

Tag and Liesl, you know we'll need to talk to the children at some point to find out what happened. We'll work with you and their doctor…"

"That's me," Liesl interrupts.

"Okay, then when the two of you think it's best, but it needs to be sooner rather than later. In the meantime, please write down anything they might tell you about what happened. I'll get my forensic people up here to check all this out. There's a lot of blood over there," Sheriff Justice points. "I'm not sure why. Do you need me to get assistance for you to get y'all down off this mountain?"

Tag glances at Liesl. She shakes her head from side to side. "Thanks, but we'll be fine. We'll walk down with 'em. I think we can do that once we all calm down. Plus, I'm not sure how you'd get us any help anyway."

Sheriff Justice scans the area, "Probably right."

"Hey Sheriff," Liesl interrupts while hugging Jase tightly. "Thanks… for saving our children." Tears stream down her cheeks.

"Yes mam. I'm glad I could."

Tag hears a murmur from Maize, "What's that?" he asks loosening his hug.

"Where's Mo?" she whispers.

"He can't hurt you anymore darling," Tag softly answers.

"He didn't hurt me. He's my friend. He saved Jase from the mean man."

The four adults are stunned by Maize's revelation.

"Did you say he saved Jase?" Tag asks.

"Yeah, the mean man was trying to hurt Jase, and Mo stopped him. I wanna give Mo a hug. He's my friend, and Jase's friend, too."

Sheriff Justice's head drops and his shoulders slump. He was certain of what he saw. Mo was violently agitated. He had just pushed his father into the gorge and was about to do the same to Jase. He had no choice but to shoot. Jase's life was at risk. There was no time to issue a warning. Mo wouldn't have heard it anyway due to the roar of the falls. Even if he did, he might not have understood.

Tag notices the anguish in Sheriff Justice's face and understands why, "Hey, we all thought the same thing. You did what you thought was best to save our children, and we appreciate it. We'll back you."

"Yes, thank you for my children," Liesl adds.

"Thank you," Sheriff Justice softly whispers. He turns his back and walks away. After a few steps they notice him rake his sleeve across his face where his eyes are located.

FIFTY-EIGHT

"Ironically," Mayor Magnolia Winter-Blossom addresses the large crowd of primarily rambunctious children spilling and running amok, to the great chagrin of their parents, outside the hastily assembled tent, "we dedicate the openin' of this wonderful playground on the third anniversary of the benefactor's tragic death. We are eternally grateful for the gift from the foundation created in her name. We..."

Tag wipes the sweat from his brow with his shirt sleeve. Even though it's shaded where he's sitting under the tent, very little breeze is circulating in Pocket Watch Valley to keep him cool on this unusually hot late July day.

Magnolia's statement causes his mind to wander back to three years ago, the day Maize and Jase were rescued. What he and Liesl call their day of rebirth as a family. Every day since then, he's thanked God for saving his children and allowing him a second chance to rededicate his life to his family and his marriage. He's often wondered how he could have been so foolish.

He stretches out his arms and rests them on the back of the metal folding chairs on both sides of him. They're occupied by Maize and Jase. They sit quietly acting like they're paying attention, but he knows they're just waiting for their cue to cut the ribbon to officially open the playground. As soon as they cut the ribbon, they'll be part of the chaos of kids gleefully enjoying all its wonderful activity stations. After all they should, they're only nine and seven years old. They need to enjoy being kids

The last three years have been difficult for their entire family, but more so for Maize and Jase. They've been faced with having to deal with issues no child should have to confront.

317

They've achieved unwanted celebrity status from their ordeal, somewhat making them freaks and causing them discomfort. Well-meaning people have a propensity to treat them with "kid gloves." This is the opposite of what the children's doctors advised. Tag and Liesl decided they needed professional help with Maize and Jase. Liesl and Tag have encouraged others to just treat their children like any other kid. It's improving. Maize and Jase are also improving. Due to his young age at the time, Jase doesn't remember much of what happened three years ago. He seems to be doing fine.

Maize glances at Tag. He smiles. She forces a nervous smile in return. Maize still struggles with being away from them. The doctors said it will improve over time. They've advised Tag and Liesl to gently nudge her into situations where she must trust others. The doctors suggested Tag and Liesl discuss with Maize in advance what good behavior by the other person looks like and then debrief her when she returns with a heavy emphasis on praising her. They're seeing progress. She's at least begun spending nights at friend's homes as opposed to always requiring they come to her home.

Tag regrets he didn't pick up Suzy's message in time to save her. It'll always haunt him, but he's come to terms with it. He knows he didn't cause her death. Mr. Jimmy did. Tag didn't want to imagine the depth of Suzy's fear, pain, and suffering, but he believed it cheapened her sacrifice if he ignored it. It's uncomfortable for him, but in a sense, imagining it honors her life and her brave deed.

From what he learned from Maize and Jase; she must've experienced a horrible death. Her body was never found to confirm their stories of her condition, but the amount of blood is evidence it was brutal. The DNA from the blood on the blanket matched her DNA. Also, her purse was found at the scene. At that time, Maize and Jase didn't know her name or who she was, but since then they've learned about her and what she did to rescue them. They haven't been fully told about her connection

318

to Tag, though. Maybe one day, when they're adults, he'll tell them more.

Tag's never confessed his fantasies about Suzy to Liesl. He's sees no need in it. Liesl's suffered enough. Also, those fantasies have now disappeared.

He wishes he could've thanked Suzy for saving his children, especially since he wasn't there to participate in her difficult decision to abort their child. It had to be a painful, lonely decision for her. It decided their fates and propelled their lives in separate directions. A direction he's thankful for today, even though it's tinged with stains of guilt and curiosity.

One trait of Suzy's he always admired was her transparency. She wasn't lying about her net worth. It's hard for him to imagine how she could've amassed so much money in a just a few years, although he knows how persuasive she could be. He admires her parents for creating a foundation with the net proceeds of her estate. He believes Suzy would be happy her money is spent supporting so many worthy causes, such as the creation of this fabulous playground for the children of Pocket Watch Valley, a place she loved as a child.

Strangely, Suzy also taught him a valuable life lesson. His memories of them together, and his desire to recreate those memories, were intoxicating. They solely involved physical pleasure. He confused pleasure with being happy. Yet when faced with recreating those pleasurable moments, he learned that merely seeking pleasure in life only ultimately generates unhappiness. It's addictive, insatiable, and fleeting.

He's learned happiness is built moment by moment, not in a moment. It thrives when it's constructed with the right priorities, unwavering ethics, caring relationships, and unselfish love. Each person's path to happiness is unique. He discovered elements of his happiness comes from simple things, such as Maize's smile and gentle spirit; Jase's unbridled curiosity and boyish enthusiasm; and Liesl's loyal devotion, forgiving nature, and warm touch. It's also a work ethic focused on helping others achieve their goals as opposed to him becoming financially successful. It's treasuring relationships with others and returning the love five-fold. It's gaining wisdom and developing compassion for others. It's the tough lessons taught by a loving God who sharpens you into a more caring, understanding, and stronger person. Happiness is truly hidden in the mundane and it flourishes with age. He's decided a better word for this type of happiness is peace. Again, it can't be judged in a moment, but it stands the test of time...

"Tag. Tag!" Tag quickly snaps to attention. "It looks like our former city councilman is a victim of another one of my rousin' speeches," Magnolia jokes. Tag flushes with embarrassment as nervous laughter erupts from those in the crowded tent. "A'right, come on, bring Maize and Jase up here to cut the ribbon to Mo Fun Park," Magnolia's holding two, enormous scissors for everyone to see.

Tag rises from his chair and hurries to Magnolia. He drags Maize by her hand while Jase follows closely behind. Magnolia hands scissors to each child when they arrive. They quickly open them and turn to the ribbon.

"Hold on children!" Magnolia cautions. "Let's smile for the pictures first. Afterall, a politician never misses a photo op!" The crowd laughs again.

As they pose for pictures, Tag catches Liesl out of the corner of his eye. He smiles. She was supposed to be sitting in the open chair next to Maize, but she's frantically chasing little Mo, who's only a year old. He would have none of that.

Acknowledgments

The caring and excellent feedback my family provided to me after reading the draft of this book was extremely valuable. Their commitment of time and attention to detail was greatly appreciated.

Also, a huge thank you to all of you who proclaimed to me how much you enjoyed my previous book. Your encouragement is my motivation to continue writing.

Made in the USA
Coppell, TX
29 March 2022

75707434R10177